Rachel pee

into a slip at a floating dock. Whalebones on the floor of the bay, from the days whaling ships used the harbor, could be seen through the clear water. As usual, the beach near the dock was bustling with penguins. A Snow-Cat, a sleek, bullet-shaped vehicle with yellow stripes painted on it, was parked just above the beach line.

As they disembarked and started up the beach toward the awaiting Snow-Cat, some of the gentoo penguins scattered, lurching and stumbling over the cobblestones. Others raised their bright orange beaks in protest.

"The penguins seem particularly jumpy today," remarked one of the crew. "Like something spooked them during the night."

Two men unloaded what looked like a body bag from the Snow-Cat and loaded it on the hydrofoil.

In the distance beyond a ridge, Rachel noticed a small hut silhouetted by the low sun. "That's the Argentinean hut," said Antonio, shouldering his overnight bag. After saying a quick farewell to them, he slipped on a pair of snowshoes and headed toward the hut.

"All aboard," one of the men said. He reached out a hand and helped Rachel climb up into the cab of the Snow-Cat.

From her seat on the Snow-Cat, Rachel could see the skittish penguins watching the receding vehicle wind its way up to Shackleton Station. What had upset them? The very air seemed to bristle with angst. She glanced over at Trevor sitting across from her, but he didn't seem to notice anything amiss.

Praise for Judith A. Boss

"...I picked up *DECEPTION ISLAND* and couldn't put it down...The novel...jumps from one adventure to another with a bit of a love story thrown in. There's a pendant with seemingly magic powers, a frozen body, and some eerie antagonists to deal with before all the pieces are put together. I enjoyed the many realistic references to Antarctica, as Boss mixes fantasy and reality to create suspense and intrigue at every turn."

~Prime Time News

Deception Island

by

Judith A. Boss

Deception Island

Contact Information: info@thewildrosepress.com

Cover Art by *Rae Monet, Inc. Design*

The Wild Rose Press, Inc.
PO Box 708
Adams Basin, NY 14410-0708
Visit us at www.thewildrosepress.com

Publishing History
First Fantasy Rose Edition, 2015
Print ISBN 978-1-62830-868-6
Digital ISBN 978-1-62830-869-3

Published in the United States of America

Dedication

To all the wonderful people I met in Antarctica
who provided invaluable information
and feedback for this book.

Chapter 1

Rachel St. Claire pulled her phone from the pocket of her khaki field jacket that hung carelessly over the back of a canvas chair next to her tent.

"Hello?"

"Rachel, this is Grace McAllister."

Rachel smiled. She liked Dr. McAllister; as a scientist she wasn't afraid to push the envelope. "What is it, Dr. McAllister?"

"Some Canadian glaciologists just discovered a body preserved in an ice cave in Antarctica. We need you to come down immediately to help us identify its origins."

"Really? Now?" Rachel pushed a strand of hair back from her eyes and glanced up at the ancient Hindu Kush Mountains looming in the distance beyond the foothills of northern Afghanistan. "How old is it?"

"Not old, as far as we can tell; just unusual—very unusual as a matter of fact. From what I hear, the body has several…shall we say…anomalies."

"Anomalies? You mean genetic?"

"Possibly," Grace replied. "We were hoping your expertise as an evolutionary anthropologist might shed some light on the source of the anomalies and the body."

Rachel hesitated. This was not the first time Grace had tried to get her to come along on one of her spur-of-the-moment trips. Then again, Grace, a noted forensic pathologist at the Brown University Medical School, did have a reputation for being in the right place at the right time. “Who else is coming?”

“My nephew Trevor from Toronto. He’s a geophysicist with the Royal Ontario Museum. Also, one of my medical students will be joining us.”

The invitation was tempting and the discovery of a body in Antarctica certainly piqued her curiosity. On the other hand, she had promised her boyfriend Richard she would be home by the end of the week. She sighed, “I’d like to but I can’t…at least not right now.”

Just then, she noticed a gold pendant lying next to a pile of papers on the camp table. She leaned closer and peered at it. Someone must have put it there earlier that morning.

“This is very important,” insisted Grace. “We have to go immediately. It’s already February, and the Antarctic summer is almost over. I’ve made arrangements for Trevor to…”

“I’ll think it over and get back to you,” Rachel said, staring at the pendant. She clicked off the phone and picked up the pendant. Had one of the symbols on it just moved? She leaned closer. The delicately curved symbols reminded her a bit of diagrams of chromosomes. But there was something else. She ran her fingers over the symbols and felt a sense of foreboding. They looked eerily familiar.

A faint whirring sound pierced the air as a small plane or maybe a helicopter appeared in the distance from behind the mountains. Rachel shaded her eyes and squinted up at it. What was it doing here? From what she had heard, pockets of terrorist cells still hid out in the mountains just over the border of Pakistan.

"It's probably part of that geological survey team," said a young man with tawny skin and a wispy black beard. He stood a few meters away, in front of the supply tent. His long quilted *chapans*, baggy trousers, and brown wool cap blended in with the drab brown landscape.

Rachel picked up her binoculars to get a better look just as the aircraft disappeared behind the crest of one of the snow-capped peaks. The scene made her think of Antarctica and Grace's phone call.

Suddenly, she felt an odd tingle in the hand holding the pendant. Startled, she dropped it. She rubbed her hand. What was going on?

The young man looked at her askance, and then went back to putting items—plastic sample bags, labels, water bottles, picks, and a geologist's hammer—into a basket. Nearby, an antiquated gasoline-powered generator chugged away, powering the ventilators that supplied air to the lower reaches of a cave. Two boys stood next to the generator watching the man prepare the basket for the day's descent into the caves.

The caves, a complex of man-made and natural limestone, had once been the hideout of the Mujahideen during the great jihad. Now all that remained of their presence were some ragged sleeping mats piled up against a dirt wall and a broken-down oil stove. An earthquake a few months earlier had created a narrow opening leading from the lower munitions bunkers into a large natural cavern. The two boys were the only helpers small enough to fit through the opening.

During their first exploration of the cavern, the boys had come upon what looked like human bones.

Initial carbon-14 dating set the age of the bones at more than fifty thousand years. Realizing the significance of the find, Dr. Abdullah Shah, who was in charge of the excavation site, contacted Rachel, who was attending a conference on evolutionary anthropology in the Middle East. Rachel agreed to extend her stay by a week in order to visit the site.

"Missy doctor?" a youngster's voice said.

Ahman, the older of the two boys, edged closer to Rachel. His younger brother, Nadir, hung back, holding onto the arm of Ahman's wool jacket.

Ahman pointed at the pendant on the table. "We found very pretty necklace in the cave yesterday," he said. "You like?"

Rachel cautiously picked up the pendant by its chain and held it up to the sunlight. The metal had an odd phosphorescent quality.

"Where in the cave did you find this?" she asked.

"Nadir," Ahman replied, gesturing toward his six-year-old brother. "He go down into a hole in the floor of the cave near where we found the bones. He was looking for the River of Jewels."

According to a Hindu myth, the underground River of Jewels led to a subterranean paradise under a white island, which some scholars believed to be Antarctica. Rachel closed her hand over the pendant. A familiar melody, faint at first, drifted through her head, transporting her to a white land, pristine and sparkling in the sunlight.

The animated chatter of graduate students arriving at the work site broke her reverie. She slipped the pendant into a clear plastic bag and set it down on the table. "It would be nice if there really was such a river, but I'm afraid it's just a myth." She could not begin to count the number of times her parents had chastised her for having an overactive imagination, and nowadays she took great care to maintain scientific objectivity.

"It is very pretty necklace for lady, perhaps very valuable," Ahman persisted. He looked back at his little brother, who stood behind him with an expectant grin. "Maybe worth nice reward for cute little boy?"

Rachel sighed. "Okay, but just this one time." She reached into her pocket, pulled out some Afghani coins, and placed them in Ahman's outstretched hand.

He smiled broadly and bowed. "Oh, thank you, thank you, missy!"

Rachel smiled despite herself as she watched the two boys skip gleefully back to the entrance of the cave. She checked her watch. She might be able to reach Richard before he left for work. Tall, sophisticated, and a descendant of the Mayflower Brewsters, Richard was an in-house counsel with Global Technology, a multinational corporation with regional headquarters in Providence, Rhode Island.

She opened her phone and entered his code.

Richard and she had been seeing each other for several months now, ever since she had moved back to Providence about five months ago to take a faculty position at Brown University. Soon after moving, she'd met Richard at a benefit party for refugees who had been displaced by flooding and tidal surges due to global warming.

Although Rachel had been hesitant to get involved with a man who seemed so much her opposite, Richard had swept her off her feet with bouquets of flowers, romantic candle-lit dinners at Capriccio, ballroom dancing at the Biltmore Hotel, and gondola rides on the river under moonlit skies. Unlike the staid faculty office parties with their carafes of watered-down wine, her time spent with Richard filled a craving for excitement in her life.

A movement overhead caught her eye. She looked up just in time to see a hawk swoop down and snatch up a scampering mouse from the brush on the other side of the ravine. She shuddered as the hawk took off, the hapless rodent dangling from its beak.

The phone hummed—twelve seconds, fifteen seconds.

Richard's answering machine picked up.

"Hello," it droned. "Mr. Brewster is in a meeting. Please hold and he will be with you momentarily."

The droning voice switched to an electronic Bach cantata.

Rachel rested her elbows on the camp table and gazed at the pendant, its luster—and its secrets—dulled by the plastic bag which held it captive. Even though she yearned for the security of a real family and home, she also thrived on the adventure of traveling to unknown places, of making new discoveries. It placated a restless spirit in her, a yearning to find out who she really was.

Just as she was about to leave a message saying she would call back, Richard answered the phone.

"Hi, Richard. I just called to say hello."

"Rachel, sorry I took so long to answer your call. I was in a meeting."

"Do you want me to call back?"

"No, the meeting can wait a few minutes. What's up?"

“Well, to start, we found this interesting pendant here at the site—with these strange cryptic markings.” Rachel paused.

She half expected him to start in on his usual lecture about how dangerous it was for a woman to be in Afghanistan given all its problems with bandits and political unrest. He was so protective of her—old-fashioned almost.

Instead, he asked, “What did the markings look like?”

“Markings?”

“The markings, the cryptic markings you found on the pendant.”

“Oh, those. I didn’t know you were interested in archaeology,” she jested.

“Rachel, I do not have time for this,” he snapped, startling Rachel with his abruptness. Lately he had seemed preoccupied and tense. He had been working late and traveling a lot on business trips.

He let out a deep breath. “Sorry, it’s just that this client…” He paused. “Of course I’m interested in your work. I am trying, really I am. In fact, I wish I was there with you right now.”

She smiled. “Maybe you can come on my next trip—that is, if you don’t mind roughing it,” she teased him. She knew Richard preferred living in the lap of luxury. “In fact, just minutes ago I got a call from…”

“Tell me more about this pendant,” he interrupted.

Rachel picked up the bag and studied it. “Well, it’s gold…in color at least. And the markings are made up of symbols like some sort of ancient language—except the symbols are striated. It’s almost like they’re a cross between Sanskrit and genetic symbols—a DNA code.”

"What do you make of it?" he asked.

She shrugged. "I've never seen anything like it. It's possible it's a forgery."

"Where is it now?"

"I put it in a plastic bag and set it with my things."

He went quiet for a second then said, "Well, I'm glad to hear you're okay."

"There's one other thing…"

"Look, can I call you back later?" he asked cutting her off. "I have to get back to my meeting."

"Sure. Love you, miss you," she said. She smiled as she put the phone back in her pocket. It was not like Richard to take such an interest in her work. Maybe he was finally coming around.

She looked up as a familiar figure approached.

"Good morning, Dr. St. Claire," Dr. Shah said, bowing slightly. "Our young friends tell me they found a pendant in the cavern."

She showed him the pendant.

"This could be valuable," he said, examining it. He handed it back. "Keep it in a safe place until we are able to send it off to the museum for further analysis."

"Okay."

"Meanwhile," he said, "I have some news for you. Lord Nigel Rathbone from the British Royal Museum in Al-Qahirah just arrived to report their findings." He gestured toward a pretentious-looking man with a neatly trimmed red mustache and wearing a pith helmet, immaculately pressed khaki pants, and a matching safari jacket.

"And?" asked Rachel.

"The geological testing sets the age of the rock and debris in which the bones were found at 185,000 years, give or take a few thousand years."

"No kidding. That old?"

"Yes. What's more, DNA analysis of the bones revealed what looked like genetically engineered genes. The only similar findings are some preliminary research by Dr. Pei-Ling Lin in Beijing involving a new method of genetic engineering using a synthetic vector."

Rachel was flabbergasted. "Genetic engineering? But how can that be?"

The findings did not mesh with current theories of human evolution that had *Homo sapiens* gradually evolving over the past 150,000-200,000 years from primitive cave dwellers to technologically sophisticated modern humans.

"The results are puzzling, to be sure," said Dr. Shah, pulling the report out of his pocket. "Here, I will leave this with you so you can look it over. My good students await me." He smiled at her, his dark brown eyes twinkling. "We can talk more after you have a chance to catch your breath."

Rachel watched as he walked away. He was at ease with his environment; this was his home, his roots. She envied people like him and like Richard. At least they knew who they were and where they came from. Adopted at the age of three, she had never known her birth parents and her adoptive parents refused to tell her anything about them. Even though she had searched official sources several times, she had found no record of her adoption.

She checked her watch again. Lunch should be arriving soon from the village. The students were moving around now, stacking their sifting baskets and getting ready for noon prayers and lunch. On the other side of the ravine, a small swirl of pale dust rose above the horizon. Picking up the report, she walked over to the mulberry tree near the ravine. A cool breeze wafted from the mountains, rustling the pale green leaves.

She sat down on a mat under the tree, the report on her lap, trying to collect her thoughts. A hum from her phone interrupted her musings. She was about to answer it when a bird flew out of the mulberry tree, startling her. It let out a shrill cry as if alarmed by something. Rachel looked around but saw nothing out of the ordinary.

Then a movement caught her eye. A woman on the path below had dropped her basket and was running back toward the village. Black-eyed beans tumbled helter-skelter down the road and into the ravine. In the village below, the men were looking up at the hills and yelling something.

"Bandits!" one of the students cried, pointing in the direction of the ravine.

Chaos broke out. Teacups clattered to the ground as the students jumped up from their mats, upsetting the low table. The students scattered like buckshot into the rocky hillside.

"Run," Dr. Shah called out to her. "Run for cover in the hills!"

Rachel glanced back toward the ravine. The dust cloud had turned into a raging dust storm. Shouts and the clatter of horse hoofs on rocks rose to a roar as four horsemen waving rifles suddenly appeared over the top of the crest on the other side of the ravine.

Rachel stared, frozen in terror, as one of the horsemen spotted her. He signaled the others and, trailing a cloud of dust, they all turned in her direction.

Chapter 2

Rachel made a frantic dash for the cave. One of the gunmen raised his rifle and took aim. She felt a painful prick in her elbow just as she ducked inside the stone opening.

She pressed back against the wall of the cave, her heart pounding. After a few moments, she poked her head outside. The gunmen were no longer in sight. She could hear their muffled shouts and falling stones as they spurred their horses down the steep slope of the ravine. It would not be long, she figured, before they would be heading up the other side of the ravine toward the archaeology site.

Sprinting from the cave, she grabbed the pendant from the table, which was less than five meters away, and took off in the direction of the hills. From the other side of the hills she could hear a mechanical whooshing sound. As she rounded a rocky outcrop, a helicopter loomed up in front of her. Startled, she stumbled backward.

Regaining her balance, she looked frantically behind her. No one was in sight except Lord Rathbone, scuttling down the rock-strewn path toward his Land Rover. The shouts of the bandits were getting louder. Looking up, she saw the helicopter coming toward her.

"Oh, shit," she gasped. She felt faint and slightly woozy.

"Hello, down there," a voice called out from above. "Are you Rachel St. Claire?"

She stared up in disbelief. She could just make out a figure in the door against the glare of the midday sun. The rush of air from the blades stirred up the dust below, making it even more difficult to see.

"Rachel St. Claire?" the figure called again, his hands cupped around his mouth. "I'm Trevor, Grace's nephew. I've come to pick you up."

"What?" She could barely make out what he was saying.

He pointed in the direction of the ravine then shoved a rescue basket out the door. "Quick, get inside the basket," he shouted.

A gunshot echoed off the sides of the rocky ravine. Panicked, Rachel lunged for the rescue basket that hung from the helicopter. The ground whirled beneath her.

She tripped on a rock and fell.

The helicopter edged closer.

Shots rang out as the bandits appeared over the side of the ravine, their horses foaming at the mouth. One of the bandits veered off after Lord Rathbone. The other three, waving their rifles in the air, took off in the direction of the helicopter.

Rachel gasped and jumped to her feet. As she grabbed for the basket again she could feel the warmth from the pendant in her jacket pocket. This time she managed to hold on to the basket and, using the last of her strength, tumbled inside.

The helicopter rose into the air, the rescue basket swinging precariously beneath it. Rachel thought for sure she was going to be sick. Then she lost consciousness.

****

An annoying buzz punctured the air. Scowling, the bandit pulled his exhausted horse to a halt and turned on his phone. The other riders came to a stop behind him.

"Did you get the girl?" demanded a woman's voice in English.

The bandit swung his leg around and slid off his horse onto the dusty ground. He dreaded having to tell his superior of their failure. As a member of the elite New World Order guards, she had a reputation for being ruthless, particularly when it came to the Aryan Project. He took a deep breath. "No," he said, "not yet."

"No? How could you possibly fuck it up?" she snapped.

"Something unexpected came up, Generalmajor Braun. A helicopter picked her up before we could get her."

"A helicopter? Where in the hell did she find a helicopter?"

The bandit unwound his turban and wiped his forehead with it. His short-cropped blond hair was plastered with sweat and dust. Cursing under his breath, he threw the turban to the ground and spat on it. "I don't know," he replied. "It just appeared from out of nowhere."

"Are you telling me someone else is after her besides us?"

"Possibly. We have the helicopter under surveillance right now."

"What about the others? Did you at least get the pendant?" The pendant had disappeared years ago. Rumor had it that Charlie McAllister had it with him when he fell into the crevasse in Antarctica. They had been keeping Rachel St. Clair under surveillance ever since, hoping the pendant would eventually find its way to her since the symbols on the pendant mirrored her genetic code. Who would have guessed it would turn up again in Afghanistan at the very site where the girl was working? Had it somehow made its way to the site through that "mythical" underground river? Hilde clenched her fists. Just the thought of having to share a planet with that genetic freak made her blood boil. God, how she hated the St. Claire creature.

"No sign of the towel-heads," grumbled the bandit. "They disappeared into the hills. However, we caught up with a Nigel Rathbone from the British Museum. He was scared shitless."

"I don't give a damn about him, you incompetent idiot. What about the fucking pendant? Did he have it with him?"

The bandit swallowed hard and looked out at the barren, rocky landscape. "We searched him, took his wallet, and roughed him up a bit to make it look like a robbery. But, no, he did not have the pendant on him."

"Damn." She paused. "Okay. Let's go back and try to figure out what went wrong. Did the girl make or receive any phone calls this morning?"

The bandit snapped his fingers at one of the other riders. "Phone calls." One of the men pulled a crumpled piece of paper out of his shirt pocket and, reaching down, handed it to him. He opened the paper and read it. "Just two: One from a Grace McAllister and the call to R—"

"Dr. Grace McAllister, Charlie's widow? That meddling fool?" Generalmajor Braun said with barely suppressed rage. “Do you know where the girl is now?”

“They landed just a few minutes ago near the Riyadh airport on the Arabian Peninsula, Generalmajor. But, don’t worry—we’re on top of it. We have people there right now.”

“What in the hell are they doing on the Arabian Peninsula?”

“We’re not sure, but…”

“Well, let me know as soon as you are. And no more fucking excuses this time. And don’t forget to fill in Ramirez on your gross incompetence.”

****

The gentle thump of the helicopter landing woke Rachel from an uneasy sleep. She flinched as she pushed herself to a sitting position. She shook her head, trying to shake off the drowsiness. Her head throbbed. The right sleeve of her khaki jacket and white blouse were torn, exposing an ugly red welt near her elbow. The shooting pain jarred her memory—the bandits, students scattering for cover in the rocky hillside, the helicopter. It all blurred together like a bad dream.

She rubbed her eyes and looked around. The rescue basket was lying on the floor beside her seat, the cable neatly coiled inside it. Two men sat in the cockpit not far from her: the pilot and another man who was engrossed in watching e-news on his mobile phone. They apparently had not noticed her regain consciousness.

As the safety straps disengaged, she lunged toward the open cargo door and accidentally tumbled to the ground. She staggered to her knees and stumbled forward a few meters before the whirlwind of dust stirred up by the helicopter blades stopped her dead in her tracks. Gasping for air, she fell to the ground again and covered her head with her arms.

The blades came to a stop. A young man with tousled hair jumped out of the helicopter and ran toward her. "Are you all right?" he called out. "Oh, God, we've killed her!" Rachel tried to speak, but her mouth was full of sand and dust. The pilot came dashing around from the other side of the helicopter. "What's up, mate? She okay?"

"I think so," said the young man uncertainly as he reached into his jacket and pulled out a flask of water. He handed it to Rachel.

She sat up and took a few sips, then threw the flask back at him. By now, her fear was giving way to fury.

"What were you trying to do, kill me?" she sputtered.

The pilot rolled his eyes. "Kill you? Are you kidding, lady? We saved your bloody life."

She glared at him and attempted to stand.

"Here, let me help you," said the young man, offering his hand. "I'm Trevor Brookenridge and this is…"

"Don't touch me," she snapped. Her elbow hurt like hell and her head was pounding. Hugging her right arm close to her body, she slowly got to her feet. "Ouch," she groaned. "Was I shot?"

Keeping at arm's length, Trevor looked her over. "That's a pretty nasty sore on your elbow, but I don't think it's from a gunshot. I don't see any blood." He stepped back and smiled reassuringly with a wide boyish grin.

"Looks like a giant bee sting, if you ask me," said the pilot with a bemused smirk.

Trevor shot him a look.

"I don't see what's so funny," said Rachel, trying hard to maintain her dignity and not to burst into tears. She felt like shit. "Someone tried to shoot me and all you can do is make a sick joke out of it?"

"Joke? Hardly," protested Trevor.

The pilot looked amused.

Rachel turned in disgust. The late afternoon sun cast a soft golden-orange glow over the rolling sand dunes that seemed to stretch for miles in front of her. In the near distance, she could hear a hum. As she turned around a wide modern highway came into view. A water tanker truck, its sides scraped clean from countless sand storms, zoomed by followed by a caravan of faded red trucks carrying oil-drilling equipment. An old white pickup truck with a camel tethered in the back passed going in the other direction.

"Here, let me help you," said Trevor, extending his hand. "The airport's in the other direction. Besides, we should get you to a medical center, have your elbow looked at and make sure you didn't break any bones or anything."

She limped past him, ignoring him. Maybe she could flag down a ride or make it to the whitewashed building on the other side of the highway and call for help.

Trevor walked along a few meters behind her. "Please," he said. "We're not here to hurt you. I thought my Aunt Grace had told you we were coming. We didn't mean to frighten you."

Rachel stopped. "Did you say your aunt?"

"Yes, my aunt—Grace McAllister. She said she had spoken to you."

Rachel studied him for a moment. She could sort of see a family resemblance—the eyes, the same smile—but she could not be sure.

"Please," he said softly reaching out for her arm. "We have a plane waiting for us."

Rachel shook her arm from his grasp. "Let go of me," she protested. "I'm not going anywhere until I know what's happening. And what about Dr. Shah and the others at the site? They may be in danger."

"They're all okay," Trevor assured her. "The story came over the news just before we landed. This fellow Lord Nigel Rathbone—you probably met him at the site—claimed he fought off the armed bandits single-handedly so the others could make their escape."

Rachel could not help but smile at the unlikely image of Lord Rathbone fighting off bandits or anything larger than a mosquito, for that matter.

"My sentiments exactly," said Trevor, grinning, as though reading her thoughts. "Anyway, the bandits got away. There's no sign of them."

Rachel looked away, not sure if she could trust him. "How convenient that the bandits arrived at the same time you did," she said.

"Wait a minute," said Trevor with a surprised look. "Do you think we arranged those bandits?"

Rachel did not answer.

"Look—we had nothing to do with that. Believe me—we were as startled by them as you were."

"Bandits?" the pilot said over his shoulder as he headed back to the helicopter. "Lady, those blokes didn't look like any ordinary bandits to me."

As she glanced back toward the pilot and the helicopter, Rachel caught sight of a large modern complex of gently arched roofs sparkling like metallic sand dunes in the bright sun. A low flying plane passed overhead. "Where are we?" she asked, shielding her eyes against the glare.

"On the Arabian Peninsula—the King Khalid International Airport north of Riyadh," replied Trevor. "There wasn't enough room for us at the airport helicopter landing area at such late notice, but they agreed to send a shuttle out here to pick us up."

Rachel rubbed the back of her neck. The magnitude of what had happened was beginning to sink in. Dr. McAllister's nephew, if that is who he really was, had probably saved her life.

"I suppose I should thank you both for saving my life," she said reluctantly.

"You're welcome," replied the pilot as he climbed into the helicopter.

In the distance, she noticed a small hovercraft heading toward them, its silver outline shimmering in the heat waves that rose from the golden sand. The hovercraft came to a stop beside them. "Hertz Terminal," Trevor said to the robodriver. The craft rose a few feet off the ground and, turning sharply, floated noiselessly toward the airport.

There was only one other passenger on board—a tall woman in an *abaaya*, a long black garment that covered her entire body except for an opening for the eyes. Oversize running shoes poked incongruously from beneath the *abaaya*. Prior to the Islamic Reformation, Saudi women were required to wear these cumbersome garments in public. Apparently some still did. Rachel thought it strange that the woman was traveling alone and not with a male relative as the old tradition dictated.

Rachel sat back and, reaching into her pocket, retrieved the plastic bag with the pendant and examined it. The symbols appeared to have shifted again. Odd. She ran her finger over the symbols. Nothing happened. She shrugged and slipped the pendant around her neck and tucked it under her blouse.

Trevor cleared his throat. "I must apologize once again," he said, "for presuming that Aunt Grace had already cleared everything with you. Aunt Grace—she does things like that—assumes that everyone is on the same page as her. But she means well."

Rachel smiled half-heartedly but said nothing.

It seemed like only seconds before they reached their terminal at the airport. The hovercraft slipped effortlessly into a glass shuttle bay. Outside, palm trees swayed gently in the late afternoon breeze.

Once inside they followed the signs to the Medical Center. The walls of the brightly lit terminal were decorated with beautifully woven Bedouin tapestries and the works of Saudi artists. Pilgrims, men and women dressed in white, on their way to Mecca strolled past them, some carrying hand luggage.

"There it is," said Trevor, pointing toward a cluster of tubular booths. "I'll be over there at Gate 3J. We have a plane reserved for us. With all this concern about terrorism, all personal planes being flown over international airspace have to be inspected, preprogrammed, and the flight plan locked in before takeoff."

Rachel frowned and pressed her hand to her forehead. At least her headache was starting to go away. "And just where exactly are we going, if you don't mind my asking?"

"Ushuaia," he said.

She stared at him. "Ushuaia—in Argentina? But I thought we were going to Antarctica."

He shook his head. "There are no commercial airports in Antarctica. They try to keep air traffic to a minimum down there. Most of the scientists and staff at the research stations on the Antarctica Peninsula travel by ship now."

Rachel eyed him skeptically. She felt torn. Part of her said to get away while she could—to book a flight for Providence. On the other hand, she felt drawn to the mysterious body that had been found in Antarctica. In addition, Trevor did seem a genuinely nice guy.

She glanced over at the CAD—Computer Aided Diagnosis—medical booths. She had never seen such sophisticated ones, but then the Saudis seemed to be ahead of the rest of the world in many ways.

"We have about half an hour until it's ready for takeoff," Trevor said.

Rachel wandered over to a vacant booth and stepped inside. She needed some time alone to think. The door slid shut behind her.

"Welcome, Rachel St. Claire," the booth cooed as it read the microchip in her shoulder. She sat back in the padded seat and rolled up the right sleeve of her blouse. The air cuffs slowly inflated, holding her arms and body securely in place. "Instructions, please."

"Check injuries from…" She paused. She had lost all perspective of time. She was not even sure it was the same day. "The past thirty-six hours," she said. Better safe than sorry.

As the booth clicked away doing its thing, soft

music played in the background. Rachel closed her eyes, relishing the solitude after the chaos of the previous hours. She could feel the comforting warmth from the machine as it soothed her injured elbow and scrapes with a medicinal gel from its soft mechanical hands.

"Diagnosis complete," the booth said. "Multiple bruises and superficial lacerations from trauma to the body. Puncture wound to elbow and loss of consciousness caused by a dart containing sedative Ripvan. Antidote being administered." A tube pressed against her upper arm and injected something. "Treatment complete."

The air cuffs hissed open.

Rachel sat up. What was this about a dart with a sedative? Why would the bandits—if that was what they really were—want to sedate her? It did not make sense.

Stepping out of the booth, she looked around for signs to the commercial terminals.

"Hey, Rachel!" Trevor called out cheerfully as he crossed the lobby. "We're all set to go."

"But…"

He gave her a concerned look. "Are you going to be okay?"

She sighed. "I'm fine. It was nothing. Like you said—just a scrape."

"That's good news," he said, taking her arm. He led her over to the window in the boarding area. Parked outside the window was a small, streamlined plane with silver flex wings shaped like the gently undulating sand dunes in the background.

He beamed. "This is the Ferrari of the sky. It's

based on the HALE-3 drone technology. We're lucky. It's carrying medical supplies destined for Antarctica from Al-noor A-awal Trading Establishment here in Riyadh and just happens to have room for a few passengers. And it has a cruising speed of 700 kilometers per hour—even more with a good tail wind. That means…" He paused to do the calculations in his head. "…with the gain in time we should arrive in Ushuaia at maybe 2100 hours tonight and the ship for Antarctica is expected to leave at 2300 hours." He grinned at her. "You're going to love it."

Rachel smiled in spite of herself. She found his enthusiasm contagious.

A Hertz attendant wearing a light wool *trobe* and a red and white checked *gutra* on his head came over. "*Ahlan Wa Sahlan*—Welcome to Saudi Arabia," he said. "Please follow me." He ushered them outside to the waiting plane. Trevor got in first and extended a hand. Rachel hesitated, and then climbed up the steps. Standing just inside the door, she looked around at the plush interior.

"Where's Dr. McAllister?" she asked.

"It's just us," said Trevor, throwing his bag into the luggage bin. "Aunt Grace is meeting us in Ushuaia."

Rachel swallowed and stepped back toward the door. Alone on a plane to nowhere with a complete stranger?

Before she could protest, the attendant closed the door.

Trevor pressed some lights on the control panel. The plane gently lifted off the runway and then turned southward toward the southern tip of Argentina and Antarctica.

Chapter 3

Sensing Rachel's uneasiness, Trevor kept to himself, checking out his gear, for the first part of the trip. Rachel estimated he was probably in his late thirties or early forties, good-looking in a boyish sort of way with unruly sandy-colored hair and an engaging smile.

Finally, her curiosity got the best of her. After all, she was stuck with him—at least until they got to Argentina or wherever they were going. She might as well make the best of it. She cleared her throat. "I hope that's not a kidnapper's kit you're working on," she said, trying to keep her tone light.

He laughed. "No, nothing so James Bondish! This is my spelunking gear."

She looked at him skeptically.

"It's for going into crevasses," he explained.

"Crevasses? But I thought crevasses were dangerous."

He shrugged. "Sometimes we have to take risks to enjoy what life has to offer."

Rachel hugged her arms to her body. "Not me," she said. "I like to play it safe."

He set down his gear and looked at her. "You took a risk coming on this trip with me—a total stranger. That took a lot of courage. And look at the site where you were working in Afghanistan—not exactly the safest place on Earth right now."

Rachel flushed slightly and looked away. "Is that why you're going to Antarctica? Because you enjoy taking risks?"

He grinned and shook his head. "Hardly," he replied. "I only take well-calculated risks." He gave one of his ropes a hardy tug.

Rachel flinched. "So," she said, "I gather you've been to Antarctica before?"

"Several times," he replied. "I'm a geophysicist with the polar sciences division at the ROM—the Royal Ontario Museum—in Toronto."

"Oh? And just what does a geophysicist do in Antarctica?"

"Study the Earth's magnetism. There's a lot of magnetic activity going on in Antarctica right now—the highest level in about thirty years." He paused, and then added, "But I'm really just a simple geologist at heart. I like collecting rocks—been doing it since I was seven."

Rachel smiled. It was easy to imagine him as a happy-go-lucky freckle-faced kid, his pockets bulging with rocks.

"Also," he continued, encouraged by her smile, "a team of British particle physicists from the Boulby Mine Dark Matter Research Lab in England are going to be down there, and I want to drop in and see what they're doing."

"Dark matter? You mean that invisible stuff that supposedly makes up most of the known universe?"

"That's the stuff." He leaned forward and pressed a button. "Hungry?" he asked. A menu flashed on a small screen directly in front of him.

Rachel nodded. She was famished. In fact, she

could not remember when she had last eaten.

"The menu is limited but very good," he said, punching in selections.

A small robo-waiter holding a bottle of red wine and glasses appeared out of a tiny door.

"Don't you just love Japanese technology?" Trevor said as he took the bottle from the robo-waiter. He uncorked the bottle, poured two glasses of wine, and offered Rachel one.

She hesitated, and then took it. May as well go with the flow since there was nowhere else to go, at least for now. On the other hand, she was not one to throw caution to the wind.

"You go first," she said after a moment's hesitation.

He grinned and held up his glass in a toast. "Okay. Here's to taking only well calculated risks—like making sure first that the wine is not poisoned." With that, he lifted the glass to his lips and drank, then set the glass down with a dramatic flourish.

Rachel laughed and settled back in her seat and took a long slow sip. "So, tell me more about yourself," she said after a few moments.

"Well, you already know what sort of work I do."

He paused as the robo-waiter placed their meals on trays in front of them and then disappeared back into the hole in the wall.

"What about you?" he asked.

"Me?"

"Yes, you. Like, where do you call home? What about your family? Where did you grow up?"

"Oh, I didn't…" She paused. "What I mean to say is that right now I live in a small apartment near Brown

University—where I work." She looked away. "To tell you the truth, I don't really have a place I think of as home."

"What do you mean?"

"I was adopted when I was young," she said, glancing down at her hands. "We moved around a lot. Not much of a childhood."

"Sorry, I didn't mean to pry."

They sat in silence for a few minutes.

Rachel thought back to her childhood and the two little boys at the site in Afghanistan. She and Richard had talked about starting a family. Actually, Richard did most of the talking. Rachel wanted to wait until she got her career off the ground. On the other hand, she had always wanted children and knew she should feel grateful for having met a man who cared so much about family.

He had even set up an appointment for her at a fertility clinic—for her peace of mind because of her age, he told her. Although in her mid-thirties, Rachel looked more like twenty-one with her lithe figure, honey blond hair, perfect skin, and wide, hazel-blue eyes flanked by dark curving lashes. The whole visit had turned out to be a fiasco. At the clinic, they had inserted a large needle into her abdomen. Before she realized what was happening, they had aspirated some tissue from her ovaries. They had wanted to put her under anesthesia to do a complete biopsy of her ovaries, but she had refused. A burly male nurse had become forceful, trying to hold her down, but she had managed to break out of his grip and get away. Richard was furious.

Rachel took a deep breath and stared out the

window. Off in the distance she could just make out another airplane—a silver speck against the bright blue sky.

"One thing still puzzles me," she said. "How did you get to the excavation site in Afghanistan so fast? I mean, coming by helicopter."

"Actually, it was a Dragonfly-class tilt-rotor aircraft."

She looked at him blankly.

"But I guess you could call it a helicopter," he conceded.

"Whatever. The fact is you couldn't have been far away."

"Ha," he said playfully. "What is this? Am I getting the third-degree from Detective St. Claire?"

She chuckled. The wine was making her feel more relaxed.

"Sorry to once again disappoint your sense of adventure," he said, "but I was working nearby in some of the caves in northern Pakistan at the foot of the Himalayan Mountains, where we hope to learn more about the early geology of Antarctica, when Aunt Grace contacted me about picking you up. As soon as we finished dropping off some supplies at one of the base camps we came right over to get you."

Rachel sat back and crossed her arms. "Ha! Likely story. And you just happen to have a helicopter at the site—I mean, are you sure you didn't fly in from somewhere less—how should I put it—less rugged?"

He laughed. "The plot thickens! Well, we needed a dragonfly tilt-rotor aircraft to get up to the cave sites. Peter—he's a pilot from Tasmania—can get a tilt-rotor into places where you'd think not even a falcon could land."

"Yeah, right," she interrupted. "And you expect me to believe that?"

"Okay, so the falcon part was a bit of an exaggeration."

She shook her head. "It still seems too much of a coincidence to me. How do I know this isn't just an elaborate plan to kidnap me?"

He grinned. "Hmmm, not such a bad idea." Their eyes met briefly, like two sparks.

Rachel laughed self-consciously. "Don't you take anything seriously?"

He shrugged. "Not usually—especially when I'm having fun."

She smiled, surprised at how much she enjoyed the banter. She thought about Richard. He was so much more serious—almost dull in comparison. She frowned and mentally chastised herself for having such a thought.

"A penny for your thoughts," Trevor said, leaning over and topping off her wine glass.

His comment caught her off guard. "I…I really don't know what I was thinking." She gazed out the window. Puffs of pale, pink clouds drifted lazily over the blue water far below. A red blinking light on a map at the front of the cabin indicated they were two-thirds of the way across the Atlantic Ocean.

She picked up her wine glass and ran her finger along the rim. "I heard that Antarctica and the sub-Indian continent were connected at one time, millions of years ago," she said, hoping to change the subject.

Trevor nodded. "True. And there may still be more of a connection than most realize."

"What do you mean?"

"Some geologists believe there are rifts, or tunnels, created by the pulling apart of the great continents, running under the Earth's crust between the Antarctic Peninsula and the Hindu Kush Mountains."

Rachel thought about the Mongolian legend and the bones they had found at the site in Afghanistan. She was about to mention them to him but then decided it was probably best not to tell him too much.

"Why not just go to Antarctica itself?" she asked.

"Well, for one thing, it's too inaccessible for the most part. Almost ninety percent is covered in ice. Even with the recent slip of a another section of the West Antarctic ice cap, much of the ice is still trapped in between the mountains, making it unstable in places."

She looked at him in alarm. "Unstable? Is it safe to go there?"

He smiled reassuringly. "No problem. We're going to the Antarctic Peninsula. It's stable—at least for now."

Rachel sat back in her seat. Truth be told, she was looking forward to working with Grace in trying to solve the mystery of this body that had been found in Antarctica. She doubted it was as unusual as the bone fragments they had found at the site in Afghanistan. However, those were just bones while the body in Antarctica was apparently still intact.

The robo-waiter came over and cleared away their dishes.

"One more glass for the road?" asked Trevor.

"Okay, but this is it for me."

The robo-waiter refilled their glasses. They both sat back in their seats, savoring the wine. Rachel ran her finger absentmindedly around the rim of the crystal glass. It gave off a pleasant, high-pitched musical tone. Her hand went to her chest as she remembered the pendant. It felt warm and comforting, even familiar.

Outside the moon was rising over the horizon. The pale moonlight reflected off the rugged snow-capped peaks of the southern Andes Mountains.

As the plane began its gradual descent, Ushuaia loomed into view, twinkling like a thousand stars in the dusky evening sky and casting golden rivulets of light out across the tranquil waters of the Beagle Channel. The plane circled over the channel and then came in for a landing at the airport.

Grace McAllister was there to greet them.

"My dear Trevor," she said, embracing her nephew once they had passed through customs. A tall, handsome woman in her late fifties, her wavy snow-white hair was swept gracefully back in a loose bun. She wore a loose-fitting quilted jacket with brightly embroidered pockets. Now that the two of them were standing together, Rachel could definitely see a family resemblance—the eyes, the same engaging smile.

Grace turned to her and extended her hand. "Rachel, how was the trip?"

"It was, ah, fine."

"I'm so sorry for the misunderstanding. Trevor told me all about it." She smiled at her nephew and gave his arm a playful pat.

Trevor returned her smile. "I'll be with you in a few minutes," he said, shouldering his bag. "I have some business to take care of."

"We'll meet you in front of the terminal," Grace said.

She took Rachel's arm and steered her toward the terminal. "By the way," she said, "you'll be glad to know I just learned Dr. Shah and the others are fine. The bandits ransacked the site but apparently didn't take anything of value."

Rachel frowned. "I wonder what they were after?"

The terminal looked like a quaint turn-of-the-century Swiss ski lodge with its sharply pitched roof and warm, woody smell. A group of skiers in Nordic sweaters milled around a luggage carousel sipping hot cider served by a Capital Cruise Lines representative. A dog meandered among them, sniffing for drugs and weapons.

Rachel suddenly remembered she needed to call Richard. She checked her phone. The messages-waiting button was blinking.

"Do you mind?" she asked Grace. "I have a phone call to make. I didn't have time before we left Afghanistan."

"Of course. I'll just be over there." Grace gestured toward a table in the airport café.

Rachel sat down on a wooden bench and entered Richard's number.

He picked up right away. "Where have you been?" he demanded. "Why didn't you return my call?"

"I…it's a long story. And I only have a few…"

"Where are you now?"

"Here, you can see for yourself." She switched on the camcorder in her phone and made a wide sweep of the view in front of her.

"Rachel, please don't play games with me. I don't have time for this. Is that an airport? What the hell are you doing in an airport?"

Rachel rubbed the back of her neck. Sometimes she wondered who the real Richard was—the exciting, fun-loving man who had swept her off her feet when she first met him, or just another stressed out, overworked corporate lawyer. However, she supposed that such doubts were normal once the initial glamour and infatuation wore off.

"I'm not coming back to Providence right away after all," she finally said, trying to sound calm. "Something came up at the last minute—a job. We're in Ushuaia, Argentina."

Richard fell silent.

Rachel hated the punishing silences that followed whenever she disagreed with him. She was about to apologize just to keep the peace when, to her surprise, instead of insisting that she come home he asked, "What do you mean 'we'? Who are you going with?"

She told him about what had happened in Afghanistan, how Trevor had saved her from the bandits and how he was Dr. McAllister's nephew and they were all going down to Antarctica to examine a body that had been found in the ice.

"What about that pendant you found in Afghanistan?" he asked.

"I have it with me. I grabbed it when I was fleeing from the bandits."

"And what about this Trevor Brokenwhatever? Are you even sure he is really who he says he is?"

"He seems like a nice enough guy," Rachel replied uncertainly.

"And that McAllister woman—I've only met her once, but there's something odd about her. I never did trust her."

"Grace? But she's a respected forensic…"

"Honestly, Rachel; sometimes you can be so naive. Think about it. Don't you think it is a bit of a coincidence that this Trevor guy, who claims to be her nephew, just happened to be there to rescue you from these probably fake bandits?"

Rachel did not answer. She glanced over at Grace, who was sipping a cup of hot cider in the café. Trevor was still nowhere in sight.

"All I'm saying, Rachel, is be careful. You are too trusting of people. I'm just telling you for your own sake: beware of wolves in sheep's clothing. And stay in touch," he added, his voice softening. "Promise me."

"Okay." She rubbed her elbow. It had started to throb again.

When she looked up, she saw Trevor and Grace walking toward her.

"Our taxi is waiting outside," Grace said cheerfully, taking both their arms as though they were heading down the yellow brick road in Oz.

Rachel sighed and glanced out the large plate glass window, catching sight of the choppy black water of the bay beyond the airport.

Chapter 4

Once outside the terminal, a small electric autotaxi drove up from behind a line of buses.

"This is ours," said Grace.

Rachel took a deep breath and, hunching over, crammed herself into the back seat of the vehicle. Trevor set his bag in beside her and squeezed into the front seat beside his aunt.

"Sorry about the cramped quarters," Grace apologized, looking over her shoulder at Rachel. "This was the only taxi available."

The vehicle headed noiselessly down a long winding hill toward a causeway. Up ahead the Andes Mountains protruded from above pine-forested slopes. Sinuous glaciers snaked their way down the rocky peaks. At the end of the causeway were two signs, one pointing toward Tierra del Fuego National Park and the other toward downtown Ushuaia and the waterfront. The taxi turned and headed downtown.

Rachel leaned forward and put her arms on the back of the front seat. "I was just thinking," she said. "Can you believe that the Umini Indians who used to live in Tierra del Fuego fished naked, even in the winter, in these near-freezing waters?"

Trevor grinned and shook his head in mock disapproval. "The naked part is intriguing, but I think I'll pass on the dip in the freezing water."

Rachel tried to ignore his comment but found it hard not to smile. He was so unlike Richard.

"But seriously," she said, "I've also heard a rumor that Argentinean geneticists have cloned an Umini from a bit of viable bone marrow. Is that true?"

"You heard right," replied Grace. "Global Genome is conducting a study on genetic adaptation to extreme cold and long periods of darkness in the winter." She pointed toward a complex of buildings clinging to the lower slope of one of the mountains. "That's Schwaben Labs, operated by Global Genome."

Rachel rubbed the back of her neck. If she recalled correctly, Global Genome was one of the subsidiaries of Global Technology International in Rhode Island where Richard worked. But, of course, Richard was a corporate lawyer and probably had no idea what was going on down here at some obscure lab in Argentina.

"But isn't it illegal to use humans for genetic experimentation?" she asked.

Grace frowned. "They claim they're not breaking the law because they destroy the embryos before they reach viability. But who knows what they're up to."

"I seem to recall the police intercepted some correspondence suggesting Global Genome might be involved in bioterrorism research as well," Trevor said.

"Bioterrorism?" Rachel shuddered and stared out the side window. The stark white buildings looked eerie in the pale moonlight.

"The Argentinean government is keeping a close eye on them," Trevor said. "But with no evidence they can't close them down or bring any charges."

Rachel sat back and closed her eyes. Her head was beginning to throb again.

After a few moments, she drooped in exhaustion. She could feel the pendant pulsating warmth against her skin. As she drifted off, she could hear the faint drone of Grace and Trevor's voices in the background as visions of ancient spirits in long ethereal robes floated through her head. It had been a long time since she had dreamt of these gentle beings who had often come to her in her childhood dreams. The beings surrounded her with their energy, beckoned to her from the other side of a river, calling to her in soft singsong voices.

A voice broke the reverie, pulling her back to the cramped back seat. She rubbed her temples; the headache was gone.

"As I was telling Trevor," Grace said, twisting around to face Rachel, "at one time there was only one large dock here. What you see now was all built after the collapse of the Ross ice shelf."

Silhouettes of fishing boats and yachts dotted the harbor. Under the blazing lights of the waterfront, Rachel could make out the remnants of the old dock jutting out of the cold water like a reef of concrete, coral, and coiled steel bones.

The taxi rolled to a stop. "Dock 3," it announced as the doors slid open.

"There's our ship," said Grace, pointing at a sleek white multi-hulled vessel moored at the far end of the dock. It looked like a cross between a large, elegant yacht and a small cruise ship. The words *Queen Maud* were emblazoned on the side. A crane was loading brightly colored containers onto the main deck at the back of the ship. "The *Queen Maud* is a combination cruise/research vessel," she explained to Rachel. "It can carry 127 passengers plus crew."

"It also has a fully outfitted oceanography lab," Trevor added.

Grace pulled her credit card from the meter, pressed the *End* button and got out of the taxi. "We have a little less than two hours to departure time," she said. "But first you two need to get to the outfitters and get some warm clothes for the trip."

"Are you coming with us, Trevor?" asked Rachel, climbing out of the cramped space.

"Part way; I'm meeting some friends at the Café Beagle just up the street."

A brisk breeze blew off the water. Rachel pulled her lightweight jacket tighter around her.

"Are you going to be warm enough?" he asked.

"I'll be okay," she replied stoically.

"It may be summer here, but the temperatures can drop quite a bit at night." He removed his jacket. "Here, take my jacket. I have another one in my bag."

Rachel put his jacket around her shoulders. It felt wonderfully warm.

Trevor took a fleece jacket from his bag, and then heaved the bag over his shoulder. "I'll be right back," he said. "May as well check it in now while there's someone out on the dock taking bags. Be back in a minute."

Grace gazed wistfully out over the harbor. An almost full moon hung in the sky over the bay, casting a magical glow over everything it touched. "My husband Charlie and I used to stroll along the old dock," she said, pointing at an area now covered by water. "That's where he proposed to me."

"I didn't know you were married," Rachel said.

Grace smiled. "Yes, I met Charlie here in Ushuaia

in 1981. I was a medical student. He was a meteorologist with the British Antarctic Survey." She fell silent, lost in her memories.

"Have you been back to Ushuaia since you married?"

"Oh, yes. The following year, Charlie and I took a honeymoon cruise along the coast of South America to Ushuaia, and then down to Antarctica."

"Sounds romantic," Rachel said. She glanced in the direction of Trevor. A steward was scanning his bag. Trevor waved to Rachel and signaled it would just be another minute.

"It was," Grace said. "It was just the first of many trips we took to Antarctica together."

"Where's he now?"

Grace sighed. "He disappeared several years ago in an accident in Antarctica—fell into a crevasse."

"Oh, I'm sorry."

"That's okay." She patted Rachel's arm. "I'm fine with it now. I know Charlie is all right."

"You do?"

"A few years after it happened, I was in an automobile accident. The car went into a skid on an icy road and went over an embankment. I was pulled up into a white light."

"You mean like a near-death experience?"

"Yes…I guess that's what you could call it. Anyway, I found myself in this beautiful paradise. And there in the distance was Charlie smiling at me, beckoning me to join him. It was so real…even more real than this. Then I felt this tug pulling me backward. Next thing I knew I was looking up at a medical team in the emergency room at Rhode Island Hospital."

"Sometimes I have dreams of a beautiful paradise and spirits calling me," said Rachel. She paused, then added, "But, of course, they're just dreams."

Grace stopped and placed her hand on Rachel's arm.

"Are they?" she asked. "Are they really just dreams?"

Rachel looked away uncomfortably. Did Grace really think there was a chance her husband was alive at the bottom of some crevasse in Antarctica after all these years?

****

Once Trevor had finished checking his bag, the three of them followed San Martin Street along the waterfront. As they walked, Rachel plied Grace with questions about the body that had been found in Antarctica.

"I really don't know much about it," Grace said. "We'll have to wait until we get there to learn more." She let go of Trevor's arm and checked her watch. "Oh, goodness, look how late it is. We need to get you to the outfitters before it closes."

She pointed toward a street that headed up a hill toward the center of town. "Antarctica Outfitters is about three blocks up that street. You can't miss it. I picked out some outfits for you because I knew you wouldn't have much time. I'll see you back at the ship, say, in one hour?" she said, turning and walking away.

Trevor offered Rachel his arm in an exaggerated display of chivalry. "Shall we do some exploring together?"

Rachel laughed. "Thank you for your generous offer, but I'm quite capable of walking up hills on my own."

The streets bustled with groups of young people in vintage black spandex, older couples walking arm-in-arm and speaking softly in Spanish, and tourists in red parkas and fleece vests flitting from shop to shop. The smell of fresh ocean air blended with the delicious aroma of *cortado*, a blend of warm milk and coffee, wafting out of the many cafés that lined the street. The sound of Papo blues music and laughter floated out as they passed.

Rachel took a deep breath. The smell of the *cortado* reminded her of Richard—that was how he liked his coffee—with lots of warm milk. She felt slightly disoriented, as if she would look up and there would be Richard standing beside her. Then she realized Trevor was talking to her.

"Maybe next time we'll have time to enjoy the music," he was saying.

Rachel looked at him blankly. "Next time?"

"Oops, watch out," he said, grabbing her arm as the street light turned red.

She jumped back up on the curb.

"See, I saved your life again—now you owe me a dance."

Rachel looked in both directions. "Except there weren't any cars coming."

"But there could have been," he teased. He gave her arm a gentle squeeze before letting go.

She managed a smile, but she could not shake the uneasy feeling that something was not quite right.

After crossing the street, they entered a brightly lit outfitters store. A display of late-nineteenth- and early-twentieth-century clothing worn by the early Antarctic explorers and scientists occupied one corner of the store. A small collection of books on Antarctica just inside the front door caught Rachel's eye. She picked up one written in German entitled *Neues aus Neuschwabenland* and studied the cover. A UFO hovered over some apparently unsuspecting penguins waddling past a woman in a Nazi uniform.

Curious, she thought. The symbols on the UFO reminded her a bit of the symbols on the pendant.

A clerk came over and greeted them. "*Buenas noches.*"

"I'm Trevor Brookenridge, Grace McAllister's nephew," Trevor said in Spanish. "You have some clothing put aside for our trip?"

"*Ah, si.*" He handed each of them a pile of clothing, then pulled some items from a rack and handed them to Rachel. "Dr. McAllister was not sure of your size," he said to her in heavily accented English.

Rachel slipped into a dressing room with the clothes and quickly made her selections. The items were packed and sent by courier to the ship.

With almost an hour left before departure, Rachel and Trevor took their time walking back, peeking in shop windows and exchanging stories about their work and Antarctica.

"Grace told me about what had happened to your uncle Charlie," Rachel said. "How he fell into that crevasse."

Trevor took a deep breath. "It happened a while back," he said. "I was just a kid at the time."

"Does Grace really think there's a chance he's still alive?"

He shook his head. "I don't know. Aunt Grace

never really got over it, or accepted that he was dead. She never remarried even though she's had plenty of suitors."

"How sad."

They walked in silence down the dock toward the *Queen Maud.* The temperature had dropped, and the once invigorating breeze had turned into a bone-chilling wind.

A Capital Cruise Lines representative met them at the top of the gangplank. "Welcome to the *Queen Maud,"* he said with a wide smile.

Grace stood just inside the door. "I forgot to give you your tickets," she said, handing each of them an envelope.

The representative checked their passports, and then ushered them over to a small machine. A bright bouquet of flowers stood on a pedestal next to the machine.

He slipped the tickchips into a small slot. A plastic magnetized card slid out of another opening. "Here," he said, "present your cruise card whenever you leave or return to the ship. It also serves as the key to your cabin. As you know, we're departing later than originally scheduled. But we'll make up some of the time crossing the Drake Passage."

"Actually, the change in schedule was lucky for us," said Trevor with good humor, winking at Rachel. "Otherwise, we might not have made it."

The representative smiled stiffly. "You're not the only people who wouldn't have made the cruise if we'd been on time. That couple there at the bottom of the gangplank right now," he said, gesturing toward the dock, "just came directly from the airport with no time to spare."

Through the open door, Rachel spotted a couple getting out of a taxi. The woman, a strapping, yellow-haired Amazon, stared in Rachel's direction and then gave a thin, tight-lipped smile. The man—silver-haired with eerie gray-blue eyes magnified by thick wire-rim glasses—studied her with the cold, detached look of an entomologist examining a bug.

Rachel felt a cold knot in the pit of her stomach.

"Are you okay?" Trevor asked.

Rachel didn't answer.

A young Filipino man in a maroon uniform appeared.

"This is Ferdinand, your cabin steward," said the representative to Rachel.

"Good night," said Grace, patting Rachel's arm. "I'm sure you'll feel better after a good night's sleep."

Smiling wearily, Rachel said her farewells and entered the elevator followed by the steward.

The scent of roses filled the air as the steward opened the door to her cabin. A red parka, along with the packages from the outfitters, was neatly laid out on the spare bed. On the dresser, set into a built-in vase, were a dozen short-stemmed roses. A small envelope was propped up against the vase.

Once the steward had left, Rachel sat down on the bed and opened the envelope.

I love you, the card read, signed *Richard*.

Rachel pressed the card to her heart. With her other hand, she ran a finger along the soft silky intimacy of the petals. After a few moments, she set the card down and took out her phone. It was late—well past midnight. Rather than risk waking up Richard, she left a message with his teleandroid thanking him for the roses and saying that she loved him too.

She set the phone on the night table beside her bed. The boat rocked gently beneath her. Feeling around in her pockets, she pulled out some Afghani coins, her portable holographic projector with the chip still in it, and a small silver box. She put the projector in the drawer and dropped the coins on top of the night table. The night table had a lip around the top to keep things from falling off should waters become rough. She opened the silver box, took out a small ring, and closed her hand around it. It was all she had—her only connection with her early childhood. Putting it back, she set the box on the night table. Then she carefully removed the pendant from around her neck and laid it down on the night table beside the silver box and coins.

Kicking off her shoes, she lay back on her bed. She was about to turn off the light when she heard a rap on the door.

As she opened the door, she caught a glimpse of the pale blond woman who had boarded the ship after them standing farther down the hall, watching her door.

"Excuse me," said the steward apologetically. "I hope you don't mind my knocking at this hour." He held out a plastic *Queen Maud* toiletry case. It contained a toothbrush, toothpaste, comb, and other travel essentials. "Your friend Dr. McAllister thought you might need this."

"Thank you," said Rachel, taking the case. As the steward departed, Rachel glanced down the hall. The woman had vanished.

Rachel shut the door and checked to make sure it was securely locked before returning to bed.

Chapter 5

Rachel awoke to the sound of clattering and creaking. Groaning, she rolled out of bed and stood. The floor heaved beneath her. It was all she could do to stay upright with the ship and her stomach pitching and rolling underneath her. She clutched her stomach as a wave of nausea struck. Staggering over to the spare bed, she grabbed the red parka and headed outside for some fresh air.

Overhead, the pale pink early morning glow lent a tinge of color to the otherwise gray, wispy clouds. She sat back in one of the deck chairs and gazed up at the sky.

One of the crew stopped next to Rachel's deck chair. "Are you okay, miss?"

She looked up at him miserably. "Just a little seasickness."

"The doctor's in the medical center, if you'd like a shot for it."

"Thanks, but I think I'll go back to my cabin and try to sleep it off."

As she struggled to her feet, Trevor appeared from around the corner.

"Hey, Rachel," he called out. He rushed over to help steady her.

She put her hand out to stop him and leaned against the wall as another wave of nausea hit. What in the world was she doing out here in the middle of nowhere? What had she been thinking when she let Trevor kidnap her? "I'm okay," she muttered. "I just want to be left alone."

Trevor looked hurt, but backed off.

From the stern area of the ship a woman's voice called, "Trev, come on. You gotta see this!"

"You sure you're okay?" he asked Rachel.

She did not reply.

He hesitated, then turned and walked away in the direction of the voice.

By the time Rachel returned to her cabin she was feeling even worse. The ship moaned and lurched, almost sending her sprawling to the floor as she crossed the cabin to the bed. As she gripped the raised lip of the night table to steady herself, her hand brushed against the pendant and she felt the seasickness subside momentarily. Surprised, she picked up the pendant. The seasickness ebbed again.

She stared at it. She knew that some so-called primitive people believed that certain amulets had magical healing powers, but as an educated person she had dismissed this as superstition. Feeling nauseated enough to try anything she slipped the pendant around her neck and lay down on the bed.

She woke five hours later. The violent pitching and rolling of the ship had subsided to a gentle rocking. Except for being hungry, she felt fine. After changing her clothes, she picked up a copy of the cruise itinerary for the day that had been slipped under her door and headed up to the café on the main deck.

When she arrived at the Café Aurora, the kitchen staff was busy replacing some of the breakfast items with sandwiches, lasagna, and a selection of soups and salads. A colorful mural of the aurora australis adorned the wall behind the buffet. Outside a cold, misty rain fell.

There were only a few people in the buffet line. She picked up a tray and plate and looked around for Trevor. She felt badly about the way she had been so rude to him earlier and felt she should apologize. After all, he was just trying to be helpful. A couple got in line behind her. Rachel recognized her as the blond woman she had seen out in the hallway the night before.

The woman turned to Rachel and said with a slight German accent, "Such a delightful buffet. You don't see real food like this much anymore."

"Yes, it's very nice," replied Rachel politely.

"My name is Hildegaard—Hilde. And this is my husband, Wolfgang Meyer—but everyone calls him Wolf."

"I'm Rachel," she said half-heartedly. She definitely was not in the mood for socializing.

Wolf reached out to shake her hand. Rachel flinched as he touched her, his handshake cold and clammy. For a brief second his deep-set, penetrating gray-blue eyes met hers. Then, just as quickly, he turned back to the buffet and began heaping slabs of roast beef and tangled strips of bacon onto his plate.

"This is our nineteenth cruise and seventh continent," said Hilde. "Right, Wolfy?"

He smiled thinly and gave her a knowing look.

"How about you?" asked Hilde, shifting her attention back to Rachel.

Rachel took a deep breath. "Actually, this is my first cruise," she said, looking around for a table.

Several were occupied by passengers—mostly older women—making plasticine penguin pins under the watchful eye of the ship's artist.

"*Ach*!" the woman uttered in feigned astonishment. "Never been on a cruise before! Wolfy, can you believe that?"

"My job is rather demanding," Rachel explained. "I don't have time for…"

"Well, you *must* join us for brunch. That would be nice, eh, Wolfy?"

"Well, actually I'm…" Just then Rachel spotted Grace sitting at a table near one of the windows. She breathed a sigh of relief. "I'm joining someone else."

"Then we must get together later," Hilde declared as if it had been all settled. She pulled a small pad out of her jogging suit and jotted down something. She handed the slip of yellow paper to Rachel, who noticed one of the ship's security guards watching them from the other side of the dining room.

"Excuse me," said Rachel. With the ship rolling beneath her, she carefully made her way over to Grace's table.

"Rachel," said Grace, looking up. "How nice to see you. Please, have a seat."

A waiter came over and offered Rachel some coffee.

Grace gestured toward a diminutive young man sitting next to her. "Rachel, this is my student Ka-Wing O'Brien. We were just reviewing some material for my book on forensic medicine."

"Hi, there," said Ka-Wing. He stood. "Sorry, I have to get going. I have an appointment to see the dry lab up on the Sky Deck. They're doing some pretty neat marine research up there."

"We'll talk more later," Grace said as he left.

"Where's Trevor?" Rachel asked, glancing around the dining room.

"Catching up with old friends," Grace said. She picked up her cup of tea and took a sip. "By the way, I saw you talking to that couple over at the buffet. Did they say who they were?"

"Oh, them," replied Rachel, rolling her eyes. "God, I'm so glad I spotted you. They wanted me to join them for brunch."

"I noticed them last night when we were getting on the ship. Odd couple, not the type you'd expect on an Antarctica cruise," said Grace pensively.

"From what I gather, they're collecting continents—like trophies."

Grace smiled. "There's always a few of them on every cruise."

Rachel glanced over at the couple. "You know, that man sitting over there with that Hildegaard woman—I think his name was Wolf something. He looks kind of familiar—those eyes."

"Oh?"

"But I can't quite place him. Maybe it'll come to me." As Rachel spoke, a premonition of dread swept over her.

Reflexively, she placed her hand on her chest. She felt the pendant through her sweater. A vision flashed before her eyes of an underground bunker, horrible and dreary, with zombie-like people pushing stretchers full of tiny deformed bodies. She pressed her palms into her eyes and shook her head, thinking it must be her seasickness returning.

"What is it, dear?" asked Grace, alarmed.

Rachel took a deep breath. "We found this pendant at the site in Afghanistan, shortly before the bandits got there and ransacked the site. And it…well…" She paused.

"Go on."

"We're not sure if it's authentic, but it is rather unusual."

"Unusual? In what way?"

"For one thing, it has symbols on it—they're sort of like ancient Sanskrit except…" She pulled the pendant out and showed it to Grace.

Grace's mouth fell open and she dropped her teacup. "Did the symbols—did they ever seem to change shape?" she asked, ignoring the tea trickling across the white tablecloth. She reached toward the pendant, stopping short of actually touching it. "And when you touch it, does it sometimes seem to have—" She paused, searching for the right words. "—to have strange powers?"

"Why, yes," replied Rachel. "How did you know?"

Grace studied the pendant. "My husband Charlie found a similar one in a snow bank up near the old meteorology station. We had no idea how it got there."

"That is so bizarre. What happened to the pendant Charlie found?"

"We were planning on taking it back and giving it to a museum. But we never made it that far." She took a deep breath, then continued, "He had it with him when he fell into the crevasse."

They sat in silence while a waiter came over to clean up the spilt tea and replace it with a fresh hot cup.

After he had left, Grace sat forward and took

Rachel's hand. "Whatever you do," she said with quiet urgency, "put the pendant in the safe in your cabin until we get to Shackleton Station. And don't let anyone know you have it with you."

Rachel glanced sideways at Hilde and Wolf, sitting at a table on the other side of the dining room. Hilde was staring at them with rapt interest. She looked away quickly when she noted Rachel looking her way.

"Just do as I say," urged Grace.

"Okay," Rachel said. Although she found it hard to imagine that thieves were lurking aboard a cruise ship to Antarctica, it was certainly possible that Hilde and Wolf Meyer were international jewelry thieves. Maybe the vague memory she had of his face was from a newspaper article. She glanced back over at the table where they had been sitting. They had disappeared.

She got up from her table and looked out the window. The rain had let up somewhat. "Well, I'll let you get back to your work. I saw on the itinerary that there's a bird talk going on now—but first I'll take care of the pendant," she assured Grace.

****

Back in her cabin, Rachel was about to put the pendant in the safe, but hesitated. For some inexplicable reason she felt safer with the pendant near her. Tucking it back under her sweater, she picked up her parka and the pair of binoculars the steward had left for her and headed up to the deck.

On the port side of the ship, sheltered by an overhang from the upper deck, several passengers with binoculars were following a pair of sooty-brown birds. Rachel pulled her hood over her head and walked over to join them. The wooden deck was slick with freezing rain.

One of the birdwatchers, a bronze-faced man with deep laugh lines and wild, sun-bleached ringlets, wore a large patch on his yellow jacket that identified him as "Byrdie" Parker, ship naturalist. "The main food of storm petrels," he was explaining, "is krill, tiny shrimp-like creatures that form the foundation of the Antarctic food chain. Everything from whales and seals to penguins depend on krill for food."

He pulled a plastic cube from his pocket. In it were embedded a swarm of small gray-green creatures that looked like tiny shrimp. "These tiny creatures form the largest biomass on Earth. If you put all the krill in the world together, they'd weigh five times as much as all the humans on earth."

Rachel watched in fascination as the storm petrels fluttered just above the surface of the water. Every now and then the petrels' long yellow legs would patter across the crest of a wave as they searched the slate-gray waters for krill.

Other birdwatchers scanned the air, each hoping to be the first to spot something exceptionally exciting. "Over there!" A wave of red parkas ebbed toward the back of the ship.

A lone albatross came into view and glided alongside the ship, riding the thermals and currents created by the ship's movement. A mere jagged line in a vast ocean, the albatross's two-meter wingspan was dwarfed by the rising swells and whitecaps. Below the ship's wake, water gushed out of the twin motors, arching up into the cold air in milky clouds. Without any detectable wing movement, the albatross turned slightly and glided gracefully across the wake.

As Rachel followed the path of the albatross, she noticed Hilde standing at the stern of the ship. Rachel pulled her hood around her face and hunched down behind the other birdwatchers.

"It's a black-browed albatross," Byrdie said. "The most abundant albatross in—" He broke off and furrowed his eyebrows. Leaning against the rail, he adjusted his binoculars to a higher resolution and peered into the thin fog.

Rachel moved over beside him. "What do you see?" she asked.

He hesitated. "I don't know. It almost looked like a periscope—but that has to be impossible. It's probably just the black edge on the wing of a wandering albatross." As he stared into the distance, a large albatross appeared, slipping in and out of the fog. A passenger pointed excitedly at the barely visible shape.

"Good spotting," said Byrdie, shifting his attention back to the birdwatchers. "It's a wandering albatross. They're enthusiastic ship followers. We'll probably pick up more of them."

Despite his air of casual cheeriness, Rachel noticed that Byrdie appeared somewhat shaken. He glanced toward the café.

Following his gaze, Rachel saw Trevor sitting at one of the tables across from a shapely woman with long auburn-red hair. Rachel felt a pang of jealousy, but quickly pushed it aside. After all, she was already spoken for.

Byrdie took a step, as if he was considering going inside, then stopped and looked back out to sea at the area where he had been looking earlier.

The passengers shifted from foot to foot trying to

keep warm. The temperature was beginning to drop and the fog thickening.

"Visibility isn't terrific right now," Byrdie said, looking around, then removing his binoculars. "This heavy fog is typical of the Antarctic Convergence—the area that marks the beginning of the Antarctic region."

"When will we start seeing penguins?" asked a plump elderly woman.

"When we get to Deception Island this afternoon. If all goes well we'll go ashore in the Zodiacs to visit the penguin colony."

"What about polar bears?"

Byrdie smiled. "Don't worry. There're no polar bears in Antarctica—or any land predators for that matter." He looked around. "Any other questions?"

Rachel frowned as the polar bear passenger raised his hand again. Even worse, Hilde had noticed her and was starting over her way, all smiles.

Rachel turned and, blending into the crowd, ducked back inside.

Chapter 6

Two kilometers to the north a small submarine, its periscope shrouded by the fog cover, trailed the cruise ship. Angel Ricardo Ramirez, a tall, handsome man with piercing blue eyes, sat on the edge of a plush velvet bench in the bridge—a small but ornate room that looked like a modernized rendition of Captain Nemo's infamous *Nautilus*. The view from the periscope was projected onto a screen that wrapped most of the way around the room.

The captain, a pencil-thin man with a neatly trimmed salt and pepper beard stood not far from Ramirez with one elbow resting on a computer console. Nearby a young man in a pale blue scuba suit sat clutching in his gloved hand a small stainless-steel cylinder with a circular lid and a digital display. A padded case with an underwater laser ice corer and other paraphernalia lay strapped on the seat beside him.

Ramirez shifted uncomfortably in his seat. As an intelligence officer for Global Genome this was his first assignment away from the luxury of a corporate office—an arrangement he greatly preferred. He frowned. He would not be here in this damned submarine if his target had not been so pigheaded and unpredictable. Now he would be answerable to Generalmajor Braun if they failed again, an unpleasant prospect to say the least.

Reaching over, he unstrapped the seat restraints digging into his shoulders. As he stood to stretch, he caught a glimpse of his reflection in the highly polished periscope column. Smiling approvingly, he ran his fingers through his dark wavy hair. Women found him irresistible, which was why he had been chosen for this particular job. A master of disguise, he could switch identities as easily as a chameleon changed color, a talent that served him well as a corporate intelligence officer. He could also speak six languages, two of them—English and German—fluently, as well as his native Spanish.

He sat back and studied the screen in front of him. The periscope came outfitted with the latest image-enhancement equipment and could see through all but the thickest fog. “Enhance image,” he said to the computer.

Tiny figures in red coats, passengers wearing the standard red Antarctic parka provided by the cruise line, flitted onto a section of the screen.

Moving forward on his seat, he studied the figures more closely, wondering if any of them was her. It was hard to tell since the high swells kept blocking his view.

When he got a clear view again, he noticed one of the red coats looking directly at him through binoculars. Startled, he was about to tell the captain to drop back when he realized they were probably just birdwatchers.

Smirking at their defenselessness, he signaled the captain to raise the periscope higher. Although this might make them easier to detect, the captain had assured him they were well hidden from view. After all, it was just a cruise ship, not a battleship. Also, he preferred living on the edge—especially when he had the clear advantage.

"Close the gap," he ordered the captain. The captain scowled, then, turning his back to Ramirez, he punched some numbers into the computer.

The craft rolled slightly as it picked up speed. Ramirez gripped the edge of the seat. He did not like the sea. Too open, too unpredictable, too dangerous. He preferred the predictable violence of human society.

As the craft lurched forward, the diver's cylinder fell to the floor with a clatter.

Ramirez leaned forward to pick it up.

"No!" cried the diver.

Before he could stop him, Ramirez picked up the cylinder, accidentally releasing the cover in the process. There was a whooshing sound as the hinged lid flapped back. A cloud of white vapor flowed out of the top of the cylinder and poured down the sides.

"Damn," muttered Ramirez as he jerked his hand back and dropped the cylinder. He examined his hand. The tips of his fingers were slightly frost bitten and one was bleeding slightly. He cursed and instinctively put his finger in his mouth to stop the bleeding.

The diver looked horrified. He started to say something, but the captain gave him a distinct leave-it-alone look. Ramirez barely had time to wonder what that was about before the diver scooped up the tube and latched the cover. Then the diver pulled a bottle out of a case, sprayed his hands, and wiped down the tube as well as the spot on the floor where it had fallen. After he had finished, he handed the bottle to Ramirez, who sprayed some of the solution onto his injured hand. He wrinkled his nose. It smelled like bleach.

The captain opened the first-aid kit and handed

Ramirez a thermal glove. “Don’t worry, it’s only liquid nitrogen,” he said in a disdainful tone. “Your hand wasn’t in it long enough to cause any permanent damage.”

Ramirez took the glove and returned to his seat, nursing his wounds. “How long before we reach Antarctica and Deception Island?” he asked impatiently.

“In a few hours. We need to allow enough time for carrying out mission Blue Ice before picking up our target.”

“Good,” Ramirez said with a smug smile. Everything was going as planned. How could anything go wrong this time? They had her in the palm of their hands.

Just then the computer spoke. “You’ve been pinged.”

“What the hell was that?” demanded Ramirez, glaring accusingly at the captain.

The captain stared at the computer screen. “How can this be? There’s nothing in this area but us and…”

“Ping. Ping,” the computer repeated, mimicking the sound of sonar hitting a ship’s hull.

“You assured me there were no subs or battleships in the area!” snarled Ramirez. “And can’t you shut that damn computer up?”

“Ping. Ping. Ping.”

The captain reached toward the button to activate the acoustic interceptor shield. Then, just as quickly, he took his finger off the button. “Unless,” he said, his eyes narrowing. “Computer, determine direction and distance of the source of sound.”

The computer dutifully churned out the requested

data.

“Damn,” said the captain. “It’s them!”

“Who? Who is it?”

“Ping. Ping. Ping. PING.”

“Jesus Christ! Do something!” cried Ramirez, his body gripped in fear.

****

Rachel shook off her wet shoes and stepped inside the café. Glancing over her shoulder, she was relieved to see Hilde was nowhere in sight. Inside, Trevor was still engrossed in his tête-à-tête with the redheaded woman. The redhead leaned forward and gave him a playful hug. Rachel unzipped her jacket and removed her gloves and jammed them into one of the pockets.

As she passed by a few tables from where they sat, Trevor looked up and smiled self-consciously at her before going back to his conversation. So much for introductions! Well, what did she expect, anyway? He’d probably been nice to her yesterday and this morning just to be polite.

Crossing the café to Grace’s table, she plopped herself down in a chair. As always, Grace was delighted to see her. A waiter brought over a selection of herbal teas.

Rachel pushed a damp strand of hair out of her eyes and secured it behind her ear.

“Try the ginger tea,” suggested Grace. “It has a nice warming effect.”

The waiter poured her a cup.

Rachel picked up the teacup and cradled it in her hands. The warmth felt good after being outdoors in the raw cold. “Please, go ahead with what you were doing. I don’t want to interfere with your work.”

Grace smiled. "You're not interfering," she said. "By the way, I thought you might be interested in this book on Antarctica. I finished it already—you can keep it."

"Thanks." Rachel picked up the ebook reader and scanned through it until she came to a chapter entitled "A Brief Political and Natural History of Deception Island." Isn't that where Byrdie said they were stopping this afternoon? She began reading.

> *Deception Island is a fifteen kilometer wide volcanic ring surrounding a spacious harbor or crater.*

She skipped ahead to the section on political history.

> *The harbor has been used as a safe haven by sealers, whalers, and expeditions seeking to establish a claim in Antarctica. During World War II, Nazi U-boats used the island as a refuge. Deception Island was later the site of both an Argentinean and a British scientific station until a series of volcanic eruptions in 1967-70 forced them to evacuate. Miraculously everyone escaped. Another station was built shortly after to monitor volcanic activity in the area. This station was destroyed in—*

A movement distracted her. Looking up she saw Ka-Wing winding his way through the café toward the table where Trevor was sitting. Byrdie had come inside and was sitting at the table next to the red-haired woman.

Ka-Wing leaned over the woman's shoulder and whispered something in her ear. She turned to him with a quizzical look, then, excusing herself from the table, left with him. Byrdie got up and followed. Trevor watched somberly as they walked toward the door to the lounge. After a few moments, he stood and came over to join Grace and Rachel.

"Hello, Aunt Grace, Rachel," he said, flashing his boyish smile. He looked at Rachel uncertainly. "I'm heading out to the talk in the Emperor Auditorium if the two of you would like to join me."

"What about your friend?" asked Rachel with forced casualness.

"My friend? Oh, you mean Caitlyn? She's heard the talk many times," Trevor replied. "Anyway, she just got a call from the sonar operator. Apparently they've sighted some unidentified object—probably a whale or something—following the ship."

Rachel stared out the window toward the stern of the ship where Byrdie thought he had seen a periscope earlier. The misty drizzle had turned into a damp sleet that covered the deck with a thin veneer of slushy ice.

****

Glaring at Ramirez in disgust, the captain raised a hand for silence.

After a few minutes, he turned to the computer. "Scramble echo," he ordered.

"PING. PING. PING. PING."

"And that's just for starters," he said with a glint in his eyes as he set about reprogramming the computer.

Ramirez stared at the captain in horror. The pings were getting louder and closer together.

"Now for the real fun," the captain said. He leaned back against the wall and slipped into a harness. "Computer, initiate program B27."

Ramirez gave a little shriek as the submarine dived and his red cushioned seat suddenly disappeared out from under him. He lunged toward the console for support, accidentally hitting some of the keys on the computer keyboard as he tumbled to the floor.

****

Caitlyn Parker burst into the room on the sky deck just below the bridge that had been set aside as a dry lab in a joint research project sponsored by the Antarctica Environmental Protection Agency (AEPA) and the International Association of Antarctica Tour Operators (IAATO). Although initially viewed with suspicion by hard-core Antarcticans, the relationship that had developed between the research scientists and the tourist industry had proved beneficial to everyone.

Captain Svenson, a tall man with thick silver hair and finely chiseled Nordic features, and dressed in an impeccable white officer's uniform with black and gold striped epaulets, had arrived just moments before. He was staring at a screen. The fuzzy red image on the screen was surrounded by an aura of yellow that turned briefly to green as it blended into a blue background.

"Let's see if it's following us," the captain said, pressing his intercom. "Crazy Ivan to starboard," he called up to the bridge. "Keep it easy."

"It's still on our tail, sir," Abe Byumba, the sonar operator, said.

"What's up?" asked Caitlyn, holding onto the doorframe as the ship pivoted slowly to the left. "Ka-Wing said it was important."

"It's an underwater object," Abe said. "The sonar on the towfish we put in the water last night picked it up. In all my years, including those in the Navy, I've never seen anything like this."

Captain Svenson frowned. "Try to make radio contact," he called up to the staff captain on the bridge.

Caitlyn walked over to the computer console and examined the image on the screen. "A large school of fish or krill or maybe a whale?" she suggested.

"That was my first thought," replied Abe without taking his eyes off the screen. "But the image doesn't match any of the species' signatures. As for a school of fish or krill, it only has one air bladder." He pointed at a dark red area in the center of the image.

Caitlyn peered closer. "Odd. It appears to be hollow."

"Whatever it is, Dr. Parker, it's been following us for several minutes now, staying two kilometers away just below the surface of the ocean." He tapped the end of a pencil on the screen. "Also, look here at how this line on top ends at the surface of the water."

Caitlyn squinted at the barely visible line jutting out of the fuzzy image.

"No response to radio contact, Captain," a voice called from the bridge.

"Hail on radio again."

"Yes, sir."

Suddenly, the image jumped from the screen, leaving only a background of blue.

"What the—?" Abe gasped. "Where the hell did it go?" He fiddled around with some controls. Then, just as suddenly, the image reappeared on the screen.

Caitlyn blinked in surprise. "What did you do?"

"Nothing."

"Can you make the image any clearer?"

"No, the object is just at the edge of our sonar

range as it is. This is the clearest image I can get it."

Captain Svenson stroked his chin thoughtfully, and then pressed the intercom button again. "Kowalski, reduce speed gradually to thirty knots and see what happens. And by the way, did you see anything out of the ordinary on the radar—maybe earlier on?"

There was a pause and then the voice responded. "Yes, sir. Come to think of it, I did see a very small blip on the surface a few kilometers directly behind us, Captain—thought it might have been an albatross or whale fin."

"Could it be a dorsal fin?" asked Abe, studying the yellow line at the top of the image. "Killer whales have prominent dorsal fins and have been known to follow ships."

"Could be, but not likely," replied Caitlyn. "The projection is too rigid for a fin."

"Rigid? You mean like a periscope?" Ka-Wing asked, pushing in for a closer look.

Byrdie looked pensive. "Earlier this morning I saw a stick-like object projecting above the water, three to four kilometers away. It was hard to see through the binoculars, especially with the fog. I thought it might be the edge of an albatross wing."

"Well, this thing definitely isn't any wing of an albatross," Abe said emphatically, thumping his fingers on the edge of the console.

"Exactly how big do you estimate the object to be?" asked the captain.

"According to the computer it's about three meters wide, not counting the lateral projections, and between two and a half to three meters high. I can't be sure of the length—maybe seven meters. I can't get a good reading because it's coming straight at us."

"If this is a killer whale, it's a monster of a killer whale—and it's traveling at one hell of a speed," said Byrdie.

Abe glanced at his watch. "Not only doesn't it fit any of the species' signatures we have for whales or porpoises, it hasn't breached in the seventeen minutes I've been watching it. And being mammals, they have to come up for air."

He stood and gestured to Caitlyn to sit down. "Here, take my seat. See what you can do."

Caitlyn sat down and started working some of the controls under his watchful eye. "Systems recalibration; check for marine species over 100kg only," she instructed the computer. Images flashed across the screen as the name of the species that matched each image appeared briefly in the upper right-hand corner of the screen.

Ka-Wing stood on his tiptoes and strained to get a glimpse of the screen. "What's happening?" he whispered to Byrdie.

"ASI," Byrdie replied, keeping his voice low. "Automatic Species Identification sonar. It gives oceanographers information on the types of marine species in the area, from zooplankton—like krill—to whales. The sonar matches the backscatter with computer data on each acoustic target."

"Recalibration check complete," the computer announced. "No match found."

The fuzzy red image flashed back on to the screen.

Caitlyn pushed the chair back and stood. "I'm as baffled as the rest of you."

Abe sat down again and studied the screen. "Could

it be some sort of underwater vessel?" he suggested. "Although it's too small for a regular submarine."

"How about a research submersible?" suggested Caitlyn.

"Maybe. But then why all the secrecy? Also, I've never heard of a submersible that can travel at this speed. Besides, the shape's wrong. Research submersibles have all sorts of instruments and gadgetry protruding from the sides. And another thing, the towfish isn't picking up any engine noise. You'd think there'd be at least some residual noise at this speed, unless this thing is using some sort of advanced electromagnetic drive."

The captain frowned. "Whatever this thing is, I think it's time to pull in the towfish and bring the ship to a full stop."

Suddenly the image on the screen switched to a school of krill and then into a series of other marine life.

Caitlyn stared at the display of changing colors like a deer caught in the headlights of an oncoming car. All of a sudden, the image burst apart into a thousand fragments of light like fireworks on the Fourth of July.

Abe fell backward in the chair, almost upsetting it.

The tension in the room was palpable as each retreated to their own hellish vision of what this mysterious object might be.

Abe wiped a bead of sweat from his forehead. "You know what I think? I think someone's playing tricks on us."

"Tricks? What are you talking about?" asked Caitlyn.

"What I mean is, I think someone is trying to

deceive us into thinking this thing on our screen is something it's not. Some of the newer ships have acoustic interceptor coatings, which are able to scramble a sonar signal to resemble something else, such as a whale. Although I've never seen one this sophisticated."

"My God," whispered the captain, staring at Abe in disbelief. "Are you suggesting that we might be under attack?"

Suddenly the range readout on the screen began rolling downward. 1.91 km, 1.90, 1.89—it read in quick succession like a motorist trying to outrun a state trooper.

"Holy Mother of Jesus!" gasped Abe. "It's heading directly toward us and closing."

The captain pressed his intercom. "Bridge, hard…"

Then, just as suddenly, the numbers stopped going down at 0.27 kilometers.

As they watched in stunned silence, the object dove down several meters and slithered underneath the cruise ship, scraping the hull slightly before coming out in front of the ship and rising to the surface again.

"Bridge, check voids for leaking!" Captain Svenson shouted into his intercom.

"No breaches showing up—yet," a voice responded.

Abe was about to say something when suddenly the image made a sharp U-turn. "What the hell?" he gasped.

Caitlyn clapped her hand over her mouth.

"It's turning back toward us!" Abe screamed. "Fuck! It's on a collision course with us."

Chapter 7

By the time Rachel, Trevor, and Grace arrived, the auditorium was almost full with passengers chatting and settling in to hear the requisite talk on ship safety and the cruise itinerary. They had just found three seats together near the back of the auditorium when Rachel's phone vibrated. She pulled it out and glanced at it, wondering if it might be Richard. It said "Unknown caller."

"Excuse me," she said, starting up the aisle toward a door at the back of the auditorium that was ajar. "I just want to find out who this is."

The small projection room was crammed with musical instruments, audio equipment, and neatly stacked music stands. As Rachel stepped inside, a man emerged from behind a large speaker. "So we meet again," he said.

Rachel jumped and dropped her phone. It was Wolfgang Meyer, Hilde's husband.

"Sorry," she stammered, picking up her phone. "I didn't know someone was using this room. I just wanted to…" She broke off. A cold feeling of dread swept over her. Through the partially opened door she could hear the squeal of a microphone and a man's voice calling for silence. She reached for the doorknob.

Wolf put his hand against the door and pushed it shut. "You got away from me once, child, but this time

I've got you," he said through clenched teeth.

"What?" Rachel asked, not sure she had heard him correctly.

"Come, child." He reached out and grasped her hand. Rachel tried to yank it back. As she did, a high-pitched scraping reverberated throughout the auditorium. The ship shuddered. An eerie silence fell over the room.

Suddenly the ship swerved, spilling passengers from their seats. A woman screamed.

From the back of the auditorium came the deafening crash of metal smashing against metal. Startled, Wolf let go of Rachel. Free from his grasp, she staggered backward, tripping over scattered instruments. "Shit, my knee!" she gasped, cradling her right knee in her hands. She could hear Wolf cursing as he tried to make his way through the tangle of scattered instruments and stands. She scrambled to the door, pushed it open, and stumbled into the auditorium—and pandemonium.

On the stage at the front of the auditorium, the program director was gripping the podium. "Please, everyone be calm," he pleaded, one hand raised in the air in a feeble attempt to restore order.

"CODE BLUE STAR," a voice called out over the intercom. "CODE BLUE STAR."

"Oh, my God, we've struck an iceberg!" someone cried.

"It's like the *Titanic*!"

"We're all going to die!"

"The lifeboats! Get to the lifeboats!"

A wave of panicked passengers flooded toward the exits.

The ship rocked a few more times and then straightened, bobbing slightly in the water.

Seeing Rachel emerge from the projection room, Trevor pushed his way up through the crowd toward her. Grace was not far behind him.

"Are you okay?" he asked as he caught up with her.

Rachel tried to stand without leaning against a wall. Pain shot through her knee. Tears welled up in her eyes.

Trevor put his arms around her to steady her.

This time, Rachel did not refuse his help.

"Here, let me have a look at that," Grace said, kneeling down. She carefully pushed up Rachel's wool slacks and examined her knee. "It looks like a sprain."

A few rows down a man was holding his wrist and groaning in agony. Farther back, a woman was sobbing, "Help! Help me, someone."

Grace stood and surveyed the chaos in the auditorium. "Stay put," she said. "I'll be back as soon as possible to wrap that knee. Trevor, if you can stay with her."

Trevor sat down beside Rachel, his body barely touching hers, and rested his hand on her shoulder. "What happened?" he asked.

"Wolfgang…Meyer," Rachel whispered. "He…" She gestured toward the open door. "He tried to…" Her throat tightened as she tried to recall what had happened.

"Tried to what?" asked Trevor, a look she had not seen before on his face. "Did he hurt you?"

"I…I don't know." Rachel said, startled by his vehemence. "I mean, he didn't actually hurt me," she added. “He just grabbed my wrist and then…I don’t know.”

Trevor scowled. He stood and went up and peered inside the projection room. “There’s no one in there now,” he said. He came back and put his arm around Rachel’s waist. “Let’s get you to a more comfortable place. Here, put your arm around my shoulder.”

He helped her toward one of the aisle seats and then sat down on the step beside her.

She wiped her eyes with her sleeve. “Thank you for being so nice after I was so rude to you this morning.”

“Hey,” he said, gently touching her arm. “It’s okay.” He handed her a clean, neatly folded handkerchief.

Rachel smiled weakly and blotted her eyes. He was probably the last man in the world to carry a handkerchief.

“Please be calm while I call the bridge,” a voice called over a speaker. The purser, a small but sprightly woman, stood at the podium next to the shocked program director. She tapped her intercom button. “Purser to bridge.”

As if on cue, the captain appeared in the doorway. His dignified presence and his confident, authoritarian air had an immediate soothing effect on the passengers. He explained that the ship had veered to avoid what appeared to be an object in the water. As it turned out, he reassured them, it was probably just a malfunction in the sonar system.

The passengers who had made it to the lifeboat stations slowly trickled back into the auditorium to hear what else the captain had to say. By now, the ship’s doctor had arrived on the scene and set up a makeshift first-aid station to one side of the stage, with the assistance of Grace, Ka-Wing, and the ship's nurse.

Before long, the panic gave way to that atmosphere of camaraderie that often follows the overcoming of a shared threat. Passengers crowded around the captain, bombarding him with questions.

With everything finally under control at the first-aid station, Grace returned to Rachel. She handed Rachel some pain medication and a paper cup full of water. Rachel swallowed the pills and glanced anxiously toward the projection room.

"I wonder what Meyer was doing in the projection room?" asked Trevor as he stood.

Rachel shook her head. "He was there when I went to check my phone. I'm not sure if he was waiting for me or just happened to be there, but he gave me quite a fright." She glanced over at Grace. "In any case, I think you may have been right, about him being a jewel thief. He was acting very suspiciously."

"We should have ship's security check him out," Trevor said.

Grace nodded, "Good idea." She handed Rachel a walking stick the nurse had brought up from the medical center. "Here, use this for the next few days. It'll take the pressure off your knee. Meanwhile, I'll be down in the Medical Center on C Deck if you need me."

Using the cane, Rachel pushed herself to a standing position. "So are incidents such as these par for the course on cruises to Antarctica?" she asked Trevor with a wry smile.

He laughed. "Glad to see you've got your sense of

humor back. Need some help there?"

She smiled and then grimaced as she made her way down the aisle with his assistance. "I guess this is just part of the risk-taking lifestyle you're drawn to."

He chuckled. "Remember, it's only well-calculated risks." Then he became more serious. "I'm going to ask your hall steward to keep an eye on your cabin tonight, just in case Meyer tries to pull another stunt like this."

Out in the lobby, the staff had almost finished clearing away the shattered pieces of glass penguins and other souvenirs that had tumbled from the shelves of the gift shop in the lobby. A robovacuum was cleaning up the mess left on the carpet. Sensing Rachel's presence, it scooted out of her way.

She stepped gingerly outside onto the damp deck. The dreary overcast had broken, revealing an azure blue sky.

"We should be seeing icebergs soon," said Trevor, scanning the horizon. "Would you like to go up to the Sky Deck and check it out? I have some work to do, but I could meet you there in an hour—that is, if you're up to it."

"Okay, that'd be fun. Meanwhile, I think I'll rest my knee."

"May I walk you to your room?"

"No. But thank you. I've kept you long enough."

"It won't take but a—"

"Trevor, I can take care of myself—go."

Trevor watched from the doorway as Rachel went back inside and hobbled past the elegant curved stairway to the elevator. "The Sky Deck in one hour," he called after her.

****

Rachel lay down on her bed, waiting for the pain medication to take effect. She pulled the pendant out from under her sweater and studied the graceful symbols. What did they mean? Who had created this pendant? The symbols looked familiar, but she wasn't sure from where. She rested the pendant on her chest. As she drifted off warmth flooded her body, taking away the pain, replacing it with visions of ancient spirits. Only this time the spirits were closer—singing to her, beckoning.

The rattling of the doorknob jarred Rachel out of her reverie. "Who is it?" she called out.

There was a pause. "Sorry to disturb you," a muffled voice said. "We're just checking the cabins to make sure everyone is okay."

Rachel could have sworn the voice had a German accent, but then again many of stewards on the ship were from foreign countries. "I'm fine," she replied. She checked the time. "Shit," she muttered. "I was supposed to meet Trevor ten minutes ago!"

By now much of the pain in her knee had subsided. She dropped the pendant on the night table. She would figure out how to use the safe later. Slipping on her parka and gloves, she grabbed her walking stick and rushed out the door.

****

The cabin door banged against the corridor wall. Hilde shot a hand out and grabbed the door before it swung shut again. Checking first to make sure no one had seen her, Hilde slipped inside the freak's cabin and shut the door behind her. After a cursory glance around, Hilde started toward the safe. Then a glint caught her eye. She noticed the pendant on the night table—

sparkling, almost teasing her. She rubbed her hands together. "At last," she said going over and picking up the pendant.

She let out a muffled cry and dropped the pendant as the blazing heat from it seared her hand. "What the fuck?" she gasped, clutching her hand.

"Someone's coming," a voice whispered from the other side of the door.

Hilda looked around frantically for something to pick up the pendant with. Seeing nothing, she gave the pendant a sharp, angry kick sending it spinning across the cabin floor. Then she scooted out the door and ducked into the cabin next door just as Trevor appeared from around the corner, followed by a steward. Trevor stopped at Rachel's door and knocked.

Hilde looked at her hand and scowled. Blisters were starting to form. She should have been more quick-witted, found a towel or something to hold the pendant. She turned to her partner. "Wolf, you distract her—try to get her away from the crowd. I'll join you later."

"Consider it done, my sweet Generalmajor," he said with exaggerated tenderness. He took her injured hand and kissed it.

****

The sight of her first iceberg, a white and blue island of ice sparkling in the sun, elevated Rachel's spirits. Light radiated from the intense blue ice like sunlight through a cathedral window. For the moment, she forgot the dull throbbing in her knee. Below the waterline, the iceberg shone like an enormous jewel through the pristine, blue-green water until its vastness disappeared far beneath the icy ocean.

Farther out, the icebergs formed a flotilla of exotic ice sculptures, each uniquely shaped by the artistry of the wind and waves. Together, the stately ice masses drifted in majestic procession westward around the great white continent.

Rachel glanced around. Trevor was nowhere in sight. However, she noticed that Byrdie had returned to his post.

"What we are seeing is literally only the tip of the iceberg—ninety percent is beneath the water," he was explaining to a group of passengers. "I'll be out here on the deck if you have any further questions." Looking around, he spotted Rachel. "Hey, Rachel—Dr. St. Claire," he called out.

Rachel was taken aback. "How did you know my name?"

"Trevor Brookenridge told me your name. Nice chap, that Trev."

"Do you know where he is right now? He was supposed to meet me here."

"No, I haven't seen him. What happened?" he asked, noticing the cane.

"I'm just a bit sore. I took a rather nasty fall when the ship swerved to avoid that phantom object."

"Phantom? Yeah, right," Byrdie muttered.

She was about to ask him what he meant when an anxious passenger tugged on his sleeve and asked, "Is that blood on that iceberg over there?"

Rachel stared at the red stains on the iceberg. For a second the awful thought crossed her mind that Trevor had not shown up because something terrible had happened to him.

Byrdie adjusted his binoculars and studied the

stains. “Well, it’s definitely not blood.”

“What is it then?”

“Algae. Some of the more northerly icebergs in Antarctica have patches of pink and green algae, which live on the surface of the ice and snow in the summer. With global warming and the temperatures rising in this area, we’re seeing more of it.”

Rachel felt a wave of relief. Shielding her eyes, she looked around again for Trevor. Where could he be? She wondered if he might have stood her up to be with that red-haired woman.

“Are we in Antarctica yet?” someone asked.

“We are,” replied Byrdie. “Deception Island is only about one hundred miles from the mainland—just a hop, skip, and a jump by Antarctic standards—and is considered part of the Antarctic Peninsula. In fact, several of the research stations on the Antarctic Peninsula are north of Deception Island. We should be able to see it any minute now.”

Rachel hobbled over and joined him and the other passengers. Setting down her walking stick, she took a seat near them on a deck chair beside a stairwell that led down to the main deck where the freight containers were stowed. A chain was draped across the top of the stairwell. She sat back and gazed out at the water. A pair of graceful white birds stood out against the blue sky. In the distance, she could just make out an island looming dark and ominous on the horizon above the frigid gray-green waters of the Southern Ocean.

Chapter 8

As the cruise ship neared Deception Island, Rachel could see heavy surf smashing against the towering black cliffs. The glaciers that clung to the sides of the dark peaks were streaked with volcanic ash.

"Look—over there," someone exclaimed. Two large barges came into view from behind the island, towing an ancient blue iceberg.

"Project Blue Ice," said Byrdie. "The flooding following the collapse of the ice shelf has left the drinking water in many of the coastal cities, especially in the developing world, unfit to drink—salinated. So the United Nations Emergency Relief Fund devised a plan to tow icebergs to the devastated areas of the world for drinking water."

"But aren't icebergs made out of salt water?"

"No. Icebergs are formed by ice from the continental glaciers. In fact, the water in the Antarctic icebergs is said to be the freshest and purest on earth."

Rachel rubbed her knee. It was starting to ache again. "I just read that the Nazis used the harbor at Deception Island for their U-boats during World War II," she said.

Everyone turned to face her.

"Let's hope there are no U-boats waiting for us now," someone joked.

Byrdie frowned and put his binoculars in his

pocket. "I have to leave now to catch my Zodiac. However, I'll be stationed at the penguin crèche if you have any questions. Meanwhile, if you want, you can go up to the Sky Deck on the bow of the ship, where you can get a better view of the Zodiacs. The crew and scientists are already heading out."

"Sky deck?" Rachel slapped her forehead. "I was supposed to meet Trevor on the Sky Deck—not down here," she muttered. She checked her watch and sighed. Too late now.

Picking up her cane, she limped over to check her Zodiac departure time on the monitor. She had been assigned to the green group, one of the later groups of passengers scheduled to leave for the island. That gave her time to go back to her cabin first and clean up and grab her life jacket.

The hall steward was sitting in a chair at the end of the hall.

As she unlocked the door to her cabin, she had the eerie sensation that something was amiss. She surveyed the room. The closet door was open. She was sure she had closed it before she left. Then she noticed the pendant lying on the floor against the closet door. Her chest tightened. Had someone been in her room? Were they still there? Or was it just the rocking of the ship that had sent the pendant toppling to the floor?

After picking up the pendant, she cautiously peered inside the closet and then checked the bathroom. Feeling sure that she was alone, she returned to the closet and proceeded to read the instructions for the safe. As she did she could hear movement on the other side of the wall from the cabin next door. She dropped the pendant in the safe. It clanged harshly against the metallic bottom, as though protesting its incarceration.

She was about to lock the safe when she had second thoughts. The pendant would probably be safer with her. Anyone who knew how to break into her cabin—if that's what had happened—might know how to break into a safe. Retrieving the pendant, she slipped it around her neck and tucked it under her parka.

Since it was still half an hour before her Zodiac departed, she decided to use the time to check in with Dr. Shah in Afghanistan and let him know she still had the pendant. She didn't mention the possible break-in. She didn't want to worry him—besides, she wasn't even sure someone had tried to burglarize her cabin or, if they had, that they were after the pendant.

After reassuring him that the pendant was safe, she asked, "Did you ever find out who those bandits were and what they were after?"

"No, they just disappeared—poof—into the desert air. There are always clever thieves trying to steal the treasures from the past."

"What about the bones—have you heard anything more from the lab?"

"Yes. The DNA analysis of the bone marrow found what appear to be genetically engineered genes," Dr. Shah replied.

"But...but how is that possible? I thought the bones were supposed to be at least fifty thousand years old."

"The lab is redoing the tests, but it may take several weeks for a complete analysis. The DNA fragments we recovered are very fragile."

Rachel took a deep breath and sat down on her bed. "This is really remarkable, Dr. Shah," she said. "It may change the way we think about human evolution." She thought about the body in Antarctica. Grace had said there was something very unusual about it. Was it some sort of pre-modern human transitional species? Would they have had the technology to do genetic engineering?

"And if you think the genetic engineering is not enough of a mystery," Dr. Shah continued, "there is yet more. Even though the foot belonged to an adult, the telomeres in the chromosomes in the nuclei of the cells are as fresh as those of a babe in the womb. As you know, every time a cell divides, a little bit of the telomere is shaved off until the cell is no longer viable. In other words, our bodies have planned obsolescence built into them."

"Are you suggesting that whoever these bones belonged to may have been able to live forever?"

"Yes, indeed," he replied enthusiastically. "It is theoretically possible—if the DNA results are correct. Indeed, some biologists think we may have had a gene at one time that kept our telomeres from shrinking as we aged and, in fact, we may still have this gene hidden somewhere in that supposedly inactive part of our DNA that has yet to be deciphered."

"But this doesn't make sense, at least in terms of the current theory of human evolution."

"Perhaps, my friend, we need to keep an open mind and rethink our old assumptions," replied Dr. Shah. "Maybe humans have devolved. Maybe people did live hundreds of years at one time, like the *Qur'an* says, in a paradise of perpetual sun and springtime."

But those are just myths, Rachel wanted to protest, but she bit her tongue. She thought back to the Hindu legend of the River of Jewels leading to a land of paradise. But, of course, that was also just a myth. She checked her watch. "I have to go, Dr. Shah, but this certainly gives us something to think about. Let me know if you find out anything else."

When Rachel arrived at the Polo Lounge, other passengers in the green group were already gathered for the briefing before boarding the Zodiacs. "Staff will be stationed around the area at key points to answer any questions you may have," one of the staff was explaining to a group of warmly bundled, eager passengers sitting in a circle around her like a group of kindergarteners getting ready to go on a field trip.

Rachel took a seat in one of the overstuffed armchairs. Wolf Meyer arrived, alone, less than a minute later and took a seat across the room. He had a green sticker on his parka like her. She looked away, hoping they would not be on the same Zodiac. The very thought of him even being near her, touching her, gave her the creeps.

She felt a wave of relief as she noticed Grace at one side of the lounge talking to a security officer. Grace had a worried look on her face. Noticing Rachel, she came over.

"I'm sorry, dear," she apologized in a low, urgent tone, "but I won't be able to go ashore. Something else has come up." She glanced uneasily in Wolf's direction.

"Oh? What?" Rachel asked.

Grace didn't answer. Instead she asked, "Will you be okay alone?"

"What about Trevor? Isn't he coming?"

"Trevor went ahead with the scientific staff. But I asked him to look out for you while he was there."

Rachel sighed. "I was supposed to meet him before we left but went to the wrong deck."

Grace patted her hand. "Well, I'm sure he understands."

Rachel did not relish the idea of going alone with her lame knee—or of being on the same Zodiac with Wolf Meyer. On the other hand, she did not want to miss what might be a once in a lifetime experience. She took a deep breath. *Come on, get a grip. You don't need some man to protect you or keep you company.* Besides, Wolf couldn't do anything with all those people around.

Grace looked over at the security officer standing in the doorway, his arms folded in a gesture of impatience. "Be careful," she said. "It's rocky there, so you shouldn't walk around too much with that knee of yours. Stay with the others. A young woman—Carmen—from the Argentinean station there will be posted near the Zodiac landing area. I already talked to her over the radio, and she'll be there if you need anything."

After being briefed, Rachel's group lined up and headed down to the exit on one of the lower decks. She glanced back. Wolf was only four people behind her. After turning in their cruise cards and having their identities verified, the passengers were each instructed to stand under a fine spray of mist and finally walk through a shallow bath of disinfectant before boarding the Zodiac.

"Precautions against carrying microbes from the ship to Antarctica," explained one of the staff as she helped Rachel walk through the tray of boot disinfectant.

Across the water, Rachel could make out a Zodiac

pulled up on shore and staff setting up orange cones. Another Zodiac was coming back toward the cruise ship. The crewmember counted off sixteen passengers. Rachel glanced behind her again. One of the security officers checking IDs had pulled Wolf Meyer out of line and was talking to him. Rachel breathed a sigh of relief. At least now he wouldn't be on the same Zodiac as her.

"Those rubber Zodiacs don't look very safe," the passenger in front of her said as they reached the bottom of the steps to the landing.

"Actually, they're very stable," the driver reassured the elderly gentleman as he assisted him onto the Zodiac. "Good thing too. The water here is barely above freezing in summer. If someone fell in, they'd begin to lose consciousness in thirty seconds. Even with a survival suit like this," he said patting the bright yellow rubberized suit he was wearing, "without the special thermal lining you'd only have maybe twenty minutes—max."

The elderly man looked alarmed.

"But not to worry," added the driver with a twinkle in his eye. "In the almost forty years Capital Cruise Lines has been operating cruises in Antarctica, we've never had a Zodiac capsize or a passenger fall overboard."

****

Once the officer had finished questioning him, Wolf went back to the end of the line behind a portly man. After making sure the man's girth obscured the officer's view of him, Wolf turned toward the wall and pulled out his two-way radio.

Hilde answered. "What is it?"

Wolf cupped his hand around the radio and said in a low voice, "They're suspicious."

"Who?"

"Ship's security. They were asking about us. Stay away from the Zodiac landing."

"Damn," Hilde muttered. "But how did they…?"

"They know about the sub. I overheard two of the biologists talking in the lounge a few minutes ago. Apparently, they'd dropped a sonar towfish overboard to track the movement of marine life and the towfish inadvertently picked up the sub. And the sub's asshole of a captain didn't have the sense to get out of its range—thought he could trick them by playing fish games."

"Damn." Hilde stared at the burglary tools—a small laser torch and a pneumatic suction cup and a pair of heavy gloves—carefully arranged on a small table beside her bed. She hoped to get a second chance while the girl was off the ship. "Forget the pendant," Wolf whispered. "Get off the ship now. I'll get the girl and meet you on Deception Island at the submarine."

Hilde scowled. She hated leaving a job unfinished. But, there was always the chance that the girl would have the pendant with her. Hilde had heard the safe opening on the other side of the wall that morning. She stuffed the two-way radio into a waterproof bag and slipped it into her pocket. Opening her cabin door, she peered cautiously down the hall. No one was in sight. She pulled her parka hood over her head and hurried toward the Zodiac storage area. At the end of the hall, she turned left down a dimly lit corridor. The door was unlocked. Finding what she wanted—a diving suit—she shouldered the yellow duffel bag and headed cautiously outside to the container area.

From the deck above, she could hear passengers talking and milling around. Then she heard footsteps. She quickly ducked behind one of the colorful containers as a security officer walked by. Waiting until she could no longer hear his footsteps, she ventured out of her hiding place and scurried across to the door and down the metal steps leading to the center raft—the metal plate between the two hulls of the ship.

Once there, she opened the duffel bag and laid out the diving gear. She frowned as she realized that the diving suit did not have the heavy thermal lining required for longer exposures in the icy Antarctic waters. Frantically she searched through the bag for it. Someone must have removed it. Damn. She glanced nervously up at the door.

Voices sounded from the deck above. Footsteps passed by the door and faded.

It would be too risky to go back and get another suit. Jaw clenched and adrenaline pumping, Hilde slipped on the diving suit and tanks and opened the trapdoor in the raft. She stared at the gray water slapping against the massive double hulls of the cruise ship. Then, taking a deep breath, she plunged into the frigid water below.

Chapter 9

The Zodiac edged up to the black sand beach. One by one, the passengers, with the help of the crew, clambered warily out of the Zodiac, taking care not to let the icy water spill over the tops of their boots. The sound of penguins squawking and a faint smell of guano permeated the air.

Once everyone was ashore, a petite woman with thick black hair pulled into a ponytail stepped in front of the group. "Welcome to Deception Island," she said. "My name is Carmen, and I'm one of your guides. Just a few simple rules to observe. We ask that you stay at least five meters away from the penguins. Also, do not remove any rocks or anything else from the island. The penguins use the rocks for nesting material."

Rachel glanced up at the penguin colony on a rocky slope directly above them. Hundreds of penguin chicks, some still sporting patches of fluffy gray down, restlessly awaited their parents' return. Some of the chicks were sitting on their rocky nests; others were squabbling over stolen pebbles. A pair of sooty brown skuas—large, robust gull-type birds—circled overhead looking for stray chicks; a skeleton not far from the protection of the crèche was all that remained of their last foray. Farther down the slope, a chick relentlessly pursued its harried parent, begging for a meal of regurgitated krill.

An inquisitive penguin edged its way toward the group.

"They're so cute," cooed a passenger, digging her camera out of her parka.

"What if a penguin comes up to you?" someone asked.

"As long as you stay still it's no problem," replied Carmen. "There're no land predators in Antarctica. So, penguins are not naturally afraid of humans and will approach out of curiosity."

Rachel leaned forward on her walking stick and began softly humming a tune. The penguin moved closer. Other penguins soon joined, mesmerized by her voice.

"Wow, you really have a way with them," Carmen marveled.

Rachel laughed self-consciously.

"Doesn't having so many people around disturb the penguins?" someone asked.

"Not really," Carmen replied. "Tourists have been coming here since 1959. A fifty-year study of the effect of tourism on the penguin colony at Port Lockroy found that tourists have no noticeable effect on the colonies as long as they obey the few simple rules I mentioned."

"Why are those penguins just standing there staring?" a passenger asked. "Are they afraid to jump in the cold water?"

Carmen looked in the direction she was pointing. "No, they love the water. They're checking for leopard seals. Remember, I said penguins have no land predators. However, leopard seals often hang out near penguin colonies, picking them off as they return from feeding at sea." She pointed out a lone seal lying on an isolated section of the beach. “In fact, that’s a leopard seal over there.”

Rachel took out her binoculars to get a better look. At almost two meters in length and with its massive head and large jaws, the seal appeared almost reptilian as it eyed the red-clad creatures before slithering to the edge of the rocky beach. As it disappeared under the water, it let out a haunting trill.

“It looks evil,” remarked a passenger with a shudder. “Do they ever attack Zodiacs?”

Carmen shook her head. “No, although they have been known to stalk scientists working out on the ice floes,” she said. “We also request that you stay within the areas designated by the orange cones. Staff members are posted throughout the area to answer your questions.”

As the last of the passengers meandered off to explore the island, Carmen turned to Rachel. “Rachel St. Claire?” she asked.

Rachel nodded.

“Dr. McAllister said you might need some assistance. We have chairs if you want to sit down. We bring them out mostly for the swimmers who want take a dip in the hot volcanic springs along the beach. I’ll go get one for you.”

Rachel shielded her eyes with her hand and searched, unsuccessfully, for Trevor. She estimated that close to eighty passengers and crew were milling around on the island, all looking pretty much alike in their standard red parkas. The cruise ship loomed large in the distance looking majestic and invincible against the snow mottled black volcanic cliffs on the other side of the harbor.

Carmen returned with a chair and helped Rachel up to a flat spot overlooking the beach.

Thanking her, Rachel sat down. "Are those edible?" she asked, pointing at the krill floating in the water among the few hardy swimmers.

"To most animals, yes; but not for humans," Carmen replied. "The fluoride in them is potentially lethal to humans. It's a good thing too. Otherwise, Antarctica would be flooded with commercial fishing, and that would be the end of our pristine environment."

"What's that up there?" asked Rachel, noticing a small compound of one-story prefab red buildings on the lower slope of one of the volcanoes not far from the penguin crèche. She could just make out two people standing in front of what looked like the main building. One was wearing a red *Queen Maud* parka, and the other, a slight man with a graying beard, was wearing a navy blue pea jacket.

"That's the new Argentinean research station, *Juan Domingo Peron*. They monitor volcanic activity in the area. I'm staying with two other graduate students in that little building way over there. If you look just to the left of it you can see the top part of a Chilean station that was destroyed by the 1967 volcanic eruption."

Rachel glanced at the twisted remains of the Chilean station, and then adjusted her binoculars to get a better look at the Argentinean station. A line of tourists from the cruise ship extended from behind the station each waiting their turn to go up in the small observation tower on top of the main building. Rachel returned her gaze to the front of the building.

For a split second, she thought she saw Richard standing in a doorway scanning the beach area. She almost dropped her binoculars in astonishment. Leaning forward in her chair, she looked again. As she did, the figure in the door quickly stepped out of view.

"Those chinstrap penguins are feisty little creatures and quite the mountaineers," Carmen said like a proud parent, assuming that Rachel had raised her binoculars to get a better look at the penguins.

Rachel set her binoculars on her lap and pondered what she had just seen. It could not have been Richard. That was impossible—he was back in Providence. She rubbed the back of her neck. She had probably just imagined she had seen him, because she was feeling guilty about being away for so long. Guilt could play havoc with one's imagination.

Raising her binoculars again, she looked back up at the station. The two men appeared to be in the middle of an argument. The man in the *Queen Maud* jacket shoved the one in the pea jacket, almost knocking him down. Another person, wearing a yellow high visibility jacket similar to Carmen's, came running over. He pushed in between them, breaking up the fight.

Rachel shifted in her chair, straining to get a better look at the passenger with the *Queen Maud* jacket. Unfortunately, his back was to her. She glanced over at Carmen. Apparently, Carmen, absorbed in admiring the young penguins in the crèche, had not noticed what was happening up at the station.

Rachel was about to say something when a movement caught her eye—someone sprinting from behind one of the windowless sheds next to the station. This time she got a good look at the person's face. It was Trevor! The others didn't notice him as he slipped out of sight.

“What was that all about?” asked Rachel.

“Oh,” Carmen replied casually. “They’re just fighting over rocks.”

“Rocks?” Rachel stared at her. Then she realized Carmen was talking about two squabbling penguin chicks.

At that moment, another Zodiac pulled up to the beach.

“It looks like I have another group of tourists arriving,” Carmen said apologetically.

Rachel watched as Carmen headed down toward the beach. The smell of snow hung in the air. Overhead, dark clouds were moving in, casting a grayish-green hue over the harbor waters. A group of passengers waited on the beach to return to the cruise ship.

She glanced back up at the station. No one in sight. Standing, she strained to get a better look over the rocky outcrops that partially blocked her view. She was dying of curiosity to find out what was going on up there. After testing her knee, she picked up her stick and started walking slowly up a narrow, rock-strewn path that passed along the perimeter of a penguin colony as it wound upward toward the station, stopping only to pick up a piece of litter that had fluttered down in the breeze.

She was so busy watching her step and being careful to give the occasional passing chinstrap the right of way that she did not notice that the path had headed up over a knoll and out of sight of the beach. In the distance, straight ahead, she could make out the other side of the island. She leaned on her walking stick and squinted. Something gleamed in one of the small, rocky inlets, hidden from view of the station. It looked like the back of a whale rising out of the water, but it seemed too close to the shore to be a whale. A small boat was heading toward it.

She was just about to get out her binoculars when she heard someone coming down the path toward her. Looking up, she saw Wolf Meyer moving rapidly toward her like a predator on the hunt.

"Stop right there," he ordered.

Aghast, Rachel snatched up her walking stick and started to run, as best she could back down the path, through a group of chinstrap penguins.

The chinstraps scattered, squawking and indignantly flapping their stubby wings.

Cursing, Wolf scrambled down the slope, taking a detour around the penguins, and grabbed Rachel from behind.

He pulled her back, pressing his body up against hers, and clamped his hand over her mouth.

Rachel tried to scream for help, but his hand muffled her call as he dragged her backward toward a skua nesting area. She fought to break loose of his grip.

"You think you can get away from me again?" He tightened his grip. "I don't think so—not this time."

A large bird let loose a jarring, raucous cry as it circled menacingly over their heads. Wolf paused and looked up.

Seeing her chance, Rachel swung her walking stick behind her and walloped him in the leg. His heavy boots deflected the blow, but still he grunted in surprise.

Recovering, he wrenched the walking stick out of her hand and flung it. It clattered down the rocky slope and out of sight. He pulled a small pistol out of his jacket and, yanking her head back, jammed it into the side of her neck. "One sound from you and I blow your fucking head off," he snarled.

A sickly sweet smell invaded Rachel's nostrils—a vaguely familiar scent of a man's cologne or aftershave lotion. Where had she smelled it before? She struggled to turn her head away from the smell.

"My, aren't you the feisty little specimen," he said, licking his lips. "Just like your mama."

Rachel froze. He knew her mother? Or was he just trying to play mind games with her?

He pressed his face into her hair and inhaled deeply. "You've grown up to be quite the little sexpot," he murmured, breathing heavily. He reached under her parka and sweater with his free hand, groping her breasts, thrusting his hot tongue into her ear.

Rachel felt like she was going to vomit. She raised her hands to her chest, trying to push his hands away. As she did, she could feel the pendant under her parka, pulsing, her silent cry for help seeming to resonate with each pulse.

His hand moved between her breasts, brushing against the pendant. "Ah, I seem to have hit the jackpot," he said, as he closed his hand around the pendant and started to wrench it from her neck.

The skua let out a shrill warning cry. Pulling back its wings, it dive-bombed Wolf, smacking him hard in the face. Its powerful wings knocked off his glasses, sending them flying.

Terrified, Rachel gasped and ducked as the tip of the wing grazed her cheek.

Wolf stumbled backward, bellowing like a wounded elephant seal, and dropped the pistol. Blood gushed from his nose. Pulling a glove out of his pocket and pressing it to his nose, he groped around for his glasses. Spotting the metal frames outlined by the white snow, he managed to stand and started staggering toward them as the skua, now joined by its mate, prepared for a second attack.

Lunging forward, Rachel brought her heel down on the ground, smashing the thick glasses.

Furious, Wolf swung at her. As he did, the two skuas attacked, one ripping at his skull with its talons, throwing him off balance. The other knocked into him with such force that he tumbled head over heels down the rocky slope, hitting his head hard on a sharp rock. He quivered slightly; then, his body went limp.

Her heart thumping, Rachel gaped at Wolf's broken body. The blood from his head and nose oozed down his face and jacket, making dark rivulets and ragged puddles on the rocky ground. The snow between the rocks began to turn a sickening shade of pink.

In the distance, she heard voices shouting.

Then she noticed a small leather pouch lying near her foot. She picked it up and shoved it into her pocket.

The two skuas circled overhead one more time, mewling softly.

Suddenly Trevor appeared from behind the rocky knoll.

"Rachel!" he cried, racing toward her. He stopped short when he saw Wolf's body.

She tried to stand, to run to him, but her knee gave out. And her walking stick was nowhere to be seen. She fell back and stifled a scream as an icy gust of wind flapped Wolf's jacket, creating the impression of a zombie coming to life.

Sprinting forward, Trevor gathered Rachel in his arms and rushed her away to a clearing near the path. "What happened?" he asked, putting his arms around her.

"The birds," she said, with a dazed expression. "He was trying to…and then the birds…" She paused. It had all happened so fast. She closed her eyes, shutting out Wolf, and sank into Trevor's protective embrace.

"He's unconscious but still alive," a woman's voice called out, pulling Rachel back to reality.

Carmen was crouched beside Meyer, her hand pressed against his head, trying to stanch the bleeding. She glanced up nervously at the birds, which were watching from their perch on top of the rocky knoll. The wind was picking up and the sky growing more menacing by the moment. "I know skuas will attack if provoked," she said uneasily, "but I've never seen an attack like this before."

One of the skuas let out a guttural cry and started to lift off but then settled down again.

"Just stay low and don't make any quick or threatening movements," Carmen said.

Rachel swallowed hard. She rubbed her knee. It was starting to ache again.

Carmen pulled out a radio. "*Manden un paramédico. Pronto!*" she urged. "*Hay un hombre herido.*"

In what seemed less than a minute, two men in yellow jackets and carrying all sorts of medical paraphernalia came into view. Working quickly and staying low, they strapped Wolf to the backboard and carried him out. Carmen followed.

Trevor helped Rachel to her feet. "Here, lean on

my arm."

"He had a gun," she whispered, tears welling in her eyes.

"A gun?" Trevor asked, an edge of anger in his voice.

"He was trying to force me to go..." She paused and wiped her eyes on the back of her sleeve. "Then those birds..." She broke off again.

"What about the birds?"

"I think they saved me. Does that sound crazy?" She looked up at him.

He put his arms around her and held her tight. "No. No. He can't hurt you again, I promise."

She stared at the bloodied ground where Wolf had been lying, then she looked up at the darkening sky. A few sharp drops of icy rain were beginning to fall.

"We should get going," she murmured.

With Trevor's help, Rachel began the slow, painful descent to the Zodiac landing.

The few remaining passengers were boarding an awaiting Zodiac. The Zodiac supervisor helped Rachel onto the last available seat. "I'll be back on the next Zodiac," Trevor called from the beach. Getting the okay signal from the supervisor, the driver pushed off in the dreary drizzle.

From the direction of the station, Rachel saw a helicopter lift off and head north in the opposite direction and out of sight.

What had happened back there? What had Wolf Meyer wanted with her? And all the strange things he had said—what did they mean? Rachel's mind was filled with confusion. All she knew was that someone on this mysterious continent meant to do her harm.

Chapter 10

The water slapped rhythmically against the side of the Zodiac as it edged up to the cruise ship. After disembarking and removing her boots for decontamination, Rachel hobbled over to Grace, who was waiting for her, a new walking stick in hand. Apparently, Trevor had already called his aunt. After Rachel told her about what had happened, Grace took her hand and asked, "Would you like a cup of tea? We can talk more in the café."

Rachel hesitated. What she really wanted was some time alone to collect her thoughts. "Thanks, but no thanks," she said. "I think I'll just sit out on the deck and rest my knee."

The light rain had passed, and the sunshine was returning. She sat down in a lounge chair next to the stairwell and mulled over what had just happened on Deception Island. What had Wolf wanted? She thought about his saying he knew her mother, and a sense of loneliness and despair welled up inside of her. God, what a lying sleaze bag he was—whoever he was. Well, at least the skuas had taken care of him.

She closed her eyes. Whenever she thought of her family, melancholy settled over her like a dark cloud. Her life had been full of deception. As a child, she used to dream that her real mummy and daddy would come and take her away with them to her real home in a land where everyone was kind.

When she was almost seven, a young man had come to the playground at her school. Whoever he was, Rachel had soon convinced herself he must be her real daddy. The next day, when school was letting out, he returned. It was a glorious day. The daffodils were in bloom and the distant church bells playing a medley of tunes. The man smiled and waved at her and gestured for her to come over.

At that moment, her adoptive father drove up in his fading red Toyota Corolla. Casting a sideways smile at the nice man—her *real* dad—she climbed into the Toyota. Then an exciting thing happened. The nice man got into his car and followed them. Rachel didn't tell her father he was back there.

That evening, the same man turned up at their house that overlooked Narragansett Bay. Rachel peeped out from behind the lace curtains in her bedroom. She was about to run downstairs when her father came outside and yelled at the man to get off his property. In the distance, Rachel heard the wail of a police siren.

The man looked nervously toward the sound and then returned to his car. "Mark my words, Mr. St. Claire," he called out from the window of the car. "We will be back to get what is rightfully ours." Then, he drove off, leaving rubber marks on the pavement. Rachel dashed outside and tried to run after the car, but her adoptive parents stopped her.

"He's a bad man," they warned her.

That night her parents hastily packed their belongings. Ignoring Rachel's tearful protests, they bundled her into the backseat of the Toyota. Her adoptive mother had sat next to her, tight-lipped and expressionless, holding Rachel, who wept inconsolably as she was whisked away, not to see her Rhode Island home again for more than twenty-five years.

Rachel opened her eyes and rubbed the back of her neck. Beneath her she could feel the gentle vibration of the ship's engines. The rocky landscape rose sharply on either side as the ship left the protection of the harbor. Icebergs, sparkling in the early evening sun, came into view as they reached open water. As she sat up to get a better look at the icebergs, a large barge towing a mountain of blue ice came into view from behind Deception Island.

The blue ice reminded her of the way the sun had shone through the wild morning glories that cascaded over the arbor that spanned the weathered front gate of their house in Nova Scotia. Rachel had passed the early weeks staring out the window of her attic bedroom watching for the man to come and get her. Before long, the dreariness of that first spring in Nova Scotia had been replaced by the warm summer sunshine and Rachel had forgotten about the man—until now.

The sound of voices from the deck below roused her from her musings. Leaning to one side, she peered through the metal rails of the stairwell to the area of the main deck where the containers were stowed. Two men in navy blue parkas stood beside one of the containers. Pressing closer to the rails, she could just make out the words "Chief of Security" on one of their jackets. Whatever they were talking about, she did not like the tone of their voices. She pulled back slightly and listened.

"What do you mean, she's missing?" the chief was demanding. His fists were clenched, his narrow, pockmarked face an ugly shade of red.

"It would seem that way," the younger officer replied stiffly.

"We're in the middle of Antarctica and this dame just disappears without a trace? Is that what you're trying to tell me?"

The younger officer did not reply.

The chief threw up his arms. "They'll have our heads if we don't find her." He yanked a cigarette from his pocket and lit it. The gray smoke spiraled upward.

Rachel shrank back. She wondered if they could be talking about her—if the people at the station on Deception Island had implicated her somehow in what had happened to Wolf. Surely, they didn't think it was her fault that those birds had attacked him.

"We've checked everywhere, sir. Her room is empty—everything's gone. We checked all the security videos around the perimeter of the ship, and she didn't get off at Deception Island."

"Then she still has to be on board, you imbecile!" The chief tossed his cigarette butt on the deck and crushed it underfoot. Picking it up, he flicked it overboard.

At that moment, Rachel's walking stick slipped and fell to the deck with a clatter. The security officers looked up. She quickly pulled her scarf around her face and lay back and feigned sleep.

She heard the sound of heavy boots coming up the metal stairs. Then, they stopped. She held her breath.

"Who is it?" the younger officer called from the bottom of the staircase.

"No one," he muttered. "Just someone taking a nap."

Rachel listened to the receding footsteps. Who hadn't gotten off at Deception Island? Curiosity getting the best of her, she picked up her walking stick and carefully unhooked the chain at the top of the staircase and made her way down to the main deck.

Looking around, she noticed a metal door with a boldly lettered sign reading: "KEEP OUT." The door was opened a crack. Her curiosity getting the better of her, she pushed it open a bit wider and peered down a metal ladder into a large, dark space. She could hear the sound of water rushing under the floor. She was about to stick her head inside to get a better look when she heard footsteps coming from behind her.

She quickly pushed the door shut, then hobbled over and ducked behind a container just as the chief came around the corner. He lit another cigarette and stood there for a moment listening. Then he checked the door to make sure it was locked and left.

Rachel waited, her heart racing. When she could no longer hear him, she slipped out of her hiding spot and hurried back up to the promenade deck.

"Rachel!" someone called out.

She turned with a start.

"I've been looking all over for you," Trevor said, jogging toward her. "How are you doing?"

"Okay," she said, flushing slightly, remembering his embrace on Deception Island. "Any word on the condition of Wolf?"

"I just heard from Carmen that they flew him to the hospital at Esperanza. That's the Argentinean station at the north end of the peninsula. They have a hospital there. Apparently Wolf is conscious but pretty disoriented—probably a concussion among other things. They're running tests on him right now."

Rachel fished in her pocket. "By the way, I found this on the ground near where Wolf fell. I think it may have fallen out of his jacket during the skua attack." She handed him the small leather pouch. "It has some rocks in it that I thought might be of interest to you."

Trevor opened it and held up one of the small rocks. "Interesting," he said. "They have some sort of crystal in them, though I'm not sure what kind." He put the rock back and pulled out a piece of black plastic. He stared at it.

Rachel peered at it. "What is it?"

"I'm not sure. It looks like a cover to a virus flask."

"A what?"

"A virus flask, small glass tubes used for carrying virus samples. I remember seeing them in Aunt Grace's lab back in Rhode Island. I wonder what the flask was doing in the pouch?"

"Maybe it's something to do with a virus that infects penguins or seals," suggested Rachel.

Trevor shrugged. "Maybe." He dropped the cap back in the pouch, closed it up and put it in a plastic specimen bag with the rocks. Then he pulled a plastic envelope of wipes out of another pocket and cleaned off his hand. When he had finished, he offered Rachel the bleached soaked pad. "Here, you might want to wash your off hands just in case."

Rachel flinched in alarm.

"Don't worry," he assured her. "Even if there were any viruses in the flask, they're almost certainly dead. Viruses can't live very long out in this balmy air. From what I understand, in order to survive, they need a host or to be kept at below freezing temperatures."

“Are you sure?”

“Pretty sure,” he said. He checked his watch. “Hey, it’s getting late. I’m supposed to meet with the scientific staff from the landing team in a few minutes. It’s just a short debriefing meeting.” He eyed her walking stick. “Do you want me to walk you back to your cabin?”

Rachel gestured toward the nearby lounge chair. “No, I’m fine. I think I’ll sit here a few more moments and enjoy the scenery.”

“Good idea. So I’ll see you soon then,” he said.

Once he had gone, she settled back and watched the icebergs drifting lazily by. So much had happened today. She pulled the pendant from under her parka and ran her fingers over the symbols. As she did, she felt warmth pulsating through her body, drawing her in, relaxing her, pushing out negative thoughts, pushing out the pain in her knee.

She closed her eyes, letting her mind drift with the feeling. A wonderful, dreamy mist embraced her. A white figure appeared, calling her. The figure reached out, almost touching her.

Her eyes popped open. Had she fallen asleep? She checked the time. An hour had gone by. She stared at the pendant. She felt good—really good—like she had just had a full-body massage.

Her stomach rumbled, reminding her that she had not eaten lunch yet. She picked up her walking stick and started toward the Aurora Café.

A waiter approached her as she entered the café. “I’m sorry, miss,” he said. “We’re closed right now. We’re setting up for dinner.”

“Oh,” said Rachel apologetically. “It’s just that, my

knee—and this was the shortest route to the, um, Marco Polo Lounge and the elevators." Actually, her knee was feeling much better. She also knew Grace enjoyed having a drink of sherry in the evening. Maybe she'd be in the lounge and Rachel could tell her about the virus flask.

Seeing her walking stick, the waiter nodded sympathetically. "Ah, the captain's cocktail party, of course." He glanced at her clothes with a questioning look but said nothing. Taking her arm, he escorted her toward the lounge.

As Rachel stepped inside, she drew in a quick breath. Trevor was standing to one side of the lounge wearing a tuxedo and looking more dashingly handsome than any James Bond actor. He was talking to Caitlyn, the redhead, who looked ravishing in an emerald green cocktail dress.

Rachel frowned and glanced down at her rumpled sweater and baggy ski pants. She felt like a total frump. She was about to sneak away when Trevor spotted her.

"Rachel!" he called.

She could feel a pang of pain returning to her knee. Taking a deep breath, she hobbled over to meet him.

"Rachel, this is Caitlyn Parker," he said, introducing his friend.

"Trevor told me what you did," said Caitlyn. "That took a lot of guts. I guess you find all kinds, including thugs and thieves, even here in Antarctica!"

"It was nothing," said Rachel, forcing a smile. "Just another Antarctic adventure, like Trevor says."

Caitlyn laughed and winked at Trevor. "She really is a trouper, just like you said."

Trevor looked embarrassed. He gave Rachel an

apologetic shrug. "Would you like a drink? Some wine, perhaps?"

"Sure, why not?" Rachel replied self-consciously.

Rachel and Caitlyn stood in awkward silence while Trevor left to find a waiter. It was broken by the arrival of Byrdie, decked out in a suit and tie.

Caitlyn beamed and took his arm. "Byrdie darling, this is Trevor's friend Rachel St. Claire. Rachel, this is my husband, R. Falcon Scott Parker."

He smiled. "Yes, we met earlier today. By the way, my friends all call me Byrdie—sort of a play on Falcon and Admiral Byrd."

Rachel looked down at her clothes. "I forgot tonight was the cocktail party. If you don't mind, could you tell Trevor I'll be back soon?"

"No problemo," said Caitlyn. "We'll be right here."

****

Rachel rummaged through the pile of clothes on the spare bed in her cabin and fished out the pouch from the outfitters in Ushuaia marked "Cruise Formal Wear." Opening it, she pulled out a silky black dress, a small black purse, a double-strand pearl necklace, and a pair of sling back pumps. The dress had a tantalizingly low scoop back and a long slit up one side.

She held up the dress in front of her and looked in the mirror. "Ooh, sexy," she cooed.

Then she noticed the fading roses from Richard on the dresser. Draping the dress over one arm, she sat down on the bed and pondered the roses and the sense of disquiet, rather than happiness, she had felt when she thought that she had seen Richard on Deception Island.

She rubbed the back of her neck and glanced at the

heap of rumpled clothing she had worn to Deception Island. It couldn't possibly have been Richard—or could it? Rachel caught herself. "Stop it," she scolded herself. Her adoptive mother had always told her that she asked too many silly questions. Of course it hadn't been Richard. He was back in Providence.

She glanced again at her image in the mirror. "Heck, why not?" she said to her image.

Feeling wonderfully naughty, she pulled off her leggings and threw them on the floor with the rest of the discarded clothes. Tonight, she promised herself, she was just going to let go and stop trying to figure everything out. For the first time in a long time, she was going to simply relax and have fun. She walked over to the mirror, brushed her hair and pinned it back, then slipped into the sexy black dress.

After removing the pendant, which did not at all go with the dress, she fastened the pearls around her neck. Then she opened a drawer and removed a pair of heavy wool socks and pushed the pendant into the toe of one of the socks. She folded the two socks together again and stuffed them back in her underwear drawer. The pendant should be safe there.

She stepped back from the dresser and admired her reflection in the mirror. Her knee felt much better. After testing it out in the new shoes, she decided to leave the walking stick in the cabin.

When she returned to the Polo Lounge, she hesitated at the door and looked around. Men in tuxedos and women in flowing gowns and fine jewelry chatted amicably and sipped from champagne glasses. Trevor, Caitlyn, and Byrdie were sitting around a low table cluttered with drinks and plates of half-eaten hors d'oeuvres. Grace and two people Rachel did not know had joined them.

In an alcove, just inside the door, the ship's photographer was busy snapping photographs of beaming couples against a romantic backdrop of moonlit icebergs.

Trevor was the first to see Rachel standing in the doorway. She felt a rush of warmth as he caught her eye.

"Rachel," he said, coming over and offering her his arm, "you look gorgeous."

She smiled and slipped her arm into his.

As they stepped through the door into the lounge, the ship's photographer stopped them.

"Welcome to the captain's cocktail party, Mr. and Mrs. Brookenridge. Trevor, I believe," he said in what appeared to be an Italian accent. He paused and looked approvingly at Rachel, as though trying to remember her name.

Rachel glanced up at Trevor, who gave her a teasing grin.

"This is Rachel St. Claire," he said, winking and giving her shoulder a squeeze.

She cleared her throat. "We're not married—we're just friends."

"Ah, such a lovely couple," said the photographer, gesturing, toward the backdrop. "Please, would you like a photograph of the two of you on this most romantic night?"

Once the photographer had taken several shots of them, Rachel and Trevor made their way through the crowded lounge to join the others. At the far end of the lounge the *Queen Maud* Concerto Strings were playing

Schubert's "Death and the Maiden."

"We saved a seat just for you, Rachel," cooed Caitlyn, thumping her hand on the cushion. "Dinner is in twenty-five minutes."

Rachel sat down in the large overstuffed chair. Trevor sat next to her on the arm of the chair.

A waiter came over and offered them champagne.

"Rachel, you look perfectly lovely tonight," said Grace, leaning forward and patting her hand.

Rachel thanked her and took a sip of champagne. The champagne, the romantic music, and the closeness of Trevor were making her feel giddy. In the window she could see the reflections of people laughing and enjoying themselves against a surreal backdrop of towering icebergs slowly waltzing by and sparkling in the evening sun. It looked like a scene from the movie *Titanic*. She sat back, her shoulder resting against Trevor's arm.

A bell sounded, calling the first seating for dinner.

****

The submarine lay in wait in a deep-water cove on the north side of Deception Island, hidden from view by the black volcanic cliffs. A Zodiac edged up to the submarine. Air hissed as the vents from the submarine's ballast tanks opened. The submarine sank slightly, leaving only the hatch exposed. The hatch flew open and a crewmember stepped out. He threw the Zodiac driver a line and pulled the inflatable onto the rounded hull next to the hatch. The man extended a hand.

Ramirez stood up in the Zodiac, holding onto the side for balance. Grimacing, he reluctantly put one foot on the black hull and grabbed the man's hand. He heard the hatch slam shut behind him as he descended the metal ladder.

"Dog the latch," the captain ordered.

The crewmember turned a handle and secured the hatch.

Ramirez took a deep breath. Stooping, he made his way over to where Hilde Braun sat shivering. She glared at him as he approached.

The captain stood next to her, his arms folded across his chest and a smirk on his face.

"Generalmajor Braun," said Ramirez, his hands spread in an apologetic gesture, "I am so sorry. Let me explain…"

Hilde shot him a menacing look, then turned and talked in a low whisper to the captain.

Ramirez bit his tongue. The only reason he had accepted this assignment was to have a chance to visit *Neuschwabenland*—the old headquarters of the glorious Third Reich, the new world order. He had seen an old drawing of it once when he was a boy in Argentina with its grand granite buildings carved out of the rock far beneath the ice sheet of the Antarctic Peninsula. He knew it was not far from here. Now the base was home to Global Genome's secret Antarctic headquarters—humanity's last great hope. He closed his eyes, trying to visualize what the base would have been like during its heyday with glistening U-boats lining the docks of the underground basin, red banners unfurled, and smartly dressed SS officers marching in the parade grounds under blazing floodlights.

Hilde turned back to Ramirez. "We have information that the girl is headed for Shackleton Station. You will capture her there and bring her to us."

He gulped. "Shackleton Station? But how will I get

there?"

"The captain will drop you off in our launch three kilometers from the station. You will have to walk the rest of the way. There is a hut where you can spend the first night while you await further instructions." She shot him a look that made it clear she would not tolerate any failure. "It's time for you to finish what you started. This time I want her brought to me. Is that understood?"

Chapter 11

Following a dinner of king crab salad, Argentinean roast beef with Jackson potatoes, and Black Forest gâteau for dessert, Grace and the others returned to the lounge to enjoy the music. Trevor stood and offered Rachel his hand. "Would you like to dance?"

Rachel pointed at her knee.

"Oh, I'm sorry, I forgot. Well, then, may I have the pleasure of your company out on the deck? I hear there's a beautiful sunset right now which is scheduled to be followed by a spectacular full moon."

Rachel laughed and took his outstretched hand.

As they slowly wound past the few remaining diners toward the lobby, Rachel wondered if this was what it was like to have one of those infamous shipboard romances. She had to admit that she certainly enjoyed his company.

"I think we should get our wraps," he said. "It's a tad chilly outside. If you'd rather wait in the lounge, I'll get your parka for you."

"Thanks. That would be nice." She handed Trevor the card to the door of her cabin.

"I'll meet you in the lounge, in a few minutes," he said.

Rachel wandered into the lounge and found an empty seat near the bandstand. As the music began, couples got up to dance. The trombonist raised the instrument to his lips as the band broke into a slow foxtrot. Rachel smiled as she noticed Grace dancing with the Texan, a rugged-looking older gentleman, who had been assigned to their dinner table.

"I'm back," said Trevor. Her parka was draped over his arm. "Are you sure you're up to this?" he asked, as Rachel took the parka.

"Sure, my knee's feeling much better." She reached into her pockets and pulled out the gloves. As she did a crumpled newspaper clipping fell out.

"What's that?" Trevor asked.

"Oh, just a piece of litter I picked up on Deception Island. It's about some event the President of the United States is attending at the United Nations headquarters in New York City later this month."

"Probably the International Climate Change Conference," Trevor said. "It's a pretty big conference with leaders and scientists from all over the world."

"Yes, that's the one," Rachel said as she tossed the paper into a nearby receptacle. She glanced at the outside temperature on the monitor in the lobby. It had climbed to a balmy seven degrees centigrade—a veritable heat wave, at least by Antarctic standards. She leaned against the lobby wall and slipped on her ski pants, then tucked in her cocktail dress.

"Here, sit down and I'll help you with your boots," said Trevor.

Rachel sat down and slipped her pumps into one of her parka pockets. "You're quite the little caretaker, aren't you?" she said.

"So I've been told—especially when it comes to damsels with bum knees." He finished fastening the last hook on her boots. "There," he said, flashing his boyish grin. "Of course, once your knee is better, you're on your own—no more coddling."

Rachel laughed. "And I'm just starting to get used to the royal treatment. I guess I'll have to come up with another injury," she teased.

Outside, the sun was suspended just above the horizon, bathing the world in soft pink light as the cruise ship maneuvered its way through the icebergs and floes. Rachel felt happier than she had in a long time. "It's beautiful," she whispered.

"Mm-m-m," murmured Trevor. He put his arms around her and gently pulled her closer. They stood in silence, enjoying each other and the magnificent scenery. A gentle breeze off the water caressed her cheek.

A couple strolled by, arm in arm, laughing softly. Rachel felt a twinge of guilt as she thought of Richard.

"Trevor?" she asked, pulling away and facing him.

"Mm-mm?"

"What's going on?"

"You mean, between us?" he asked hopefully.

"No, I mean with Wolf. What do you think he wanted?"

Trevor took a deep breath and shook his head. "I don't know."

Rachel stepped up to the railing and scanned the horizon. In the distance, a humpback whale broke the surface and then disappeared again beneath the dark water. "I saw something in a cove on the other side of Deception Island—out of sight of the station. I just remembered it now. At first I thought it might be a whale, but I think it may have been a submarine of some sort."

Trevor leaned against the railing, his face solemn. "I noticed it, too. Caitlyn thinks it may have been some sort of small submarine or submersible that scraped the *Queen Maud* earlier."

Rachel looked at him in alarm. "But I thought it was a sonar malfunction."

"Maybe, maybe not. They're not sure."

"But what would a submarine being doing here in Antarctica?"

He shrugged. "I don't know. If you ask me, I think someone's involved in some sort of illegal activity—maybe something to do with fishing or mining the ocean floor—and doesn't want to be caught. We probably stumbled on the vessel by accident."

Rachel stared out over the black water, a dark foreboding growing in her. "Do you think it has any connection to Wolf?"

Trevor put his arm across her shoulders and gave her a playful squeeze. "Hey, Wolf's gone. He can't hurt you anymore. So let's enjoy this beautiful evening while we can."

An ice floe drifted by. A crabeater seal stretched out on the floe lifted its head and briefly checked them out, then fell back into slumber. The surreal beauty was almost hypnotic.

"Just one more question, I promise," she said, turning back to Trevor. "Did you find out any more about those rocks that Wolf had in his pocket?"

He took a deep breath. "Yes. For one, they are a highly magnetized rock—probably a blend of neodymium-iron-boron ore and an unknown crystalline structure."

"Is that unusual?"

"It's highly unusual. I've never seen this particular type of ore before. However, I do know that neodymium magnets are many times more powerful than the old steel magnets. Our instruments went crazy when we got near those rocks. We looked at them under the microscope in the Sky Lab and there seem to be microbes living among the crystals."

"Like viruses?" she asked. "Maybe that explains the cap from the viral tube."

He shook his head. "Viruses can't be seen under ordinary microscopes."

He paused as a group of passengers in evening gowns and warm wraps strolled by. A security officer was stationed inconspicuously at the stern of the ship.

"One more thing," Rachel said. She told him about the incident with the two security officers and the door that led to a large, dark space under the cargo deck.

Trevor listened without interruption. "And you said they were looking for a woman?" he asked when she had finished. "I heard a rumor that one of the passengers is missing."

"Missing? Do you think maybe someone fell overboard or was left behind on Deception Island?"

He shook his head. "I don't really know. Aunt Grace may know more about it."

Rachel shifted restlessly.

He put his arm around her again. "Cold?" he asked. He motioned toward a wide teak deck chair. "Hey, let's have a seat," he said, sitting down.

Rachel looked down at his boyish face smiling up at her. She had to admit, she found him pretty hard to resist.

Noticing her hesitation, he scootched over in the

chair to make room for her.

"But we just met," she protested. "What will people think?"

"Who cares what other people think," he said, reaching up and taking her hand.

She laughed. "You never give up hope, do you?"

"Nope," he said cheerfully, patting the empty space in the seat beside him. She sat tentatively on the edge of the chair. The evening was too beautiful to waste worrying about the feelings of someone who wasn't here. In fact, Rachel rationalized, she would not be surprised if Richard was out cavorting with some other woman at this very moment. Despite his constant doting and even possessiveness, he had always seemed ambivalent toward her. But she supposed a lot of men were like that—afraid of commitment, yet not wanting to be alone. She glanced over at Trevor. He grinned and winked at her. She smiled back in spite of herself. He didn't seem ambivalent—that was for sure. After a brief hesitation, she settled back in the deck chair.

Trevor pulled a warm Polartech blanket from the foot of the deck chair up over them, and put an arm around her shoulders. With their bodies pressed together, they watched the stars peeking down at them through the wispy clouds. The gentle breeze and rocking motion of the ship made Rachel feel both giddy and romantic.

"A penny for your thoughts," she whispered.

Laughing softly, he put his hand under her chin and raised her face to his. "I was thinking about how beautiful you are," he whispered as he gently brought her lips to his.

She melted into his embrace, all thoughts of

Richard erased from her mind.

Soft music drifted from the lounge as they floated into that sweet netherworld between friendship and love. The lights from the ship twinkled on the water, dancing to their own music.

The music stopped. Rachel opened her eyes. In the silence she heard a faint, clear tone above the rhythmic swishing of the ship's water jets. She sat up. "Did you hear something?" she whispered.

Trevor opened his eyes a crack. "Hear what?" he asked, his voice low and sexy.

"The sound—there it is again."

He leaned forward, resting his cheek against her hair and listened. "What does it sound like?"

"Like wind chimes or one of those Buddhist prayer bells. It's very faint."

"I can't hear it," he said, shaking his head. "Sorry."

Rachel scanned the horizon, looking for the source of the sound. In the distance, through the silver blue twilight, she could just make out the white cliffs of the Antarctic Peninsula. The light from the rising moon filtered through the low clouds, casting a magical aura over the ice-capped mountain peaks that rose up behind the cliffs. "Maybe it's all in my head," she finally said.

He pressed his ear up against the side of her head. "Nope," he said. "I don't hear any wind chimes in there either."

She smiled and turned to look at him. "So what's the verdict, doctor? Am I going crazy? Is my head full of magnetic rocks?"

He chuckled. "The verdict is unanimous. You're maybe just a little bit crazy—in the best sense of the term." He pressed his lips to her forehead and stroked her hair. Rachel closed her eyes and nestled her head against his shoulder.

Suddenly, he stopped.

"What is it?" she asked.

"Now I hear it too," he said, staring out over the water.

"What do you think it is?"

"I don't know. Maybe whales? There are a lot of humpback whales in this area."

For the next hour, they sat together in each other's arms, listening to the music of Antarctica, until the long twilight finally transformed into the brief darkness of an Antarctic summer night. A security officer in a blue parka walked by and smiled at them, then continued on her rounds.

****

Under the cover of the darkness, a small boat pulled up to a rocky beach several kilometers southeast of the cruise ship. The top of the boat opened like the petals of a giant Venus flycatcher. A man dressed in a white, insulated jumpsuit poked his head out and glared at the water lapping against the edge of the launch. "Can't you get any closer?" he growled.

The driver looked amused.

Hanging onto the guide ropes on the boat, Ramirez climbed cautiously over the side and scuttled up onto dry land.

The boat closed and backed away, leaving him alone in the icy darkness. After skirting the edge of the ice cliff for a ways, the boat submerged and disappeared under the cliff.

Checking his GPS unit, Ramirez started up the rocky slope, disturbing some sleeping penguins. They stirred, making soft cooing noises and rustling their wings. One penguin poked at his boot with its beak.

"Shut up, goddamn it," Ramirez hissed, giving the hapless penguin a swift kick. The other penguins, sensing danger, fell silent as the strange new predator in their midst picked his way up the rocky slope toward the snowy ridge above, cursing under his breath as he went.

Chapter 12

Rachel and Trevor awoke to the sound of passengers traipsing across the deck. The sun was up and the sky a clear blue. The ship had slowed to a crawl.

"Whales!" someone shouted, pointing at a spray of mist. The column of water faded into the white backdrop of snow cliffs. It was followed by another burst of mist as a five-ton humpback calf surfaced near its mother, much to the delight of the passengers.

Rachel rubbed her eyes and looked around. "I can't believe we fell asleep out here," she said. "Good thing we didn't freeze to death."

Trevor rolled onto his side and propped himself on one elbow. "Mm-m-m," he said, rubbing her back. "I felt as snug as a bug in a rug. Couldn't imagine a more perfect way to spend a night."

She laughed. "Such a romantic."

"How's your knee feeling?"

She stood and put her weight on the knee. Nearby, a whale raised its fluked tail and brought it down with a large splash.

"Actually, much better," she said, looking in the direction of the whale. Beyond, the white tongue of a glacier jutted out into the cobalt blue water. The whirling blades of a helicopter broke the stillness. She shielded her eyes with her hand and looked up.

"That's the ice captain," said Trevor as he sat up and stretched. "He flies ahead to check out the ice conditions—make sure we can get through these channels safely."

Rachel walked over to the railing. The water on the sides and in front of the ship was strewn with remnants of pack ice and bergy bits—chunks of ice broken off decaying icebergs. "This is spectacular," she said.

Trevor carefully folded the blanket and replaced it on the double lounge chair.

"I'll be back in a few minutes," Rachel said. "I don't want to miss any of this."

Back in her cabin, she washed up and changed into a warm sweater and wool slacks. Then, on an impulse, she checked the dresser drawer just to make sure the pendant was still there. She was about to put it back, when her mobile phone rang.

"Hello?" she answered, setting the pendant on her night table.

"Rachel, this is Richard."

Rachel felt a pang of guilt—like she had been caught in an illicit act. "Richard," she said, regaining her composure. "I tried calling you. Where are you? You sound out of breath."

"I've been really busy. I have a train to catch for a meeting in Washington. You know how it is."

"Yes, I suppose," she said. Richard was always heading off to somewhere. He probably spent more time traveling here and there than in Providence.

"How's Antarctica?" he asked.

"Oh, I really love it here. It's so…"

"I miss you," he interrupted, "I can't wait to see you again."

Rachel wasn't sure what to say. Richard and Rhode Island seemed so far away now—like they belonged to another lifetime. "I'll probably be back in the next week or so," she finally said.

"Hopefully it'll be sooner than later," he replied.

Rachel sighed and absentmindedly reached over and picked up the pendant.

Without warning, the room swirled about and the word "danger" flashed through her head like a neon sign. Startled, she dropped the pendant. It clattered to the floor. From the hall outside her cabin, she could hear voices and laughter. She took a deep breath. Probably just a voice in the hall she had heard.

"What's going on?" asked Richard. "Is something wrong?"

Rachel rubbed the back of her neck. "It's just people out in the hall making noise. Look, I have to go."

She set her phone on her dresser. Then she leaned over and picked up the pendant. Nothing happened. Putting it around her neck, she tucked it under her sweater and headed back up to the deck. She needed some fresh air to clear her mind.

Trevor arrived five minutes later, two blueberry scones in one hand and cup of tea and a cup of coffee balanced in the other.

"Would you like some?" he asked, offering her a scone and the coffee.

"Thank you," she said, taking the hot cup of coffee.

The early morning sunlight reflected off the brilliant white snow and ice cliffs as the ship moved at a leisurely pace through a wide channel.

Nearby, passengers clustered around Byrdie.

"Whaling," he was telling them, "was carried out in the Antarctica area from the mid-nineteenth century up until the 1960s. The whales were hunted almost to extinction. Between 1900 and 1910 alone, the ships operating out of the whaling station on South Georgia Island killed 22,000 humpbacks."

Rachel shuddered at the image of this pristine corner of the world soaked in blood, the shores littered with rotting whale carcasses.

"Good morning, kids," said Grace, joining them.

"Morning, Aunt Grace," Trevor said.

Grace turned to Rachel. "The chief of security wants to talk to you."

"Me? Why me?" Rachel asked.

"It seems Hilde Braun is missing, and the chief says he saw you talking to her yesterday. He thought you might know something."

"Hilde? You mean that obnoxious woman from the breakfast line?"

"That's the one. I also told him about what had happened with Wolf Krause, in the auditorium. He already knew about the incident on Deception Island."

"Krause? But…but I thought his last name was Meyer."

Grace shook her head. "Turns out Wolf and Hilde were using assumed surnames. They even had fake ID microchips implanted in themselves."

Rachel frowned and set down her scone. "I seem to have lost my appetite," she said.

Grace patted her arm. "It's not that he suspects you of anything, dear. We've been invited to the captain's quarters for lunch, and he's arranged a brief meeting with Chief Armstrong before we eat. I can come early too if you prefer me to be there."

"I'd like to come as well, if you don't mind," said Trevor.

****

A steward in a crisp white uniform greeted the three of them at the door to the captain's suite. The room was paneled in teak. Pictures of the *Queen Maud* in Buenos Aires, Antarctica, and various ports along the Mediterranean along with pictures of the various crews and a map of Antarctica hung above a side table. A large window with a panoramic view of Antarctica dominated the outside wall. Captain Svenson stood in front of a window talking to two security officers.

"Please come in," he said, "This is Dexter Armstrong, our chief of security, and this is Antonio de la Cruz, one of the senior security officers. During the off-season Antonio works for the Special Forces police office in Buenos Aires."

"I hear you're also something of an expert on the political and military history of the Antarctic Peninsula," Trevor said, reaching out and shaking Antonio's hand. "It's nice to finally meet you in person."

Armstrong gestured for Rachel to take a seat on a small sofa by the window. The chief pulled up one of the dining room chairs and then said, "Dr. McAllister told me earlier you said the man you knew as Wolf Meyer looked familiar."

Rachel nodded. "Yes, but it was just that. I've never seen him before."

"Tell me about what happened in the back of the auditorium and on Deception Island," he said.

Rachel told him everything she remembered.

"What do you think he wanted?"

"I don't know. Maybe a piece of jewelry I was wearing—a pendant."

The chief looked unconvinced. "He had your picture in his wallet," he said, studying her face for a reaction. He pulled the photo out of his pocket and handed it to her.

She stared at it incredulously. She recognized it as one taken by a *Providence Journal* photographer at a fund-raiser, shortly before she had met Richard. "I have no idea why he would have my photo," she finally said, handing it back to the chief.

"Can you think of any possible connection at all?" the chief asked.

Then she remembered Wolf telling her he knew her mother. "There is something else," she said, hesitantly.

He leaned forward in his seat. "Go on."

"Well, he did say something about knowing my mother." She looked down at her hands. "Actually, I thought he was just making it up to upset me—to throw me off guard."

"So you have no idea what he meant?" Antonio asked.

She shook her head. "No, I told you—I never saw him before until a few days ago—at least not that I remember."

"One of our security personnel," the chief said, "saw you in the breakfast line yesterday morning talking to Wolf and Hilde Braun, his mistress. He also saw Hilde hand you a slip of paper. Do you remember that, Miss St. Claire?"

Rachel squirmed in her seat. "Yes, but I didn't even read it. I lost it or misplaced it before I had a chance to look at it."

"Any idea of what may have been on it?"

"I don't know—probably her phone extension or cabin number. She wanted to get together, but I wasn't particularly interested."

The chief produced the crumbled piece of paper. "It says, 'Meet me on the back deck outside the café in one hour.'"

"How did you…" She broke off and glanced over at Trevor. He stood with his back to the wall, his arms crossed and his eyes on the chief. She wondered what he must be thinking. He was probably thinking she was some sort of criminal or unsavory character.

"You left it on your tray," the chief said. "One of our security officers picked it up after you left."

"But…" Rachel didn't know what to say.

"She really doesn't know anything," Grace said, leaning forward in her seat. "I think she's told you all she knows."

The chief looked intently at Rachel for a few moments then glanced at Antonio. "Okay, maybe it's time we told you who they really are. Wolf's real name is Erwin Krause; Wolf is his nickname. He's a senior-level geneticist with Global Genome and also a member of Triple A."

"Triple A?" Rachel looked puzzled.

"It's the *Alianza Anticomunista Argentina*," Antonio explained, "not to be confused with the more benign automobile travel association. It's a white supremacy organization formed by the Nazis and Nazi sympathizers in Argentina following World War II."

"Nazis? Is this some kind of a joke?" Rachel asked. She glanced at Trevor to see if he was smiling, but he looked dead serious. He gave her a strange look, as if he wasn't sure who she was. She felt a sick knot in her stomach. What was going on? Did he know something she didn't? She felt like she had fallen through a time/space warp into a Kafka novel.

There was a knock at the door. It was Ka-Wing arriving to join them for lunch.

The chief stood. "I have to get back to work," he said. "Antonio can fill you in if you have any more questions."

The captain motioned toward the table. "Please, why don't we all sit down?"

The steward returned and placed a mixed green salad in front of each of them. In the center of the table, next to a vase of fresh flowers, was a basket brimming with French baguettes, whole wheat rolls, and slices of sun-dried tomato bread. Rachel helped herself to one of the rolls.

"Tell us what else you know about this Hilde Braun and Wolf Krause," Grace said, turning to Antonio.

"Well, we know Hilde Braun is Wolf's mistress and also a high ranking officer in the secret paramilitary New World Order organization, which is associated with Triple A."

"Fortunately, Antonio thought he recognized them when they came on board in Ushuaia," the captain added. "Then we got that call from you Grace about the incident in the auditorium and we've been keeping a close eye on them ever since."

"What are they doing on this ship?" Trevor asked.

"I can't tell you why they were on the ship, although I do know they booked the cruise at the last minute, like you, and that they're both Argentinean and of German descent. As you probably know, following World War II, many of the top Nazis fled to Argentina where then-President Juan Peron set them up with new identities and jobs. Millions of dollars in gold and other wealth were also allegedly smuggled from Germany into Argentina in 1945."

Ka-Wing's eyes widened. "Whatever happened to it?" he asked.

"Most of it was never found."

"But what's all this have to do with why Hilde Braun and Wolf Krause were on this ship?" asked Rachel. "And why did he attack me?"

Antonio shrugged. "I can't answer your last question. Maybe he was trying to steal your jewelry or just having a bit of warped fun with what he took to be a helpless young woman." He shook his head in disgust. "Who knows what went on inside his sociopathic head?"

"What's all this about him being a Nazi sympathizer?" Trevor asked.

"It's a long story. To give you a bit of background, Germany's history in Antarctica actually goes back a century when they sent explorers down here. The Nazi presence in Antarctica dates from 1933 when they sent the ship *Schwabenland* to Antarctica to claim sovereignty over the continent. In fact, there was a popular myth circulating shortly after the war that Hitler had survived in a subterranean cavern in Antarctica."

"Hitler here in Antarctica?" asked Ka-Wing, staring out the window as though expecting Hitler to suddenly materialize.

"He could have been. We don't really know."

The steward returned with their main course.

"But why would they be interested in Antarctica now?" Trevor asked.

Once the steward had left, Antonio wiped his mouth with his linen napkin and continued, "Because it was—and still is—the perfect place to start a new world order. Remember, Hitler believed the German race—what is sometimes mistakenly called the Aryans—had become weakened because of interbreeding with what he regarded as genetically inferior groups such as Jews and Slavs. Antarctica, being uninhabited by humans, is a perfect place for them to carry out secret genetic experiments for reestablishing a pure Aryan race."

Rachel glanced out the window at the icy landscape.

"What do you mean about the Germans being *mistakenly* called the Aryan race?" Ka-Wing asked. "I thought they were one and the same."

"That's a common misperception," replied Antonio. "Hitler actually believed there was a super race—the Aryans—living under the Earth. He even went as far as sending an emissary to Tibet, where there was supposedly some sort of portal to this world, seeking pure line descendants of this Aryan race. The swastika is actually one of the oldest symbols in the world and may even be of Aryan origins."

"Didn't you write a paper on the Aryans once?" Grace asked, turning to Rachel.

Rachel nodded and set down her fork. "From what we know, the Aryans were an advanced civilization that settled in India and the Middle East well over five thousand years ago. Legend has it they just appeared one day from out of the holy Ganges River. Apparently, they introduced the Sanskrit language. The term *svastikah* actually comes from the Sanskrit word meaning 'fortune.' Then, the Aryans just disappeared."

"Does anyone know what happened to them?" Trevor asked.

Rachel shook her head. "Not really. Their existence was dismissed as a myth for many years. Then writings on genetics, attributed to the ancient Aryans, were unearthed near a Buddhist temple in Tibet. Turns out the Aryans' genetic knowledge was very advanced. They wrote of the *bija-bhaga*—DNA that was unique to them—even describing it in such detail it could be translated into modern genetic language."

"Speaking of a super race living under the Earth," said Grace, "according to Admiral Byrd's diary he flew almost three thousand kilometers beyond the South Pole to a land where he was greeted by peaceful and beautiful albino beings, or at least that's what he claimed. It was his belief he had penetrated the inside of the Earth."

Rachel looked skeptical.

"You can read the excerpts from his diary in the history of Antarctic I gave to you," she added.

"It looks like someone was living here," Antonio said. "We found maps and photographs of German bases in Antarctica in the Argentinean naval archives. If we can believe them, there were about eight thousand Germans stationed here during and shortly after World War II. The United States Navy sent Admiral Byrd to Antarctica in 1946-47 along with thirteen naval ships. The official mission of these visits was to establish the United States' claims in Antarctica. The unofficial mission was to seek out and destroy any Nazi presence."

Captain Svenson pointed out the window. "See the large island over there?" he said. "That's Wiencke Island. There's a small British station just on the other side of it, known as Port Lockroy, established in 1943 by the British military to keep an eye out for Nazis. Now it operates as a tourist stopover. The British also had a base on Deception Island."

Rachel gazed out the window at the white cliffs towering majestically above the ship as it passed through the channel on its way to Paradise Harbor. White and blue icebergs drifted dreamily by. How could such a serene and seemingly untouched place like this be the scene of so much violence and deceit, she wondered.

"What became of the Nazi plot to take over Antarctica?" Ka-Wing asked.

Antonio shook his head. "We don't know. We still haven't been able to locate any of their alleged bases."

"But *surely* any abandoned Nazi bases would've been spotted by now," Rachel protested. "With all our modern satellite and tracking equipment, I mean, it's been well over half a century since the Nazis were defeated in World War II."

"Not if the bases were underground," suggested Trevor. "Remember, the Germans were expert engineers. They built massive underground munitions factories in Germany in the 1930s and 40s."

Rachel was not convinced. "Okay, say that I accept your theory that the Nazis are alive and well here in Antarctica. What does all this have to do with Krause?"

"To tell the truth, it's not the Nazis who concern us

right now," replied Antonio. "It's their heirs—white Aryan supremacists, like Dr. Krause who, by the way, has a degree in genetics and virology."

"Are you saying Krause might be some sort of neo-Nazi bioterrorist?" Rachel asked.

Antonio nodded. "He's a member of the Party of the New Purity—*Partido de la Nueva Pureza.* By that they meant racial purity—ridding the gene pool of genetic defects, as they define them. The PNP is connected, mainly through the Internet, to a worldwide coalition of white supremacist terrorist groups. The organization has since gone underground, but we know they're still active."

"Did you find out anything else about Krause?" asked Grace.

"Yes. It turns out he's the grandson of the infamous Dr. Joseph Mengele, who fled to Argentina following World War II."

Rachel shuddered. Maybe that's why he looked familiar—maybe she'd seen a picture of Dr. Mengele somewhere.

Everyone sat in silence, each lost in their own thoughts, as the steward cleared away the plates then returned with coffee, tea, and plates of dainty confections.

Grace took a sip of tea and then asked, "But what about Hilde Braun? What's her connection to all of this?"

"She started working with Global Genome about twelve years ago, as an intern," Antonio replied. "From there she rose to become one of the top brass in their security division—as well as Krause's mistress."

"I just remembered something," Rachel said.

"What is it, dear?" asked Grace.

"When I was out on the back deck yesterday morning—it was just as we approached Deception Island—I think I might have seen Hilde down on the main deck carrying some sort of yellow duffel bag—but I'm not sure it was her."

"One of our Zodiac driver's gear is missing," the captain said. "And it was stowed in a yellow duffel bag."

"But we checked the security cameras and no one went off the ship except to visit Deception Island," Antonio reminded him. "And all the Zodiacs are accounted for."

"Actually, I believe there *is* a way to get off this ship without being detected," Trevor said.

"How?" asked Antonio, leaning forward.

"Well, I know this sounds far-fetched, but Hilde Braun may have escaped through the trapdoor in the center raft."

"What's that?" asked Ka-Wing.

"It's the metal plate between the two hulls. There's a small trap door in it that's used to inspect the outside of the hulls," Trevor explained.

"Are you suggesting she did this while we were out at sea?" asked Antonio. "Wouldn't she get caught up in the engines and killed?"

"Not necessarily," replied the captain, stroking his beard pensively. "The momentum from the fall would have pushed her below the jets. And the ship was going relatively slowly at that point. Still, it is unlikely she would have survived. From what one of the Zodiac drivers told me, the thermal lining in the duffel bag was not intended for long exposure to the cold water. I would give her maybe one in a thousand chances—at best—that she could reach Deception Island alive."

Antonio looked at Rachel. "There's still one more thing unexplained," he said. "Why did Wolf Krause have a photo of you in his pocket?"

Rachel rubbed the back of her neck. "I don't know. I told you, I never saw him or heard of him before." However, even as she said it, she could not shake the horrible feeling she *had* seen Wolf Krause before. A raw dread squeezed her chest, numbing her. Her knee began to ache again.

"Are you okay?" asked Grace, reaching out and taking her hand.

Rachel let out a deep breath and stared out the window. In the dark recesses of her memory, Wolf looked up at her with a sinister smile. He was coming to get her. Coming to get her and take her away.

Chapter 13

After washing up, Rachel gathered up her ebook reader and headed topside. She needed to keep her mind busy to shut out the Wolf, lurking in the shadows of her memory, getting ever closer.

The ship bustled with activity. Passengers staying on for the remainder of the cruise were out on deck or assembled in the Polo Lounge waiting for the Zodiacs to take them on a tour of the Chilean Station and Paradise Harbor. Byrdie was at his usual post, a sandwich in one hand and his binoculars in the other.

Rachel found a deck chair with a view of the harbor. Sitting down, she flicked on her ebook reader and typed in search terms "Byrd" and "journal." She scrolled down the log to the entries purportedly made by Admiral Byrd on February 19, 1947. It read:

2/19/1947: 0190 hours: Both magnetic and gyro compasses beginning to gyrate and wobble, we are unable to hold our heading by instrumentation...1000 Hours: We are crossing over the small mountain range...Beyond the mountain range is what appears to be a green valley with a small river or stream running through the center portion. There should be no green valley below! Something is definitely wrong and abnormal here!...1050 Hours: The external temperature indicator reads 74 degrees Fahrenheit... 1130 Hours: Ahead we spot what seems to be a city!!!!

This is impossible!

Rachel scrolled to the next entry and continued reading.

"Hey, Rachel," a voice said.

She looked up.

"Trev was just looking for you," Byrdie said. "He asked if I'd keep an eye out for you. He's going over some old maps with Antonio and Caitlyn right now."

Rachel stood and scanned the horizon. Rocky beaches and dazzling blue indentations and caves in the edges of the glaciers punctuated the white shoreline. "Can we see the cave where the body was found from here?" she asked.

"No, it's farther down the bay—maybe four kilometers—in a cove, between here and Almirante Brown, the Argentinean station, where we'll be mooring for the night. I'll be taking you to the cave in the morning."

"So what do you know about this body?"

"Not much—just that a tourist on the last cruise spotted it during a Zodiac tour of the harbor."

Rachel thought about Hilde and wondered if some passing cruise ship or tourist would find her body washed up on a remote rocky beach.

"At first they thought it was the body of a skier who had wandered off course," Byrdie said, "and fallen down a crevasse and got washed out there."

Rachel raised an eyebrow. "A skier?"

"There's a hotel and ski resort nearby. You'll see it once we get into the harbor. A team of glaciologists from Shackleton Station came and retrieved the body. It almost started an international incident, since the Antarctic Treaty requires all scientific research to be open, so they have to allow the scientists from the other stations access to the body, which they haven't done so far."

"Why not? Do they suspect foul play?"

Byrdie shook his head. "I don't know."

Rachel blinked in surprise as the ship rounded the point of land. There, on a spit of rocky land across an inlet from the Chilean station, stood a large modern building glistening brightly against a backdrop of glaciers. In addition to the official-looking scientific vessels, two large steel-hulled sailing yachts and a luxury motor yacht were moored in the inlet. There was also a small cruise ship—a converted Russian icebreaker that offered adventure tours. The clanking of the halyards against the masts blended harmoniously with the rhythmic sloshing of the water against the ship and the cry of the kelp gulls circling overhead.

"This is incredible," she said. "Except for the glaciers, I feel more like I'm in Newport, Rhode Island, than in Antarctica."

"That's the Antarctica-Hilton Hotel/Ski Resort," said Byrdie. "It was built two years ago. There was a lot of resistance to it at first, but it meets all environmental standards. Most of the hotel's energy needs in the summer months comes from solar power." He pointed to a row of three sleek turbine wind generators standing at the top of a rise above the hotel. "The rest of the power comes from those turbines."

Once the cruise ship was securely moored, a barge eased up to the stern. Crew from the ship busied themselves unloading containers with the purple Hilton labels and others with the red, white, and blue Chilean labels. Workers from the hotel and nearby station supervised the loading of the containers onto the barge.

Trevor appeared and took a place at the railing between Rachel and Byrdie.

"Hey, Trev, there you are," replied Byrdie, jabbing him playfully with his elbow.

"Through with your good-byes?" asked Rachel, smiling.

"No need to. We'll be picking up the ship again at the Argentinean station after we visit the cave."

"Oh? Why can't we just take the Zodiac to Shackleton Station from the cave? I thought it wasn't far from here."

"Not as the skua flies," said Byrdie. "But by boat, it's a different story. It's at the far end of the bay on the other side of those mountains. The people from Shackleton are picking up their cargo at the Argentinean station. It'll be easier for us to go back with them."

Passengers, some toting skis, lined up waiting to go ashore on the Zodiacs. Grace emerged from behind the line and came over and joined Rachel and the others.

"Look!" someone cried out as a pair of brightly colored paragliders appeared over the edge of a snowy crest. The bright colors contrasted with the stark white of the glaciers and the pastel blue sky.

Byrdie studied the skiers through his binoculars. "It's the New Zealand team. The New Zealand and Norwegian teams are here practicing for the Trans-Antarctic skiing competition."

"Kiwis," said a fair-haired young man. "Those New Zealanders. They'll do anything for a thrill." He smiled flirtatiously at Rachel.

Suddenly Rachel remembered where she had seen

Wolf Krause before. A clammy fear slithered across her chest, constricting it. She squeezed her eyes shut and swallowed hard.

Trevor took her arm and, drawing her close, glared at the skier.

"What is it, dear?" asked Grace. "You look as though you've seen a ghost."

"I…I remember where I saw him—Krause—before," she whispered.

Grace took her elbow and directed her toward some deck chairs. "Let's go sit over there where there's more privacy."

Rachel slumped down in one of the chairs. She felt numb.

"Go on, dear," Grace said. "Tell us what you remember."

Rachel closed her eyes again, trying to shut out the image of a smiling Wolf Krause standing there waving to her. "He came to my school," she said in a barely audible voice.

"Your school?" asked Trevor. "What do you mean?"

"I thought he was my real dad." Rachel's voice quavered. Then she told them about what had happened and how she had been whisked away in the middle of the night.

"So it *was* him," muttered Grace under her breath.

Trevor gave his aunt a questioning look.

Rachel shook her head and buried her face in her hands. "How could I have been so stupid?"

Trevor put his arm around her shoulders. "It wasn't your fault. You were just a little girl with a dream of finding her real parents."

"And he had my photo too." Rachel looked up at Grace. "Do you think maybe he *is* my real father?" she asked in horror.

Grace let out a deep sigh and gazed out across the water. "No, I don't think so," she said. "I think something else is going on—something to do with you and the pendant—but I'm not exactly sure what."

Rachel wiped her eyes with the back of her glove.

Grace leaned over and patted her hand. "If you give me a blood sample, I'll check your DNA against his. I'm sure the doctor at Esperanza will send me a sample."

Rachel smiled weakly. "Thank you."

Trevor gave her shoulder a gentle squeeze. "Hey, even if Wolf Krause is your biological father, it doesn't matter. You are your own person—a wonderful person. And no one can change that."

They sat in silence watching the skiers lining up on the gangplank. *Who am I really?* Rachel wondered. Nothing seemed real anymore.

****

The following morning, Rachel woke up late. Every time she had started drifting off to sleep during the night, visions of Wolf and dank, underground caverns filled with crying, deformed babies would drift through her head and she would wake up with a start, her heart pounding.

Sitting up, she took the pendant from the night table and slipped it around her neck.

Grace was sitting in the cafeteria when Rachel arrived for breakfast.

"I was just going to go wake you up," Grace said. "The Zodiac's leaving for the cave in half an hour."

Rachel plopped down in one of the chairs. “Sorry. I didn’t sleep well.”

“Are you sure you’re up to going? You don’t have to come if you don’t want to.”

“No, I want to come.”

A waiter came over and poured Rachel a cup of coffee and offered her a basket with an assortment of muffins and bagels.

“By the way, how’s your knee?” asked Grace.

“The pain seems to be gone.”

“You should wrap it anyway before we leave. The beach is rather rocky, and we wouldn’t want you twisting it again.”

****

When Rachel arrived at the departure area, their Zodiac was just returning from dropping off a load of passengers at the Chilean Station. Caitlyn and Byrdie were waiting on the platform at the top of the gangplank.

Byrdie waved and moved over to make room for her.

“I was just wondering,” Rachel said after a few moments, “about something you said earlier, Byrdie.” She hesitated, not sure how to word the question. “Did Trevor really ask you to keep an eye on me?”

“Oh, it wasn’t Trev’s idea,” interjected Caitlyn. “His aunt instructed him to keep an eye on you. It’s one of the reasons she asked him along—to keep track of you.”

Rachel winced. “What do you mean? Like to spy on me?”

Byrdie scowled at his wife. “Caity, that wasn’t necessary.”

Caitlyn shrugged.

"Time to go," called Ka-Wing excitedly from the Zodiac.

"What's going on?" asked Trevor, joining them.

"Nothing," mumbled Rachel as she pushed past him.

****

As the Zodiac pushed off, clouds were settling over the tops of the mountains, and it began to snow lightly. The filtered sunlight cast a silver gauze over the snow and water.

"Hey, how're you doing?" Trevor asked Rachel once they settled in.

Rachel forced a smile. "Fine," she lied. It was bad enough she might be the progeny of a ruthless neo-Nazi bioterrorist. Now, on top of that, she had to learn that Trevor might have just been pretending to care about her in order to keep her nearby.

Before long, the clouds parted and the sun returned. Brilliant bergy bits, the last remnants of once majestic icebergs, gleamed like blue diamonds scattered across the water by some divine artist.

"It's easy to see why they named this Paradise Bay," said Grace, smiling.

Byrdie cut the motor. "Listen," he said, cupping his hand to his ear.

The bergy bits made soft crackling sounds as the air, which had been trapped for thousands of years, escaped from its icy blue prison.

"Awesome!" exclaimed Ka-Wing, leaning over the edge of the Zodiac. "It sounds like Rice Krispies."

"Look over there," said Byrdie. He pointed toward a pod of humpback whales in the middle of the bay clustered inside a circle of bubbles, their cavernous mouths stretched wide open. Inside the circle, a cloud of krill and plankton swarmed and swirled like miniature synchronized swimmers.

"What are they doing?" asked Ka-Wing.

"Cooperative feeding," he replied. "The whales dive down in a circle and exhale a ring of bubbles which rise to the surface and form a net that traps the krill. Then all the whales have to do is come back up, open their mouths and strain the trapped krill through the plates of baleen inside their mouths." He pulled out his camera. "Caitlyn would've loved this."

Rachel looked at him and frowned. But he didn't notice.

Grace reached over and patted Rachel's hand. "Don't worry, dear, we'll get this Wolf Krause business all sorted out," she said. "You'll see."

Rachel closed her eyes. She could feel the pendant through the fabric of her parka, pressing against her, warming her. She began softly humming a childhood lullaby, trying to ease the tension, trying to shut out the world and all the confusion she felt.

One of the whales broke from the feeding circle and slipped beneath the water.

Byrdie was just about to start up the motor when the humpback surfaced near the Zodiac.

"Whoa!" cried Ka-Wing, falling backward into his seat.

"It's okay," said Byrdie, retrieving his camera. "Humpbacks often come up to Zodiacs."

"I think the whale's looking at you," Trevor said to Rachel.

She opened her eyes. The giant eye gazed back at

her. As their eyes locked, she heard the same gentle tinkling sounds she had heard the night before out on the deck. All her tension evaporated, and she felt enveloped by a warm, soothing light. Then the whale seemed to nod slightly before slipping back beneath the calm blue water.

Rachel put her hand to her chest, feeling the pendant. For a brief, peaceful moment she felt like she had come home.

Byrdie started the motor.

"How much farther is the cave site?" asked Grace.

"About five minutes, I'd say. You should be able to see it any moment now." He steered the Zodiac closer to the shore through the broken bits of ice. A leopard seal watched them from an ice floe. Byrdie gestured toward a wide beach strewn with rocky outcrops and irregularly shaped hunks of ice. "It's right over there."

The beach ended abruptly at an ice cliff punctuated by irregular, triangular openings to caves and tunnels that had been sculpted by melt water. As the Zodiac neared the beach, the leopard seal slithered off its floe and popped its ugly head out of the water beside the Zodiac.

"A leopard seal," said Byrdie. "Not quite the friendly visitor, like the humpback."

"Is it dangerous?" asked Ka-Wing warily.

"Not usually," replied Byrdie. "As long as we keep our distance."

The seal edged closer and sniffed the pontoons.

Byrdie revved the engine to scare off the interloper. The seal disappeared under the Zodiac. After steering the Zodiac along the beach a bit farther Byrdie pulled into a shallow cove and tethered it to a large rock on the beach.

Checking first to make sure the leopard seal wasn't lurking nearby, they climbed out of the Zodiac and, grabbing their gear, headed up the beach to the opening in the ice cliff where the body had been found. The gravelly beach crunched under their boots.

The sunlight shone through the blue ice that formed the walls and ceiling of the cave. Rachel felt as if she had stepped inside a sapphire. Several tunnels ran off the cave. A line of melt water zigzagged across the rock-strewn floor.

Trevor advanced a few steps and pointed up. "There's a large opening that heads upward," he said. "The body could've fallen into a crevasse farther up the glacier, then washed down here with the spring melt water."

Grace looked up. "Seems a likely explanation," she said, setting down her gear. She hesitated, then leaned over and pushed her hand into a narrow opening, maybe six or seven inches wide, near the bottom of the wall, and felt around. Kneeling, she peered inside with her flashlight. "Or he—the body—could have come from underground and gotten swept up in the melt water. This opening goes down as far as I can see."

Trevor looked doubtful.

Grace stood. "In any case," she said, wiping the dirt off her hands, "don't wander off. It's easy to get lost in these caves. Ka-Wing, why don't you stay here and help me? Rachel, you go with Trevor—see if you can find any other evidence of where our subject may have been or what he was doing. It's possible he was still alive shortly before his body was found."

Trevor pulled two headlamps from his pack and

handed one to Rachel. "Come on, let's go exploring."

She reluctantly took it.

He put his headlamp on and walked over to examine one of the walls. Then he carefully spread out his geologist's gear on the ground—an ice pick, laser hammer, tool belt, hand lens, field guide, and an assortment of plastic bags. Using his laser hammer, he coaxed several rocks out of the blue ice and put each of them in a separately marked bag. "We're always on the lookout for meteorites," he explained to Rachel. "Antarctica is the best place to collect them. They strike the ice sheets and glaciers and get buried in them where they're preserved for hundreds of thousands of years."

Rachel leaned against the ice wall and looked around. It seemed incredible that this ice had been here longer than the pyramids of Egypt. Squatting down, she pulled out a magnifying glass and brush and studied the floor looking for clues to the mystery man's appearance. But she found nothing.

"I'm going to check out this tunnel over here," Trevor said after several minutes.

Rachel glanced over at Grace and Ka-Wing, engrossed in their work picking through the debris.

Trevor hesitated. "Are you all right?" he asked.

"I'm fine," Rachel replied. She felt confused, no longer sure of whether they were friends or if he was merely keeping track of her. Was it possible he thought she was actually part of some Nazi conspiracy?

"Okay," he said with a shrug. "You can come with me or stay here, whichever you like. I'll just be around the corner."

Trying to put him out of her mind, she ran her hand across the cool translucent surface of the wall. Had the person whose body they found perhaps leaned up against this very wall?

She reached under her jacket, pulled out the pendant, and pressed it against the ice. She could feel the warmth of the pendant glowing against the ice, drawing her in and through the blue crystals. She heard the music again and began humming, floating. A woman in white materialized out of the ice, smiling, with outstretched arms—singing the same lullaby Rachel had been humming on the Zodiac. Just as Rachel was about to take her hand, she felt something pulling her back through the wall, back to the cave.

She opened her eyes and blinked in bewilderment. There was a barely perceptible mist around her feet. What was happening? Grace and Ka-Wing were no longer in sight. Except for the dripping of melt water and the faint fizzling of Trevor's laser pick, it was completely silent.

She slipped the pendant into her pocket and began walking toward the sound of the pick, but then stopped. She really didn't feel like being with Trevor right now. She stooped and peered inside an opening in the wall.

Noticing another tunnel leading off the cave parallel to the face of the ice cliff she entered it, hoping to find Grace and Ka-Wing. As she made her way through it, she thought about the strange experience she had just had. Who was the woman in white? She sensed that the woman held the secret to her childhood. Her thoughts shifted to what Caitlyn had said earlier about Trevor. She was getting more and more worked up over the incident when she came to a split in the tunnel.

She stopped. Icicles hung from the ceiling like stalactites. The bright blue had faded to a dark indigo color. She realized she was heading into the center of the glacier. She would have to turn around and head back. The pendant, she thought. Maybe that could guide her back. She reached into her pocket. It wasn't there! It must have fallen out of her pocket somehow. She would have to retrace her steps and find it.

Remembering the headlamp Trevor had given her, she pulled it out of her other pocket and switched it on. She could just make out another split in the tunnel farther back. As she swung the light around, her heart sank. The whole place was honeycombed with tunnels.

She took a deep breath. "Think, think," she said aloud, trying to drown out the sound of her thumping heart. Cupping her hands to her mouth, she called out for help.

No answer. She called again, louder. This time she was answered by a sharp crack as a dagger of ice broke off from the ceiling and smashed to the floor in front of her.

She fell back with a shriek and threw her hands over her head. Panic pressed in on her, threatening to suffocate her. Swallowing hard, she turned off the headlamp and looked around, trying to determine which direction was the lightest.

A light caught her eye—a faint blue light. She stumbled toward it. As she rounded a bend in the tunnel, she saw an opening and beyond it the blue water of Paradise Bay.

Elated, she sprinted toward the light. She was about to burst forward into the daylight when she heard a scraping sound, followed by a low grunt.

She paused and listened. But all she could hear was the soft swish of the water against the edge of the rocky beach and the occasional plaintive cry of a skua. Far off in the distance a hydrofoil skimmed across the bay and passed out of sight. The Zodiac was nowhere to be seen.

She cautiously ventured outside. Just then a roar pierced the air. She screamed and shrank back against the ice cliff as a seal lurched up, exposing its sharp canine teeth.

Chapter 14

Rachel flung the headlamp at the seal and took off down the beach as fast as her legs would carry her. From behind, she could hear the crunching of gravel. Her chest pounded as she stumbled across the rocks and chunks of ice. On the beach ahead, she spotted a large rock outcrop. Ducking behind it, she crouched down and picked up a jagged rock.

She held her breath. She thought she heard someone calling her name. Could it just have been the trill of a leopard seal? The crunching on the gravel got closer.

She was preparing to throw the rock at her pursuer when Trevor appeared from behind the outcrop.

"Rachel?"

She felt a rush of relief. Then she remembered. He was just keeping an eye on her, as Grace had told him to do.

"Are you okay?" Concern filled his face. "What happened?"

"Nothing! Now will you leave me alone? A leopard seal scared me, that's all."

"May I sit down?" he asked.

She hesitated and then, feeling unreasonably churlish, moved over slightly to make room for him. She *was* relieved to see him, after all. Even if he was here at Grace's request.

"I take it that's a yes?" he asked, squatting down beside her.

She glanced up at the sky. The sun had vanished behind thick clouds and a cold wind was blowing off the mountains. Fluffy white snowflakes drifted down from the silver sky. She shivered and hugged her knees to her body.

"Cold?" Trevor asked, noticing she was missing a mitten.

Why did he have to be so nice? She shook her head.

He reached into his pocket and took something out. "Here, I found…"

"I told you I'm fine," Rachel snapped. Jumping to her feet, she started back down the beach.

"Rachel," he said, catching up to her. "Talk to me."

She kept walking. She didn't want to talk to him right now. She needed time to think, to be alone and sort out her feelings.

"What's bothering you?" he persisted.

"Bothering me?" she said without breaking stride. "The only thing that's bothering me is *you*. Now, please leave me alone."

"I can't. And will you please stop taking off on me like this?"

She stopped and swung around to face him. "Oh, that's right. I forgot. It's your job to *stalk* me."

"Is that what this is all about? Look, I'm sorry. Byrdie told me what Caitlyn said. It was…"

"Is that why you've been so nice to me? Because your aunt told you to be?"

"No—I really like you. And Aunt Grace didn't ask me to spy on you, if that's what you're thinking. Just keep an…"

Rachel threw up her hands. "Oh, I see, you *like* me. Well, *excuse me* if I thought it was something more." She kicked a chunk of loose ice, shattering it.

His jaw tensed. "Look, you're the one with the fiancé." He picked up a rock and tossed it into the water. It skipped several times before sinking. "You know, this hasn't been easy for me," he said. "I didn't know I was going to fall for you."

Fall for her? Rachel's breath caught. She felt a lump in her throat. She swallowed and turned away. He couldn't mean it. Could he?

"What is it you want from me, Rachel?" he asked.

She stared out at the blue bay, wondering if she could trust him. "I don't know what I want," she finally said. "Maybe it was a mistake my coming here to Antarctica in the first place. I mean, Richard…" Her voice trailed off.

Trevor looked upset. "Look, nobody's keeping you here against your will. If you really want to leave, I'm sure Aunt Grace can arrange to have you go back with the *Queen Maud*." He picked up another flat stone and sent it skipping across the water this time with more heat than before.

A Weddell seal broke the surface, checking to see if the rock was edible. Rachel realized it was probably the same seal she had startled earlier by the ice cliff. It looked a lot less daunting now.

Trevor paused, possibly encouraged by her silence. "Is that really what you want?"

She lowered her eyes. Her head was beginning to throb. "I don't know what I want," she repeated, her voice catching.

Trevor started to reach out to her, then hesitated. "I understand you're upset about what's happened in the past few days," he said, dropping his arm back to his side, "But can't we just talk about this?"

Rachel sighed. It was clear Trevor was not going to drop the subject. "Okay," she said. "Why don't you start by telling me why Grace asked you to keep an eye on me? I'm quite capable of taking care of myself, you know. Or do you think I'm some sort of neo-Nazi conspirator?"

"Of course not," he said. "It's just…well, she thinks you might be in some sort of danger."

Rachel raised an eyebrow. "In danger? From what?"

"I don't know. She didn't tell me. My aunt chooses her own time for divulging information."

"How do I know I can trust you?" Rachel asked. "Maybe you're all part of some stupid terrorist plot. After all, you're the one who kidnapped me and brought me to Krause."

Trevor shook his head. "I'm not part of any plot," he said. He sat down on a large rock near the edge of the water.

Further down the beach Rachel could see Grace and Ka-Wing heading to meet the Zodiac, which had just pulled up. "I think we should get going," she said, brushing some snow from her parka. "They're probably wondering what we're doing here."

"I don't care what they think. I care about you and what you think. They can wait." He paused, waiting for a reply.

Rachel remembered how much she hated it when Richard gave her the silent treatment. She opened her mouth, but the words didn't come.

"If you were upset about something," he said, breaking the silence, "why didn't you just say so right away, instead of pretending like nothing is wrong? My parents always taught us never to go to bed mad."

"Well, aren't you the lucky one to have such perfect parents," sniped Rachel. She immediately regretted her sarcastic tone. She sat down on the edge of the rock next to him and put her bare hand up to her mouth and blew on it, trying to warm it. It was starting to ache from the cold.

Trevor took off his mitten and handed it to her. "Here, I have extra ones in my pack."

"Thanks," she said, reluctantly accepting it. "Anyway, we're going to get in a Zodiac, not a bed."

Trevor flashed his boyish smile and moved closer. "Well, as for the Zodiac not being a bed, look at it this way. We've already spent a night on a deck chair. Maybe it's time to move on to a Zodiac."

Rachel laughed despite herself. Then she burst into tears. "How could anyone care about me? I don't even know who I am—who my real parents are or where I came from."

He pulled a clean handkerchief out of his pocket and handed it to her. "I care about you," he said softly.

She blew her nose. "I'm sorry," she said. "I just wish I knew what was going on."

He put his arms around her and pulled her closer. "Me, too. So, are we friends again?"

She nodded. "It's just that, sometimes I just feel so confused."

"I know," he said.

She smiled weakly. "I guess it's a good thing you

were keeping an eye on me or I might have been halfway to the South Pole by now—*under* the ice sheet."

Trevor grinned and kissed her on the forehead. "I'd follow you to the ends of the earth if I had to. Of course, I may end up doing that if you keep running away from me like this."

She laughed and pushed her hair back from her eyes. Down the beach, she could just make out Grace waving at them, and she realized she must have come quite a way before exiting the ice cave. "How'd you know I was here? How'd you find me?"

Trevor reached in his pocket and pulled out the pendant. "It showed me the way."

He placed the pendant in her hand.

She closed her hand over it and held it to her heart. She felt warm and good. Her suspicions of Trevor fell away like a calving glacier collapsing into the ocean. She slipped the pendant around her neck, then hugged him. "But where did you find it?"

"By one of the walls in the cave. When I picked it up the symbols moved. I just followed its direction—sort of like a compass—" he kissed her hair and whispered in her ear, "—leading me to you."

"You're such a romantic," she said, snuggling into his embrace.

****

By the time the Zodiac was loaded and ready to go, the wind had pushed the pieces of floating ice toward the shore, creating a barrier between them and the open water. Byrdie stood, searching for an opening in the ice. Small, choppy waves slapped the sides of the Zodiac. He slowly edged it between the ice and the shore until he came to a narrow opening. Then, revving the engine, he turned the Zodiac toward the open water. "Hold on."

Rachel gripped the lines on the side of the Zodiac. The bow rose in the air as it pushed its way through the loose ice, sending slivers of icy water into the air.

"Did you find anything in the cave?" Grace asked Rachel once they were safely in open water.

Rachel did not feel like telling her about getting lost in the tunnel or explaining about how the pendant had led Trevor to her. "No, nothing," she said, glancing sideways at Trevor.

He smiled back at her but said nothing.

"Me neither," said Grace. "But it was interesting seeing where the body was found."

Rachel nodded in agreement.

****

By the time they reached the Almirante Brown Argentinean station, the snow had stopped and the sun was peeking out from between silver clouds.

The *Queen Maud* sat moored out in the harbor like a glistening, white iceberg. Crewmen unloaded containers onto a hydrofoil pulled up to the stern of the cruise ship.

"That's the boat we're taking over to Shackleton Station," said Trevor.

Rachel swiveled in her seat and pushed back her hood. She took out her binoculars and studied the Argentinean station. It looked so vulnerable perched on the rocks in front of a huge glacier.

"What are those things in the building over there?" someone asked.

"Oh, those are elephant seals," Byrdie replied. "They've taken over the old helicopter hangar. The

Argentineans found it easier to build a new hangar—with doors—than to evacuate the seals and end up battling the environmentalists, to say nothing of irate bull elephant seals."

They laughed.

"The original station was destroyed by fire. Story is someone set it on fire because they couldn't stand the thought of having to winter over again. The winters here can be pretty brutal."

Rachel shuddered and put her hand to her chest, feeling the pendant safe and sound under her parka. She was glad she didn't have to winter over on that desolate beach.

****

As Ramirez rounded the crest of the snow-covered hill, he spotted the hut. He removed a glove, pushed back his hood, and checked the hut out through his binoculars. It appeared to be empty. Beyond the hut, he could just make out Shackleton Station, the low sun reflecting off the glass dome that enclosed the station.

Lowering his binoculars, Ramirez licked his lips and ran his fingers back through his hair. He thought about Wolf Krause in the hospital at Esperanza and cursed Rachel St. Claire's uncanny good luck in escaping him. He was glad he did not have to deal with her again, at least not just yet. First, he had to get those old mining maps of the tunnels under Shackleton Station from the hut.

Walking just below of the crest of the hill until the hut was between him and Shackleton Station, he climbed back up and trudged through the snow toward his destination. Approaching the hut, he drew his gun. As he did, a slip of yellow paper fell from his pocket into the snow. He cautiously pushed the back door open. As he stepped into the foyer, he could smell something burning—a sweet smell. Damn, he had been told the hut would be empty. Peering nervously around the corner, he surveyed the room. No one. Then he noticed a door going off the room beyond the sitting area. A shuffling sound came from the other side of the door. Gripping his gun, he edged toward the door. Taking a deep breath, he kicked the door open.

"Whoa, man," a voice called out.

Ramirez spotted a skinny, pimply-faced youth, sitting cross-legged and stoned on the floor. Beside him was a plastic bag of what looked like marijuana joints.

"Hey, man—this isn't my grass," the kid protested in slurred speech. "I—I just found it here."

Ramirez glared at him. Damn, now he would have to kill him. He couldn't take the chance. Even though the kid was stoned, he might be able to identify Ramirez.

The kid laughed nervously and, swaying slightly, reached up and held out a joint from the bag. "Hey man, put that gun away—it's just grass. It's all yours if you want."

Smirking, Ramirez reached out to take the joint. As he did, he grabbed the kid's arm.

"Hey, man, what the—?"

Pulling the kid forward, Ramirez whacked him on the side of the head with the gun.

The kid grunted in surprise. Drops of blood trickled from his nose onto the wooden floor as he crumpled to the floor.

After making sure no one was in sight, Ramirez dragged the kid outside, out of view of the hut behind a boulder protruding from beneath the snow. Cursing beneath his breath, he arranged him so it looked like he had fallen and banged his head on the rock. Then he placed the bag of joints in the kid's pocket. The kid moaned softly. "Hey, man," he mumbled. "It's c-cold."

Ramirez glanced up at the sky. A light snow was beginning to fall. At least there was some advantage to this Godforsaken icebox—the snow would cover up his tracks. He looked back at the kid, who was still now, and scowled. Thanks to him, he would have to go back to the hut and clean up the kid's bloody mess.

Chapter 15

The early dinner sitting was already under way by the time Rachel and the others boarded the *Queen Maud.*

"I'll see you at the hydrofoil," Trevor said, going ahead of them. "I just need to say good-bye to Byrdie and Caitlyn. And I'll grab some sandwiches for our trip to Shackleton."

"Have you finished packing yet?" Grace asked Rachel as they ascended the gangplank.

Rachel shook her head.

"Come on then—I can help you."

While Grace folded and packed the clothes on the spare bed, Rachel sorted out the items on her dresser and night table. She picked up the silver case with the ring and opened it, suddenly feeling an urge to connect with her roots.

"What's that?" asked Grace

"It's a ring," Rachel said, taking it out of the case. "I was wearing it when I was found as a child." She handed the ring to Grace.

Grace pulled a small magnifying glass out of her pocket and examined the ring. "Interesting symbols on the band," she said. "They almost look like a DNA code."

Rachel took the magnifying glass and squinted at the ring. "You're right," she said, "Amazing—I'd never noticed that before." She reached inside her sweater and pulled out the pendant.

Grace leaned forward and studied the pendant. "The marks on the ring do look a little like the symbols on the pendant," she said. "I wonder if there's any connection?"

"You know, I noticed the marks as a child," Rachel said. "They just looked like pretty squiggles. My adoptive parents took it to a jeweler—or at least they said they did, maybe just to get me off their backs."

"And what did the jeweler say?"

"He said it was just a pretty design and didn't contain any information about where the ring came from. After that my parents put the ring away in a safe deposit box and I didn't get it back until after I graduated from college." She paused, then added, "Following the death of my parents."

"I'm so sorry about your parents," Grace said.

Rachel nodded and ran her fingers along the edge of the ring.

"It is a pretty ring," said Grace, her eyes fixated on it as though expecting it to do something.

"I keep it locked away in a drawer in my room at home," Rachel said, "except when I travel overseas. I guess I take it as sort of a good luck charm." She slipped the ring on her little finger and glanced over at the flowers on her dresser. "Richard once asked me if I was wearing anything special when they found me as a child. I said no. I suppose I should have told him the truth, but it was just that…I don't know."

Grace patted her hand. "It's probably a good thing you didn't tell him."

"What do you mean?"

Grace looked away. “We all need to keep some things about ourselves secret. It adds to the mystery.”

Rachel was wondering if she should tell Grace about the mysterious powers of the pendant when Grace reached for their parkas. “We should be going,” she said. “The hydrofoil is scheduled to leave soon.”

When they arrived, Trevor and Ka-Wing were already on board. Trevor stepped forward to help Rachel and Grace with their bags. Rachel blushed as his hand brushed hers.

Just as the hydrofoil was about to push off, Antonio came running up, carrying a small overnight bag.

“Hold up,” called a crewmember, “one more passenger coming on.”

Antonio jumped aboard.

“What’s happening?” asked Trevor, catching the overnight bag Antonio tossed to him.

Antonio paused to catch his breath. “There was a report of a light last night in one of the windows of the Argentinean hut near Shackleton Station,” he replied. “A scientist saw it when he was coming in from the field. The manager of the Almirante Brown Station asked if I’d go over and investigate.”

“What’s so unusual about a light in the window?” asked Rachel.

“Nothing, except no one is supposed to be staying there at the moment.”

“Spooky,” said Ka-Wing.

Rachel stared out over the icy water. Enough disturbing things had already happened. Despite this latest unsettling news about the light in the window, she was excited to at last be on her way to Shackleton

Station to do what she'd been brought down to Antarctica to do—examine the mysterious body and try to determine its origins. She had a feeling that learning more about the origins of this mysterious body might give her some clues to her own origins.

Turning, she noticed Grace talking to an older man with a stubble beard and graying hair. Grace signaled for her to come over and join in the conversation.

"Mr. Slocum here is one of the staff who was at the station when they brought in the body from the ice cave," Grace explained to Rachel.

Slocum reached out and shook Rachel's hand. "To tell you the truth," he said, "I don't know much about it. It was in a body bag when they brought it to the station. But I do know Dr. M is really looking forward to you guys coming."

"Believe me, we're just as anxious to find out more about the body as he is," Grace said.

Slocum guffawed. "To tell you the truth, I think he's getting a little creeped out, spending all that time alone in the medical center and morgue with that body."

After listening for a while longer, Rachel rejoined Trevor on the front deck. He had put together a makeshift picnic on a packing crate, complete with a red checked tablecloth he must have "borrowed" from the *Queen Maud*.

"This is quite the spread," Rachel said. He smiled and handed her a sandwich and a bottle of sparkling water. She sat down on the opposite corner of the crate from him and took a bite of her sandwich. Richard would never have done something like this. To him, picnics were for commoners. Besides, he hated any kind of wildlife—too noisy and dirty for his taste.

Rachel smiled to herself as she recalled his horrified reaction when a seagull had pooped on his head when they were walking along the sea wall in Narragansett. She had laughed until she had almost wet her pants.

She glanced over at Trevor who was watching a pair of seals float by on an ice floe. She hoped she had not given Trevor the wrong idea earlier that she was somehow romantically interested in him. She had a fiancé. She had made that clear…or had she?

Then she heard a soft, sweet humming sound and felt the pendant pulsating slightly against her skin—as if it was drawing her to the station, just as it had led Trevor to her at the cave site. “Did you hear that?” she asked, turning to Trevor.

“It’s the same sound we heard the other night,” he whispered.

She nodded. She could feel the motion of the hydrofoil skimming over the water. Chunks of blue ice floated lazily in the water as the hydrofoil maneuvered between them. Overhead, a flock of Antarctic terns flew by, silhouetted against the pale pink sky.

“This whole place is amazing,” she said, then stood and crossed to the railing. “It’s just so incredibly beautiful here.”

The hydrofoil rounded the end of a glacier and turned into a fjord flanked on both sides by snow-covered mountains that sloped gently down to the water. The evening sun cast its pastel palette on the snowy landscape. A large colony of blue-eyed shags, chanting like a choir of Benedictine monks, was settling in for the night on the narrow, guano-streaked ledges of a rock cliff.

As the hydrofoil progressed up the bay, the

mountains became steeper and more rugged. Glaciers threaded their way between the mountains down to the bay.

"Isn't this hydrofoil cool?" said Ka-Wing, stepping up to the rail beside her.

A pair of skiers appeared at the top of one of the slopes and waved to the hydrofoil.

Ka-Wing leaned over the railing and waved back.

Rachel gazed at the white landscape. It was like a blank sheet of paper waiting to be written on—pure possibility.

****

Shackleton Station was located near the end of a fjord overlooking a sheltered harbor. Magnificent glaciers, jutting gracefully out into the blue water of the bay, bordered the sheer cliff at the end of the fjord. Behind the cliff, the ice-capped mountains that formed the spine of the Antarctic Peninsula rose to over a kilometer in height and disappeared into wispy clouds. Shafts of golden light from the setting sun danced on the white valleys between the mountains.

Unlike the other stations Rachel had seen, which consisted mainly of clusters of low orange buildings, Shackleton Station was enclosed in a large geodesic dome made up of solar and glass panels that mirrored the surrounding sky and mountains.

Rachel peered over the rail as the hydrofoil eased into a slip at a floating dock. Whalebones on the floor of the bay, from the days whaling ships used the harbor, could be seen through the clear water. As usual, the beach near the dock was bustling with penguins. A Snow-Cat, a sleek, bullet-shaped vehicle with yellow stripes painted on it, was parked just above the beach line.

As they disembarked and started up the beach toward the awaiting Snow-Cat, some of the gentoo penguins scattered, lurching and stumbling over the cobblestones. Others raised their bright orange beaks in protest.

"The penguins seem particularly jumpy today," remarked one of the crew. "Like something spooked them during the night."

Two men unloaded what looked like a body bag from the Snow-Cat and loaded it on the hydrofoil.

In the distance beyond a ridge, Rachel noticed a small hut silhouetted by the low sun. "That's the Argentinean hut," said Antonio, shouldering his overnight bag. After saying a quick farewell to them, he slipped on a pair of snowshoes and headed toward the hut.

"All aboard," one of the men said. He reached out a hand and helped Rachel climb up into the cab of the Snow-Cat.

From her seat in the Snow-Cat, Rachel could see the skittish penguins watching the receding vehicle wind its way up to Shackleton Station. What had upset them? The very air seemed to bristle with angst. She glanced over at Trevor sitting across from her, but he didn't seem to notice anything amiss. She shuddered and pulled her jacket more tightly around her.

Chapter 16

The next morning Rachel jumped out of bed and dressed as fast as she could. She put on the wool slacks she had worn the day before along with a pale blue cotton and silk sweater set Grace had picked out for her in Ushuaia. Then she took the pendant out from under her mattress, where she had put it before going to sleep, and slipped it around her neck and tucked it under the sweater. She thought of Trevor. He had suggested they meet for breakfast, but Rachel felt it better not to spend so much time with him, given the circumstances, and told him she had a breakfast meeting with Dr. M and Grace first thing in the morning—which was sort of true. Grabbing the map of the station and an energy bar from a basket on the desk, she headed toward the medical lab.

The green-tiled lab was located off the medical examining room in the basement of the station. Grace already had everything set up and ready. "We still have half an hour before meeting the station's chief medical officer, Dr. Morganthal, in the morgue where the body from the cave is stored," she told Rachel. "Do you mind if I just drop by the marine biology lab and say hello to an old friend? You can come if you like."

The marine biology lab was located just down the corridor from the medical center. A briny, slightly fishy smell hung in the air.

“Dragnet!” Grace called out as she spotted Ian Duffy across the room packing some gear.

The burly marine biologist had coarse hands, a bushy red beard, and a warm smile. He dropped what he was doing and lumbered over to greet them.

“Scully, me lass,” he chortled, giving Grace a big hug. “I heard you were coming.” He stepped back. “This here is Dr. Sutchin Singh. He’s the winter-over doc who’ll be replacing Dr. M. Sutchin just came in on the helicopter from Palmer Station a few days ago.”

“Pleased to meet you,” said Grace. “This is my colleague, Rachel St. Claire.”

Rachel figured Dr. Singh, a soft-spoken young man with jet-black hair, copper-colored skin, deep brown eyes, and delicate features, was probably straight out of residency.

Dragnet grinned and extended his large hairy hand. “And what brings you to Antarctica, lassie?” he asked Rachel.

She was about to tell him when Grace cut her off. “This is her first trip to Antarctica,” she said. “Rachel’s an evolutionary anthropologist from the States and she’s here on a sort of working vacation—as my guest.”

“This is my first trip to Antarctica too,” said Sutchin, smiling at Rachel.

“Spot any more UFOs lately?” Dragnet teased Grace with a twinkle in his eye.

She laughed. “Not recently.” Then she grew more serious. “By the way, have you noticed anything strange going on lately?”

He stroked his beard. “Come to think of it, just yesterday our ROV—that’s a Remotely Operated Vehicle—picked up a large object at the bottom of the bay. The object was too regular and smooth to be natural. But before we could zoom in and get some photos or measurements, it vanished from sight."

"What do you think it was?"

He shrugged. "Could have been an instrument malfunction."

Grace pursed her lips. "There seems to be a lot of that going around."

Dragnet took Grace's elbow. "Come, I want to show you something."

While the two of them caught up on old times, Rachel looked around. Shelves of specimens in bottles, earmarked reference books, racks of micro-centrifuge tubes, electronic equipment, and an assortment of nets lined the walls of the lab. Aquariums filled with tiny swarming creatures sat along black-topped lab tables. "Save the Krill" posters, family photos, and outdated calendars hung above the aquariums.

"Trevor would love it down here," she said, more to herself than to anyone else. She couldn't wait to show this place to him.

Sutchin cleared his throat. "So you're an evolutionary anthropologist?" he said. "I've always been interested in anthropology."

"It's a fascinating field."

"I'm doing a fellowship in immunology at Oxford. While I'm here, I'll be doing research on the immune system. Wintering over tends to weaken the immune system."

Rachel glanced at the large aquarium that stretched across the front of the lab. The morning sunlight filtered through the blue-green water reflecting in swirling movements off the white walls. Odd-looking creatures—diaphanous, speckled jellyfish and translucent ice fish with fins like fairy wings—drifted past pink and coral starfish.

"I'm especially interested in viral infections," Sutchin said.

"Oh?" Rachel recalled Antonio had told them Krause had a background in virology. There was also the black cap they had found on Deception Island.

"I have some photographs of viruses with me. Would you like to see them?"

"Sure."

"They're over here." He walked over to a tiny desk in the corner of the lab, pulled out a pile of photographs and carefully tacked them to a large board above the desk.

"Beautiful photographs," she said putting her hands on the desk and leaning forward to study them. She wished now she had not turned Trevor down for breakfast. He probably knew more about this stuff than she did.

Sutchin pointed at a virus coated with what looked like peppercorns. "Here, this is one of my photos. See these spiked projections? They use them to attach to the host cell. They have an incredible ability to sense the right cell."

"What type of virus is this?" asked Rachel, indicating a photo of another virus with a long graceful tail shaped like the symbol for infinity.

"That's Ebola II—it somehow mutated from the original Ebola virus. I got this photo from the CDC's collection."

Rachel had read about Ebola II—sometimes referred to as the doomsday or Andromeda virus—and had seen photos of its victims, blood oozing out of their eyes, mouth, and other body openings. Over a million people, mostly in Africa, died before the World Health Organization was able to develop a vaccine for Ebola II. White supremacists referred to the deadly viruses that emerged out of the jungles of Africa—AIDS, Ebola, the Marburg viruses—as the "African karma." Rachel shuddered. It reminded her of Wolf and Hilde and their white supremacy connections.

Sutchin motioned toward another photo. "This may interest you."

"What is it?"

"It's the Ratonera virus from the rain forests in Central America. The virus silently invades the germ cells—the ovaries—of rodents so it's inherited by all subsequent offspring; thus the virus is ensured of immortality. A brilliant strategy—something we haven't been able to achieve with all our biotechnology."

"Pretty ingenious," Rachel said. She picked up a picture from the desk. It looked like a child's drawing of some sort of disembodied boogey monster—a multi-sided, semi-transparent geometrical figure with spikes that looked like golf balls suspended on tees sticking out of the pyramidal top. "And what kind of virus is this?" she asked.

"That's a hypothetical chimera virus—a maximally virulent or deadly virus. It's something, isn't it? This one here was genetically engineered in a lab in South Africa."

"Is it worse than Ebola II?"

"Almost certainly. It would have the potential to wipe out humankind. On the other hand, a maximally virulent virus could also be engineered to be selective about whom it kills, since it doesn't want to kill its target host. For example, it could target a particular segment of a population based on differences in their genome."

Rachel was about to ask Sutchin about the likelihood of viruses surviving here in Antarctica when the return of Grace and Dragnet cut their conversation short.

"I regret we have to get going, Scully," Dragnet was saying. "But please feel free to stay and have a cuppa tea or coffee."

He swung a duffel bag of equipment onto his back and headed out the door beside the aquarium to join his team, who were outside packing their equipment on a sledge.

Above the door, a small security camera recorded his departure.

"Sorry to have abandoned you like that," said Grace, once Sutchin had returned to his work. "Did you enjoy your talk with Dr. Singh?"

Rachel nodded and helped herself to some coffee. "So what's this Scully business?"

Grace chuckled. "My nickname—after Dr. Dana Scully, the FBI forensic pathologist on the old TV show *The X-Files*. My husband Charlie was Spooky—Fox Mulder's nickname—because of his interest in, well, I guess you could call it the paranormal. Everyone eventually gets a nickname here."

"The paranormal?"

Grace nodded. "Charlie believed the earth is hollow based on the astronomer Edmund Halley's theory that the inner Earth is a series of concentric hollow spheres with a red sun at the core."

"Interesting hypothesis," replied Rachel.

Grace paused a second then said. "Dragnet was telling me they found a body early yesterday morning not far from the Argentinean hut."

"How horrible. What happened?"

"One of the scientists coming in from the field the night before thought he saw a light in the window of the hut. When they went to investigate in the morning, the hut was empty, but they found a body nearby beside a boulder—it was a nineteen-year old boy—Andrew Marley—one of the kitchen helpers."

Rachel winced. "Was that who was in the body bag they were loading on the hydrofoil?"

"I'm afraid so."

"How did he die?"

"I spoke to Dr. M this morning and he said it was an accident. Apparently Andrew was high on drugs—there were large amounts in his blood—and he slipped and hit his head on a boulder."

"And what do you think?"

"I don't know," Grace replied, rinsing out her cup. "I wish they hadn't taken the body away so soon. I would have preferred the chance to do an autopsy on him. But they wanted to get the body to the *Queen Maud,* where they have a morgue, so they could get it back to his family and England for burial as soon as possible."

As they headed down the corridor toward the morgue, Rachel noticed a sulfurous odor coming from a dimly lit section of the hall where the walls were unfinished granite rock.

"What's down there?" she asked, wrinkling up her

nose.

"Who knows?" replied Grace. "The area under this section of the station is riddled with tunnels.

"Tunnels—what kind?"

"They were here before the station was built. Some are natural; others are from illegal drilling operations. But, at least someone's getting some use out of them. I hear a group of dark-matter scientists have set up a temporary lab in one of the old tunnels."

"Why here in Antarctica?"

"From what I understand, it's easier to detect dark matter underground since the Earth's crust blocks out the background noise," replied Grace. "For some reason the Earth's crust is unusually thin in this section of the Antarctica Peninsula. I'm sure Trevor can tell you more about it." She stopped at the morgue and tapped on the door.

A thick-necked, bespeckled man opened the door. With his hawkish nose, thinning brown hair combed back, and green scrubs he looked like a skua peering out from a bush.

They stepped inside. The morgue was located in a small, windowless room and consisted of a row of cupboards lining one wall, a large sink, a stainless steel gurney, and a cart draped with a white cloth. It was probably one of the few rooms in the station where posters and photos did not clutter the walls.

Ka-Wing was already there chatting with Dr. Morganthal, or Doc Morgue for short according to his nametag. Rachel decided to stick to the nickname Grace used—Dr. M.

"Glad you could make it, Dr. St. Claire," Dr. M said. He opened one of the cupboards and pulled out two sets of pale green scrubs, hair covers, and neoprene gloves, and handed them to Rachel and Grace along with two clear plastic face shields. "Just in case," he said. "You never know what diseases this thing might be carrying."

After suiting up, Grace opened her black case and arranged her autopsy instruments on the cart while Dr. M slid out a tray holding the body and unzipped the body bag. With the help of Ka-Wing, he transferred the body onto the gurney.

The corpse's hair was as white as newly fallen snow and the skin translucent like frosted glass. There was something about it that was not quite human, yet at the same time the body seemed familiar. Rachel thought about what Antonio had said earlier on the ship about Hitler's belief in a race of fair-haired Aryans living beneath the Earth.

"I hope I did the right thing by calling you," Dr. M said as he switched on the surgical lamp. "I haven't had much experience with autopsies, and I know you're an experienced forensic pathologist."

Grace stared at the body.

"I told you there was something very peculiar about this body," said Doc M.

"Yes, well, you're certainly right about that," she said. "I hadn't realized the extent of the anomalies. Let's start by having Dr. St. Claire do her anthropological workup before we do the autopsy and compromise the body."

She reached into her black case and handed Rachel some instruments. "I brought an Anthrop scanner and calipers for you, since you didn't have much time to pack for this trip."

Rachel felt a thrill of excitement at the thought of finally getting a chance to examine this mysterious body. Taking the instruments, she set them down on the table beside the body. She studied the face with its fine bone structure and perfect skin. Who was this being? And where had he come from?

"Be careful," cautioned Dr. M, furrowing his brow. "We don't know how the thing died, or if it's carrying any diseases. No one in their right mind would go out in this cold wearing only a thin gown."

Rachel pulled down her plastic face shield and positioned the scanner over the body. That's when she heard it—the tinkling of music like she had heard on the ship that night with Trevor, then again on the trip over here—faint at first, then louder, closer, clearer. She drew back, her mouth hanging open in surprise, and touched her hand to her chest. Was it the pendant? No, the word had clearly come from the body. The pendant felt warm.

"What is it?" asked Grace.

"I thought I heard the body say my name," Rachel whispered.

Dr. M looked skeptical. "I didn't hear anything."

"Your name?" asked Grace.

Rachel looked at her. "Well, not exactly. He didn't use words. It was more like a thought—a musical thought—like telepathic."

Dr. M rolled his eyes.

Rachel rubbed the back of her neck. "Maybe I'm just tired." She placed the scanner over the body again, trying to keep her hands steady. However, try as she might, she could not get the music out of her mind—sweet, seductive music, like a mantra, drawing her in. It took all her strength to resist and to concentrate on the work she had been brought to Antarctica to do.

"Whoever this is," she said after several minutes, trying her best to sound calm and professional, "I don't think he's from this region. He seems poorly adapted to survive in such a cold climate."

"What do you mean?" asked Ka-Wing.

"Well, for one thing, with such fair skin the radiation from the sun here would have done far more damage. Yet his skin is in perfect condition—no sign of sun damage. And look." She pointed at the hands. "There's webbing between the hands as well as the toes."

"You mean, like its aquatic?" asked Ka-Wing.

Rachel shook her head. "I doubt it, but I don't really know," she said. "It might just be a birth defect. Some humans are born with webbing between their fingers and toes."

"There is a theory—the Aquatic Ape Theory," Grace said, "that humans evolved as aquatic primates."

They watched in silence as Rachel took more readings and measured the body.

"What else did you find?" asked Grace, once Rachel had finished.

Rachel straightened up and lifted her face shield. "Well, he's definitely hominoid," she said. "Also, I don't see any overt signs of disease. He seems in perfect health. In fact, I'd say *unnaturally* healthy. Not even frostbite or hypothermia."

"You said this thing is hominoid," said Doc M. "But is it human?"

"He," interrupted Grace. "*He's* a person, not an *it* or a thing."

"Whatever," replied Dr. M with a wave of his hand. "Okay then, is *he Homo sapiens* like us?"

Rachel shook her head. "I don't know. Like I said, he's definitely hominoid, but whether or not he's the same species as us, we'd have to first—"

"But if *he's* not *Homo sapiens* then what sort of creature is it?" interrupted Dr. M.

"What I said was he has some anomalies, but whether or not they fall outside the range of the human genome, that's the question. We'll have to do a more detailed workup of his genetic material to find out." She paused. A puzzled expression came over her face as she read her scanner.

"What is it?" asked Grace.

"According to my readout, the body is over two thousand years old."

"There must be a mistake," said Doc M. "The cadaver's much too well preserved to have been dead that long."

"I didn't say he'd been dead that long," Rachel replied. "That's his age." She pulled the holographic imager out of her pocket, set it down on the cart next to Grace's black bag and plugged the scanner into the imager. The scanner made a soft whirring sound as it transferred the data into the imager.

There was a knock at the morgue door and Trevor's voice came over the intercom.

"What is it?" asked Dr. M impatiently.

"I'm going to get some lunch, then go out to the Argentinean hut to see what Antonio's up to, if any of you want to come with me," answered Trevor.

Rachel glanced at the clock on the wall. It had been almost three hours since they had arrived at the morgue.

She was starting to feel weary, and her stomach was a bit unsettled, probably from the stale air in the morgue. She shivered slightly. The chilly air in the morgue felt creepy, claustrophobic. Also, she didn't relish being at the autopsy. Taking measurements of mummified corpses and bones was one thing, but the thought of watching someone cut into flesh gave her the willies—although maybe she would learn more if she stayed. Then again, maybe Antonio would have some news about Krause's gang of terrorists and why he had been after her.

"Why don't you take a break and go with him, dear?" said Grace, patting her arm. "We'll be taking a break soon."

"Ka-Wing?" Rachel asked as she washed up. "Want to come with us?"

"Thanks, but I think I'll stay here and help out," he said. He obviously didn't have her aversion to slicing open bodies.

Grace smiled at her protégé. "This will be a good opportunity for you, Ka-Wing, to practice making incisions for autopsies." Ka-Wing picked up the harmonic scalpel and prepared to make the first incision. As Rachel watched out of the corner of her eye, Ka-Wing carefully placed the tip of the scalpel against the upper left part of the chest, just under the shoulder.

"What baffles me," said Doc M, "is that there's no sign of rigor mortis after four days."

Grace nodded pensively. "It is strange. I was watching while Rachel was doing her work-up, and I wonder if he is even dead. He might be in some sort of deep catatonic…"

"Holy Jeepers!" cried Ka-Wing. He jumped back and dropped the scalpel.

"What is it?" asked Rachel, wiping her hands dry at the sink.

"His finger," Ka-Wing gasped. "It twitched when I touched his body with the scalpel!"

Rachel dropped the towel in the sink and hurried over to the autopsy table.

Grace studied the body for a few moments and then checked it for vital signs. Nothing.

"Is he alive?" Rachel asked, rubbing the back of her neck. Inside, she felt an odd mixture of hope and fear. Who—or what—was this strange being? And why was it having this effect on her?

Grace was talking. It took Rachel a few seconds to focus on what she was saying. "…movement could have just been what's known as post mortem movement—reflexes that mimic voluntary movement after the patient is dead." She turned to Rachel, who was still staring at the body as though she expected it to rise from the dead. "Why don't you go ahead on your walk to the hut with Trevor? We're going to take a break—grab a spot of tea. I think we could all use a bit of a break right now. I'd also like to take some more photographs of the body and send the data we have so far to Brown Medical School before we start the autopsy again."

"Okay," Rachel said, reluctantly. She wanted to stay in case the being might be actually alive, but she was exhausted, feeling punchy, and badly needed a break. Grace was probably right. The movement was almost certainly post mortem movement. What else could it be?

****

As Rachel stepped out into the hall to join Trevor, the hair on her neck stood up; her skin prickled. She wasn't sure what had alerted her. Perhaps a sound or flicker of movement in the shadows down the hall from a gap in the rock wall, or the odd sixth sense that someone was watching her. However, when she looked nobody was there.

"What is it?" asked Trevor, glancing in the same direction.

She pulled her cardigan closer around her. "I thought I saw something move," she said. Maybe it was the dampness or the smell of sulfur in the air making her jumpy.

"Come on," said Trevor, taking her arm. "Let's get out of here."

Chapter 17

Fluffy cumulus clouds floated lazily through the sky, creating an ever-changing quilt of silver and white on the snow. From the snowy ridge above the station, they could hear the soft whoop, whoop of the windmill blades that provided power to the station.

"I've reserved a Ski-Doo for us," said Trevor. "Or, if you prefer, we can walk. It's about a kilometer. I have some compact snowshoes in my pack, in case we need them. I always carry a spare."

Rachel smiled at him. Always prepared like the good boy scout; she liked that about him. "In that case," she said, "I'd rather walk."

"Me, too. I like the snow."

She took one of the pairs of snowshoes from him, glad to see they were the newer, smaller, more flexible kind, and strapped them on.

"How'd it go at the morgue this morning?" asked Trevor as they reached the top of the ridge above the penguin colony and started out across the snowfield.

"Interesting, to say the least," Rachel said. She told him about the body in the morgue.

"What do you make of it?" he asked once she had finished.

She shook her head. "I'm as baffled as the rest of them," she said. "And how'd your morning go?"

"Pretty good. We ran some tests on the rocks from

Deception Island—the ones you found on Wolf Krause—and found magnetized microorganisms living in the crystalline structure. I took some of the crystals down to the Dark Matter lab and they're packed—and I mean, densely packed—with dark matter."

"Dark matter? How could you tell?"

"When we put the rocks under the cryogenic dark matter search spectrometer, the crystals emitted a sort of rippling misty glow—magnetic energy as it turned out—almost like the aurora. It was so bright you could actually see the glow from across the room."

"That's amazing."

"The guys in the lab say they'd never seen anything like it."

"Were the rocks meteorites? Maybe the microbes in the crystals are some sort of alien life form which lives only in dark matter."

Trevor shrugged. "It's hard to know. We've found magnetized microbes in rocks elsewhere on Earth."

"But here in Antarctica? How could anything survive at such cold temperatures?"

"Actually, scientists have found organisms living beneath four kilometers of ice in the Lake Vostok area near the South Pole."

As they trudged on toward the hut, they pondered the meaning of the findings running the gamut from there-has-to-be-a-logical-explanation to speculations of an alien invasion.

"I've always had a soft spot in my heart for those gray aliens from the UFO movies," joked Rachel. "If it's an alien invasion, I hope they're behind it."

Trevor laughed. "Well, I've always thought it would be the alien rocks that turned out to be the higher life form."

"Oh, really?" She scooped up a handful of snow and tossed it at him.

"Hey! What are you doing?!"

"Isn't snow theoretically a type of rock?"

"Oh, boy, now you're in trouble," he said, dodging another snowball. "No more Mr. Nice Guy."

She giggled. "Catch me if you can." She tried to run as best she could wearing snowshoes, when *thunk*—Trevor tackled her, knocking her face down in the snow.

"Let me up," she squealed as she tried to reach around and push snow in his face.

"Not until you say 'uncle,' " he said, pinning her to the ground.

"Is this any way to treat a lady?"

"Yeah, right, some lady. Come on—say 'uncle' or it's a snow sandwich for you."

"Okay. Okay. Uncle! I give up!"

He let her go.

Rolling over, she pushed a handful of snow in his face. "Sucker!" she laughed. She hadn't had so much fun in years.

Trevor looked so surprised she could not help taking pity on him. She sat up and, removing her mitten, gently wiped the snow from his face. His skin felt warm and sensual. She wanted to stroke his skin, explore even more of him. His hand brushed hers as he pulled some snow out from under his collar.

She felt her face flush as their hands met. Their eyes locked for a brief second, his questioning. All she could think about was kissing him.

Instead she offered a too-cheery "Hey!" and

struggled to her feet, deliberately ignoring the look of confusion on his face. Her own confusion was enough to handle right now. "We'd better get going. Antonio's expecting us."

As they approached the Argentinean hut, one of the snowy sheathbills nesting on the front porch fluttering its wings nervously. White, pigeon-like birds with stubby beaks and pinkish wattles on each side of their faces, they looked more like they belonged in Central Park or Kennedy Plaza in Providence.

"*Hola!*" called Antonio through an open window. "Please, go around to the back so we don't disturb our fine feathered friends."

Antonio went around to the back door to greet them.

"Any action last night?" asked Trevor, knocking the snow off his boots before he entered.

"Nothing. It was as quiet as a *velorio*—a funeral," replied Antonio, closing the door behind them.

The hut was pleasantly warm and woody smelling.

Trevor tucked his boots beneath the bench in the foyer. Then he stuffed his hat and gloves into his pockets, and hung up his parka on one of the hooks above the bench. "Did you find any clues about who might have been here the other night?" he asked Antonio.

Antonio shook his head. "But I do know someone has been here recently."

"How do you know that?" asked Rachel, sitting down on the bench.

"Because I could not find a single fingerprint. I've never seen a research hut as clean as this place."

"Do you think maybe that young man they found

not far from here may have cleaned it?" Trevor asked.

"Not likely. Dr. M ran a blood test and he was pretty stoned at the time of his death. I think someone else was here."

Rachel pulled off a boot. It fell with a thud onto the wooden floor. A piece of yellow paper was stuck to the bottom. "What's this?" she asked, leaning over to peel it off.

Wait," said Antonio. Taking a pair of small forceps from his pocket, he removed the paper from the boot. He held it up to the light and studied it. At the top was a barely visible imprint of a DNA helix with the initials GG superimposed over it. The letters RAMI were handwritten in large letters at the bottom of the scrap of paper, but the rest of the word was torn off.

"This is the insignia of Global Genome," Antonio said.

"Isn't there a facility in Ushuaia that belongs to Global Genome?" asked Trevor.

Antonio nodded. "That's right—Schwaben Labs." He turned the paper over. "The paper must have been buried by the snow yesterday, along with any footprints." He slipped it into a small notebook with plastic sleeves then gestured toward a door leading from the vestibule. "Meanwhile," he said, "please come in."

"Cozy," said Rachel as she stepped into the main room. Colorful native tapestries from Argentina and posters from international science conferences hung on the cream-white walls. In the middle of the room was a large Formica table surrounded by six wooden chairs. A cast iron stove burned in one corner of the hut. A desk made out of metal file cabinets and floor planking stretched along the window overlooking the verandah. An old laptop computer sat in the middle of the desk beside a cup of steaming tea.

"May I fix you a cup of tea?" asked Antonio, moving the kettle back to the center of the stove. He put some small pastries on a plate and set them on the coffee table in front of a brown leatherette couch. "Please, help yourself to some *paselitos*."

While Antonio busied himself in the kitchen area, Rachel nibbled on a *paselito*. Flickering movements on the wall at the other end of the room caught her eye. Looking over, she saw a large plasma television. The sound was muted. Scenes of terrified, pleading women and children being brutalized and dragged away by soldiers filled the screen. Trevor was standing, with a half-eaten *paselito* in his hand, watching the film.

Rachel averted her eyes and sat down on the couch.

Antonio set down the two cups, picked up the remote control, pointed it at the screen, and pressed STOP. "Sorry," he apologized. "I forgot it was still playing. It's Luis Puenzo's *La Historia Oficial,* a documentary about the Dirty War in Argentina."

"The Dirty War? What was that?" asked Rachel.

Antonio frowned and stirred his tea. "A war of the government against its own people. Thousands were kidnapped by the military junta, including pregnant women and children snatched from their homes in the middle of the night. Some of the people were sedated and hurled out of airplanes into the sea."

"Pregnant women? Children?" Rachel sat forward on the edge of her chair. "When did this happen? Were they ever found?"

"1976 to 1983," replied Antonio, "and no, most of

them were never found or accounted for. They seemed to have disappeared off the face of the earth."

Rachel's chest tightened. "1983—that's the year I was born," she said. Her parents had once told her she was from south of South America, or something confusing like that. Rachel wondered if they meant Argentina because she was blondish and there was a large German population there. She wished she had pushed them harder for more information.

Trevor picked up the two cups of tea. He handed one to Rachel, then sat down beside her.

"It was one of the most disgraceful chapters in our history," Antonio continued. "That we, the good people of Argentina, did not stand up to them and stop it."

Trevor looked thoughtful. "You said earlier—one reason you were coming down here was to investigate the possibility that some of these white supremacist groups might be infiltrating Antarctica."

Antonio nodded. "That's right—maybe setting up quarters in some of the old Nazi underground bases—if in fact they exist."

"Do you think there's a connection between the Dirty War and what's going on now?" asked Rachel.

"It's possible," Antonio replied. "The Argentinean Special Police recently uncovered documents revealing that the PNP—the Party of the New Purity—was involved in the kidnappings that took place back in the Dirty War. We think they may have funded the kidnappings using Nazi gold smuggled into Argentina at the end of World War II. Apparently, the PNP has connections, mainly through the Internet, to other white supremacist groups throughout North America and Europe. Together they make up a loose coalition known as the New World Order."

He walked over to the desk. Picking up the laptop, he brought it back to the coffee table and pressed the enter key. The screen flickered on. "I pulled up the documents from our police files on some of the top members of the organization. Here's the photo and background information on Wolf Krause."

Rachel winced and stood. She leaned forward and examined the picture more closely. The mere mention of Wolf's name gave her the creeps, even though Grace had said she doubted he was her father. But if he wasn't her father, why was he so interested in her? And what had he meant when he said all those years ago when she was a child, *We will be back to get what is rightfully ours*?

Trevor reached up and touched her arm. "Hey, are you okay with all of this?" he asked.

"I'm fine," she said, taking a deep breath and sitting down again. "Go ahead. I need to find out what's going on."

"Here are the photos and profiles of all the heads of the Ushuaia-Antártida division of the PNP," said Antonio, scrolling down the screen. "We know that they moved their headquarters to Ushuaia several years ago, which might mean, like you said, they've infiltrated Antarctica."

"Or they are expanding their operation here," said Trevor.

"Could be, but how and where we don't…" Antonio stopped in mid-sentence and tapped the screen with his finger. "That man there. Angel Ricardo Ramirez." He pulled out the slip of yellow paper from his notebook. "The letters RAMI on this slip of paper might be the first part of Ramirez.'"

Rachel stared at the fuzzy picture of the bearded man on the screen: something about him looked familiar—his eyes maybe.

"Says here his father's Spanish and his mother's family Argentinean…had connections with the Nazi expatriate community there," said Trevor.

"Like Krause," muttered Antonio.

"Ramirez was born in 1974 in the United States… Washington, D.C.," read Trevor, "where his father held a middle-level position with the Spanish embassy. When Angel was eight, his parents were killed in an automobile accident, and he went to live with his maternal grandparents in Argentina."

"I remember now. I met him once, very briefly," said Antonio.

"It goes on to say that after his parents' death he became obsessed with right-wing ideology and that he was a troublemaker at school—a skinhead. Then he turns up again several years later in Buenos Aires as a member of the new underground PNP organization. And—get this—he was initially rejected for membership in PNP because his great-grandmother on his father's side was from Morocco." He looked up at Antonio. "Not lily-white enough for them, I guess."

Antonio snorted. "I wonder how he got around that one."

"Maybe he convinced them he was a bastard."

Antonio smiled wryly and shook his head. "He's certainly that. He's a pretty slippery character—keeps disappearing. As I recall, he was last seen somewhere in the States."

Rachel stiffened. That was it—the photo reminded

her of a younger version of Richard. She rubbed the back of her neck. What was wrong with her? Was she losing her mind? She was starting to see Richard look-alikes everywhere. First Deception Island, now here.

"We're lucky we have any photo of him," said Antonio. "This one's old and he's wearing a beard, probably fake. But I can tell you one thing—he's a real *vibora*, a snake."

"I wonder if he has any connections to Global Genome," asked Trevor.

"Speaking of Global Genome, did you hear about the six missing scientists?"

Trevor set down his teacup. "No. When did this happen?"

Antonio clicked off the laptop. "Only a few hours ago," he said. "They were attending a conference on emerging viruses, which was sponsored in part by—surprise, surprise—Global Genome, at the Universidad Nacional de Ushuaia. They were taking a boat excursion into the Laguna Bombilla on the coast of Tierra del Fuego as part of the conference's extracurricular activities when the boat simply disappeared—no radio contact, nothing. They have a search party out for them now."

Trevor checked his watch then glanced up at Rachel. "Speaking of search parties," he said, "we have to get going. Grace will be expecting you."

"I'm glad you could find time to come here," said Antonio, standing. "I will do some more research on this Ramirez character and get back to you if I find out anything new."

Chapter 18

By the time Rachel and Trevor started back, the sun had melted most of the new snow, leaving large pit marks of slush and mud mixed with penguin guano. When they arrived at the station, the top of the dome was open, like the iris of a giant eye gazing heavenward. A shaft of golden sunlight streamed through the opening. The large main building formed a crescent around the back half of the dome. Several smaller buildings, mostly labs and maintenance buildings, were located along the perimeter of a large courtyard inside the dome. A brick-red jogging and walking path meandered around the courtyard and buildings.

"Trees? In Antarctica?" asked Rachel, noticing two people in fleece pullovers playing cribbage on a bench under some trees in front of the botany building.

"Beech trees—*Fagus antarctica*," said Trevor. "We found fossils of them in rocks here on the Peninsula. They're the same species as those found today in Tierra del Fuego."

They crossed the courtyard to the main building. The polished floors of the lobby gleamed with granite salvaged from the blasting for the foundation and basement of the station. A large black and white photograph of Shackleton's ship *Endeavor* balanced precariously on a massive slab of ice, hung in the entryway across from the boot room.

The door to the medical center was locked when Rachel and Trevor arrived. The hours on the door said it would reopen again at 7:00. Rachel tapped on the door. No one answered.

Trevor checked his watch. "It's only 5:30. Shall we grab an early dinner and then try to find Aunt Grace?"

After a scrumptious dinner, accompanied by lively speculation about the day's findings and a surprisingly good wine from a biodegradable box, Rachel and Trevor retired to the lounge, which was connected to the cafeteria by a wide arched doorway. A window overlooking the mountains of the Peninsula ran the entire length of the lounge. The window sloped gently upward, like the wing of a swan, as it followed the contour of the dome. The air smelled warm and good, like hot buttered popcorn and cinnamon.

A group of young people, mostly techies, sprawled out on couches and armchairs in front of a large screen TV amid half-drunk mugs of beer and hot cider and bowls of popcorn, watching the latest Antarctica horror flick, *The Return of the Thing*. At the other end of the lounge, four weary-looking people sat bowed over mugs of cocoa at a table next to a slightly water-damaged piano salvaged from an abandoned Chilean research station.

Grace was sitting on a couch in front of a wind-powered fireplace. Rachel sat down beside her.

"Can I get you something to drink?" asked Trevor, picking up the empty glasses and cups on the table.

Rachel watched as Trevor wove his way over to the bar.

"By the way," Grace said, "we got a DNA sample

from Krause and compared it to yours. He's definitely not your father."

Rachel breathed a sigh of relief and sank back into the deep cushions.

Trevor returned with a glass of wine, and cup of Red Rose tea for Grace.

"We also got the DNA results back from the patient downstairs," said Grace, taking the tea from Trevor, "and they were most remarkable—to say the least."

Rachel sat forward, unsure if she had heard her correctly. "Patient?" she asked.

"Yes. It turns out the 'body' is alive—in a deep state of something like hibernation. We moved him immediately into the recovery room in the medical center. Dr. M and Ka-Wing are monitoring him. They'll let us know if there are any changes."

"This is incredible," said Rachel, barely able to contain her excitement. "Tell me, what did you find out from his DNA analysis?"

"He has almost the same configuration of chromosomes as *Homo sapiens* except…well, as you know over 95% of our genetic material is non-coded or what's popularly called junk DNA."

Rachel turned to Trevor. "Junk DNA consists of repeated sequences of DNA that some biologists think may be key for development of new species or new traits during evolution," she explained.

"Sort of like the free storage space in a computer hard drive where new programs can be added?" asked Trevor.

"Yes, something like that."

"Except," Grace said, "our patient's non-coded

DNA is more complex than ours. It has a cadence to it that's almost rhythmic in its pattern. The geneticist who analyzed it said it was unlike anything he's ever seen."

Rachel sat forward in her seat. "When I last talked to Dr. Shah he mentioned they'd found what appeared to be genetically modified DNA inserted into strands of non-coded DNA in the bones we found in Afghanistan. And he described them in the very same way—rhythmical—like music."

"Interesting," said Trevor.

"You know, the idea that human evolution has been a straight line from less to more complex has recently been called into question," Rachel said. "For example, the cranium capacity of both late Neanderthal man and Cro-Magnon man are significantly larger than those of modern humans. And just recently an archaeologist in Palestine unearthed two 160,000 year-old hominoid skulls with brain cases well above those of modern humans."

"What are you suggesting?" asked Trevor. "That we've somehow devolved?"

Rachel stared at the flames in the fireplace. "It's been assumed, based purely on lack of evidence to the contrary, that all early humans up to 3000 BC were primitive cave dwellers eking out a living by clubbing ailing antelope or whatever over the head with crude stone tools. But maybe…" She paused and glanced over at Trevor, uncertain of how far to carry her speculations. Richard used to get annoyed when she went off on tangents like these. Just stick to the facts, he would tell her.

"But maybe what?" asked Trevor.

"I'm just speculating, but recent DNA evidence

suggests that modern humans—*Homo sapiens*—may have appeared suddenly, at least relatively speaking, about 160-200,000 years ago. I'm only conjecturing, but maybe something happened that led to a sudden leap in evolution. It's even possible early humans were *more* advanced than us."

"What do you mean by 'something happened'?"

"I don't know—new genes introduced somehow—maybe a virus or…" She hesitated.

"Or deliberate genetic engineering?" Grace suggested.

Rachel shrugged. "It's just a wild idea."

"Maybe not," mused Grace.

"Did you say earlier it was about 10,000 years ago when our brain started decreasing in size?" asked Trevor.

"More or less," Rachel replied.

"That's not long after there was a period of global warming that led to a dramatic rise in sea level," he explained. "In fact, the sixteenth century Piri Reis map shows the coast of Antarctica, something we didn't have the technology to map through the ice until just recently—which suggests the coastline of Antarctica was probably ice free at the time the map was made."

Rachel had heard about the Piri Reis map. It was dismissed by scholars as an unexplained mystery and therefore irrelevant.

"Ten thousand years ago," said Grace pensively. "That's just about the time Atlantis is alleged to have disappeared."

"Atlantis?" asked Rachel, startled by the sudden change in topic. "What does the legend of Atlantis have to do with this?"

"Maybe nothing; but one has to keep an open mind—it's the first rule of good detective work," Grace gently chided her. "You know, according to some scholars, the lost continent of Atlantis was here on the Antarctic Peninsula."

"Here?" Rachel stared out the window at the endless expanse of snow. "How could an advanced civilization survive here?"

"It wasn't always this cold," Trevor reminded her.

Rachel sat back and considered this. "There's just so much we don't know." She paused, then continued. "For example, there's this myth in India about an underground river—the River of Jewels—that runs through the middle of the earth from the Hindis River to a white island."

"Yes, I've heard that myth," Grace said. "Some people think that white island may have been Atlantis."

Rachel shook her head. "I don't think so. If there was such a place surely we would have discovered evidence of it by now."

Grace poured herself another cup of tea, then said, "Unless it sank beneath the sea, as legend has it."

Rachel looked puzzled.

"What I mean is that Atlantis might be *below* Antarctica. Many cultures have myths about the inner Earth being inhabited by an advanced race of albino humans—perhaps not unlike the body downstairs."

Rachel stared at her in disbelief. "Are you suggesting we might have come from inside the Earth? But that's impossible!"

Grace took a sip of tea and looked Rachel in the eye. "Just because it doesn't fit our current paradigm, dear, doesn't mean it's impossible. As you said yourself, lack of evidence doesn't prove something didn't exist. My feeling is that if an idea gets people riled up, it's worth exploring. And don't forget Admiral Byrd's diary," she added.

Rachel sat back and folded her arms. She felt like they had gone beyond the acceptable bounds of scientific speculation. But then their patient downstairs certainly didn't fit the current scientific paradigm. Moreover, neither did the bones they had found in Afghanistan. As unlikely as it seemed, was it possible there was some connection between Antarctica and the bones they had found in Afghanistan, with their evidence of having been from a genetically-engineered humanoid species? And what about her own genetic anomalies? Even though her parents had dismissed them as insignificant, she had always felt otherwise—that she was different from other kids. She stared at the flames in the fireplace, safely contained behind a Pyrex shield. Maybe it wasn't as quiet and peaceful here in Antarctica as she had thought.

After a moment's silence, Grace placed her hand on Rachel's. "There's more I have to tell you about the results of your DNA analysis." She glanced over at Trevor.

He started to stand.

"No," said Rachel reaching up and touching his hand. "You can stay." She turned to Grace. "It's okay with me if Trevor hears whatever you have to say. I trust him."

"Thank you," Trevor said, sitting back down. Rachel could see he really meant it.

Grace looked back and forth between the two of them and smiled.

Rachel flushed as it occurred to her that Grace might be playing matchmaker. Which irked her a bit since Grace knew about her involvement with Richard. But then it was clear from the one time they had met that Grace and Richard had not exactly hit it off.

Grace took a deep breath. “Okay—the DNA results show that for the most part you’re the same as the rest of us; except…” She paused.

“Except what? Tell me.”

“Except you have some similar strands of genetic material in your noncoded DNA as does our patient.”

Rachel stared at her in stunned silence.

“I need to study the results further, but I’d say…”

“But, how? Are you saying I’m some sort of genetic freak of nature?”

Grace paused, searching for the right words. “You’re as human as the rest of us only—I guess you could say—more so.”

“Some consolation,” Rachel said glumly. Her head was spinning. She wondered if Grace knew more than she was telling her. She glanced over at Trevor but she could see he was just as surprised by the news as she.

“How can you know all that just from the preliminary results?” Trevor asked. “Maybe there was some sort of error.”

Grace sighed. “We reran the tests with another blood sample from you in case there was a mistake. We got the same results.”

Rachel took a deep breath and looked down at the ring on her baby finger.

“Look at it this way,” said Grace, patting Rachel’s hand. “We all have untapped potential. Even us so-called normal humans are often capable of achieving far more than we give ourselves credit for."

"That's right," said Trevor, taking Rachel's other hand. The ring echoed the words *right, right, right* in her head as he gently squeezed her hand, reassuring her.

"Being different can be a blessing or a curse," Grace said, "depending on what you decide to make of it. This could also explain why you've never been sick in your life and why you healed so fast from the sprain to your knee."

"And the unusual powers you have over the pendant," Trevor added. "Or it has over you."

Rachel forced a smile. She wondered if the symbols on the pendant and her ring held some sort of secret to her past.

Just then, a group of people came and sat down on some couches not far from them.

The lounge was getting more crowded, people milling around, chatting and laughing. Someone played the piano—a lilting waltz. Outside, it was beginning to snow. The gently swirling snow muted the vivid colors of the sunset.

Now that Rachel had had a few moments to process what she had just learned about herself, it didn't seem so bad. She had spent so much of her life trying to be normal, rather than focusing on who she really was. She pressed her fingers against the pendant tucked beneath her sweater. As she did, she heard the music again and she felt the presence of the spirits closer, much closer now. This time it felt right—like Trevor had said—as it was meant to be.

"Well, I'll be off," Grace said. "It's late and there's something I want to check out. I'll leave you youngsters to enjoy yourselves. Meanwhile, I'll let you know if there are any changes with our patient."

"Night, Aunt Grace," Trevor said, standing and giving her a kiss on the cheek. He sat back down and put his arm around Rachel's shoulder.

On her way out, Grace stopped to say hello to Dragnet Duffy. From there she headed down to the basement to the medical center.

"Expedition coming in!" someone shouted. People crowded around as the Norwegian ski team entered the lounge looking like Nordic gods and goddesses straight from the World of Asgard in their sleek racing outfits.

"What's up?" Trevor asked one of the maintenance men who had come over to warm his hands in front of the fireplace. Frost clung to his ragged beard.

"There's a blizzard blowing in," he said, "and the skiers decided to seek shelter for the night rather than risk continuing on to the ski lodge at Paradise Harbor."

Rachel glanced out the window. It did not look that bad outside.

"Bloody wimps," growled a man, flopping down on the couch where Grace had been sitting. One of the others squeezed in beside him. Trevor moved closer to Rachel.

"I remember a storm we got caught up in on the plateau near the Pole," the man boasted, as though it was the highlight of his life. "Temperature forty below. Wind was so bloody strong it blew us right off our feet."

At a nearby table, a heated debate broke out between some of the British support staff and the Norwegian skiers about who was the greatest South Pole explorer in Antarctica's heroic age: the British Robert Falcon Scott or the Norwegian Roald

Amundsen.

****

While the debates and tales of adventure raged up above, a dark figure emerged from a concealed doorway in a dreary, unlit section of the basement. A woman, a scowl etched across her pale face, stood just inside a tunnel not far behind the figure. "You'd better get it right this time," she threatened. Then she disappeared back into the tunnel.

Ramirez flinched and mumbled something under his breath. Skulking along the narrow corridor, he stopped at the door to the morgue and tried it. It was locked. He cursed. He had read that there were no locked doors in Antarctica. God, how he hated this place! He pulled a small case out of his jacket and set about picking the lock. It opened with a click. Pushing the door open, he stepped inside and eased it closed behind him.

The air inside was unpleasantly cool and smelled slightly of formaldehyde. He flicked on a light switch. There were two small doors in the far wall beside the autopsy table. He walked over and pulled open the first cadaver drawer. Empty. The body had to be in the other drawer. He froze as he heard a woman's voice and footsteps outside the door.

Pulling out his gun, he flicked off the light and stepped behind the door.

After what seemed like an eternity, but was probably only a minute, the footsteps and voices receded and he heard the door to the room next door—the medical center—open and shut again. Ramirez took a deep breath. He had better work fast. But first, he needed something to carry the body in. He checked out a nearby closet and found a body bag on a shelf beneath a strange, gauzy robe. Pushing the robe aside, he grabbed the body bag. Returning to the second door, he took a deep breath, and eased it open. His face fell. The cadaver drawer was empty!

Chapter 19

After listening for almost an hour to the Antarctic veterans swapping stories of their most harrowing storm experiences, Rachel stood and stretched. "Well, I'm going to bed. See you in the morning," she said.

"Would you like me to walk you to your room?" asked Trevor, starting to stand.

"No, thank you, I'm fine," replied Rachel, blushing slightly. "I think I need some time alone."

As she headed up to her room, the recessed lights in the ceiling filled the corridor with a soft glow. Hearing footsteps coming up behind her, she turned around.

"Oh, my God," she gasped. "Richard!"

"Surprise!" he said.

She stared at him. She felt bewildered, thrown off by his sudden appearance. The photo she had seen of the terrorist Ramirez flashed through her mind. Then, just as quickly, it was gone and Richard stood in front of her, smiling, as large as life.

He spread out his arms so she could hug him. "Aren't you glad to see me?"

Rachel did not move.

He put his hands on her shoulders and kissed her on the cheek. His hands and lips felt cold on her skin.

She drew back. "What are you doing here?"

"I flew from Providence into Palmer Station, where

I met with a client and then caught the helicopter coming over here this morning."

"A client? Here in Antarctica?"

"That's right. We're thinking of expanding our energy business. And when I heard about the opportunity to come down here, of course I volunteered immediately—since it would give me a chance to see you." He smiled. "I miss you."

Rachel stepped aside to let someone pass.

Richard looked up at the security cameras and frowned. "Not much privacy here."

"Let's go into my room," suggested Rachel. "We're blocking the corridor."

He followed her into the room and closed the door behind them. He glanced around. "Not much space."

"It's sufficient," she said with a shrug. She sat down on the edge of her bed.

"It's better than what I have," he said, frowning. "They put me up in the temporary guest quarters where I have to share a room with three other men." He took a seat in the chair next to the desk.

After spending a few minutes catching up on what had been going on in Providence since she had left on her travels, he asked, "Are you having a good trip?"

"It's been strange," she said, starting to relax. He seemed so much more interested in her work than he had before. Maybe she had misjudged him. Traveling all the way down here to Antarctica just for an opportunity to see her and putting up with all the inconveniences seemed so uncharacteristic of him. She smiled and patted the bed beside her.

He came over and sat beside her.

"I don't even know where to start," she said.

He took her hand. "I'm listening," he said.

Rachel told him all about the strange object that had been following them and how it had struck their ship, and about Wolf Krause attacking her, and how Hildegaard Braun had mysteriously disappeared from the ship, and about Antonio and the piece of yellow paper they had found outside the Argentinean hut with the letters RAMI on it.

The color drained from Richard's face. He let go of Rachel's hand and ran his fingers through his hair and glanced nervously toward the door. Rachel could hear people talking in the hall.

"Are you okay?" she asked, touching his cheek.

He licked his lips. "Ah, I…I'm just worried about your safety." He forced a smile. Small beads of sweat glimmered on his forehead near his hairline.

"Are you sure?"

"Yes, of course. It's just that…" He paused and took a deep breath. "It's just that I couldn't wait to give you your surprise."

"Another surprise?"

He pulled a large diamond ring out of his pocket and held it out to her. "Rachel Marie St. Claire, will you marry me?"

Rachel stared at the ring, speechless.

"Let's get married, as soon as possible," he said with a tone of urgency.

"I…I…" Rachel had dreamed of this magical moment ever since they had met at that cocktail party, and now she was struck with indecision. "I'll have to think about it," she whispered. "This is so sudden."

His jaw tensed. The silence that followed was as long as it was awkward. "Okay," he finally said. "Fair enough." He set the ring down on the bed beside her then stood and brushed off his trousers. After checking his hair in the mirror, he headed to the door.

She jumped up. "Wait, I'm sorry. Please don't go yet."

Turning, he took her by the shoulders and kissed her on the forehead. "Good night, darling," he said. "You have a lot to think about, and I have important work to do."

He had never called her darling before. It made her feel both giddy and uncomfortable.

"When will I see you again?" she asked.

"I'll find you, maybe at lunch. I have some business to do for my client, so I'm going to be rather busy." He glanced in both directions before stepping out in the corridor and disappearing.

Rachel rubbed the back of her neck and walked over to the window. Richard showing up and then proposing to her was so unexpected. Tiny flakes of snow drifted back and forth in the air as if they did not have a care in the world. She hoped it did not turn into a full-blown blizzard, but she knew from the weather forecast that this was probably just the lull before the storm.

****

The blizzard hit with full force during the early hours of the morning. The wind shrieked down the sides of the mountains and over the glaciers, whipping up the snow from the ground. Icy sleet pounded against the dome like millions of tiny knives trying to break in.

Rachel stared out of the cafeteria window and wondered how much punishment the dome could withstand. Picking up a tray, she looked around for

Richard. He was nowhere in sight. Then she spotted Trevor sitting with Grace and Ka-Wing. After filling her coffee mug and selecting a raisin scone, she walked over to join them.

"Rachel, dear," said Grace. "How nice to see you. I'm just on my way down to the medical center."

"It looks like our patient might be recovering consciousness," said Ka-Wing. "Last night his eyes fluttered a bit. This is so-o cool!"

"That's great news!" said Rachel, debating whether to skip her coffee and head straight down to the medical center with them.

"We have to be careful not to let anyone else know about the status of our patient," said Grace in a hushed tone. "I'm worried that any flurry of publicity might compromise his recovery. It's probably best we don't all go down together—it would call too much attention. We have to keep him isolated for now. We're not sure if his immune system can withstand germs from us."

Rachel nodded and sat down at the table. "Okay, I'll be down in a few minutes then. There's something I wanted to tell Trevor first anyway."

"Take your time," Grace said as she and Ka-Wing left.

"This is great," said Trevor. "What a breakthrough." He reached across the table and touched Rachel's hand.

She pulled it away, and then picked up a knife and spread some jam on her scone. "You'll never guess who turned up last night," she said, avoiding his eyes.

He shrugged. "I don't know. An alien hybrid?"

She smiled. "No, silly. It was…it was Richard."

"Who?"

"Richard…you know…from Rhode Island."

"Him? Here in Antarctica?"

"That's right."

Trevor did not say anything.

"Well, I think it's very romantic that he came all the way down here to see me," she said, trying to sound chipper. "And to propose."

Trevor's face fell. "Did you accept?"

"I told him I'd think about it." She took the diamond ring from her pocket and showed it to Trevor. "Not that he came all this way just to propose," she explained. "He's also doing some work for a client at Palmer Station."

Trevor looked skeptical. "A client in Antarctica?" He ran his finger across the ring band and then examined the tiny letters inside the ring band. "This looks like twenty-four carat gold," he said, frowning, "something you can't get in the States or Canada. Where'd he buy this ring? Did he buy it in Argentina?"

She scowled and took the ring back. "I don't know. What difference does it make anyway? At least our engagement's official now." She hadn't meant to say that. She just said it out of anger at Trevor's petty reaction.

He let out a deep breath and sat back in his chair and folded his arms. "Well, I guess congratulations are in order," he said without enthusiasm.

"What I meant to say is I'm thinking about it. I haven't said 'yes' yet."

He forced a smile. "Hey, it's your life. I wish you the best of luck in whatever you decide."

Rachel picked up her coffee mug and cradled it in her hands. "Thanks for being such a nice guy about all this," she said. "I hope whatever happens we can still be friends."

He poked at his oatmeal with his spoon. "Yeah, right," he said glumly. "That's me—Mr. Nice Guy."

****

The door to the medical center was locked when Rachel arrived. She knocked. Dr. M pushed aside a curtain and peeked out of the small window in the door. Unlocking it, he showed her to a recovery room off the main examining room. The patient was lying in a warming bubble used to treat people with severe hypothermia. Grace was sitting beside him.

Rachel washed up then tiptoed over and put her hands on the bubble. The patient was lying pale and serene as though suspended in time. She felt a strange kinship to him although she could not say why.

"He's still unconscious," said Grace in a low voice.

Rachel sat down on a stool next to her. After a few moments of silence, she turned to Grace and told her about Richard and how he had proposed to her.

Grace reacted with only slightly more enthusiasm than Trevor. "You say he flew into Palmer Station two days ago?"

"That's right. He took a plane to Palmer Station and then caught a helicopter here."

Grace frowned. "That's interesting, because there's no airport at Palmer Station—just a helicopter pad. And when we arrived I checked both the hydrofoil and helicopter passenger lists for the past three days—because of the disappearance of Hilde Braun—and the only new people who came in by helicopter were Doctor Singh and a Canadian artist—an Inuit woman—with the Antarctic Artists and Writers Program."

Rachel shrugged. "I guess I just misunderstood what Richard…"

At that moment, the door flew open and Ka-Wing burst in. "What's happening?" he asked.

Grace pointed at the monitors. "Not much improvement in the past few hours," she replied. "We may as well open the warming bubble; it doesn't seem to be making any difference." She pressed a button and the bubble slid open.

Rachel rested her hand on the patient's shoulder. She could feel the pendant warm against her chest. For some reason, she was no longer wary of him or the music that flooded her thoughts when he was near. Then she realized he was trying to tell her something.

"He wants the robe he was wearing when you found him," she said, turning to Grace. "And his name is Ome. It's more of a musical tone than a word."

"Wow! How'd you know that?" asked Ka-Wing.

"I don't know," replied Rachel, shaking her head. "Maybe it's some sort of telepathy. I think it has something to do with this pendant. Here, you try it."

She took off the pendant and handed it to Ka-Wing.

He held it and leaned close to Ome.

"Nothing," he finally said. He handed it to Grace.

She tried too, but nothing happened with her either. "It seems like the pendant has some special connection to you," she said, giving it back to Rachel.

Ome stirred slightly.

"Quickly," Grace instructed Ka-Wing. "Go get the robe. I think it's still in the morgue!"

Chapter 20

Unable to get Rachel off his mind, Trevor took a break from his work to visit the library and check out some things on the Internet. The only computers in the station connected to the world wide web were in the library and station manager's office. With Internet crime on the rampage, SCAR (the Scientific Committee on Antarctic Research) had chosen to develop its own closed system—THAW, or The Antarctica Web.

There were a few other people in the library, including a tall, dark-haired man standing at the other end of the library.

Trevor sat down at one of the terminals and typed in the search terms "Richard Brewster" and "Boston." Finding nothing of interest, he typed in "Richard Brewster" and "Global Technology International," returning several hits. He was surprised to learn, among other things, that Global Technology had been contracted by the United Nations to provide the technology for towing icebergs from Antarctica. However, there wasn't much on Richard except that he was an in-house counselor for GT and had been there for less than a year. How long, he wondered, had he and Rachel been dating?

The tall man's phone rang.

Trevor cleared his throat and pointed at a sign on the wall reading NO PHONES. The man glared back at him, his cold blue eyes narrowing. After saying something to the person on the other end, he got up and left, bumping Trevor's chair forcefully on the way out, almost knocking him over.

****

While Grace monitored Ome, Rachel studied her data from the day before. From the other side of the door, they could hear Dr. M and Ka-Wing talking to someone who had broken a finger while unloading some equipment from the hydrofoil.

"This is amazing," whispered Rachel. "His cranium is 1830 ccm—well above the normal range found in *Homo sapiens*." She pointed at her iPad. "Also, his bone density is much lighter than that of an average human."

"So, what's your professional opinion?" asked Grace. "Is he a different species or just a subspecies which has been isolated from the wider human gene pool for a long time?"

Rachel shook her head. "I don't know. I'll need to run more comparisons against the findings from the Human Genome Diversity Project."

Grace removed her stethoscope and placed it on Ome's chest. Even though his vital signs were electronically monitored, she had never gotten out of the habit of double-checking the heart rate with her stethoscope. "What's this?" she said, pointing at a barely visible design in the robe. She took a magnifying glass from her bag and handed it to Rachel.

Rachel took the glass and held it over the robe. "It looks like a pattern of some sort. And look here," she said stepping back so Grace could view it. "I'm pretty sure this is the same pattern that's on the pendant!"

Once Dr. M's patient was gone, Rachel slipped out of the medical center. She wanted to do more research on the patterns in the robe and pendant. As she turned down the hall leading to the library, she spotted a familiar figure. "Richard!" she called out.

He turned around. He had a haggard look and dark circles under his eyes. He looked at her hand and noticed she was not wearing the diamond engagement ring. He frowned.

She reached up and felt his forehead. "You don't look well. You even feel a bit feverish."

He brushed her hand away. "I've just been very busy," he replied tersely.

Rachel stepped back, alarmed by his curt behavior. "Is that a rash on your hand?" she asked. "You should have Doctor M look at it."

"It's nothing," he said, shoving his hand in his pocket. "Just stress."

"Oh, I'm sorry," Rachel said. "I have an idea. Why don't you take a break from work and meet us—Grace and Trevor and me—in the lounge for cocktails at… say four o'clock?"

He took a deep breath and rubbed his temples. "You're right. I need to unwind. Things just are not working out with my client as I had planned. I didn't sleep well last night. And to top it off, I've got this damn headache."

"You poor thing," said Rachel sympathetically.

"So how's the work going with the body?"

Rachel shrugged. "Nothing definitive on it so far."

He smiled weakly. "Look, I'm sorry for being so brusque with you," he said, stepping forward and giving her a perfunctory hug.

"Four o'clock then?"

"I will see you then." He hesitated, and then said. "By the way, do you still have that pendant you told me about—the one you found at the site in Afghanistan?"

Rachel put her hand to her chest. She was about to show the pendant to him when a voice inside of her said *No*. "I gave it to Grace to keep safe," she lied.

"Oh? Well, I would like to see it if you can get it. You know how interested I am in your work. I mean, I've heard so much about that pendant."

Really? From whom? Rachel wondered, but felt no need to antagonize him. "I'm not sure where she put it. I think in a safe somewhere until we can return it to Dr. Shah." Rachel looked down at her feet. She felt badly about lying to Richard.

"I see," he said. He gave her a peck on the forehead, and then disappeared down the hall.

Rachel felt a surge of loneliness. She twisted the child's ring on her little finger and wondered what Trevor was doing. She was pleasantly surprised when she entered the library and saw him sitting at one of the terminals.

"Hi, Trevor."

He swung around in his seat to face her. "Hey, Rachel."

"What are you doing?" she asked, peering over his shoulder.

"Just some research on dark stuff," he replied as he quickly logged off. "But I'm done now."

"Oh. Well, I just saw Richard and we're meeting for drinks in the lounge at four o'clock. Want to join us?"

Trevor folded his arms and leaned back in his

chair. "Wouldn't you rather be alone with him?"

Rachel pulled up a seat and sat down beside him. "Come on," she said. "Don't be such a sourpuss. I thought we were friends. I want you to meet Richard."

He heaved a deep sigh. "Okay," he said. "I'll be there."

****

Trevor was in the lounge promptly at four o'clock. Rachel was already there, dressed in a soft green silk blouse, which she had purchased on the cruise ship. Her hair was swept back and pinned with hairpins Grace had given her. Trevor stopped by the bar on the way to her table and got a mug of Molson ale and a glass of wine for Rachel.

"You look gorgeous, as always," he said.

She took the glass of wine from him and smiled. "Thanks. I hope Richard feels the same way. Here, I picked up a bowl of nuts for us and some salsa and chips."

"So, is that what Richard likes…nuts and salsa and chips?"

"No, he's more the shrimp cocktail type, except they don't have those items on the menu here."

Trevor grinned. "Probably a good idea given that krill—Antarctica's version of shrimp—is poisonous to humans." He took a seat next to her. "So how was your day?"

Rachel glanced around to make sure no one was in earshot. A few tables away a group of scientists, affectionately known as beakers in Antarctica, sat quietly sipping tea and munching on tiny decrusted cucumber and marmite sandwiches. Leaning forward on her elbows, she said softly, "We discovered some really interesting things about our patient. His name is Ome, by the way."

"How do you know?"

"He told me."

"Told you? What do you mean? I thought he was in a coma."

"He is. But…I felt his voice in my head." She paused and took a sip of wine.

"In your head? Like telepathy?"

She shrugged and nodded.

"You know, you're pretty amazing," said Trevor, flashing his boyish grin.

"Well, I don't know about that. It just happened. I think it had something to do with the pendant…and maybe those extra genes." She laughed self-consciously then paused, wondering if he would ask where the pendant was; everyone else seemed to be so interested in getting their hands on it.

Instead, he said, "I'm glad it's looking out for you, or at least seems to be."

"Actually, I'm not wearing it right now. I left it in my room. It would show with this blouse, and the rules say we're not supposed to bring expensive jewelry to the station. So I hid it under my mattress."

"Good idea," he said.

They sat in silence, enjoying each other's presence. After a few minutes, Trevor checked his watch. "I don't think Richard's going to show. Do you want to get out of here, go down to the Hot Tub Pub maybe?"

"The what?"

"The pub in the basement. It's in one of the old tunnels off the corridor just past the morgue. It's sort of a makeshift bar next to a hot tub fed by some underground mineral springs."

"Ah. So that explains the sulfur smell. I thought the tunnels might lead to hell."

Trevor laughed. "Don't worry," he reassured her. "Most of the tunnels are closed off now, except for the one leading to the Dark Matter Lab and a few others. No demons can get to us from down below."

"But what if Richard turns up late?"

He raised his eyebrows. "So we miss him and have some time to ourselves—you know, to get to know each other better as *friends*."

"You're bad," she said, trying to keep from smiling. "But go ahead. I think I'll wait a bit longer for Richard…and Grace. She's coming after her shift ends at four-thirty."

"Okay, I'll wait too then."

"Oh, there's Grace now," Rachel said, waving to her.

"Rachel and I were just talking about demons in the basement and renewing our friendship in the Hot Tub Pub," Trevor told Grace as she joined them.

Rachel laughed. As she did, she caught sight of someone else walking toward the table.

"Hello, Rachel," said Richard. His eyes narrowed as he recognized Trevor.

"Richard," she said, "this is Dr. Grace McAllister and my friend Trevor Brookenridge."

"Yes, we already met in the library," said Trevor stiffly as he stood and extended his hand.

Richard glared at him, then sat down on the other side of Rachel and put his arm possessively around her.

After some initial small talk, Trevor turned to Richard and said, "So Rachel tells me you're descended from the Mayflower Brewsters. And you went to law school at Harvard University?"

"That's correct," he said.

"You must remember the Big Dig, then."

"Of course," Richard replied in an irritated tone. He raised his hand and snapped his fingers for service.

A pallid young woman with spiked green hair came out begrudgingly from behind the bar. Her nametag said MADISON and below in large letters SMOKER GIRL.

"A round of drinks for everyone," he said.

Once the drink order was complete, Trevor continued, "So the Big Dig was in full swing when you were in law school. What was it like living there at the time—with all that going on—that is if you were actually there?" he added with a note of challenge in his voice.

Richard didn't reply. Rachel glared at Trevor.

Smoker Girl returned with their drinks.

Richard picked up his shot glass of whisky and tossed it back. Then, he turned to Grace and said, "I understand, Dr. McAllister, that you came down to do an autopsy on a body which was found over at Paradise Harbor."

"Where did you hear that?" Grace asked, taken aback.

"Rachel mentioned it to me," he replied. "I gather the body's still here at the station?"

"Yes and…" Rachel started to reply.

Grace cleared her throat and shot Rachel a look.

Rachel fell silent.

Richard's jaw tensed. "Well, if you don't want to talk about it," he said. "I was just trying to make conversation. Maybe I should just leave you all to yourselves." He sat forward and put his hands on the table as if getting ready to stand up.

"No, please," said Rachel, putting her hand on his.

"I remember hearing about the Big Dig when I was in high school," persisted Trevor, "but never knew exactly what it was. Maybe you can tell me. I've always wanted to know."

"Trevor, will you stop…"

Richard shoved his chair back and stood. "No—it's okay, Rachel," he said, putting his hand on her shoulder. He turned to Trevor. "I had better things to do back then than watch a bunch of stupid archaeologists dig for bones, Mr. Brokenridge," he replied coldly. "Now, if you'll excuse me, I have important work to do." He strode briskly out of the lounge."

"I can't believe how rude you were to Richard," Rachel said to Trevor, feeling furious.

"Me? Rude? It seems to me he was the rude one."

"That doesn't justify the way you acted. You could see he didn't want to talk about that stupid 'Big Dig.' Why did you have to keep pushing him? And what did you mean by asking him if he was actually there? Honestly, Trevor—that was uncalled for." She got up to leave.

"Well, at least I'm not a liar."

"What are you talking about?" she demanded.

"Tell me, why did Richard say it was an archaeological dig?"

"Probably to get you off his back," she snapped.

"In case you don't know, the Big Dig was the construction to replace the main highway through Boston—creating the worst downtown traffic jam for a decade. And that's not all he lied about. He never lived in Bos—"

"You know Trevor, you're not always right. Did it ever occur to you that Richard really didn't know? He might have had better things to do than watch people making piles of dirt and rocks…like you."

"Sorry, but I don't accept that. It's sort of like being in Hiroshima in 1945 and not noticing the atomic bomb go off. And another thing, why is he so interested in the body?"

Rachel threw up her arms in frustration. "For God's sake, he was just trying to make conversation." By now people in the lounge were beginning to stare at them. Rachel glared back at them then started toward the exit. "And will you please stop following me?"

"I can't believe you don't see what a phony he is," Trevor called after her.

She spun around to face him. Her eyes welled up with tears. "Oh, so now *I'm* the idiot."

"No, Rachel. I didn't mean it that way."

"Leave me alone. I wish I'd never met you."

Trevor winced. "Rachel, I'd never do anything to hurt you," he said softly. "I love you."

She bit her lower lip, trying to hold back the tears. "I'm sorry you feel that way," she said.

Chapter 21

Try as she might, Rachel could not stop thinking about how Trevor had said he loved her. In all the time they had dated—what was it now? Almost five months?—Richard had never told her he loved her. After an hour of tossing and turning in bed, she heard a soft tap on her door.

She checked the clock. It was almost midnight. “Who is it?” she called.

“It’s me.”

She hesitated. “Richard?”

“Yes, let me in.”

Getting out of bed, she opened the door. Richard started to step inside, but she blocked his way.

“Aren’t you going to let me in?” he asked, trying unsuccessfully to push past her.

Rachel stood fast. “I have a question for you.”

“What is it now?” he asked impatiently.

She took a deep breath. “Richard, do you love me?”

Richard was caught off guard. “I…I…”

Rachel searched his face for the answer she wanted to hear—or maybe didn’t want to hear. She didn’t know anymore. But it wasn’t there. “Get out,” she said under her breath.

“Rachel, can we just talk about this?”

She shoved the door shut and leaned against it—

half hoping he would knock again and half dreading he would. She listened as his footsteps receded down the corridor. Then she flopped down on her bed and cried herself to sleep.

****

The VLF underground radio connecting the hideout below Shackleton Station to Global Genome's underground base let out a low hum. Hilde leaned forward and flicked it on.

"Seth Legere here," a man's voice said. "What the hell's going on up there? The people in the laboratory can't wait forever. We need the subject's Aryan DNA and the code on the pendant in order to complete the second phase of Project Blue Ice."

Hilde sucked in a breath. "We're planning on delivering the goods tomorrow at the latest. And if Ramirez doesn't come through this time, I'll take care of it myself."

****

The following afternoon Rachel found Richard holding a glass of whiskey as he sat on a couch in the lounge next to the window. She noticed the rash on his hand had worsened and he was sitting stiffly, as though in some pain.

He did not say anything when he saw her approach.

She sat down beside him and folded her hands, not sure of how to broach the subject of his trip to Shackleton Station. There was probably a logical explanation, she told herself. But how could she ask without upsetting him or having him think she didn't trust him?

Richard's eyes narrowed as he noticed Trevor walking toward them.

"Hi," said Trevor, keeping a distance.

"Hi, Trevor," said Rachel. She glanced nervously at Richard.

"Don't worry, I'm not going to stay," said Trevor. "I just came over to apologize for what I said last night. I was out of line. Sorry."

Richard dismissed Trevor's apology with a wave of his hand. "I'll let it go this time," he said. "But from now on, stay away from my fiancée."

There was an awkward silence.

"I…I have to go," Rachel finally said. "I have work to do down in the medical center."

Richard scowled. "You're spending a lot of time there. What is so fucking interesting down there? That damn body you came down for, is that where you're keeping it?"

Rachel did not respond. She had never known Richard to be so rude, and she did not have to put up with it.

"I see," said Richard, setting his whisky glass down with a bang. "Okay, if that's how it's going to be." He got up to leave, but not before warning Trevor once more time. "Don't mess with me, boy," he said, poking Trevor hard in the chest with his index finger. "I meant what I said."

Trevor stared defiantly at Richard's back as he stormed from the lounge and disappeared out of sight.

"I'm sorry," said Rachel. "I don't know what's gotten into Richard lately. I don't think he's feeling well. And I'm sorry too for the way I acted earlier."

Trevor started to sit down. "I guess we're all a bit tense."

Rachel put her hand over the seat beside her.

"Look, maybe it's best for both of us right now if we stay away from each other," she said. "Until this all blows over."

He paused, then reached out to touch her shoulder, but she pulled away. "Okay," he finally said, as he turned to leave.

Rachel stared out at the whirling, chaotic snow. She felt confused. Why was Richard being such a jerk? He had always seemed so charming and debonair when they were out together in Providence, the perfect gentleman. She didn't understand what had gotten into him, or why he was even here, for that matter. Just who was this mysterious client Richard was working for in Antarctica? Or had he just made that up, like the airplane trip to Palmer Station? After several minutes, she stood and slowly made her way down to the medical center.

She found Ka-Wing sitting by himself at a small metal table, diligently studying a medical ebook. He greeted Rachel enthusiastically, glad for the company.

"How's Ome doing?" she asked.

"Terrific. He's been moving a bit."

She watched Ome for a few moments and then flicked open her e-pad to record what Ka-Wing was saying.

"His temperature is…" Ka-Wing stopped in mid-sentence. "Holy jeepers!" he cried, jumping up. "He's waking up!" He raced out of the room to fetch Grace and Dr. M.

Rachel set down her e-pad and stepped cautiously over to the bed. As she took Ome's hand, he opened his eyes and looked up at her.

****

Ramirez waited and watched. He had been crouched inside a hidden opening to one of the abandoned tunnels for almost half an hour. His joints ached, his head pounded, and his stomach did not feel much better. But he had to wait for just the right moment. He could not risk botching the job again. Every so often, someone would appear in the hallway on the way to the Hot Tub Pub. Two scientists from the Dark Matter Lab passed by, prattling on about renewable energy resources. He watched as Dr. M left the medical center and Rachel entered several minutes later. No one noticed him hidden in the shadowy recess.

Suddenly the door to the medical center swung open and Ka-Wing rushed out. Ramirez narrowed his eyes, like a predator ready to strike. Only the body and her in the room now.

Two birds with one stone. Things were looking up at last. Once Ka-Wing was out of sight, Ramirez crept down the hall toward the medical center. This time the door was unlocked. Grabbing a cloth and a small bottle from his pocket, he slowly opened the door to the recovery room.

Chapter 22

"Rachel! Wake up," droned a distant voice.

Her eyes fluttered open. She was lying on the bed in the recovery room. Furniture had been toppled, scattering medical equipment and papers across the floor. Grace and Dr. M were standing over her.

"Thank God you're okay," said Grace, checking her eyes with a pen light. "No sign of a concussion."

Rachel blinked. "Wh…what happened?"

"We found you in the other room, face down and unconscious."

"Did it—that creature—do this to you?" asked Dr. M with a scowl.

"Creature?" Rachel looked puzzled. "You mean Ome? Oh, no. He *warned* me there was danger. But it was too late. The next thing I knew, someone grabbed me from behind and then…" She looked around the room. "Where is Ome? Is he okay?"

"He's disappeared," replied Dr. M.

"You don't remember anything else?" asked Grace.

"No…not until I woke up and saw you."

"I don't know who could have done this to you," Grace said. "Ka-Wing is up with the station manager right now looking through the security tapes for the outside doors from the past hour. Unfortunately, the camera in the hallway outside the medical station had been tampered with and wasn't working."

"With that blizzard outside, the creature couldn't have gone far wearing only a thin robe," said Dr. M.

Rachel reached up to massage a kink in her neck. "The pendant! It's gone."

Grace reached into her pocket. "It's right here. We found it lying next to you." She handed it back to Rachel.

"It must have fallen off in the struggle," said Dr. M.

"Now you just rest a while, dear," said Grace. "I'll be right here beside you."

Exhausted by the turmoil, Rachel lay back and closed her eyes. She ran her fingers across the pendant. She couldn't tell if it was her fingers moving or the symbols. However, she somehow knew that Ome was okay and she would see him again.

When she awoke, it was late evening. Grace sat beside her, skimming through some notes. The room was neat again with everything in its place.

"Be careful," said Grace, resting her hand gently on Rachel's arm. "You've been through quite an ordeal."

"Where is everyone?" asked Rachel, rubbing her eyes and propping herself up on her elbow.

"Richard dropped by early on to see how you're doing, but I haven't seen or heard from him since. He wanted to stay with you, but I thought it would be better if one of us doctors stayed. He didn't look well at all. Besides, he was very upset…agitated. He blamed Trevor for all this—for bringing you down here in the first place."

Rachel shook her head. "I don't know what's wrong with him these days."

Grace gave her hand a gentle squeeze. "You know, dear, Trevor cares very much about you. He's already been by several times to check on you."

"Maybe this whole thing is my fault," Rachel said. "I shouldn't have led him on the way I did."

"Now, there's no blame to be laid here. Trevor is quite capable of making his own choices."

There was a tap at the door. Grace got up and opened it.

Trevor poked his head inside. "I just wanted to see how you're doing." He hesitated. "I hope you don't mind."

"No, come on in," Grace said. She stood and offered Trevor her seat. "Would you mind staying with Rachel while I check to see if security has any new information? I'll be back in a few minutes." She left the room.

"Well, I guess you're stuck with me for a while," Trevor said, smiling awkwardly. He sat down beside the bed. "How are you doing? Aunt Grace told me what happened."

Someone walked by in the hall. Rachel shot a worried glance toward the door. She knew how jealous Richard could be—or least she did now.

"Look, I don't want to make any trouble for you with Richard," Trevor said, standing. "I'll go as soon as Aunt Grace gets back."

"You probably should. You know, he blames you for all this, since it was you who brought me here."

Trevor drew back, as if he had just been punched in the gut. Anger flashed across his face, before he contained it. "I'm sorry all this happened," he said in a low voice. "I truly am."

Rachel felt terrible. She did not mean that she personally blamed Trevor—just that Richard did. She wanted to say so, but…she suddenly burst into tears as the realization came tumbling in on her that she was falling in love with Trevor.

The latch on the door clicked and Grace came in.

"Look, I better get going," Trevor said, looking lost. "I'm sorry I upset you."

"What was that about?" Grace asked, once he had left.

Rachel sat up and blew her nose. "I'm just feeling a little confused," she said.

"Well, you wouldn't be normal if you didn't after all that's happened," Grace said, patting her hand. "And you're probably ravenously hungry on top of it. Come on, let's get you upstairs and get some food in your stomach, unless you'd rather rest more or have me bring something down from the cafeteria."

"No, really, I'm feeling much better now, and, you're right, I'm famished."

****

Rachel sat down at one of the tables in the cafeteria while Grace went to fetch her supper. It was late and the cafeteria was almost empty. From where she sat, Rachel had a good view of the lounge area. Trevor was sitting in one of the armchairs listening to a group playing a lively jig. Some of the people were dancing to the music, including Duffy, the red-bearded marine biologist.

Grace returned and set a plate of macaroni and cheese in front of her. "The Canadian blue plate special," she said. "Something nice and bland to settle your stomach."

“Thanks,” said Rachel.

Grace pulled up a chair and sat down beside her.

“Why don’t you go join your friends?” suggested Rachel.

“Oh, I don’t mind staying here with you.”

“Please. You don’t have to watch me eat. I’m fine now.”

“Well, if that’s what you want,” said Grace reluctantly, “but make sure you let me know if you need anything. I’ll be just inside the lounge.”

While Rachel ate her dinner, she watched the people enjoying themselves in the lounge. Trevor looked over a few times. Knowing he wanted to come over sent a warm surge through her, but she pushed the feeling aside. This was not a good time. What if Richard turned up?

Shoving aside her empty plate, she gazed at the snow swirling wildly against the indigo twilight sky. She remembered how only a few weeks ago she had dreamed of marrying Richard and living happily ever after in a neat Victorian house overlooking Narragansett Bay. He had seemed so charming then, so composed and in charge—and now it was as if she didn’t even know him.

She sighed and thought of Ome. Was he still somewhere in the station? Was he even alive for that matter? She closed her eyes, trying to communicate with him somehow, but nothing happened. Suddenly she remembered she had left her e-pad with the data on Ome in a drawer in the medical center. What if the intruder came back looking for it? Picking up her dish, Rachel dropped it off and headed back down to the basement.

As she turned down the hall, she saw a tall figure leaning against the wall near the medical station. He was holding his stomach. “Richard, what are you doing here?” she asked, recognizing him. His face was a ghastly shade of gray and he had a bump on his forehead.

“Are you okay?” she asked cautiously, keeping her distance.

“I’m not feeling very well. It is probably the flu, or maybe something I ate. I had shrimp cocktail with my client earlier and—” He broke off in mid-sentence and, holding his stomach, groaned slightly.

“Do you want me to go upstairs and get Dr. M or Grace?”

“No, I saw the station doctor earlier. He’s an idiot; he doesn’t know anything,” Richard muttered. He straightened up and stared at her as if he had just noticed her.

She shifted restlessly and glanced down the empty hall. “Any luck in locating the person who attacked me?”

“No, but I found out something else that might interest you,” he said tersely. “I had my assistant back in Providence do some research on this Trevor friend of yours. Turns out he’s a Nazi hunter—a lunatic.” He fumbled in his pocket and pulled out a folded piece of paper. His hand trembled as he flashed it in front of her. Then he stuffed it back in his pocket before she had a chance to read it.

Voices and laughter drifted down the corridor from the Hot Tub Pub. Richard glanced nervously in that direction.

“For your own good,” he said, “I want you to stay

away from him."

"Look, Richard, we have to talk about us and—"

"For Christ's sake," he said, cutting her off, "the guy's delusional. There are no Nazis around. World War II ended over seventy years ago."

Rachel felt bewildered by his hostility. "Richard, what's going on here? I've never seen you like this before. I'm going upstairs to get Grace so she can take a look at you."

"I do not need a fuckin' doctor," he said between clenched teeth. He reached for her hand.

She instinctively pulled it away.

"I told you, I feel fine now," he said. "Can't you see that this Trevor guy's trying to turn you against me?" He glanced furtively over his shoulder. His eyes had a cold, haunted look to them. Beads of sweat stood out on his brow, even though it was cool in the hallway.

Rachel looked up at the security camera in the hall and noticed it was still broken. She felt a twinge of fear. "I have to go now," she said. "I'll tell Grace you're down here." She looked around for a way out. This was one time she wished Trevor had followed her.

Richard looked disoriented by her rebuff. "No… no, I have something to show you," he insisted in a low voice. He pointed toward the unlit end of the hall. "It's a surprise."

"You mean the hot springs? I already know…"

"No, farther down. You'll like it." He brushed back his disheveled hair with his hand and forced a smile. His smile looked grotesque in the cold, harsh light of the corridor.

Rachel started to walk away. "Please, I have to go now."

He blocked her. All pretense of friendliness vanished. "Go?" He grabbed her wrist. "Where do you have to go in such a hurry?" he demanded.

She tried to pull away. "What is this? Am I a captive?"

He squeezed her wrist harder. "Of course not. Why won't you just cooperate? Why do you always have to be so damned stubborn?" Then he noticed the chain that held the pendant. "What's this?" he asked, grabbing the chain between his fingers.

"What's what?" she asked, jerking back from him. As she did, the chain snapped. The pendant clinked to the floor and rolled down the corridor, settling against the stone wall.

"What's wrong with you, Richard? Let go of me!"

His demeanor suddenly changed.

"Wait, please don't leave me," he said, backpedaling. "I haven't been feeling well lately and things with my client aren't going all that well and…" He paused and looked her in the eye. "And you don't know how much I need you right now."

Rachel was not falling for that. Not now. "You've never needed me before," she said under her breath. "Why now?"

Scarcely were the words out of her mouth when she regretted she had said them. His jaw tensed. His face hardened and the veins in his forehead stood out as he grabbed her arm.

She tried pulling back, but to no avail. "Let go of me, Richard," she protested. "You're scaring me."

"You heard her," said a voice from down the hall.

They turned around. It was Trevor.

"I told you to stay away from her," snarled

Richard.

Trevor stretched out his hand. "Come on, Rachel. Let's get out of here."

Richard stepped between them, knocking Rachel back against the wall.

Grabbing Richard's shirt with one hand, Trevor drew back his fist and hit Richard square in the jaw. Richard stumbled backward, grunting and clutching his chin. Blood trickled from the corner of his mouth.

The noise had attracted the attention of the people in the Hot Tub Pub, who gathered around looking for some entertainment.

"Whoa, dude—way to go!" shouted one of the techies, cheering on Trevor.

Regaining his balance, Richard staggered to a half-standing position and pulled a scalpel out of his boot. As the crowd gasped, he lunged at Trevor, grazing his arm. Trevor grabbed the hand holding the scalpel and jerked Richard toward him, punching him hard in the solar plexus with his other hand. Richard, too weak to fight back, dropped the scalpel and collapsed to the floor, writhing only inches from where the pendant lay, obscuring Rachel's view of it.

"Finish off the bloody bastard," someone yelled.

"Stop it!" cried Rachel. "Stop it before someone gets killed." She gave the onlookers a disgusted look, then turned and ran up the stairs.

Miserable and confused, she stumbled into the lobby. What was Richard doing with that scalpel? Even worse, how could she have fallen for him in the first place?

Crossing the lobby to the boot room, she grabbed her parka and gloves and went out into the covered courtyard. Her head was swimming. She needed to get away, to get a breath of fresh air. Outside, the wind howled and the icy snow clawed at the dome like a demon trying to rip it apart. The dome creaked ominously under the fierce pressure.

She drew her parka tightly around her and stepped into the vestibule that enclosed the outside door. A security camera recorded her movement. There was a storm warning light on beside the door. Pulling up her hood, she pushed open the outside door. The snow stung her face and the bitter cold took her breath away.

She closed the outside door and quickly stepped back inside.

"Hey, what do you think you're doing?" barked a gruff voice from behind a bearded face. "Don't you know there's a bloody storm alert on?"

"Sorry, I just…"

The man scowled at her. Then he walked away, muttering something about damn women and the good old days when Antarctica belonged to the men.

Rachel unzipped her parka and stepped back into the courtyard. A movement near the grove of beech trees caught her eye. She saw someone in a red coat disappear behind the botany building. There was someone else as well, but Rachel only caught a glimpse of the other person's feet. From around the corner, she could hear them scuffing along the path, like the person was drunk, followed by what sounded like a muffled scream. Or was it just the sound of the storm?

Rachel paused and listened. However, all she could hear was the shrieking of the wind outside the dome.

Chapter 23

When Rachel awoke the next morning, the storm had passed and long rays of sunlight sliced through the dispersing clouds. As she reached for her clothes, she realized the pendant was gone. Then she remembered it had fallen off during the scuffle yesterday.

After quickly dressing, she headed down to the basement and searched the hallway. But the pendant was nowhere to be found. Back upstairs, Rachel found the cafeteria abuzz with the news of the fight between Trevor and Richard. To add fuel to the rumor mill, Richard was missing. First Ome, now Richard had disappeared.

Through the door to the lounge, she could see Antonio talking to Grace. Trevor was standing in front of them with his back to the fireplace. Grace was holding something—a photograph perhaps?—studying it as if she thought she might recognize the person in the picture, but then, shaking her head, she handed it back to Antonio.

Nearby, people at one of the tables were eyeing Rachel and whispering. Frowning, she wrapped a muffin in a napkin, picked up her coffee mug, and headed out to the courtyard. It was chilly inside the dome, but quite bearable with her fleece pullover. People with huge backpacks of gear were milling around in the courtyard, preparing to go out in the field.

Now that the blizzard had passed, the station took on a renewed urgency, especially for the summer-only scientists who had just a few weeks left before returning home. She walked over and sat on a bench under a beech tree.

Someone touched her gently on the shoulder.

Looking up, she saw Trevor.

"I thought I might find you here," he said. "I have something of yours."

Her heart skipped a beat. "The pendant?" She moved over on the bench to make room for him.

He held out his hand. "Sorry. Just the chain. I was hoping you had the pendant."

"Thanks," she said, trying not to show her disappointment.

"I found it last night in the hallway not far from the medical center."

"I looked for the pendant this morning, but couldn't find it." She sighed and put the broken chain in her pocket.

"Do you think Richard might have taken it?" he asked.

Rachel rubbed the back of her neck. "I don't know. He did seem pretty interested in it." She paused. "I don't know if you've heard, but Richard has disappeared. Apparently he didn't return to his room last night."

"Yes, Aunt Grace told me at breakfast." Trevor took a deep breath and sat down beside her. "Hey, I'm sorry about yesterday," he said.

"Yeah, well, I wouldn't be surprised if Richard was on his way back to Providence by now…probably with the pendant," she said with some bitterness.

"But why would he want the pendant?" Trevor asked.

She shook her head. She had no clue. "I think he was angry because I wouldn't agree to marry him. He probably saw it lying there on the floor and took it to spite me. He can be like that sometimes."

"More than sometimes, it seems." Trevor leaned over and picked up a beech leaf off the ground. "So it's over between you two?"

Rachel nodded. "I know I've been behaving like a real idiot. It's just that I've…" She paused.

"It's okay," he said. "No need to explain." He reached over and handed her the leaf.

She smiled. "Thanks. I'll add it to my collection of Antarctica memorabilia. By the way, I saw you and Grace with Antonio in the lounge this morning."

"Oh? You should have joined us. He came over about half an hour ago—the storm alert is off now. He says he has reason to believe Ramirez is here in Antarctica, possibly even in this area."

Rachel looked startled. "You mean the neo-Nazi terrorist? Here?"

"But it's unlikely he's actually here at this station," Trevor added. "The head of security checked the guest and staff directory as well as the security camera pictures, and everyone's accounted for. Except Richard, of course."

"Well, I hope they find him soon. It's creepy to think a terrorist might be lurking around." She took a long sip of coffee and then asked, "Any word on Ome yet?"

Trevor nodded. "Sort of. We figured out how Ome escaped."

Rachel perked up. “Oh? How?”

“Through the door from the marine biology lab.”

“But I thought all the outside doors except the main door were locked during storm alerts.”

“They are,” he said. “Normally the magnetic locks only open automatically if the temperature falls below or above a certain temperature—in case of fire or power failure. Somehow, Ome seems to have opened it. Whatever happened, it’s probably the last we’ll see of him.”

“Maybe not,” Rachel said pensively.

“What do you mean?”

“I don’t know how I know it, but I think we’ll be seeing Ome again.”

They sat in silence, watching the Norwegian team pack their colorful parafoils on sleds.

After a few minutes, Trevor cleared his throat and said, “Look, I’m really sorry about Richard and the way I acted last night.”

She shook her head. “No, you were right. I don’t know what I ever saw in him.” She touched his arm. “I’m just sorry you got hurt.”

Their gazes met, and she felt a surge of warmth.

“It’s just a scratch. Wanna see my scar?” he asked, a mischievous twinkle in his eye.

Rachel felt like hugging him for being there for her. Instead, she smiled and ran her fingers along the contour of the leaf on her lap.

He leaned toward her and took her chin in his hand. She hesitated—what about Richard? But then wasn’t it as good as over between them? Of course it was.

Her breath caught as Trevor kissed her lightly on her lips. She felt lightheaded when he drew her closer, then kissed her harder. Her heart beating wildly, she wrapped her arms around his neck, her body melting into his.

Footsteps.

Startled, Rachel pushed away and jumped to her feet, feeling both confused and embarrassed. “I think I hear someone coming.” For a split second she feared it might be Richard, seeking her out, until she spotted a young woman pushing a cart.

“Anyone we know?” Trevor asked, standing as well and placing a hand under her elbow.

Rachel let out a silent sigh of relief, grateful for Trevor’s easygoing personality. Another man might have taken offense at her skittish behavior. “Just the girl from the kitchen. You know, the one we call Smoker Girl?”

“Who could forget her?” Trevor said, smiling. He offered Rachel his arm. “How about taking a short walk around the courtyard?”

“How about we get a cup of coffee instead? I think I could use another cup.”

As they crossed the yard, Smoker Girl trudged past them on her way to the compost heap behind the Botany Building.

****

“Oh, my Gawd! Oh, my Gawd!” A frenzied wail pierced the air just minutes later as Smoker Girl staggered wide-eyed into the cafeteria.

Nearly everyone stopped what they were doing to stare at her. Rachel set her cup down at an empty table and glanced at Trevor, still holding a cup of tea and looking at Smoker Girl.

“A…a body! A dead man!” Smoker Girl cried,

shaking her hands frantically. "In the compost pile!" She collapsed into a chair and buried her face in her hands. Someone broke free of the crowd to sit down beside her and offer comfort as pandemonium nearly broke out and most everyone else rushed into the courtyard, Trevor and Rachel among them. Antonio was the first to reach the body. Trevor and Rachel weren't far behind, but given the enclosed space of the compost area, were still too far away to see much of anything. Only one arm and the top of a head protruded from the pile of composted garbage. Antonio crouched before the body and brushed the rest of the compost off the face. He inhaled sharply and made the sign of the cross.

"Stand back," shouted the station manager. "Let the medical staff through."

Dr. M and Grace edged their way over to Antonio through the crowd of bystanders, while Rachel and Trevor moved back with the crowd.

"Oh, no!" the usually unflappable Grace gasped when she saw the body.

"You know this person?" asked Antonio.

"Yes, but—"

Why didn't you tell me he was here?" Antonio asked.

Grace gave him a puzzled look. "You didn't ask."

"Back it up, everyone, there's no need to be gawking." The station manager tried unsuccessfully to herd the spectators back toward the cafeteria.

Grace turned and glanced around the crowd, spotting Rachel.

Rachel tried to come closer, but Grace held up a hand. "Rachel, dear, you don't need to see this," Grace called out, moving her body to a spot where Rachel could now see nothing. “Trevor, would you take Rachel back into the cafeteria? Please?”

“Of course. Rachel—”

She pulled her arm out of Trevor’s grip. “What’s going on? Why doesn’t’ she want me to see the body?”

“Come on, Rachel, Grace is right. We don’t need to see this. Let’s go finish our coffee.”

Rachel held steadfast. “You go back if you like, but there’s no way I’m leaving. What if it’s someone we know?” She looked around. Why else would Grace be shielding her from seeing the body? “Where’s Ka-Wing?” she asked. Feeling frantic, but not knowing why, she started searching the crowd for his familiar face.

“All right.” Trevor’s voice was grim. “There’s a spot against the wall where we can stand and be out of the way.” Rachel nodded. She still couldn’t see much of anything, but she would at least be able hear what was going on. “For now,” she relented, stepping back. She rested her hand on Trevor’s shoulder and stood on her tippy toes, straining to get a glimpse of the body. But no luck. Grace and Dr. M had now moved in a way that blocked her view of the entire body. She looked at Trevor, to ask if he could see anything, but his face was turned away, looking toward a group coming back from the field.

“What happened?” Rachel heard Dr. M ask Grace, as she set her medical bag down and removed a pair of surgical gloves. Slipping on the gloves, she knelt down beside Dr. M and examined the body.

“He’s been dead for a while. I’d say at least twelve hours, maybe more.” Grace ran her hands down the back of the dead man's head and neck. "Blood," she said, holding up her hands.

"How do you think he died?" asked Antonio. "Do you think it might have been…?" Antonio paused, and then said something in a low voice that Rachel could not hear.

"Possibly," Grace replied.

"Look at this," Dr. M said. "There's an unusual rash on the hand and arm."

Sutchin, who had just returned from the field, joined them.

Dr. M stepped back so Sutchin could examine the body.

"What do you think?" Grace asked.

"The rash may be from a viral infection," Sutchin replied. "Had the victim been complaining of nausea? Aches or stiffness?"

"He came into the medical center a few days ago complaining of stiffness in the joints and a headache," replied Dr. M. "I thought it might be flu, so I sent a blood sample off to the World Health Organization Epidemic Intelligence Service. We're required to report any suspected viral infections."

"Did you get the results back yet?" asked Grace.

"I haven't checked my email yet today. To tell you the truth, I forgot about it. He didn't come back, so I just assumed his symptoms had cleared up."

"The rash could also be caused by krill poisoning," said Grace. "I saw it once when I was the winter medical officer at Rothera Station. The cook had a breakdown—polar madness they call it—and tried to poison the station manager. Fortunately, the station manager survived the attempt on his life."

"Well, there's only one way to tell." Dr. M pulled a small tube out of his medical bag and took a blood sample. He passed it to Ka-Wing, who had just arrived.

Sutchin and Ka-Wing left with the vial of blood.

"Make sure to check your email while you're down there," Grace called after them.

Spotting Rachel and Trevor, Antonio went over to join them.

"Who is it?" Rachel asked.

"His name's Ramirez—Angel Ricardo Ramirez," Antonio said.

Grace stood up and looked back toward Antonio, her eyes widening. "Who…who did you say it was?" she asked, sounding very confused.

Just then she spotted Trevor and Rachel still in the vicinity. She moved to quickly block Rachel's view of the body once more, but by then Dr. M had stood and moved away as well, giving Rachel her first glimpse of the dead man's face.

"Oh, my God," she gasped. "It's Richard!"

Chapter 24

The hydrofoil was pulled up to the dock, the marine biologists unloading gear and specimens: buckets of krill, black-finned ice fish, and Antarctic spiny plunder fish. The sun hung just above the horizon, the sky turning a pale pink in anticipation of nightfall.

Rachel stopped at the edge of the dock to watch the marine biologists unload the trawl net from the back of the hydrofoil. As she stood there, she contemplated once more Richard's grisly death. She shuddered. No one deserved to suffer that way. No one. She took a deep breath and glanced over her shoulder. Were there other terrorists, possibly Richard's murderer, at the station this very moment? And were they after her as well? Grace and Antonio seemed to think so.

Rachel thought back to earlier that afternoon, when Grace had finally sent Ka-Wing back up to the cafeteria to bring her and Trevor down to the medical center. At first, Grace had suggested Trevor take Rachel back to her cabin to rest and recover from the chilling shock of the morning's events, but Rachel had felt a very strong need to be around people, instead of alone with her spiraling thoughts and growing fear.

She looked up at the fading sky and rubbed her arms, still reeling from the revelation that Richard was not whom he had pretended to be—that he had been deceiving her all this time.

If that wasn't enough, when she and Trevor had joined them in the medical center, Antonio and Grace had dropped another bombshell.

"We think it was Hilde Braun who killed Richard," Antonio explained as they stood together beside the thankfully empty examination table. Rachel didn't know what she would have done if she'd seen Richard naked and cut open on the autopsy table.

Antonio brought her attention back to the present with the stunning revelation that Grace had found some strands of blond hair and a broken nail with clear nail polish on the collar of Ricardo Ramirez's jacket.

"But isn't Hilde dead?" Rachel asked, taken aback. None of this made sense.

Antonio shook his head. He told them apparently Hilde had survived the plunge through the door in the center raft of the cruise ship and made it to Deception Island and from there to Shackleton Station.

"But there are plenty of women at the station who have blond hair," Rachel protested, "including me."

"Yes, including you," Grace replied, turning to her. "Think about it, Rachel. The killer was wearing a red *Queen Maud* jacket, which both of you own. The body was probably staged so it would look like you murdered Richard."

"Me?" Rachel felt numb. She just couldn't wrap her head around the idea of Richard in league with that horrible Hilde Braun. Now, even worse, someone wanted to frame *her* for Richard's murder? Was this all a bad dream? More like a nightmare.

She took as deep breath as Trevor put his arm around her waist. His arm was the only thing in the room that felt sure and solid at that moment.

"But Rachel was with me all morning," he said.

"We know Rachel didn't do the killing," Antonio reassured them.

Grace then went on to explain that Antonio also suspected Hilde of being a neo-Nazi and already had her under surveillance.

Antonio shook his head. "Apparently the surveillance did not work well enough, if she could kill someone and not be seen doing it!"

In the strained silence that followed, Rachel wondered if she was losing her mind. Believing any of this would be hard on a good day. Right now she was not in the mood for any of it. Richard was dead, and she…she…

"Have you determined yet how he died?" Trevor asked quietly, breaking through the tension in the room.

"It appears to be krill poisoning," Grace said. "But we still need to complete the autopsy."

Rachel felt a chill as she remembered Richard telling her he was meeting a client for shrimp cocktail. But, who was the client? Could it have been Hilde Braun? She shuddered and shook her head. Impossible. But then until an hour ago, she'd thought the same about Richard being a neo-Nazi.

Now Hilde was trying to frame her for Richard's murder. But why?

Antonio pulled out a map and spread it out on the examination table. "We need to get you to safety in case Hilde Braun and her neo-Nazi cohorts are after you, Rachel."

"Don't forget her interest in your connection to that pendant," Grace added.

"But I don't have it!" Rachel said, bewildered. Why would anyone want her pendant badly enough to kill for it?

"All the more reason to take precautions. If somehow Hilde does have the pendant, it might not work without you."

"What do you mean? Work for what?"

Grace shook her head. Another dead end. No one knew.

Antonio then explained he had made arrangements for the Norwegian ski team to take Grace and Ka-Wing to an abandoned hut several kilometers from the station. He pointed at a spot on the map. "Given favorable winds, their parasails are capable of safely carrying two people over the rough ice fields and crevasses," he reassured them.

"You mean Grace and Ka-Wing are in danger too!" Rachel asked.

"We don't know. We can't be sure. But neither can we take that chance. As long as Ramirez's—Richard's killer is on the loose, we'll have to operate on a worst case scenario basis."

"What about Rachel?" Trevor asked. "How do you plan to get her to safety?"

"We can't have all of you leaving at one time since that would arouse suspicion," Antonio said, rolling up the map. "Once Grace and Ka-Wing are safely on their way, you and Rachel can escape using the old mining tunnels."

"And then what? I'm supposed to run, be looking over my shoulder, for the rest of my life?" Rachel asked.

"Well, no, it's just—"

"What about using me as bait?"

Everyone looked at Rachel.

"What if you use me as bait, to draw out Hilde from wherever she may be hiding."

"Rachel," Trevor protested. "You're not thinking clearly. If Hilde killed Richard, then—she'd have no qualms about…"

Rachel held up a palm. "I don't want to hear it. This is my life we are talking about, and I'm not going to spend it on the run. We either come up with a plan, or I'm not going anywhere until Richard's killer is found and captured."

Two hours later, they left the medical center, a rough plan formulated. It wasn't the best, and Rachel knew it, but—deliberate deception or not—her conscience wouldn't let her just walk away if Richard's death had anything to do with her. Who could be next? Grace? Ka-Wing? Trevor?

If, as Grace and Antonio believed, the killer was indeed after Rachel, then by all means she wanted to get this over and done with. And besides, if the killer wanted her dead, she'd already be dead, wouldn't she?

So here she stood, feeling like a worm on a hook, staring at the rocky snow-capped mountains across the bay. She glanced over her shoulder one last time. No one unusual in sight. Would this even work?

It didn't matter. This was her only chance, and she had to try. If this failed, anyone who was after her would know she was on to them.

After taking a final deep breath, she stepped onto the dock. It swayed slightly under her weight. Grace's friend Ian Duffy paused when he saw her, and gave her a thumbs-up. She smiled back weakly as the burly marine biologist began stuffing the net into a large oblong bag.

****

Down the beach, behind a rocky outcrop just beyond the penguin colony, a figure wearing white camouflage coveralls over her red *Queen Maud* parka watched the marine biologists through binoculars. An all-terrain Sno-Cat pulled up to the dock, momentarily blocking her view of it—and her prey. When Hilde finally got a glimpse of the dock again the biologists were loading a big, long canvas bag onto the Sno-Cat.

Hilde's eyes narrowed as she surveyed the scene. That idiot Ramirez. Who had he thought he was dealing with?

Meanwhile the St. Claire freak still stood at the far end of the dock, staring melodramatically out over the water. Missing her lover, was she?

The Sno-Cat now loaded, it took off toward the station with the biologists plodding along behind it. The hydrofoil took off in the opposite direction. When both were out of sight, Hilde stepped from behind the rock, keeping low. The snow on the mountains across the bay glowed blood red in the setting sun. A skua, like the one that had nearly killed Klaus, lifted off its nest, circled overhead, and let out a warning cry. It was all Hilde could do not to shoot the damned beast.

She glanced back toward Rachel. She did not seem to notice the skua. She just stared straight ahead, like the stupid freak she was. Lifting up the rope that cordoned off a protected botanical area, Hilde stooped and went under it, crushing fragile snow-covered dendrite lichen and mosses under her heavy boots. When she reached the dock area, she paused beside the boathouse, checking once more to make sure she had not been seen. There was no one, except Rachel and some penguins preening their feathers and settling in for the night.

Hilde's jaw tightened. Silently she stepped out into the open and moved stealthily across the beach to the dock. She could barely make out Rachel now; just a silhouette against the setting sun. The dock tilted slightly under her weight as Hilde stepped onto it. She pulled a small stun gun from her coveralls and gripped it tightly, ready to shoot in case her target noticed the movement.

But Rachel St. Claire did not move. She just kept staring ahead at the dark, choppy water.

Just keep daydreaming, you stupid girl, just one more minute and you're mine.

Hilde inched forward along the dock until she reached her quarry. In triumph she shoved the gun deep into Rachel's back.

The gun went straight through as though passing through a ghost.

"What the—?"

Losing her balance, Hilde fell forward, tripping over something hard. The ghostly image of Rachel shimmered and faded away. Hilde looked around, bewildered. There was no one there. She was all alone on the dock.

Then she spotted what she'd tripped over. Her fury building, she crawled over and picked it up. It was a portable holographic projector. Her heart pounded with rage as she threw the projector into the water then pushed herself to her feet. Beside the dock she noticed a net lying in the water—the same net the marine biologists had supposedly been putting into the oblong bag.

Her heart pounded and adrenaline pulsed through her body. Son of a bitch. She'd been set up.

"Put your hands over your head, Hilde Braun," ordered a male voice behind her. "I'm placing you under arrest for the murder of Angel Ricardo Ramirez."

Hilde swung around and saw the outline of a tall figure standing at the other end of the dock, a revolver pointed at her. As she did, she switched her stun gun to kill and fired it. It was a wild shot—a shot in the dark—but it hit the man in the shoulder.

His eyes opened wide in shock as he toppled backward onto the rocky beach. Blood gushed from his shoulder, turning the snow between the pebbles a deep red.

A spotlight flashed on, and suddenly people brandishing guns rushed at her from the boat shed.

Looking frantically around for an escape, Hilde leapt off the dock and into shallow water at the edge of the shore, then raced for her life along the icy, pebbly beach, zig-zagging wildly to avoid being shot, until she reached the ice cliffs.

Then she disappeared.

Chapter 25

Trevor was waiting anxiously in the medical center, when Rachel appeared, her face flushed and her hair tousled from the trip up from the dock hidden in the net bag. A piece of seaweed clung to the sleeve of her parka.

"Quick," said Trevor, jumping up and slipping a backpack onto her shoulders before she had a chance to say a word. He shoved a headlamp into her hands then stepped into the corridor, looking both ways. Waving at her to hurry up, they headed for the steel door that sealed off one of the old abandoned mining tunnels that threaded their way under the station. As they had discussed during their whirlwind planning session earlier in the day, he'd already loosened the bolt while waiting for her to arrive from her stint as a decoy at the dock, and it now slipped open easily.

Together they moved rapidly through the abandoned tunnel. As they made their way through the narrow passage, Rachel couldn't stop thinking about Richard. His deceit, his betrayal—his completely inexplicable association with Hilde. By now Rachel's numbness and denial had turned to anger. The more she thought about it, the more she began to believe Grace was right. Hildegard Braun and Richard Ramirez had been stalking her, together, for some reason. She didn't know which to feel more—anger at his betrayal or pity for them both. One dead, the other hopefully in custody and charged with murder.

Then again "Richard" had been a façade—not a real person, but a role player with an act designed to trap her into falling for him. And he had asked her to marry him! So that he could do what? Kidnap her? Kill her? What did he want of her?

The anxiety of it all made her chest tighten, squeezing her, suffocating her. She stopped and tried to take a deep breath. Up ahead she could see the beam of Trevor's flashlight.

"How much longer?" she called out in a thin voice.

"I think I see the end up ahead," he called back, shining his flashlight down the length of the tunnel. He came back and took her hand. "Are you all right?"

"I'm fine. Just…overwhelmed by it all."

His voice gentled. "It's not much farther."

The tunnel came out near a nanutuck, an outcrop of granite rocks, a few kilometers from Shackleton Station. By the time they emerged, the short Antarctic night had set in.

Removing her headlamp, Rachel leaned back against the rocky outcrop. "We actually pulled it off!" she said, gulping in the fresh cold air.

Trevor smiled. "We make a good team."

"So what's next?"

"We're meeting Aunt Grace and Ka-Wing at an abandoned meteorology station about twenty kilometers from here. Byrdie and Caitlyn are picking us up there."

"Byrdie and Caitlyn from the *Queen Maud*?"

He nodded. "If anyone is after us, they'll have the Shackleton helicopters under surveillance as well as the regular teams leaving from there. Caitlyn's out doing a survey of the whales anyway. A short detour overland shouldn't raise any suspicion."

Trevor pulled a tent from his backpack and set it on the ground.

Rachel looked through her pack. "I don't seem to have a tent."

He shrugged. "It's a two-person Scott tent. Everyone shares tents here in Antarctica; it's warmer and makes for less to carry." He pulled out his sleeping bag. "The sleeping bags can be used separately or zipped together to make one double sleeping bag," he said with a grin. "You know…in case it's *really* cold out."

Rachel raised an eyebrow and looked into her backpack. "Well, at least I have my own sleeping bag." She shivered and pulled her fleece balaclava over her mouth and nose. "Br-r-r. It's cold out here once the sun sets."

Trevor pointed at a panel inside her lapel. "You can regulate the temperature on your outer gear to suit your own comfort level," he said. "It's equipped with nanosensors. The boots and gloves automatically adjust to your body temperature."

Rachel could feel the warmth of his breath on her cheek as he showed her how to regulate the sensors on her parka. "Mmm," she said. "I'm already feeling more cozy and comfy."

He laughed. "Let's get this tent set up." After selecting a level spot, he pressed a release lever on the tent and gave it a shake. It popped open.

In a matter of minutes, the two of them had the tent secured, the sleeping bags spread out, and the small Primus stove set up and going. It was already becoming pleasantly warm inside the tent. Trevor pulled out a pot and began preparing some dehydrated soup.

Rachel unzipped her parka and looked at the two sleeping bags lying side by side.

He handed her a cup of hot soup and a hard roll. "I hope you don't mind sharing a tent," he said. "If you'd rather, I can sleep outside. The sleeping bags are good up to -20° Celsius."

"No, it's okay," she said, cradling the warm cup in her hands. "No need to be a martyr and risk freezing to death. I trust you."

He picked up his cup and sat down on the sleeping bag beside her. "Speaking of trust," he said, "what went through your mind when you discovered Richard had been murdered?"

"I…I was shocked, of course—by the whole thing—and the realization that Richard was really Ramirez." She felt a fresh wave of anger as she thought of his betrayal, of how he had used her. What a fool she had been. She let out a deep breath, trying unsuccessfully to put him out of her mind.

They sat in silence, sipping their soup.

Rachel glanced up as a soft light pulsated through the walls of the tent and then faded, only to be replaced by a brighter light. "What's that?"

Trevor poked his head out of the tent. "The aurora australis—southern lights," he said. "It's earlier than usual this year, probably because of all the magnetic activity in the area. Want to go outside and watch for a while?"

After putting their parkas on, Rachel and Trevor crawled outside and sat beside the tent.

The whole sky was ablaze with a kaleidoscope of

color. The aurora billowed pale green and pink overhead like curtains in a breeze, as it had for a million years.

"This is amazing," said Rachel. "Beyond beautiful."

"Like you," Trevor whispered, drawing her closer.

She laughed softly and snuggled up to him, all thoughts of Richard's betrayal eclipsed by the splendor of the aurora.

Trevor gazed up at the ribbons of gold rippling across the star-lit sky. "Did you know that, according to Norse mythology, Frea, the most beautiful of all Norse goddesses, is said to have rode the aurora from heaven to Earth?"

"Sounds romantic."

"Of course, it's only one theory regarding the aurora."

"And what's the competing theory, may I ask?"

"It's not nearly as romantic."

"Tell me anyway," Rachel said, loving being with someone she could discuss science with.

"Well," he said, "some scientists think the magnetic activities are coming primarily from inside the Earth. The Earth is just a big magnet, you know, possibly a hollow one at that."

Rachel looked skeptical. "With a sun at the center? Is this the hollow-earth theory Grace talks about?"

He shrugged. "Who knows what's down there? Right now it's all just speculation."

She hugged her arms to her body and gazed up at the lights dancing across the sky. *So much we don't know about the very Earth we inhabit.*

"How are you doing?" Trevor asked. He rubbed

her hands through her mittens, pressing her ring against her finger as he did.

Then she heard it again. The music—like the tinkling of bells they had heard that evening from the deck of the *Queen Maud.* She looked at Trevor, who was still holding her hand.

"Yes, I hear it too," he said.

"What do you think it is? Is it the aurora?"

"I don't know." He paused. "Maybe it's the music of the spheres—the Earth, the whole universe, singing in perfect harmony."

She smiled and gave him a gentle nudge in the ribs. "You know, you sound just like your aunt. You're such a romantic for a scientist."

"They say the best scientists have a romantic streak. It keeps us from getting in a rut in our thinking."

Streamers of color shimmered across the sky. The lights in the sky flickered and then exploded into a magnificent show of color. Flares of crimson red leapt out of the dusky blue horizon as brilliant green and purple banners danced in and out of the stars. Another pause and then a veil of color pulsated across the sky.

They sat for several minutes watching as the ribbons of light swirled above them, bathing the white landscape in a magical kaleidoscope of color, before they crawled back in the tent.

Unable to fall asleep, Rachel propped herself up on her elbow and gazed at Trevor lying next to her in his sleeping bag. He looked so handsome, so solid and dependable—someone she could always count on. Feeling flushed with desire and conflicting emotions, she reached out and touched his cheek.

"Hey," she said softly.

He stirred.

She moved closer and put her arms around him. "How about showing me how that double sleeping bag works?" she whispered in his ear.

He opened his eyes and gently touched her cheek, her lips. Then he sat up and unzipped the inside edges of the two sleeping bags and zipped them back up again so they were one. Lying down again, he turned toward Rachel and drew her closer.

She pressed into him as they kissed first tentatively and then long and passionately.

****

They awoke to bright sunshine. After preparing a breakfast of blueberry pancakes, Trevor filled a pot with snow for coffee and drinking water for their trip.

Rachel crawled out of the tent and looked around. The sky was arched with wispy cirrus clouds. Only the occasional rocky outcrop and the somber granite mountains in the distance broke the dazzling white that extended as far as the eye could see.

She sat down beside the tent and took a sip of her coffee. As she did, she heard a pattering noise coming from behind the tent and felt something touch her. She let out a gasp, almost spilling her coffee. Looking over her shoulder, she saw a large bird with a hooked beak eyeing her cup of coffee. She froze, not sure if it was dangerous.

"Trevor?"

"You okay?" he called from inside the tent. He emerged from the tent holding a bag of water. "It's just a giant petrel," he said, as though it were an everyday occurrence.

Rachel let out her breath. "For a moment there I

thought it might be Hilde sneaking up on us."

He laughed. "Those petrels are pretty ugly," he said. "But, unlike Hilde, they're harmless…at least to humans."

Rachel smiled. Twisting around to face the petrel, she broke off a piece of energy bar from her pocket and held it out to the bird. It snatched the piece from her hand and retreated a few meters to check it out. After scarfing it down, the petrel flew off to rejoin its friends.

Trevor knelt down beside her. "Here," he said. "This hydration pack goes inside your parka."

Rachel unzipped her parka and sat forward.

"Your body heat keeps the water from freezing so you have a constant source of drinking water," he explained as he arranged the pack. "This tube clips onto the inside of the shoulder of your parka. You can reach the end through here when you need a drink."

She shivered slightly. A brisk breeze was coming off a nearby glacier.

Trevor checked her temperature controls once more, then started to zip up her parka. "Also," he said, "don't forget to wear your snow goggles once we get going. Snow blindness can be pretty painful. And you already know how to use your…"

Rachel stroked his cheek. "Thank you, Mr. Mom," she said, zipping up her parka the rest of the way. "I think I'll be okay. I'm a big girl."

He grinned, then kissed her. "Indeed you are. Let's get this tent down so we can get under way. We have a lot of ground to cover today. There should be two pairs of skis and poles waiting for us somewhere just inside the tunnel."

"I'll go get the skis if you take care of packing the

tent."

"Deal." Rachel jumped up and started toward the tunnel.

"Wait," he called after her, holding up a flashlight.

"What?"

"Here—you'll need a torch so you can see."

****

Hilde Braun inched her way along the rocky ledge. Below, an icy stream snaked through a narrow channel. Her pale hair was matted and her white insulated jump suit filthy and torn, letting in the chilly air. She had spent the previous night huddled on the ledge, trying in vain to catch some sleep. She was cold and hungry, and her back and legs ached from constantly having to stoop over.

She removed her gloves and pulled out the map of the tunnels running under Shackleton Station and studied it. The tunnel she was in was off the edge of the map. Cursing, she crumpled up the map and tossed it on the ground. She looked around. It was too dangerous to go back. They would almost certainly be waiting for her at the edge of the ice cliffs near the station. Like a true soldier, she would rather die than surrender or be captured. She had no choice but to push forward and hope *this* tunnel would eventually lead to the underground complex. She patted her pocket. At least she had the pendant Ramirez had stolen. He'd gotten that much right. That was one consolation.

Hunching down, she slithered through an opening in the tunnel. The stone felt cold and jagged against her fingers. On the other side of the opening, the ledge made a sharp descent. Losing her footing, she plunged down the slick, rocky surface. She flailed wildly as she tried to break her fall. Her headlamp tumbled off as she hit the hard rock at the bottom.

Slowly, painfully, she got up and groped around. The low ceiling pressed down on her. Fortunately, the headlamp had not broken in the fall. Picking it up, she directed it at the spot where the stream disappeared through a slit in the wall. Looking behind her, she realized with growing dread that she would not be able to climb back up the slippery incline to the opening.

Chapter 26

The snowy terrain sloped gently upward as Rachel and Trevor pushed on toward the old meteorology station. Only the swish of their skis and the hollow crunch of hard snow disturbed the pristine silence. Ahead, a glacier spilled down a valley between two rocky peaks like spilt milk frozen in time. Even though the glacier was several kilometers in the distance, the wide-open vastness and clear air left the impression it was only a short distance away.

Trevor stopped and stuck his poles in the snow. Checking his GPS receiver, he surveyed the scene. "We'll have to go up that glacier," he said. "It'll be easier than going over those peaks." He reached around to a side pocket in his backpack, pulled out a bag of trail mix, and offered some to Rachel.

She removed her snow goggles and outer mittens, and helped herself to some.

"How are you doing?" he asked. "Do you want to stop for lunch now or go a bit longer?"

"I'm fine," she said. "I feel like I could keep going forever."

He glanced up at the sky. A halo of ice crystals circled the pale yellow sun. Clouds were beginning to form in the distance. "Good," he said. "We should probably keep moving as long as we can while this weather holds."

As they approached the glacier, Trevor stopped once again to study the terrain. Small crevasses webbed the ground between the glacier and the snowfield they had to cross. "We'd better rope up," he said. "We don't want to take any chances. You can't always see the crevasses. Sometimes the opening is covered with a shallow bridge of snow."

He set down his backpack and pulled out a thick length of rope about five meters long. After tying one end around his waist, he turned to Rachel and said, "Okay, lift your arms." He tied the other end around her waist, then stepped back and pulled her toward him.

She stumbled forward into his arms.

"Just making sure it's secure." He grinned.

"This isn't some sort of ruse to keep me from running off, is it?" She raised a bemused eyebrow.

He laughed and pointed toward a rocky outcrop. "Over there. I see a perfect place to have a romantic picnic for two." Then he grew more serious. "Remember to stay in my tracks when we cross this crevasse field."

By the time they reached the outcrop and had lunch, it was mid-afternoon. Rachel sat down on the rock while Trevor packed up and melted snow to replenish their hydration packs. A silver glint in the snow caught her eye. She stepped off the rock, onto the snow, and walked forward a few steps. Leaning over, she reached down for a metal object sticking out just inside a large, shallow depression in the ground.

Trevor looked up just in time to see the snow at the edge of the crevasse collapse and Rachel disappear from sight. The sudden jerk of the rope on his waist pulled him across the stove, sending the pot of hot water tumbling to the ground.

"Rachel!"

Recovering his balance, he grabbed the rope. Pulling it back toward him, he rushed over to the edge of the crevasse and threw himself down spread-eagle on the snow. He peered down into the blue light. Rachel was hanging just below the edge, covered with loose snow and clutching a long metal stake that protruded from the wall of the crevasse.

"Grab my hand!" he shouted.

As Rachel reached up with her free hand, the stake snapped loose. She screamed as she plunged another few meters. Luckily, the rope broke her fall. Looking up at him in speechless terror, she dangled from the end of the rope, swinging wildly, the stake in one hand.

****

Hilde Braun crouched on the narrow ledge and stared at the rock wall at the end of the tunnel. She pressed her palms to her eyes and fed off her rage at Rachel St. Claire, whose erratic behavior had left Wolf permanently disabled. How could they have failed yet again to get the girl? It should have been simple. But every time they got close, something would interfere with their plans. Then Grace McAllister and her goody-two-shoes nephew had to turn up.

Then she remembered the pendant.

Yanking off her tattered glove, Hilde reached into her pocket and pulled it out by the piece of string she had put on it in place of the missing chain, being careful not to touch the pendant itself. It glistened in the cold light of her headlamp. As she held it out, she let out a shriek as she felt herself sucked into an icy void.

When she came to, she found herself back in the

tunnel. Except it was not quite the same. A flicker of light at the end of the tunnel caught her eye. She squinted at the light. Why hadn't she noticed it before?

Placing the pendant around her neck so it rested outside her parka, she mustered her remaining strength and lowered herself into the shallow stream. She gritted her teeth as the icy water rushed in through a tear in her boots. Burning with hardened determination, she waded through the water to the end of the tunnel.

Etched into the dank rock wall she could just make out a symbol like the one on the pendant. She reached out and put her hand on the symbol. Nothing happened. Then she slipped the pendant from around her neck and dangled it against the rock.

The wall groaned, like a mighty giant woken from a deep sleep. Startled, she jumped back, dropping the pendant into the water. Cursing her clumsiness, she bent over and felt around for it. As her gloved hand closed around the pendant, the wall slowly began to grind open.

****

"Hang on to the rope and I'll pull you out," shouted Trevor.

As soon as Rachel appeared over the edge of the crevasse, he secured the rope to a nearby rock. Reaching out, he clasped her under her arms and pulled her back from the edge and up onto the rocky outcrop. He held her close until she stopped shaking.

She rested her forehead against his chest. "I'm sorry," she whispered. "You warned me."

"Hey, it's okay," he said, stroking her hair. "We've all fallen into crevasses out here one time or another. That's why we rope up."

Rachel wiped her eyes with the back of her mitten. “All I could think of was how Grace’s husband had died when he fell into a crevasse.”

Trevor shook his head. “No, no, that was different. They weren’t roped up, and the crevasse was much deeper. Uncle Charlie was trying to save a young woman who had fallen in and was lying unconscious on a ledge several meters below the opening.”

“What happened to her?”

He paused and then said, “Neither of them survived.”

Rachel thought about Ome and how his body had washed out in that ice cave at the bottom of a glacier. “Did they ever find their bodies?”

“They recovered the body of the young woman. But they never found Uncle Charlie’s body. I was only seven at the time, but I remember it as clearly as if it happened yesterday. It was 1986.” He looked up. The wind was starting to pick up slightly.

“1986? That’s the year I was adopted,” said Rachel. She closed her eyes and tried to envision the young woman she had seen calling to her in her dreams.

He surveyed the crevasse field. “It happened not far from here—over near the old meteorology station where we’re headed.”

He bent over to pick up the pot that had rolled off the rock. As he did, he noticed the stake lying near the edge of the crevasse. Using his ski pole, he pulled it toward him. The aluminum stake was a little over a meter long and topped by a flat oval with a swastika engraved on it. He turned it over and wiped off the snow. Scratched into the back of the oval was the date January 1939.

"What is it?" asked Rachel.

He frowned. "It's a claim stake. It must have been dropped by the Nazis in 1939 when they flew over Antarctica, or what they called *Neuschwabenland*."

Rachel shuddered and pulled her knees closer to her body. The jagged granite outcrop had taken on a sinister overtone. She wondered what else might be lurking behind the next rocky outcrop. Overhead, ominous clouds had replaced the blue sky. A cold gust whipped her hair across her face.

"Come on, let's get going," said Trevor, reaching for his skis.

The incline grew steeper and each step more difficult as they switch-backed up the snow-crusted lower slope of the glacier. After an hour of grueling climbing, Trevor signaled for them to stop. "Time to exchange our skis for crampons," he said. He removed his skis, took off his backpack, and pulled out two pairs of sixteen-point cleats.

Rachel watched him strap the spiked crampons to his boots. "Those things look pretty dangerous," she said.

After strapping their skis to their backpacks, they started again across the icy slope, using their ski poles for balance. This time the going was much slower and the cold air stung their lungs. Every so often, they came to an area where the glacier was swept clean by the wind, and they had to maneuver carefully across the glassy, blue surface of exposed ice.

The air grew colder and the wind stronger as they ascended the glacier. Every so often, the wind would stop and an eerie silence would follow. Then, with an explosion, a gust would shriek down the face of the glacier, slapping at their parkas and whipping the snow into violent swirling clouds. At times, the wind was so bad that Rachel could not even see Trevor up ahead of her. It was like hiking inside a steam room—except for the bitterly cold temperature. Fortunately, he had roped them together during their last rest stop so they would not become separated.

By early evening, they reached the top of the glacier and sought shelter from the wind just below the top of a rocky ridge. Trevor crouched to conserve body heat. Rachel huddled beside him, her exhausted body pressing against his. He put his arm around her and drew her closer.

Up ahead lay a vast snowfield. The low, thick cloud layer diffused the light, dissolving all features into a shadowless white, making it almost impossible to see crevasses.

"We'll stay here for the night," he said. "It's too dangerous to travel in this weather."

****

The Norwegian ski team arrived at the old meteorology station by mid-morning. After making sure Grace and Ka-Wing were settled in, they bid their farewells and set off again across the great white expanse.

Several kilometers to the west, Trevor and Rachel sat surveying the scene through binoculars. From the top of the windblown ridge, they could just make out the old meteorology station on the other side of the snowfield. Beyond the station was a ridge of mountains, their lofty peaks rising until they were lost in the clouds.

A flock of snow petrels flew overhead on their way

north from the polar plateau where they had raised their young.

"Winter's setting in soon," said Trevor, lowering his binoculars. "Time for the birds to start moving north before the whole continent becomes encased in ice."

"When is Byrdie picking us up?" asked Rachel nervously.

"Tomorrow morning, weather permitting."

****

The trek down the icy slope to the snowfield below was almost as treacherous as the trip up the glacier. However, once on firm snow their progress was rapid. The wind fussed and swirled around them, like a fastidious housewife sweeping the snow clean of their ski tracks and restoring the pristine whiteness.

By the time they reached the meteorology station, Grace and Ka-Wing had already started dinner. Cans of peas, fruit cocktail, beef stew, and other provisions lined the wooden shelves. Even though meteorologists had not used it for several years, the small hut was kept well stocked with food for scientists and any other travelers who might need to use it for refuge during a storm.

While Grace heated up their dinner, Rachel examined the dog-eared photos of the meteorology teams tacked to the walls. "Why was this station abandoned?" she asked Grace.

"The meteorology stations are all automated now." Grace set down her wooden spoon, and came over and pointed at a photo of four figures standing in front of the meteorology tower. "This is my Charlie. He's the good-looking one on the left." She turned and stared out the window at the white landscape as though expecting to see him. "He disappeared into a crevasse, just over there."

"It must have been terrible losing him that way." Rachel paused then continued. "Trevor told me you think Hilde Braun may have killed Richard—or, I suppose I should say Ramirez."

Grace nodded. "It was a vicious, drawn-out killing. Whoever did it must have really had it in for him."

Rachel shuddered. Even though Richard had deceived her and used her, she *had* at one time cared for him.

"I remember Sutchin saying something about a possible viral infection," said Trevor.

"That's right," replied Grace, "though that isn't what killed him." She poured herself another cup of tea. "And there's one other thing. It was a genetically engineered virus."

"I wonder where he picked it up?" asked Ka-Wing.

"Your guess is as good as mine. Sutchin sent the printout of the viral genome to the EIS—Epidemic Intelligent Services. They're sending a team of epidemiologists down to pick up the body."

Rachel shifted uncomfortably in her seat. Several companies were in the process of creating genetically engineered viruses, including Global Genome. There was a lot of public protest over it, primarily because of the fear that the technology might fall into the hands of bioterrorists.

"Well, enough talk of viruses," said Grace. "Let's get you kids some supper. You must be famished." As she headed toward the stove, a floorboard squeaked. She stopped and pushed on it with the heel of her boot. It gave slightly under the pressure.

"What is it?" asked Trevor.

"I don't know."

Trevor fetched a screwdriver from a drawer. Kneeling down, he pried up the loose floorboard and reached down into the murky darkness below the floor. "There's something down here," he said. He lifted out a metal box and handed it to Grace.

She set it on the table and opened it. Inside was a gun in a waist holster.

Ka-Wing's eyes widened.

"It's an old Colt .22 handgun," said Grace, furrowing her eyebrows.

Rachel stared disapprovingly at the gun. "But I thought weapons weren't allowed in Antarctica."

"They aren't, except in exceptional circumstances," explained Trevor. "That's probably why this one was kept hidden."

"Wow," said Ka-Wing. "Can I hold it?"

"But why would anyone need a gun here?" asked Rachel. "I thought there were no land predators in Antarctica."

Grace glanced toward the window. "They must've been afraid of something—but what?"

Rachel stepped back as Grace pulled the gun out of the holster.

"Don't worry," said Grace, inspecting the gun. "It's not loaded."

"There's something else down here," said Trevor from the floor. He pulled out a plastic case of .22 long shells.

"Do you guys know how to use that thing?" Ka-Wing asked.

"Aunt Grace went to the police academy as part of

her forensic training," replied Trevor with a touch of pride. He stood and wiped off his hands.

A flickering movement outside the window caught Rachel's eye. In the distance she saw a tiny black speck hovering over the top of the glacier they had crossed the previous day. "What's that?" she asked, pointing. "More migrating birds?"

Trevor pulled out his binoculars.

"I bet it's the plane coming to rescue us," said Ka-Wing, opening the front door and waving his arms in the air.

Trevor's mouth fell open. He dropped his binoculars.

"What is it?" asked Grace.

"I don't know, but that's no airplane."

Chapter 27

Grace grabbed Ka-Wing's arm. "Quick, get back inside." She slammed the door behind him.

Rachel stared in disbelief at the object hovering above the horizon. It had not occurred to her they might still be in danger. Their escape had seemed so perfectly executed.

Trevor rushed over to the stove and shut it off, then turned off the lantern on the table. The hut went dark.

The object descended and was now below the reach of the sun's rays. It looked dark and foreboding, like a blemish on the landscape. Then it turned sharply and started heading directly toward them.

"Holy jeepers!" cried Ka-Wing, jumping back. "What's that?"

"Close the curtains," shouted Trevor. "Before it spots us." He ran over and pulled the curtains closed.

Rachel glanced anxiously around the room. Grace stood by the door, her hand still poised on the knob. Trevor pressed his hand on Rachel's shoulder. "Get down," he whispered. She crouched on the cold floor under the window and fiddled nervously with her ring. The wind stopped, and a soft tinkling light filled the room.

She got to her knees and peered out through the crack between the curtains and window frame. The object was less than a kilometer from the hut now. She could hear a faint humming coming from it.

"What is it?" asked Ka-Wing, his eyes wide with alarm. "It looks like a flying saucer."

Trevor examined it through his binoculars. "It may be some sort of magnetic levitation or anti-gravitation machine," he said. "But it's still too far away to tell."

"What do you mean—an anti-gravity machine?" Rachel asked.

"MLM—a magnetic levitation machine. It uses diamagnetic levitation which allows it to float weightlessly in the magnetic field. But I thought they were still in the experimental…" Trevor suddenly broke off and grabbed Rachel's arm and dropped to a squatting position beneath the window.

"What's happening?" she asked, pulling loose from his grip.

Before he could stop her, Rachel opened the curtains slightly and peered outside. Suspended in midair, less than four meters away, was a large silver disc. A dazzling beam of white light shot through the window of the hut. She gasped and ducked down, but not fast enough to avoid the light.

Time stood still. She felt herself floating through a tunnel of white light. Singsong voices whispered inside her head as the light enveloped her, pulling her upward toward the disc.

"Rachel," cried Trevor. He seized her hand and yanked her back down.

She collapsed to the floor beneath the beam of light. Then, just as suddenly as it had appeared, the light faded away. The disc veered off in a pulsating glow, splitting up into six shimmering balls of light before completely disappearing, leaving behind only the Antarctic dusk and an eerie silence.

Trevor put his arms around Rachel. She rested her head on his shoulder. Her face was as pale as a ghost. Her eyes had the look of someone coming out of a hypnotic trance. "All will be well," she whispered in a monotone.

"W-what did you say?" asked Ka-Wing.

Grace knelt down in front of Rachel, checking her over for injuries. "What happened?" Grace asked.

"I don't remember. Except…" Rachel hesitated.

Trevor rubbed her hands between his. With the stove off, it was getting uncomfortably cold in the hut. "It's going to be okay," he said softly.

Grace went over to the window and cautiously opened the curtains a little wider and looked out. All she saw was the pale purple snow. "It's gone." She took a deep breath. "Look, why don't I fix some hot chocolate?" she said, with forced cheerfulness. "It'll help relax us."

She groped her way over to the stove, turned on the burner and filled a pan with half-melted snow.

Rachel shivered. The sparsely furnished hut looked ominous in the flickering blue light from the burner. Placing her hands on the cold floor, she pushed herself to a standing position and looked out at the descending twilight, wondering if the object would return. The stars looked pale and distant against the deep indigo sky. The wind was picking up and eddies of crystalline snow danced across the ground. After a few moments, she closed the curtains. "What if the object comes back?"

Ka-Wing glanced nervously at Trevor. "Where do you think it came from?"

He shook his head. "I don't know."

Grace pursed her lips. "What about the recent sightings of UFOs over Lake Vostok—do you think this might be related?"

"UFOs? In Antarctica?" said Ka-Wing.

"Where's Lake Vostok? Is it near here?" asked Rachel, taking a seat at the table.

"Not really. It's a huge freshwater lake under the polar plateau near the geographic south pole," explained Grace. She lifted the pan of hot liquid off the stove and poured the hot chocolate into four cups. "UFOs began appearing there in the 1990s, shortly after drilling began to reach the lake. Also," she added, glancing up at Trevor, "unexplained magnetic disturbances have been found at one end of the lake."

"There could be many explanations for those phenomena," replied Trevor.

Grace handed him a cup of chocolate. "Exactly my point," she said. "And what else would you call that thing we just saw?"

Trevor shrugged. "You may be right. We really don't know what's going on under the polar ice cap." He offered his cup to Rachel.

"Well, enough talk," said Grace, walking over to the row of bunks that lined one wall of the hut. She spread out her sleeping bag on one of the lower bunks. "I think we should lie low for a while and see if our visitor returns. Not much else we can do at this point."

****

Hilde stepped warily through the narrow opening in the wall into a wide tunnel. A dim light came from the left arm of the tunnel. To the right, the tunnel climbed upward into darkness. Swinging her light back to the left, she began picking her way through the rock-strewn tunnel toward the light.

As she approached the source of the light, she spotted a familiar landmark. She could not believe her luck. It was the underground submarine basin.

With a burst of energy, she sprinted toward the light. When she arrived, she found herself on the opposite side of the narrow inlet to the basin. Across it were several docks and beyond them a densely packed complex of drab stone buildings. The words *Global Genome, Neuschwabenland* were carved in large letters above the doorway to the main building. An old Nazi flag was draped in front of the massive structure.

Once home to a secret Nazi base, the complex had been abandoned in the 1950s. The only access for the submarines was through an underwater channel deep under the ice sheet of the Antarctic Peninsula not far from where Shackleton Station now stood. The entrance to the base was so well hidden that neither the British nor the Americans had been able to find it. All that was left now of those glorious days was the hull of an old U-boat at the far end of the basin.

The old Nazi base had remained empty and forgotten for over two decades until Wolf Krause's grandfather, *Opa* Mengele, revealed the location of the base and the hidden stash of gold to his daughter, Gerta Mengele-Krause, Wolf's mother, shortly before his death. The timing was perfect. The world was getting too nosy about their experiments in genetic purity, and it was time to go underground. Argentina was in a state of chaos in the late 1970s and it was easy to pull it off, as well as to obtain more than enough subjects for their vital research. Someday, Hilde mused, the world would understand and thank them. But, for now, they had to operate in secret.

Two sleek mini-submarines were moored at the first dock. A group of dignitaries stood nearby. Tomorrow was the big day—the unveiling of the Aryan project. Of course, the girl was supposed to have been captured by now.

Hilde clenched her fists. God, how she hated the freak and that idiot Ramirez. Well, at least he was out of the way now. She took a deep breath, trying to calm down.

Across the basin, she noticed a thin man in a captain's uniform standing at the end of the dock, next to two men in khaki guard uniforms. They were watching something large slithering through the water.

Looking around, Hilde tried to get her bearings. Then it struck her. She had only been here a few times, but as she recalled a sheer rock wall bordered this side of the inlet. Odd. She took the pendant from around her neck. It lay cold and lifeless in her gloved hand. She had heard rumors that there was a portal somewhere near here to the inner Earth and the Aryan cities. Not long after they had reopened the station, an Aryan had been captured in the water on this side of the basin. He escaped shortly afterward, but not before they had managed to get some of his DNA.

Then there was Charles McAllister—Grace's husband. He had escaped through a portal several years ago as well. He had been wearing this pendant—or one just like it—at the time. Actually, escaped wasn't the correct word. One of the guards in pursuit of him had shot him through the back of the neck just as McAllister was heading through the portal. That was the last they had seen of the portal—and him.

Chapter 28

Rachel did not sleep well that night. From the bunk above, she could hear Trevor's soft breathing. She rolled over onto her side and pulled her sleeping bag over her head. She missed the closeness and warmth of his body. When she finally did fall asleep, she dreamt of spirits calling to her from the other side of a river. Ome was there. The flying disc was hovering over the bank of the river, its light sweeping back and forth across the landscape like the beam of a giant lighthouse, seeking her out. Then, just as it caught her in its beam, the ground gave way and a dark blue void opened up beneath her.

She awoke with a start, her clothes damp with sweat and heart pounding. Light filtered in from outside.

Stepping onto the cold wooden floor, she quietly fetched a clean fleece top and a pair of heavy socks from her backpack. After dressing, she tiptoed over to the window. The uneven snow formed a medley of gold, lavender, and coral in the early morning sun. Above, the pale blue sky was streaked with pastel clouds.

"Are you okay, dear?" asked Grace sleepily.

Rachel turned and looked at her. "I'm fine."

Grace propped herself up on her elbow and checked the time. "Well, it'll be time to go soon anyway."

After a leisurely breakfast of hot cereal and rehydrated applesauce, they cleaned up and packed. Rachel noticed Grace seemed distracted, constantly glancing out the window and scanning the ground as though expecting something to miraculously appear from under the blanket of snow. Trevor watched her, a look of concern on his face. Why was he so focused on Grace? And then it hit her. Rachel felt a stab of sympathy for Grace. Coming back to the place where her husband had died in a crevasse must be hard for her. She glanced at Trevor and wondered how she would feel if she lost him. The thought made her feel strangely empty inside.

"Look, over there," cried Ka-Wing. He pointed out the window at a speck of red far off on the horizon.

Trevor grabbed the gun from the counter, startling Rachel. But he looked like he knew how to use it as he moved toward the window. There was so much she didn't know about this man she was falling for, and fast.

"It looks like a Twin Otter ski plane," Trevor announced. "Probably Byrdie and Caitlyn. We should get down to level ground. It'll be easier for them to pick us up."

Ka-Wing flung his pack over his back and headed for the door.

"There's no rush," Trevor called after him. "It's still a long way off. And watch out for crevasses."

But Ka-Wing was already outside, running down the gentle slope to the flat snowfield below. A thin layer of silvery fog hung suspended like fairy dust just above the ground at the bottom of the slope.

They picked up their gear and followed Ka-Wing. The snow crunched under their feet, and their breath made little eddies of silver steam in the cold air as they hurried along.

Rachel was the first to catch up with Ka-Wing. She took a deep breath. *It's so beautiful here.* She felt stronger here in Antarctica, as if she were drawing energy from it. Looking back, she smiled and waved at Trevor and Grace, who had just reached the bottom of the slope.

A split second later, there was a deafening roar as a snow bridge collapsed beneath her feet, leaving a gaping wound in the snow.

Ka-Wing vanished before her eyes.

A sickening feeling hit Rachel in the pit of her stomach as the ground disappeared out from under her. A torrent of snow cascaded downward, carrying her down with it into a dark blue void.

****

Hilde cupped her hands around her mouth. "Over here!" she called. The air tossed her words back, taunting her.

No response. The men at the dock across the basin didn't seem to hear her.

She screwed up her face in annoyance. Well, if they couldn't hear her, at least they should be able see her. Turning her headlamp on full force, she flashed it on and off.

The captain took a few steps toward the end of the dock and stared. Then, turning abruptly, he strode back down the dock to where one of the men in khaki uniforms stood guard and said something to him. The guard squinted out across the water in Hilde's direction.

Then the two of them headed toward a launch tied up at the dock. Climbing in, they started across the basin.

"At last," Hilde muttered to herself.

The launch came to a stop at the water's edge a few meters away. The man in the khaki uniform stood in the launch. His hand groped the air, like a mime feeling along an invisible wall.

"Are you blind?" screamed Hilde. "This is no time for games!"

The captain and the man in the launch exchanged puzzled looks. The captain edged the launch in her direction. His eyes looked straight through Hilde as the launch drifted slowly past her.

Infuriated at what seemed to be a childish prank, she clambered down to the edge of the bank and thrust her hand out to seize the arm of the captain. As she reached her hand past the waterline, she felt an odd prickling. Instead of making contact with him, her hand struck something soft and electric feeling. She shuddered and pulled it back.

The captain stared in astonishment at the slight ripple in the sheer rock wall. Then the distortion faded just as quickly as it had appeared.

Bewildered, Hilde reached toward the water once more. Again her hand struck something. Only this time it did not leave a mark. "Oh, fuck," she muttered in disbelief. "The rock wall is an invisibility shield probably put here by the Aryans—and I'm on the wrong side of it."

At length, the launch turned and started back to the dock. A feeling of cold dread flooded over Hilde. She straightened up and stared at the captain, who was looking back in her direction.

"Help! Help!" she cried.

But no one heard her.

****

Pain knifed through Rachel's knee as an icy ledge several meters from the mouth of the crevasse broke her fall. It took a moment for her to realize what had happened. Her heart pounding, she crept forward and cautiously peered over the edge of the narrow ledge. Ka-Wing was lying in a heap several meters beneath her on a larger ledge that jutted out from the ragged blue walls of the crevasse. Below, the ice seemed to go on forever until it disappeared into an inky blue void. She quickly pulled herself back from the edge.

From above, Trevor stared down in shocked silence. Grace dropped the skis she was carrying and ran toward the crevasse. A jagged line opened up in the snow, reaching toward her. Grace plunged through it into the crevasse. The snow beneath Trevor's feet slid forward, like a mini-avalanche, carrying him and his backpack with it.

Rachel glanced up just in time to see Grace hurtling through the air followed by Trevor. They landed with a thump next to Ka-Wing. The icy ledge creaked under their weight. Rachel gasped and covered her mouth.

Trevor was the first one to move. Getting to his knees, he wiped the snow off his parka and looked around.

"I'm up here," said Rachel, her voice shaking.

Grace sat up and rubbed her head.

"Hang tight. I'll be there in a moment," Trevor called up to Rachel. "I think I have enough rope to get us out of here."

Rachel hugged her knees to her body. Ragged walls of blue ice soared upward on both sides of the crevasse like abandoned skyscrapers from some long-forgotten civilization. About ten meters above her the sun shone through what was left of the snow bridge, bathing the crevasse in a soft blue glow. Massive icicles hung from the lip of the crevasse like bizarrely misshapen gothic chandeliers.

She shivered as thoughts of a ghastly death in this frozen grave flitted through her mind. She wondered where Byrdie and the plane were and if they had seen them. Below, she could hear Trevor talking to Grace and Ka-Wing.

"Don't move," he was telling them. "Let's get the two of you tethered to the wall, so you don't fall off the ledge." Picking up his ice hammer, he drove a set of ice screws into the wall just above the ledge.

After tethering Grace and Ka-Wing to the wall, he put on his crampons and belt with his equipment and rope. Reaching up as high as he could, he drove the curved pick of his axe into the ice. Wrapping the leash on the axe around his wrist, he stepped off the ledge and kicked the spiked front of his crampons into the ice wall.

Rachel's heart leapt into her throat. She half expected him to plummet into the darkness.

He looked up and tried his best to give her a reassuring smile. Using his axe and ice hammer, he planted pitons along the way as he slowly crawled up the wall toward her. Just as he was about to pull himself over the edge of her ledge, a loud sound like a rifle shot rang out.

A chunk of ice the size of a refrigerator plunged

past them, grazing the edge of the ledge where Grace and Ka-Wing were huddled. The ice ricocheted off the crevasse walls below them and, with an ear-shattering boom, broke into a thousand pieces.

Rachel screamed.

Grace and Ka-Wing's faces froze in terror as their ledge gave way with a large crack. It plunged into the crevasse below, leaving them dangling from the ropes that held them to the walls.

"Hold on," cried Trevor. He hastily secured a line to the nearest piton and swung back down to Grace and Ka-Wing. "Grab my hand," he urged, stretching out his arm.

Ka-Wing balked, frozen in midair.

Grace stretched out a hand to Ka-Wing. The line creaked and groaned under their weight. Then the ice corkscrew bolts that held them in place broke loose with a snap and Grace and Ka-Wing plummeted downward into the blue void. Trevor's backpack and the rest of his spelunking gear went tumbling down after them.

Rachel stared in horror as they faded into oblivion. She tried to stand, but her legs were like rubber. The whole crevasse felt like it was spinning. She fell backward against the wall and buried her face in her hands.

A minute later Trevor appeared over the edge of her ledge.

Rachel reached out for him and let out a cry of relief.

He pulled himself up beside her and put his arms around her. "They should have held," he whispered in stunned anguish. "The screws should have held."

After a few moments, he pushed himself to a kneeling position. Taking an ice screw from his belt, he began driving it into the wall.

A shudder from above. Rachel glanced up toward the mouth of the crevasse. The icicles had taken on a more menacing look, like giant claws reaching out for them.

The wall moaned slightly as Trevor drove another screw into the ancient blue ice. Once that was done, he began threading his remaining rope through the loops.

Just then, a deafening crack filled the empty air.

Before Rachel could open her mouth to scream, they were hurtling headfirst through space. The rope slid out of the screw heads and uncoiled downward behind them like a giant serpent as they plunged into the cold, empty darkness.

Chapter 29

Rachel landed on what felt like a cushion of warm air. A thin sliver of light filtered down from the top of the crevasse. She sat up and blinked. Trevor was lying beside her. A faint silvery mist surrounded them. She wondered briefly if she was dead. She rubbed her eyes. When she opened them again, the glow was gone and the ground beneath her cold, hard, bone-shattering rock.

Trevor pushed himself to a standing position. “Are you all right?” he asked.

“I think so,” said Rachel.

He flicked on the flashlight he had attached to his belt. “Aunt Grace? Ka-Wing?” he called out.

“We’re over here,” replied a small voice.

He shone his light in the direction of the voice. Grace and Ka-Wing were huddled together a few meters away.

“Where are we?” asked Rachel, glancing anxiously at the rock walls. The air around them was cold and heavy.

Grace came over and shone her light up into the crevasse. “Well, we’re not going to get out of here by going back up, that’s for sure.”

Trevor glanced upward then lowered his flashlight and peered around in the dim light. There was only one way they could go. “I guess we have no other choice but to see where this tunnel takes us.”

"Are we going to get out of here alive?" Ka-Wing asked, clearly trying to control his panic.

"We at least have to try," said Grace, touching his arm.

Trevor ran his hands along the dark, smooth walls. "Basalt," he said. "It looks like we're inside an old lava tube except—it's smoother, almost soft in texture." He pulled out his e-pad and jotted down some notes.

Ka-Wing shuddered. "What if the volcano erupts?"

"It's unlikely," replied Trevor. "This tube hasn't seen a lava flow in centuries."

"Well, let's see where it takes us," said Grace, gathering up her gear.

Rachel looked around. "Do we really need to bring all this gear? What about those crampons you're wearing? I don't think we'll need them down here."

"We may as well take all this stuff for now," Trevor replied, pulling two spare headlamps out of a side pocket of his pack. He handed one to Rachel and one to Ka-Wing. Then he removed his crampons, slipped them into an empty side pocket and swung his pack onto his back. "You never know when some of this gear might come in handy."

Moving in single file, they followed the pathway created by the lava flow. The descent was gradual and winding. As the hours wore on, they moved more slowly. Each turn lead them farther down into the depths of the Earth.

The close quarters of the tunnel were beginning to make Rachel feel claustrophobic. But not Trevor. The tunnel provided a never-ending source of interest for him. Every once in a while he would stop and examine the rock walls.

"I've never seen anything like this," he said. "The walls are giving off some sort of luminescent magnetic energy."

"Like the kind you described from the dark matter in that crystal from Deception Island?" asked Rachel.

He smiled. "Could very well be."

Trevor's enthusiasm helped ward off the despair and fatigue that was setting in. Even Grace, with her indomitable energy and optimism, was starting to slow down.

Just when Rachel thought she could go no farther, the tunnel widened out slightly—then split. To the right it sloped gently upward. On the left, it continued its descent.

Grace unzipped her parka and wiped her forehead with the back of her hand. "I wonder how deep we are," she said. "It's getting warmer."

Rachel forced herself to take a few deep breaths. She could almost feel the weight of the rock and ice above, pressing down on her.

Ka-Wing took off his backpack, let it drop to the ground, and sat on it, resting his forehead in his hands.

"Maybe we should rest for a while, get something to eat," said Grace. She pulled out the last of their trail mix and divvied it up among them.

Rachel spread her parka out on the smooth floor and sat down, her shoulders slumped with fatigue, and ate her meager portion.

"Shall we split up and check out the two tunnels, maybe meet back here in an hour?" suggested Grace.

Rachel leaned back against the stone wall and shook her head. She did not know how much longer she could keep going. It seemed so futile.

Trevor came over and sat down beside her. “Hey,” he said tenderly, touching her dust-streaked cheek.

Rachel closed her eyes and leaned into his hand. He put his arm around her and pulled her closer. “It’s going to be okay. All will be well—remember, you said so yourself.”

Once they had finished eating, Ka-Wing stretched out on the lava floor and fell immediately asleep. Grace sat down next to him, gazing off into the distance, lost in thought. Suddenly a faint glimmer caught her eye. She leaned forward and noticed a small metal object resting against the wall of the lava tube.

Trevor had noticed it too. He got up to look.

“What is it?” Grace whispered.

“It looks like a watch.” He picked it up and handed it to her.

“Oh, my God,” cried Grace. “It’s Charlie’s watch!” She smiled like a lovesick teenager and held the watch to her chest. “I knew he was still alive.”

Rachel’s mouth fell open in disbelief. Charlie? Even if Grace’s husband had survived the fall into the crevasse, he couldn’t have survived down here all these years with no food and water. Or could he? By now, she was sure this was no ordinary lava tube. But what was it then? She remembered Grace telling her Charlie had found a pendant similar to hers—perhaps even the same one. She sighed. If only she still had the pendant. Had whoever killed Richard stolen the pendant as well? It didn’t matter. It wasn’t here to help them find their way out. They would have to manage on their own.

But first they needed to get some rest.

****

When Rachel awoke several hours later, the

luminescent mist had reappeared. Trevor was asleep next to her. Grace was busily inspecting the opening to the tunnel that split off from the one they were in. She had also managed to heat some water for tea and coffee. The stove and her lantern gave off a soft, pleasant glow. Trevor stirred. Rachel removed his parka that he had draped over her and put it across him. Leaning over, she kissed him gently on the cheek. Then she stood, being careful not to disturb him, and went over to help Grace.

"How are you feeling, dear?" whispered Grace.

"Much better," replied Rachel softly. She poured a packet of instant coffee into a cup of hot water and took a sip, then set out the other cups.

Ka-Wing opened his eyes and stretched. He looked in better spirits as well. "Anything I can do to help?"

"How about finding something for breakfast?"

After a breakfast consisting of coffee, tea, and chocolate chip cookies from Ka-Wing's stash of goodies, they split up. Ka-Wing and Grace took the spur tunnel that went upward, while Trevor and Rachel continued in the other direction.

The tunnel wound steadily downward for half a kilometer until it came to an opening into a smaller tunnel. A stream of water gushed out of the opening and snaked along the rock-strewn floor of the main tunnel. Trevor inspected the entrance. "My guess is that this large rock here used to block the entrance to this tunnel," he said.

Rachel studied the marks on the edge of the rock and the floor of the tunnel. "You're right," she said. "Look, fresh scrape marks." She glanced around. "Someone else has been here—and recently."

"I'd say only a matter of a day or two at most,"

added Trevor. He peered into the narrow opening. “It doesn’t look very promising. What do you think?” Receiving no answer, he turned around.

Rachel had already gone on ahead. “Over here,” she called excitedly. “I found footprints in the mud. Who knows—maybe this tunnel connects to one of the old mining tunnels leading back to Shackleton Station.”

Trevor came over to investigate the footprints. He frowned, but said nothing.

Rachel turned off her headlamp and searched the semi-darkness. “Sh-h,” she whispered. I think I see lights.” She paused. A faint scent of salt water hung in the air.

****

Hilde sat with her back to the stone wall and glared at the pendant. In disgust, she stuffed it into her pocket. It was useless, at least in her hands. They would have to get the girl. Several hours had passed since the launch had turned back, leaving her stranded on the edge of the basin. Her only hope was that the launch would come back or that she could find some other way through the barrier between her and the basin.

She closed her eyes. The rush of adrenaline that had kept her going until now had taken a nosedive, plunging her into despair. Maybe this was hell, she thought. Time drifted by. An eerie silence flooded her.

At long last, she pulled herself together. Gathering up every ounce of strength she had left, she started back toward the tunnel, hoping to find another way into the complex.

Just then, she heard a noise coming from the tunnel.

Chapter 30

As they reached the end of the tunnel, Rachel stopped and stared at the complex of stone buildings across the underground basin. “What is it?”

Pressing his back against the tunnel wall, Trevor peered cautiously around the corner at the basin. “It may be the old underground Nazi base Antonio was talking about—except...” He cocked his head, listening. Reaching into his parka, he pulled out the gun and inched forward to get a better look.

“Halt!” a voice cried out.

Trevor wheeled around and found himself looking down the barrel of a laser gun. Startled, he stumbled and slipped on the wet rock. A loose boulder fell from the wall, jamming his right leg beneath it. The Colt .22 flew from his hand and skidded across the ground. He swore and grit his teeth. Hunching forward he tried to push the boulder off his leg, but to no avail.

Rachel dropped her backpack and rushed over to help him.

“Don’t move. Or your boyfriend’s toast,” hissed Hilde.

Rachel froze—her hands in the air and her heart in her throat.

Hilde chuckled. “Is this what you’re looking for?” She pulled the pendant from her pocket and dangled it in front of Rachel’s face.

Trevor groaned. Gathering all his strength, he pulled his left foot back and kicked the Colt .22 toward Rachel.

Rachel stared down at the gun.

"Pick up the gun. Rachel, please."

"Shut up, you filthy pig," Hilde snapped at him. She kicked him in his side then turned back to Rachel. "Go ahead, freak," she ordered. "Pick up the gun."

Rachel did not move. Her whole body was frozen with nightmarish fear. A cold sweat broke out on the back of her neck as if Hilde's icy stare had reached out with long tentacles and touched her, paralyzing her.

Hilde's face contorted into a hateful scowl. "Pick up the goddamn gun," she shrieked, stomping her boot on the ground.

Rachel cringed. Too terrified not to obey, she forced herself to stoop down and pick up the gun. As she did, she glanced over at Trevor, moaning softly and drifting in and out of consciousness. Seeing Trevor that way—it was as if a door opened inside her and she crossed some threshold of inner strength and resolve. Her blood surged; her fear melted away. She didn't care about the pendant anymore or anything else except getting the two of them out of here safely.

Straightening up, she pointed the Colt .22 at Hilde. Her hand trembled slightly as she positioned her finger on the trigger.

Hilde threw her head back and laughed. "Go ahead, freak. Pull the trigger."

Rachel did not move.

"You don't have the guts, do you? You can't shoot me because you're genetically programmed with Aryan DNA to be a pacifist."

Genetically programmed? Rachel's mouth went dry. She felt a numbing chill spreading through her body.

Hilde laughed again, a laugh that set Rachel's teeth on edge. "I can't believe this! You really don't know you're a genetically engineered prototype?"

Rachel tried to protest, but no words came out. The rank smell of the damp, stale air filled her nostrils.

"You're merely a pawn—a carrier of pure Aryan DNA," said Hilde, encouraged by the effect her words were having on Rachel. "An instrument in a greater plan to create a new, even better Aryan race that will rise to its rightful place of political ascendancy and domination over the world."

Aryan DNA? Rachel's head was spinning. The gun felt heavy in her hands. Then she remembered Richard's—Ramirez's—obsession with having her checked out at a fertility clinic. At the time, Rachel had thought Richard was angry because of the way they had tried to coerce her into submitting to a medical procedure she hadn't agreed to. Now she realized he was probably angry because they *had not* succeeded in subduing her.

"Richard?" she whispered. "Was he in on this?"

"Richard? You mean that idiot Ramirez?" Hilde said with scorn. "Of course he was. We managed to extract a few good ova from you when you visited the fertility clinic in Providence. Everything would have worked out except that blundering idiot Ramirez didn't store them correctly and the eggs were no longer viable by the time they arrived at the labs of Global Genome."

Rachel swallowed hard as a wave of nausea struck her.

"Oh, dear. Your meddlesome colleague Grace McAllister didn't tell you?" clucked Hilde. "Why, she's the one who kidnapped you when you were merely a toddler—her and that brainless husband of hers."

"G-Grace?" whispered Rachel incredulously.

Hilde shook her head in mock sympathy. "Tsk-tsk. I wonder why the good Dr. McAllister did not tell you the real reason she lured you down here to Antarctica. Why, my dear, it is because you are genetically programmed with homing genes in your Aryan DNA. They're just using you to get to the Aryans in the middle of the Earth." She pulled out the pendant again and dangled it in front of Rachel's face. "The only thing missing was you and this pendant to activate the portal to the inner earth."

Rachel felt numb. She looked past Hilde, trying to make sense out of what she had just heard. From across the basin she could make out a man in a white captain's uniform and two men in khaki uniforms, holding what looked like night-vision goggles, standing next to one of the launches. They were getting into the launch. She felt a stab of hope. If she could only hold off Hilde until they came to the rescue. Mustering all of her courage, she forced herself to stand steady and keep the gun trained on Hilde. "Why should I believe you?" she asked in a shaky voice

Hilde's face transformed into a grotesque imitation of motherly concern. She gestured behind her at the buildings across the basin. "Because, child, that's where you were created. You are part of a great plan to save humanity—a great new step in human evolution."

Rachel paled. Created? Here? Was that all she was—some sort of lab animal? A genetically engineered freak of nature? She felt like she was going to pass out. Still, she held onto the gun. She glanced over at Trevor. He wasn't moving.

The launch was halfway across the basin now, heading in their direction.

"See?" said Hilde, motioning over her shoulder. "They're coming to rescue us, to take you home to your real family." She turned her gun toward Trevor. "But first we need to purge the world of degenerates." The laser beam glowed red on his forehead like a Hindu *tilaka*. "No need to keep this useless pig around anymore. Why don't we just put him out of his misery?"

Rachel gasped in horror. A shot rang out.

The laser gun flew out of Hilde's hand and spun across the ground as the bullet from Rachel's gun struck it. Hilde's mouth fell open, her face clouded with disbelief. Shrieking with rage, she lunged at Rachel.

Rachel dropped the Colt .22 and stumbled backward.

Hilde grabbed her hair and forced her to her knees. "You won't get away from me this time, you freak!"

Rachel could taste the blood in her mouth as Hilde bashed her head against the rock floor. Then, letting go of her hair, Hilde reached for Rachel's throat. In the split second before Hilde's hands could close, Rachel rolled out from under her. With lightning speed, Rachel thrust her hand into the side pocket of Trevor's backpack and pulled out a crampon. Swinging around, she smashed it across the side of Hilde's face.

Hilde fell backward, shrieking in pain, blood spurting from her shattered face. The hand that held the pendant swung out toward the water.

There was a soft pop and a flash of light as the pendant hit the shield between the bank and the water. The shield shattered with a sound of a cannon. Shards of glassy sparks sprayed outward. The pendant swung back and fell with a clatter onto a rock near the edge of water. Before she could regain her balance, Hilde toppled through the tear in the shield and into the cold water.

The men in the launch gaped in astonishment as Hilde's arm, then her whole body, suddenly appeared out of nowhere.

"*Oh, mein Gott!*" one of the men in khaki yelled. "I think it's Generalmajor Braun!"

Hilde groped frantically for the rocky shoreline of the underground basin just as a leopard seal lurched forward, its nostrils flared, its teeth bared. Seizing her hand in its powerful jaws, it tore off two of her fingers. Hilde let out a bloodcurdling scream and fell backward into the water. The churning water turned bright red. Hilde's head bobbed up as she gasped for air. The seal lunged at her again. Instead of finishing her off, the monstrous seal grabbed her in its sharp teeth and shook her from side to side, then tossed her into the air like a toy.

One of the men in the launch raised his gun, trying to get a shot at the seal.

Rachel recoiled in horror as Hilde disappeared beneath the foaming waters only to resurface again, her bloody, mangled face twisted in terror. The seal came up from under her, preparing to fling her flailing body into the air again. This time the guard in the launch got a clear shot.

Trevor moaned. Her heart pounding, Rachel rushed

over to him and knelt down beside him. He was barely breathing. Pressing her back against the boulder, she grunted and slowly pushed it off his leg.

"My leg. I can't move," he gasped before losing consciousness again.

Rachel gave his arm a gentle shake. "Trevor?" No response. She flicked on the headlamp lying on the ground beside him.

Then she remembered her ring and how it had healed her knee. It was her only hope. She reached down and pressed the ring against his broken leg. "Please, please, be okay," she whispered.

He let out a low groan and opened his eyes.

Rachel felt a wave of relief.

Sitting up, he rubbed his head, seemingly unaware that moments ago he'd had a broken leg. "What happened? Where's Hilde?"

Rachel glanced over her shoulder in the direction of the water. There was no sign of her.

By now the men in the launch had reached the wall. One of them was searching the water for Hilde. The other two were pointing at the headlamp beside Rachel and talking excitedly to each other.

However, Rachel did not notice. A whirlpool of conflicting emotions tugged at her. Taking a deep breath, she looked Trevor in the eye and started to ask, "Is it true what Hilde said about your…"

"Turn off the light," he whispered urgently.

"What?"

"Look behind you."

Rachel spun around just as one of the guards raised his gun and aimed it at the spot where she and Trevor sat.

The guard pulled the trigger.

Nothing happened.

"W-what?" Rachel gasped, clutching her heart.

Trevor studied the guard for a moment and then took out his magnetometer. Standing, he tossed a small stone toward the water with a flick of his wrist.

"What are you doing?" cried Rachel. "We have to get out of here!"

Ignoring her, he took a few cautious steps toward the water until he was face to face with the guard. Then Trevor reached toward him as Rachel watched in horror. Her knees turned to jelly, and she collapsed to the ground.

Trevor turned back to her. "It's okay, it's okay," he said softly, taking her in his arms. "They can't see or hear us. They don't even know we're here." He pointed toward the basin. "There's some sort of energy field between us."

Rachel opened her eyes. The men from the launch were less than five meters away and did not even seem to notice Rachel and Trevor. One of them was leaning over the edge of the boat, trying to hook the seal's already bloated and bloody body, which had surfaced nearby.

"I think it's some sort of invisibility shield," said Trevor. "My guess is they can only see the wall behind us and not us—unless we turn on a light. It also seems to muffle sound."

Rachel sat up slowly and rubbed the back of her neck.

"At least we're safe for now," he said tentatively. "We should probably stay put until Aunt Grace and Ka-Wing find us. Hopefully they heard the gunshot."

"Are you sure we're safe? What if those men from the launch find a way through the shield like Hilde did?" Rachel asked. Then she noticed the pendant lying on the bank at the edge of the water. "Look! The pendant!"

Trevor walked over, picked it up, and examined it. "There's a crystal in it," he said. "It looks like the ones we found on Deception Island." He handed the pendant to her.

As she held it, the pattern began shifting.

"What did you do?" he asked in astonishment.

"I didn't do anything. Here, see if it does it for you." She pressed the pendant into his hand. The movement stopped.

Trevor shook his head. "It must be responding to something in you," he said passing the pendant back to her.

The crystal was glowing brighter now through the translucent pattern. "Hilde said it was some sort of key to the Aryans in the middle of the earth. Ome had similar patterns in his robe."

"A key?"

"I wonder if…" Rachel's words trailed off as she remembered what Hilde had said about Grace and Trevor.

"Wonder if what?" he asked.

If she had to choose, she would rather believe Trevor than that horrible Hilde. She was about to tell him what Hilde had said about her having been born here when Grace and Ka-Wing appeared, breathless from the tunnel.

"We thought we heard a gunshot," said Grace, catching her breath.

Ka-Wing glanced anxiously at the men in the launch, who were feeling their way along the shield, looking for a way in. "What's going on?" he whispered.

"Come on, let's get out of here," said Trevor.

However, when they tried to find the entrance back into the tunnel they could not. It was gone.

A faint scraping noise caught Rachel's attention. She turned just in time to see Hilde burst though the tear in the invisibility shield.

Hilde clung desperately to the edge of the opening with her one good hand. With a Herculean effort, she pulled herself through and crumpled to the ground, gasping in a pool of blood. Then she spotted the Colt .22 lying only inches from her face.

"Run," shouted Grace, pointing at an opening that had just materialized in the wall a few meters away. A faint glow, like a mist, surrounded the opening. Grace leapt through with Ka-Wing close behind. Rachel stared in amazement as they disappeared. Before she could protest, Trevor seized her arm and pulled her through the opening.

Rachel felt a sharp tug as if an invisible hand had grabbed her and sucked her into a churning vortex. She tried to scream; but no sound came out.

The next thing she knew she was standing next to Trevor and the others in a huge underground cavern that went on as far as the eye could see.

Chapter 31

Stretched out in front of them was a plaza with a parade ground. The warm air was heavy and still. People milled around like ants. No one seemed to notice them. A larger-than-life statue of Adolph Hitler looked down approvingly from its granite podium in the middle of the mosaic-tiled plaza.

A massive granite edifice wrapped around three sides of the plaza. With its rows of neoclassical arched doorways and windows, and contrasting stark and heavily guarded roofline, the palatial structure looked like a forced marriage between a Roman temple and the Pentagon. A group of dignitaries stood at the top of the steps to the main building. The word *Neuschwabenland* was carved in stone above the large main entrance. Through the open side of the plaza, Rachel could see a structure that looked like a scaled-down version of the Coliseum flanked by granite barracks. The whole bizarre scene was lit by floodlights mounted high on the ceiling of the massive cavern, creating the effect of pillars of light cascading down from heaven.

Rachel wondered if it was all a hallucination. It seemed so unreal.

"Where are we?" whispered Ka-Wing, his voice thin with fear.

"It looks like we're inside the complex we saw from the other side of the basin," Trevor said in a hushed voice.

The crowd fell silent as an imposing barrel-chested man in a black Nehru jacket stepped up to a podium at the top of the steps. “This is a great day!” he said in English in a booming voice. A screen behind him translated his words into both German and Spanish. “Project Blue Ice has been a grand success. Our work here will usher in the greatest advance in human evolution—and with little time to spare. With the progressive pollution of the gene pool, each generation is sicklier and less intelligent than the one before it. Working together, we *can* save the human race from extinction.”

Wild clapping.

He raised his hands for silence. “Project Aryan—the final step in the purification of the human race—will begin shortly and with it the coming of the glorious New World Order. We will rise again, a magnificent pure Aryan race like humanity was meant to be!”

The crowd again erupted into cheers.

Meanwhile, Grace had spotted a large blue laundry bin parked under a nearby overhang. “It may hold clean uniforms,” she said, gesturing for the others to come over. She took off her parka and, searching through the bin, selected a clean white lab coat. Then she took her medical bag out of her backpack and put it over her shoulder. She stuffed her parka and the rest of her gear in the bottom of the bin below the uniforms.

The others followed her lead. Ka-Wing put on a lab jacket and pants while Rachel and Trevor each slipped into a pair of dark blue coveralls. Rachel had just finished ziplocking her coveralls when a nearby movement caught her eye.

Two guards in khaki uniforms were heading in their direction. "You over there," a thickly muscled guard called out.

Too terrified to react, Rachel just stared at him.

The guards looked suspiciously at Ka-Wing. He shrank back.

One of the guards turned to Grace. "*Begrübung*, Dr. Schwartz," he said, greeting her. He motioned toward Ka-Wing and asked in German, "What is he doing here?"

Grace glanced dismissively at Ka-Wing with an expression of amused disdain and said something in German.

They laughed.

"What did you say?" asked Ka-Wing once the guards had moved on.

"He asked what you were doing here. Apparently he thought I was one of the visiting doctors."

"So what did you tell him?"

"I told him you were one of the mutants from the lab and that I was taking you out for a walk—like a dog."

Ka-Wing looked hurt. "A dog?"

"How did you know there was a genetics lab here?" Rachel asked suspiciously, recalling what Hilde had said.

"It was a shot in the dark," Grace replied. "At least now we know they're doing genetic experiments on humans here."

Rachel doubted it was just a shot in the dark. She was about to say so when she remembered what Antonio had told them about Wolf Krause—that he was a neo-Nazi and also a genetic engineer with Global

Genome. Grace had probably just put two and two together.

Trevor touched Rachel on the shoulder and pointed toward the open side of the plaza. Standing there was the captain from the launch. Rachel gasped and stepped back behind one of the fluted columns. They watched as he strode toward the entrance to the main building.

The roar of the crowd had reached fever pitch by now.

The captain approached one of the guards and said something to him. The captain glanced nervously over his shoulder as the guard scuttled up the stairs and relayed the message to the speaker.

The crowd fell silent.

Raising his arms, the man in the black Nehru jacket urged them to work even harder to bring about the New World Order. After ordering them back to work, he disappeared through a huge brass door.

The crowd broke up, some heading out of the plaza toward the barracks, others lining up in front of the many doors that opened out onto the plaza. Rachel glanced toward the open side of the plaza looking for an escape route. No luck. The guards had fanned out across the entrance and were checking each person who passed through.

"Quick," urged Grace. "We need to blend in. Get in one of the lines."

Heads lowered so to be inconspicuous, they walked over to the end of the nearest line. A few of the people looked at them askance, but nobody said anything.

"Damn," whispered Trevor. "The guards are scanning peoples' irises at the door."

Rachel felt fear closing in on her as the plaza began

to empty out. Another eight people to scan and it would be her turn. She pressed her hands against her chest, trying to fight off the rising panic. As she touched the pendant through her coveralls, she felt a warm glow and her attention being drawn to a nearby set of steps leading down to a small basement door. A faint glow materialized from the bottom of the door, beckoning her.

She touched Trevor's arm and nodded toward the basement door. Grace and Ka-Wing had just noticed it too.

The next person in line stepped forward to be scanned by the guard. "Now," whispered Trevor. "While the guard is busy, move toward the basement door, staying out of sight against the building."

The four interlopers slipped out of line and edged along the building and down the stairs. Crouching to stay out of sight, Trevor tried the door. It was locked.

"It looks like this door hasn't been opened for years," said Grace, running her hand along the edge of the doorjamb.

"It's an old magnetic lock," said Trevor. He turned toward Rachel. "Try the pendant. Maybe it'll activate the lock."

Rachel reached into the neck of her coveralls, pulled out the pendant and pressed it against the lock. It clicked open.

****

Hilde lay on the cold stone floor at the edge of the basin, struggling not to slip into oblivion. The pain was excruciating. The hole in the shield had closed up behind her. She could just make out the muffled shouts of the men from the launch as they tried to find a way to reach her. Then the shouts faded, and she was alone.

After several minutes, she pushed herself to her knees with her good hand and sat back with a long groan. Tearing a section out the lining of her jacket, she bound up her open wounds as best she could. Once that was done, she picked up the Colt .22 and slowly stood.

She grit her teeth against the unrelenting pain.

She was a warrior, and she was going to complete her mission if it was the last thing she did.

Chapter 32

Rachel stepped cautiously inside the door. The air smelled close and musty. Grace flicked on her penlight. A narrow, dusty concrete staircase led upward.

The landing at the top of the staircase opened into a short, dark passageway with two doors going off it. The passageway ended abruptly, blocked off by a crudely constructed brick wall. The closest door was padlocked. They moved to the second door. Like the outside door, it had a magnetic lock, which looked like it had not been used in years. Rachel used the pendant to open that as well.

They entered a small, dingy room with soundproof panels on the ceiling and walls, and a large glass window at one end. There was a broken console under the window and five rather rickety wooden chairs lined up facing the window. Next to the window was a doorframe with the door removed. The opening had been paneled over with cement blocks.

Ka-Wing suppressed a sneeze. "Sorry," he murmured, rubbing his nose. "I have an allergy to dust."

Suddenly the room next door lit up and the window jumped to life.

"Shit!" gasped Rachel, grabbing Trevor's arm and ducking down. Grace quickly switched off her penlight and dropped down beside them.

"W-what's happening?" stammered Ka-Wing.

"Shh," Grace whispered. She rose to her knees and peeked through the window. Rachel joined her. A dozen people stood around a wood paneled room dominated by a large mahogany conference table. A silver tea set and an assortment of pastries were set out on a tray on an ornately carved side table along one of the windowless walls. The man in the black Nehru jacket stood at the head of the conference table, his back to the mirror, studying a monitor. Guards were stationed on either side of the door.

"I don't think they can see us," Grace whispered. "It seems to be a one-way mirror, like the kind used for viewing criminal interrogations." Moving slowly, she got up and sat down on one of the chairs facing the window.

Ka-Wing cautiously eased himself into a chair next to Grace. Grace opened her medical bag and took out a silver disc the size of a quarter. She pressed it against the lower edge of the window.

Rachel looked nervously at Grace. "What's that?"

The thin, crackling sound of voices drifted through the disc.

"A sound bug," replied Grace in a low voice.

"Like spies use?" asked Ka-Wing.

"Yes, but it can also be used by physicians in emergencies—to listen to the heart for valve leaks."

Rachel moved back from the window and, checking first to make sure the chair would not collapse under her, sat down beside Trevor.

"The room on the other side was probably a large interrogation room when the Nazis occupied this place," speculated Trevor. "It looks like it's been converted into a conference room."

Just then a priggish woman with iron gray hair swept back in a tight bun stepped up to the one-way mirror and, pursing her narrow lips, pinched her cheeks, mere inches from the four of them watching her from the other side of the mirror.

Grace studied the woman. "She looks familiar," she whispered.

The woman headed back to the table and sat down next to the man with the Nehru jacket. The others refilled their cups and drifted toward their designated seats.

Once everyone was seated, the man in the Nehru jacket began speaking. "This is a momentous occasion and we welcome you, our esteemed guests, as leaders in your field, to join us in our noble endeavor. But first—introductions. I'm sure you all know me by now. I'm Seth Legare, chief administrator of Global Genome's Antarctic facility. On my right is Dr. Winston Vaughn, the brains behind Project Blue Ice."

Grace looked shocked. "Virus Vaughn?" She leaned forward to get a better look at him. "He's older now, but I'm pretty sure it's the same man."

"Who is he?" asked Ka-Wing.

Grace frowned. "An epidemiologist. He used to work for the CDC—Centers for Disease Control—in Atlanta. Brilliant man, but ambitious and unscrupulous—an unabashed bigot."

"Used to work for the CDC? What happened?" asked Rachel.

"He was terminated—suspected of stealing samples of viruses from CDC and selling them to terrorists. That was several years ago. But before he could be brought to trial something happened." Grace hesitated, trying to remember.

"What?" asked Ka-Wing.

"He was killed in the September 11th Twin Towers terrorist attack on New York City. At least, that was the official explanation of his disappearance." She pointed at the gray haired-woman sitting on the other side of the man at the head of the table. "And so was she—supposedly killed in the attack. I knew I'd seen her face before."

"What's her name?" asked Trevor.

"Mercedes Santos, one of the world's leading molecular virologists. She had even been nominated for a Nobel Prize for her work on artificially altering viruses to make them more virulent—preemptive science, she called it, staying one step ahead of bioterrorists." Grace studied the faces of the other people around the table. "The only other one I recognize is the young man at the other end of the table—Dr. Jaewon Kim, a young geneticist who was recently nominated as the scientist of the year in South Korea."

"And what about the man in the black jacket—Seth Legare?" whispered Rachel.

Grace shook her head. "I've never heard of him."

"He sounds American—maybe from the Midwest," Trevor suggested.

Seth Legare continued his introductions. Most of the other people sitting at the table, as it turned out, were physicians and scientists from various parts of the world. The woman the guard had apparently mistaken Grace for out on the plaza was Gisela Schwartz, an embryologist with the Institute for Human Medical

Genetics in Austria. Rachel noticed that most of them, like Dr. Kim, seemed ill at ease—even frightened. They were also wearing clothing that seemed inappropriately casual for the occasion. She suspected Legare was using the term "guests" rather loosely. She wondered if they might be the scientists from the conference in Ushuaia who had mysteriously disappeared during the boat tour in Tierra del Fuego.

Once the introductions were finished, Seth Legare stood again. He touched the monitor in front of him. The wooden paneling on the far wall slid back to reveal eight screens. Diagrams and photos flashed onto the screens, including a stunning photograph of a blue iceberg sparkling in the sunlight. Voices drifted through the sound bug.

"Project Blue Ice," Legare explained to his guests from the other side of the mirror, "was so named because the virus is transported to the target areas in icebergs, such as this one, which are being towed to water-impoverished areas of the world. The virus is initially transmitted by drinking water melted from the icebergs. Secondary infections occur through contact with excretions—saliva, sweat, blood, mucus—from the infected person. And, thanks to the marketing genius of our very own Mr. Frankie Vanzetti," Legare said, gesturing toward one of the visitors from the Global Genome headquarters, "blue ice cubes will soon be all the rage among the jet set, thus ensuring rapid dispersal of the virus throughout the world."

Rachel winced, remembering the melted ice from the bergy bits they drank on the *Queen Maud*. Was it infected? And what about the unknown infection Richard had somehow picked up? Could it have been caused by this virus?

"In fact," Legare said, checking his watch, "just hours from now the company catering the International Climate Change Conference in New York City, which is being attended by hundreds of scientists and political leaders from around the world, will be serving our blue ice cubes in the drinks."

Rachel glanced around the tiny room where they were hiding. Her heart sank. It was almost certainly too late to warn the people at the conference.

"Virus?" asked Dr. Dzobo Kwansy, a South African epidemiologist with the United Nations World Health Organization. "But why? And aren't you worried about starting a pandemic?"

Legare gave him a condescending smile. "We will be getting to that in due time," he said. "And now, if I may continue?" With Dr. Kwansy silenced, Legare gave a brief overview of the project, beginning with the alteration of a harmless virus found in microbes in rocks from Deception Island.

Then it was Dr. Vaughn's turn to speak. "I'd like to start by addressing Dr. Kwansy's concern about a worldwide epidemic," he said. "I can assure you that this won't happen since the Blue Ice virus infects preferentially."

He pressed the monitor on the table. A ribbon of DNA flashed onto one of the screens. "This is the AMI-1 gene. Caucasians and other fair-skinned people are lacking the leucine amino acid in position 437—right here. The loss of this one protein is responsible for hypo-pigmentation or fair skin. The virus only attaches itself to germ cells—sperm and ova—carrying the AMI-1 gene with leucine in position 437. No other cells. Once the virus enters the germ cells, it renders people with heavily pigmented skin sterile—unable to replicate."

The room fell silent as the guests pondered the implications of what they had heard.

Dr. Kim looked skeptical. "But won't the World Health Organization get suspicious when so many people at the environmental conference get sick at the same time and there are similar outbreaks in the areas where the ice is being towed?"

"No, that's unlikely," replied Dr. Vaughn. "The early clinical signs of the virus—headache, rash, nausea, mild fever—manifest in less than half of those infected, and the symptoms are not severe enough for most people to seek medical attention. And even if they do, it's unlikely to raise an alarm, since the initial symptoms disappear in a few days and will probably be dismissed as flu."

"But why would you want to make people of color sterile?" demanded Dr. Kwansy.

Dr. Vaughn narrowed his eyes. "Because, Dr. Kwansy, pigmentation is a throwback to our primitive animal nature—a sign of degeneration. We can only move forward in our evolution by getting rid of the degenerates."

"This is ludicrous," he protested, "and immoral."

Dr. Vaughn's face turned red. "Calling the kettle black, are we, Dr. Kwansy?"

Dr. Kwansy started to say something, but, noticing the guards glaring at him, instead wiped the beads of sweat off his brow. He glanced around at the others sitting at the table. Except for Dr. Kim, they all looked away.

Clenching his fists by his side, Dr. Vaughn said, "I think you get my point. The bloody massacres in Africa—tribes killing tribes, the kidnapping and selling of fellow Africans into slavery, AIDS brought on by sexual promiscuity and drug dealing. And the United States—the evil empire with its rising crime rates, dropping IQs, and a degenerate for president. And you have the audacity to call me immoral?"

The room fell silent.

Dr. Santos broke the silence. "We understand your concern, Dr. Kwansy, but it's misplaced, I assure you." She regarded Dr. Vaughn with admiration. "And I think you could show a bit more respect and gratitude. You wouldn't even have had the privilege of being here at this historic meeting if you hadn't been on that boat tour in Tierra del Fuego with all your esteemed colleagues here. As for your accusation that this is immoral we are simply doing a preemptive strike as it were, outwitting nature by doing a controlled plague and one in which no one dies. So you see, Dr. Kwansy, no one in your family is going to be harmed."

"We're actually doing your people a favor," added Dr. Vaughn, "allowing the Negroes who are living now to rise out of poverty unshackled by huge families. Granted, this will be the last generation of Negroes, but survival of the fittest is a natural part of evolution."

Dr. Schwartz raised her hand slightly and asked, "But won't the authorities begin to suspect something's amiss when it's only dark-skinned people who are getting sick? Or not having children?"

"Not at all—or at least not at first," replied Dr. Vaughn, with an air of smugness. "The outbreak will be blamed on the poor hygiene habits of Negro degenerates. As you may recall, investigation into the cause of AIDS and the search for a vaccine was delayed for years because it was believed to be a queer disease caused by their disgusting promiscuous lifestyle."

"Jesus," whispered one of the other guests. "This is insane." She shut up immediately as one of the guards took a step toward her.

The man beside her, a thin bespectacled man, shifted uncomfortably and crossed his arms in defiance, but said nothing.

Dr. Vaughn's presentation was interrupted by a tap on the door. Someone handed one of the guards a slip of paper. He brought it over to Seth Legare, who opened and read it. A smile spread across his face. Then he said to Dr. Vaughn, "Please continue."

"What about the Jewish problem?" asked Frankie Vanzetti. "Will this take care of it?" He obviously did not share Dr. Kwansy's misgivings.

"Good question, Frankie," Dr. Vaughn said, pressing the monitor. A picture of a multi-sided entity flashed onto all eight screens. "I present the Aryan virus."

From the other side of the mirror, Rachel's stomach twisted into a knot as she recalled the photo Sutchin had showed her at Shackleton Station of a chimera virus engineered for maximal virulence.

"My God," said Grace in a low voice.

They listened in horrified silence as Dr. Vaughn continued. "Phase II, also known as Project Aryan, will take care of the Jewish problem, as well as human suffering caused by disease and ignorance. The Aryan virus will live in accommodation with white populations in their germ cells. In contrast to the Blue

Ice virus, it will attach itself only to the germ cells of those who *lack* the leucine protein in the AMI-1 gene—in other words, fair-skinned people. Instead of rendering the host sterile, it will alter the genome of the germ cells. Thus, to answer your question, Frankie, it will purge the DNA of Jews of its Jewish filth. All the hosts' children and their children after them will inherit the genetic changes from the virus—an enhanced immune system, health, beauty, and intelligence. In thirty to forty years, with the exception of a few isolated groups of people, the human race will be permanently changed—purged. Thus, we will achieve our next step in evolution—a new super Aryan race."

"That is, if our own cleverness doesn't destroy us first," muttered Dr. Kim under his breath.

"Perhaps," interjected Dr. Santos. "But right now Project Aryan is our only hope for the survival of the human species."

"When will the Aryan virus be ready?" asked Frankie Vanzetti.

"I'll defer to you on that one," said Dr. Vaughn, motioning toward Seth Legare.

He stood. "Very soon," he replied, holding up the slip of paper the guard had handed to him. "The subject who is the carrier of the Aryan DNA we need to insert into the virus—a Miss Rachel St. Claire—is here in the complex as we speak."

Rachel was so surprised she almost cried out.

Dr. Kwansy stood and banged his fist on the table. "This is insane! I demand that you take us back right now. Kidnapping is a capital offense."

Dr. Kim nodded in agreement.

Legare made a barely perceptible movement with

his head.

The two guards stepped forward and, placing their hands on Dr. Kim's and Dr. Kwansy's shoulders, lifted them out of their seats and escorted them from the room.

Frankie Vanzetti brought his hands together. "Bravo!"

"A toast," cried the geneticist from Global Genome. A waiter appeared with a tray of bubbling champagne glasses.

At that moment, Ka-Wing sneezed. The chair collapsed beneath him, clattering to the floor and taking him with it.

Chapter 33

Seth Legare spun around, dropping his glass of champagne. Cupping his hands, he pressed his face against the mirror. The others in the room stared at the mirror as if it was haunted.

Grace grabbed Ka-Wing's arm and dragged him toward the door. Trevor and Rachel were already out in the hall.

"There's someone on the other side of the mirror!" Legare shouted to the guards. "Shoot out the glass!" The mirror thudded and pinged as a round of bullets pummeled it.

The people in the room screamed and ducked down as the bullets ricocheted off what was apparently a bulletproof mirror.

"Damn," Legare said, scowling at the pockmarked mirror. He turned abruptly and shouted to the guards. "Alert everyone to be on the lookout for intruders."

****

Ka-Wing slumped back against the dusty wall in the passageway. "It's all my fault," he moaned, stifling another sneeze.

"Look!" said Rachel. She held up the pendant so the others could see it. The symbols had shifted and now pointed at the padlocked door.

Grace shone her penlight at the door. The padlock hung open.

The door led into another abandoned passageway lined with holding cells. The faint scent of death lingered in the air. Each cell was dimly lit by small grids in the ceiling. The remains of human skeletons lay curled up on the floors of the cells.

"What is this place?" asked Ka-Wing, putting a hand over his mouth and nose.

"Oh, my God—Charlie!" Grace cried out, rushing toward the first cell. Then she hurried to the next cell and the next, studying each skeleton. When she finished, her eyes filled with tears of relief.

Trevor gave his aunt a hug.

Grace wiped her eyes. "Charlie had lost the index finger on his left hand in a boating accident," she explained. "And all these skeletons have ten fingers."

"Look, there's a door at the end of the hall," exclaimed Ka-Wing.

Rachel felt a surge of hope.

The steel door opened into a dusty reception area. On the far side was another door that sagged on rusted hinges. A harsh, unnatural light filtered through the crack between the door and the frame.

Trevor stretched upward and peeked through the crack.

"What is it?" asked Rachel.

"It's some sort of courtyard," he said, "It appears to be surrounded on all sides by buildings except for that archway which has a guard."

From behind, they could hear the bulletproof glass shattering, followed by the sound of shouts.

Her hands shaking, Rachel held the pendant up to the light. The symbols were shifting again.

"Look," said Grace, pointing at the bottom of the

door. The glowing mist had rematerialized.

Ka-Wing glanced nervously over his shoulder. The shouts were getting closer.

Waiting until the guard at the courtyard archway was distracted by a call on his walkie-talkie, Trevor slipped outside. The mist edged forward like a ghostly cat toward a set of double doors ten meters away. Engraved in German in the stone lintel above the door were the words “Fourth Reich Chamber of Art.”

“I think it’s telling us to go this way,” whispered Rachel, pressing her hand against Trevor’s back.

The others followed as she dashed across the courtyard, up the stairs, and through the double doors. The ornate German baroque foyer was decorated with mosaic panels framed by bands of gold oak-leaf crowns. Beyond it, through a set of glass doors, was a grand hall with a high vaulted ceiling. The mist curled through the doors, urging them through.

Except for the Roman and Grecian statues, which gazed complacently down at them from dusty recesses between crumbling fluted columns, the only person around was a museum guard, an elderly gentleman dozing fitfully behind a large antique desk. Tapestries celebrating the victories of Alexander the Great hung on the wall in a large alcove behind the desk, along with more recent woven renditions of German victories and Greek and Roman mythical figures whose faces in some cases bore an uncanny resemblance to that of Hitler.

“This is really creepy,” whispered Ka-Wing.

Rachel checked the pendant. It pointed toward a dried-up ornamental fountain in the center of the grand hall. “This way,” she said softly, being careful not to disturb the sleeping guard.

They followed the mist past paintings by Leonardo da Vinci, Rembrandt, and Rubens—no doubt stolen by Nazi forces from occupied countries during World War II—past displays of other classical and renaissance paintings and artifacts, past rooms filled with Hitler's own art. Their footsteps echoed ominously on the cracked marble floor. The mist curled around the fountain before ending in front of a large painting of a Madonna figure holding a blond, blued-eyed Christ child on one knee and, in her other hand, a brass standard with an eagle perched on a globe emblazoned with a swastika.

Rachel felt a knot tighten in her stomach as if she were in the presence of pure evil.

Trevor pushed on the wall around the edge of the painting.

"What are you doing?" asked Ka-Wing, glancing furtively around.

"Checking to see if there's a passage behind the wall. The Nazis probably built in an escape route or hideaway in case the Americans or Brits discovered their underground base."

"What's that?" whispered Rachel, cupping her hand to her ear.

"The underground base, you mean?"

"No—listen." She pointed in the direction they had just come from.

A sound, faint at first. Shuffle, thump, pause, shuffle, thump.

"It's probably just the museum guard," said Grace.

Shuffle, thump.

Suddenly Hilde appeared from around the fountain,

her bloody and disfigured face etched in pain. She jerked to a stop as she spotted them. Her good eye flashed with hatred like a deranged Cyclops from hell.

Rachel's mouth went dry and a rush of blood pounded in her veins.

Hilde turned and cried out in a broken voice, "Guards! They're over here!"

Ka-Wing gasped and stumbled backward against the painting. As his head struck the swastika on the globe, the painting swung open, revealing a secret passage. The mist flooded into it like water behind a broken dam, carrying them with it down a polished stone chute at breakneck speed, spiraling downward into the murky darkness.

Rachel could hear the painting slam shut behind them. Just as she felt she was going to faint from vertigo, the chute leveled out. The mist thinned to a trickle, depositing them on the floor of what seemed to be a closet. The air was heavy and stale—almost asphyxiating.

She sat up and blinked. Hilde was nowhere in sight. Grace was kneeling, her arm around a terrified Ka-Wing, staring at a slightly ajar door. Trevor stood next to them. A hand-lettered sign with the words "*Kinderkrippe*" hung on the door.

An unearthly wail from the other side of the door shattered the eerie silence.

Rachel's heart jumped; the hair on the back of her neck stood on end. "W-what was that?"

Trevor tiptoed over to the door and peeked through the crack. Steadying himself against the cold metal frame, he opened the door just far enough to edge through to the corridor on the other side. He pressed up against the wall as a nurse wearing a starched white uniform and a blank, listless expression walked past him, oblivious of, or perhaps not interested in, his presence. In her arms she held an infant swaddled in a blanket. Trevor ducked back inside.

The nurse was followed a few moments later by another woman in a white lab coat carrying a tray of vials. She turned down a large brightly lit corridor. As her footsteps faded, the mist returned, curling out the door like a beacon guiding them through the eye of a storm.

Rachel stepped warily into the corridor. Numbers were painted above each door leading off it. The tepid, recycled air smelt of antiseptic and urine. With its low ceiling and white tile walls, tinged yellow with age, it reminded her of a subterranean insane asylum from an old horror movie. The steady whoosh of the air recyclers and the harsh fluorescent lights only added to the oppression. Across the hall, visible through a large viewing window, was a nursery lined with plastic bassinettes, a baby in each, some grotesquely malformed.

Rachel stopped short. A wave of nausea swept over her.

Trevor reached out and took her arm. “What is it?”

“I-I’ve been here before,” she replied in a quavering voice.

Chapter 34

Rachel leaned against the cold tiled wall, her head spinning. Maybe Hilde *had* told her the truth about Grace. She removed the pendant from around her neck, stuffed it into the pocket of her coveralls and zipped it shut.

Grace looked puzzled. “Which way now?”

“Did you say you’ve been here before?” Trevor asked Rachel, as though unsure he had heard correctly.

Rachel took a deep breath. “There’s something I need to know before we go any further.”

“What? We have to get out of here before someone sees us,” Ka-Wing cried. He looked beseechingly at Trevor. “Take the pendant from her,” he urged.

Trevor looked at her uncertainly and shook his head. “It doesn’t work with anyone else.”

“Tell me about my mother,” Rachel demanded, looking Grace in the eye.

The dull thud of footsteps echoed from one of the side halls. Or, was it just the pounding of her heart? Rachel could not be sure. She swallowed hard and glanced up and down the bleak hall. There was no one in sight. Turning back to Grace, she said, “Hilde Braun said you kidnapped me and that this is my home. Is that true?”

Grace slouched, her head bowed, as if she had been punched in the stomach.

Just then, two men in white uniforms appeared from around a corner far down the hall. They were pushing a stretcher with a tiny, deformed, barely alive body on it.

Rachel blanched.

"Let's get out of the hall," said Trevor, grabbing her arm.

They slipped back into the closet, leaving the door slightly ajar. Through the crack, Rachel watched as the two men and stretcher vanished around another corner.

Grace steepled her hands and pressed them against her forehead. "Hilde's right," she finally said. "You *were* born here."

Rachel sucked in a sharp breath and steadied herself with one hand on the wall. Until now, she had hoped against all odds that Hilde was lying. On the other hand, it had become clear over the past several days that Grace knew more than she was letting on. "Was my mother a terrorist or neo-Nazi?" she asked.

"Hardly," Grace replied, reaching out for Rachel's hand.

She pulled back. "I want to know the truth."

"What do you mean, 'the truth'?" Trevor asked, staring at them. "What's going on here?"

"Your mother, Angelina," said Grace in a subdued voice, "was one of the children kidnapped during the Dirty War in Argentina. The kidnappers used the older girls as surrogates for genetically engineered embryos."

Rachel slumped back against the wall of the closet. She felt utterly drained. She closed her eyes and pressed the heels of her hands into her temples in an attempt to fend off the memories. Visions crept into her consciousness of glass Petri dishes, microscopes, tight-lipped doctors in white jackets, and women—her mother—the woman in her dream—in hospital johnnies sitting somberly in plastic chairs along one of the walls, waiting for their appointed time. After a few moments, Rachel opened her eyes and asked, "Where's my mother now?"

Grace shook her head.

Rachel's throat tightened and her eyes filled with tears. Her head was reeling.

Trevor shot his aunt an accusing glance. "Why didn't you tell her sooner?" he demanded.

Grace raised her hands in a gesture of apology. "All I can say, Rachel, is that your mother loved you very much. She found the pendant, one like yours or maybe even the same one, and by some miracle made her way with you in her arms to the surface and the meteorology station. I took you back to Rothera Station, but your mother refused to come with me. Charlie stayed back with her. She was worried her captors had followed her and she didn't want them to find you. She took a blanket from the meteorology station and wrapped it like there was a child inside and acted as a decoy. Her pursuers fell for it—at least long enough for us to escape. She jumped into the crevasse to escape them. She gave her life to save you—because she loved you so much."

Rachel pushed her nails into the palm of her hands to keep from crying.

Trevor put his arm around her. Rachel buried her face in his shoulder.

"The terrorists would have made her talk. They had their ways," said Grace. "They planned to breed you as soon as you came of age, and she didn't want that to happen to you. Charlie went into the crevasse to find her but…" Grace fell silent.

Outside in the hall Rachel could hear the moaning squeak of the stretcher as it passed by on its return trip. In the distance, a baby cried. Rachel glanced in the direction of the sound. "Was she my real mother, I mean genetically?"

"Oh, yes," replied Grace. "They took her eggs, as well as those from other prisoners, and genetically engineered them with DNA from an Aryan scout they had captured."

"What do you mean—an Aryan scout?" asked Ka-Wing.

"From what I understand, someone like Ome. Anyway, the scout later escaped. You, Rachel, were the only one who survived of the thousands of genetically engineered embryos."

Rachel stepped back and looked at Trevor. "Did you know about this?"

"The only thing Trevor knew," interjected Grace, "was that you might be in some sort of danger and that you were probably being followed. That's all. He didn't know why or anything about your background except what you've already told him. Given who we're dealing with, the less people knew, the safer it was for all of us."

Rachel began to cry softly, despite her best efforts to hold back her tears.

"Hey," said Trevor, gently resting his hands on her shoulders. "I meant it when I said it made no difference to me where you came from."

"Thank you," she whispered, knowing he meant it. At least there was one person she could trust. She wiped her eyes. She had so many questions. But there was no time for answers, for at that moment the closet door creaked open.

They froze.

Standing in the doorway was a gray humanoid creature. The creature reached out its long, thin arms, its large, black eyes full of sadness.

Rachel did not move. For some reason she was not afraid. Electricity pulsed through her as their hands met. The creature's fingers ever so gently touched the ring on her baby finger. Memories from her early childhood flooded her. The nursery, the genetics lab, the endless rounds of probings and medical tests, the mutant grays who cared for the children—the only touch of kindness in an otherwise heartless and sterile existence.

"Eingrau?" she whispered in astonishment.

The gray nodded. Then it turned and stepped out into the corridor. Looking back, it tilted its head slightly.

"What does it want?" asked Trevor.

"It wants us to follow."

With Rachel and the others not far behind, the gray moved swiftly down the corridor coming to a stop just before Room 10. It tapped the tiled wall with its long finger. Then, holding up three fingers, it pointed first at a narrow, almost invisible door carved out of the wall directly across the hall, and then pointed down at the floor.

"What's it trying to tell us?" whispered Grace.

"I'm not sure." Rachel put her fingertips on her temples, trying to read Eingrau's thoughts. "Something about three floors below, I think."

Just then, they heard footsteps coming up cement

stairs from one of the side passages, followed by the clink of a key in a gate.

Trevor gestured toward a set of swinging doors that led into a side corridor. “This way,” he urged.

They made it just in time. The wrought iron gate swung open and a guard appeared, his hand resting on his holster.

Rachel peeked through the crack between the swinging doors. Then she noticed the gray was not with them. “Where’s Eingrau?” she whispered. The door creaked slightly as she rested her hand lightly on it, trying to get a better view of the hallway.

The guard stopped abruptly and looked around. “Halt, slave!” he shouted as he spotted the gray.

Eingrau made a melancholy cooing sound and tapped the wall and pointed downward once more, this time with greater urgency as though it wanted to make sure they understood. Then, Eingrau started loping toward the guard. Rachel stared. She had never known a gray to be in any way aggressive or disobedient to an order.

The guard pulled out his gun and took aim.

Rachel heard a thud as Eingrau fell to the cold floor.

“Eingrau!” she gasped. The swinging door moaned as she started to push it open.

Trevor pulled her back. “Sh-h,” he whispered.

The guard froze as though he had heard a ghost. Hearing nothing else, he walked over and gave the gray a kick with the toe of his boot. Satisfied it was dead, he took out his radio. “Lieutenant Schmidt to control,” he said. “Send someone down here to dispose of a mutant body.”

The disposal team, the two men in white who had passed by earlier with the stretcher, appeared in a matter of seconds.

Rachel watched, her heart heavy with grief, as the two men lifted Eingrau's lifeless body onto the stretcher, as though it was nothing more than a sack of potatoes, and carted it off.

The guard started to leave, then hesitated and glanced suspiciously at the set of swinging doors.

"Damn, he's coming this way," whispered Trevor, backing away from the door. "Come on. Let's get out of here."

They raced down the wide corridor around a corner and another and through a door into a modern, well-lit laboratory. The place had an ominous aura; the air smelt unpleasantly sterile. No one seemed to notice that the four of them had entered or, if they did, they did not seem to regard their presence as suspicious.

Rachel looked around, trying to get her bearings. "I know this place," she whispered. "Except…" She leaned on Trevor's arm for support, fighting the impulse to turn and run. Unlike the dreary, rundown nursery area, the bright, modern laboratory looked recently refurbished. To her left, the plastic seats were gone where the women, her mother, had once waited for their turn to be forcibly inducted into motherhood. They had been replaced by mechanical surrogate mothers that sat lined up passively, without complaint, their metal wombs open and ready to receive the next generation of genetically engineered embryos.

Glass-fronted cupboards and metal cabinets took up every bit of available wall space. On the wall across from them, glass jars containing embryos preserved in formaldehyde stood in grim rows behind locked glass doors.

Cluttered black lab benches jutted out into the center of the room. A few dozen scientists and technicians, assisted by grays, were busy at workstations studying readouts on spectrophotometers, peering through the eyepieces of microscopes, or transferring genetic material using pipettes from color-coded cryogenic vials to nearby Petri dishes. A small group of men and women in crisp white lab coats and silk ties and scarves congregated at a workstation at the far end of the lab, discussing a holographic image of a strand of DNA. The dull hum of the air vents muffled the sound of their voices.

A gray, pushing a utility cart, walked up and down among the lab benches, carefully placing the covered Petri dishes on the cart. With the cart full, the gray headed toward a large stainless steel door at the other end of the laboratory and disappeared behind the door.

"The culture room," whispered Grace, buttoning up her lab coat. "Once the viable eggs reach the embryonic stage, they'll be transferred to a surrogate and…"

Before she could finish, one of the many doors off the lab swung open and a gray emerged, holding the hand of a small child who was crying softly. The gray nodded slightly at Rachel as it walked past. Rachel turned and stared as the gray headed down the hall toward the nurseries. She rubbed the back of her neck. Had it said something about saving the children? How could *she* do it? She glanced at the others but no one else seemed to have heard.

"We don't get attached to the subjects—the children," a young technician, who had just come over and stood next to one of the mechanical surrogate mothers, was explaining to one of the guests they had seen in the conference room. “Most of them are going to die anyway.”

The guest appeared disconcerted. “Die?”

The technician smiled. “Don’t think of it as killing, doctor. Think of it as saving the world. The subjects donate their lives to science and the betterment of humankind. What more noble sacrifice than to give one’s life so others may live?”

At that moment, the technician glanced toward the door and noticed Rachel and the others watching her.

Chapter 35

Grace snatched up a report lying on a table next to the door and pretended to be studying it.

The technician walked toward them with an outstretched hand. “Dr. Schwartz? Dr. Kim?” she asked tentatively.

“Ah, yes, of course,” Grace replied, smiling graciously. “We were told by Seth Legare that we could have a tour of your biohazard lab. He was interested in our feedback on the facility.”

The technician looked delighted to be of assistance. She glanced questioningly at Trevor and Rachel’s blue coveralls.

“We…we’re here to…” Rachel stammered, trying to think of something to say.

“Yes, I know,” interrupted the technician, “to fix the alarm on the freezer thermostat in the biohazard lab. It keeps going off for no apparent reason. We didn’t expect you to get here so soon.” She looked around. “Where are your tools?”

Trevor grinned and winked playfully at her. He pulled out his magnetometer and held it up quickly before returning it to his pocket, hoping she would think it was part of the tools of an electrician’s trade.

She blushed, hardly noticing the magnetometer. “My name is Felice,” she said, smiling flirtatiously at Trevor. “I was just transferred here three days ago and haven't met everyone yet. And you are?"

"Clark," said Trevor, holding out his hand, "Clark Kent."

Rachel jabbed him in the ribs with her elbow.

"Pleased to meet you, Clark," replied Felice. "Ah—maybe we can…"

"See the biohazard lab?" interrupted Grace, checking her watch and feigning impatience. "We don't have much time."

"Oh, yes, of course, Dr. Schwartz. It's this way."

Felice led them down the hall to a door with a biohazard sign. Pressing her thumb against the lock pad, she opened the door. "I'll be back in about half an hour." She smiled at Trevor as she turned to leave.

"It looks like you have an admirer," Rachel said, as Trevor held the door open for her and the others.

He shrugged. "What can I say—a good looking guy like me must be quite the catch down here." He winked and nudged her in the ribs. "Don't you agree?"

Rachel laughed and rolled her eyes. She wondered now how she ever could have doubted his sincerity. Stepping into the small white room that served as the biohazard lab staging area, she looked around. Along one of the walls was a row of hooks with pale blue biohazard suits, most with names on them.

Grace took down one of the nameless suits.

"What are you doing?" asked Ka-Wing.

"I'm going into the lab to look for the virus so we can make an antidote," said Grace.

"I'll help you," replied Ka-Wing, reaching for a suit.

"And I want to check out the freezer alarm," said Trevor as he looked through a drawer of stainless steel instruments for makeshift tools. "Maybe see if I can permanently disarm it—and the cooling unit on the freezer." Finding what he needed, he began to suit up.

"You coming?" he asked Rachel.

Rachel paused. She wanted to be with him; she did not relish the idea of being alone in this place. At the same time, she really did not want to put on one of those bulky suits. What if she put it on wrong and got exposed to some sort of deadly virus? And besides—she didn't know anything about viruses or freezer alarms. "I'll stay here and keep watch," she finally said.

Grace handed her a copy of the report she had picked up back in the lab. "You might be interested in looking through this while you're waiting. It's an overview of the two projects put together for the so-called guests."

After slipping into the biohazard suit, Grace pulled down her facemask and closed the front seal, which snapped shut automatically. Then she picked up an air regulator—a steel canister with a shoulder strap—and put it over her shoulder. Trevor and Ka-Wing followed her lead. The heavy door to the biohazard area swung slowly open as they entered through the airlock to the hot—contaminated—side.

Once inside, Grace put on insulated gloves and, with Ka-Wing's assistance, began checking out the freezers. Using forceps, she took out a rack of small test tubes from one of the freezers and read the labels. Then she pulled out some of the tubes and placed them in a stainless steel cylinder. A white cloud poured out of the cylinder as she opened it.

Meanwhile, Trevor set about examining the alarm system, which he discovered was wired to a Building

Automation System (BAS) that would sound an alarm in a central control room if the temperature in the freezers rose above a certain point. After temporarily disabling the freezer alarm by pressing the silencing switch, he took a small pair of scissors from his pocket and cut the low-voltage wire leading from the BAS control panel to the freezers. Working quickly, he rewired and reprogrammed the digital temperature controls on the fronts of the freezers to read out the wrong temperature so as not to arouse suspicion. Then he disabled the cooling units for the freezers.

"How's it going?" Grace asked Trevor as she sealed the cylinder and put it in her pocket.

"Just about done," he said. "Hopefully by the time they discover that the thermostat on the freezer has been jammed and the cooling motors disconnected, the viruses will be dead."

A blue light bathed their facemasks as they exited through the decontamination area and stepped into a shower containing ultraviolet light and soap. The room smelled like chlorine bleach. After showering while still in the biohazard suits, they removed the suits and placed them in a discard pan.

"You'll never guess what they're doing," said Rachel, holding up the report as they reentered the staging area. "They've vaccinated themselves against the Aryan virus. And they've developed a 'master race' strain of the Aryan virus, just for themselves, minus the genes for pacifism."

"That means they'll be able to take over the world without resistance," said Ka-Wing.

"Hopefully we can stop them," Trevor said. "But first, let's get out of here before our new friend returns."

He walked over to the door and opened it a crack. Then he stepped out into the corridor and signaled for the others to follow.

Once outside, Trevor turned to Rachel and asked in a low voice, "What's the pendant say?"

She pulled it out and examined it. It pointed in the direction of the swinging doors between the laboratory and nursery areas.

"Let's go," said Grace.

As they passed the door to the main laboratory, they could see Dr. Santos and Seth Legare talking angrily to Felice, who was looking very frightened and confused.

They picked up their pace. Fortunately, there were no guards around.

Once they were safely on the other side of the swinging doors, Rachel looked at the pendant again. "It's pointing toward that door opposite the wall where Eingrau was tapping."

Rachel walked over and pushed on the door. It was stuck. Like so many other doors in the complex, it had not been used in years.

From the laboratory area, they could hear distant shouts and doors opening and closing. Then the voices receded as the search parties headed off in opposite directions.

"Here, let me try," said Trevor. Pulling himself up to full height, he turned his shoulder toward the door and rushed it. The narrow door snapped open, banging against a stone wall. He barely managed to keep himself from falling headlong down a rough, curving set of stairs cut into the wall.

He tried to push the door shut behind them, but the impact had bent the hinges.

"Leave the door," said Grace, flicking on her penlight. "We have to get out of here before the guards catch up with us."

Trevor took out his headlamp and started down the narrow, dark stairs. The first level looked like an old storage area. The air was thick and musty. Boxes and crates stood piled and rotting against the damp stone wall. Discarded bassinettes and cribs were heaped in a corner.

Ka-Wing peered anxiously down the second set of stairs, which grew narrower as the steps descended into the gloom. He looked scared and exhausted.

Rachel did not know how much longer she could keep going either. She squeezed the pendant in her hand. As it pressed up against the baby ring, she could feel the energy coming from it. She reached out and placed her hand on Ka-Wing's shoulder.

"It's okay," she said. "Eingrau said to go down three levels. And we can trust Eingrau."

From above they heard the search party heading into the nursery area.

They descended the two remaining flights of narrow steps in single file. Rachel could make out the hollow pounding of boots in the nursery hallway three floors above. But that wasn't all. She held her breath and listened. In between the yelling and pounding of boots, she heard another familiar sound. Shuffle, thump. It was coming from near the top of the stairs.

The stairs ended next to a narrow opening cut into the stone wall. Rachel and the others squeezed through and out onto an abandoned railroad track. Rubble crunched beneath their feet, stirring up a foul, dank smelling dust.

Trevor squatted and examined the old tracks. "Could have been used for mining at one time," he said. "Or transportation."

A scraping sound follow by a thud came from behind them.

Heart pounding, Rachel squinted in the direction of the opening in the wall.

"What was that?" whispered Grace, straining to hear the sound. However, the only sound was the slow dripping of water from the roof of the tunnel.

Ka-Wing cringed. "This place gives me the creeps. It reminds me of the abandoned tunnels in the old New York subway."

Trevor shone his headlamp up and down the tracks that disappeared into the darkness. "I think I see something down there," he said, gesturing for the others to follow him.

They started down the tracks, carefully picking their way through the rubble. After a short distance, the tunnel opened out onto a wide platform about a meter above the tracks. Hoisting themselves up onto the platform, they looked around for an escape route. Unlike the two higher levels, which were hewn out of rough stone, the walls along the platform were tiled—or at least had been at one time. Most of the tiles had fallen off the walls and lay in the dust and rubble at the bottom of the wall. Those remaining were cracked and discolored. A wide crumbling concrete staircase behind a padlocked accordion-style iron gate led up from the platform.

Trevor picked up a rock and smashed the rusted

padlock. He started up the stairs, which came to an abrupt end at the first landing, blocked by a rockslide.

"We're trapped," moaned Ka-Wing as he watched Trevor come back down the stairs.

Trevor stopped and studied one of his instruments in the light of his headlamp. "According to my calculations," he said, "that wall over there at the end of this platform is directly below the spot where Eingrau was standing."

Rachel held up the pendant. It too pointed at the tiled wall at the end of the platform.

As they reached the spot, a misty glow appeared as the base of the wall.

"Try putting the pendant against the wall," urged Grace.

Rachel did as told. Nothing happened. She paused and listened. She thought she heard a noise coming toward them from down the tracks.

Ka-Wing glanced furtively over his shoulder, and then back at the wall. By now, the mist was curling up the wall like smoke from a campfire. "We have to do something. Maybe we should just try rushing the wall," he said.

"What are you talking about?" Rachel asked. She thought for sure Ka-Wing had finally gone off the deep end. "We can't just walk through a solid stone wall."

"Like Harry Potter in…" Ka-Wing started to say.

A metallic click caught their attention. Rachel turned around just in time to see Hilde burst into view, holding the Colt .22 and relentlessly dragging herself up the track toward her prey with the guards not far behind her.

A bullet exploded over their heads and smashed

into a tile, sending the shattered pieces spraying.

Rachel screamed, almost dropping the pendant.

With supernatural strength, Hilde dragged herself up onto the platform. "Now I got you just where I want you, freak," she hissed. She raised the Colt .22, trying to steady it against her injured arm.

The stone wall suddenly shimmered like a veil in a gentle breeze. Rachel rushed toward it. Grace followed, with Trevor and Ka-Wing right behind. They disappeared into the misty veil.

Shrieking with rage, Hilde lunged at the wall. Rachel could feel her hot breath and hear her heavy panting behind them as they slipped through the barrier.

Chapter 36

Rachel stared in astonishment at the crystalline pillars that rose, like luminescent Buddhist shrines, from the floor of a magnificent grotto. The beauty of each exquisite formation was breathtaking. As they took a step forward, the walls shimmered in a display of color as dazzling as the aurora. Rachel could feel the calming energy surging through her. It was such a stark contrast to the place they had just come from, that she wondered if it was all a mirage or hologram or, even worse, some sort of neo-Nazi trap.

"Where are we?" she asked, looking around.

"I don't know," Trevor replied. He ran his hand along the wall they had just passed through and then pulled out his magnetometer. "This is incredible. The crystals in the wall are radiating magnetic energy." He paused in thought. "You know, I think we may have just passed through dark matter."

"Dark matter? But how can that be?"

"Clive Wesley, back at the Dark Matter Lab at Shackleton Station, thinks there's a concentration of dark matter in the crystals we found on Deception Island. He also thinks it's somehow connected to the intense magnetism at the poles." Trevor crouched and examined the floor of the grotto with his magnifier. "They look like the crystal in your pendant," he said. Taking a clean plastic bag from his pocket, he carefully placed pieces of crystal from the floor inside the bag and slipped the bag into his pocket.

Rachel closed her eyes and rested one hand on the pendant. She could feel herself being drawn in by the magic of the grotto. She felt almost giddy.

Trevor smiled at her and gave her arm a gentle squeeze.

"Where's Ka-Wing?" asked Grace, looking around.

"He has to be somewhere," said Rachel. "We all came through the wall together—or at least I think we did." She checked the pendant. It pointed toward the far end of the grotto. "Maybe he's over there."

Just then, she heard another sound, barely perceptible, from the wall behind them. She cupped her ear and listened. A scraping, shuffling sound like someone—or something—tapping, clawing, moving inside the wall. She thought she heard a faint cry—a woman's voice: "Help! Help!"

"What is it?" asked Trevor.

"I don't know," replied Rachel, searching the grotto wall for the source of the sound. "Maybe it's just my imagination, but I thought I heard Hilde's voice coming from inside the wall."

"Over here," called Grace from the far end of the grotto.

As Rachel and Trevor caught up with her, Rachel spotted Ka-Wing staring up at a circular, mist-covered portal.

"Thank God," cried Grace, rushing over to him. "Are you okay?"

He nodded dreamily without taking his eyes off the portal, which was bordered by what looked like giant lotus petals. Each golden petal was inlaid with crystals and engraved with symbols similar to, but not quite the same as those on the pendant. Inside the portal, a silvery mist created a barrier between them and whatever was on the other side.

“What happened?” asked Trevor.

Ka-Wing turned, noticing them for the first time. “I don’t know,” he finally said, as though coming out of a trance. “I remember going through the wall. Hilde was right behind me and I turned back to try to…to stop her from following us. It was dark and spooky. And then…” He paused, trying to remember what had happened.

“And then what?” asked Grace.

“Yes, now I remember—then Ome appeared and put out his hand. I thought it was an angel at first. I reached out and grabbed his hand. And he pulled me through the darkness to here—beside this portal.”

“What happened to Hilde?” asked Rachel, glancing nervously around. She shuddered at the thought that Hilde might be in the grotto with them.

Ka-Wing shook his head. “Ome reached out to save her too, but the light, his light—I think it was too much for her. She screamed as though she was in terrible pain. It was awful. She threw her arm over her face, like the light was burning her eyes, and then—she fell backward.”

“Fell? To where?”

Ka-Wing paused. “I don’t know. That’s all I remember.”

“Well, thank God you’re safe,” said Grace, patting his arm.

Ka-Wing gazed at the portal again.

“I think it’s some sort of musical notation,” Rachel

said. She ran her fingers across the symbols on the gold petals. The mist began to gently swirl. Soft soothing tones filled the grotto. The symbols glowed and shifted in response to her touch, as though locked in a dance with the mist and her. Holding the pendant in her other hand, she began to hum. The silvery mist pirouetted in harmony with her.

They listened, transfixed by the beautiful melody.

Rachel smiled. "You know, my mom—my real mother—used to sing a tune to me as a small child. I'd forgotten all about it until now." She began softly humming the tune.

The crystals grew brighter, flickering and dancing with the music. The portal shimmered open, revealing a dazzling white light.

After a brief hesitation, Rachel stepped through it into the light. A warm breeze brushed her cheek. Above her was blue sky and beyond a lush green valley. Mountains rose in the distance.

The others followed.

"We did it!" cried Ka-Wing

"I can't believe it. We're back on the surface," Rachel said in amazement. However, even as she spoke, she knew this was no ordinary earthscape. The colors were too vivid, almost surreal. A sense of peace, of lightness, of timelessness pervaded everything. Soft music filled the air. The music was coming from a nearby river, sparkling like the one in her dreams. She thought about the Afghani legend of the River of Jewels.

Trevor moved closer and put his arm around her shoulders. "It's the same music we heard that night on the ship."

She smiled and leaned into his embrace. "And when we saw the aurora—the music of the spheres—remember?"

"Yes, the music of the spheres," repeated Grace dreamily. Then she pulled herself up straight and shook her head, as though trying to shake off the spell cast by the mystical beauty of the music and landscape. "But first," she said, "we have to figure out where we are and what to do next."

"I think I see a path on the other side of the river," said Rachel.

"Let's go check it out," said Trevor. He took a bounding step forward and then stopped in surprise. "This is incredible," he said, staring at the ground. "The gravity is much lighter here."

Rachel smiled fondly at him—always the scientist. She took a tentative step toward him. He grabbed her around the waist as she almost flew past him. They both laughed.

After several tries, they adjusted to the strange new sensations, and together they made their way down to the river. The grass was thick and green like moss and the air fragrant with the scent of roses and hibiscus flowers.

Rachel stooped and felt the water. It was soft and warm and inviting, almost like down feathers. She stepped into the water and began wading to the other side.

"This is amazing!" she called out to the others. "It's not like any river I've ever been in before."

"Hey, wait up," Trevor called.

When they waded out onto the narrow sandy beach on the other side, they were barely wet.

Joining arms, the four of them started up the path through a meadow blanketed with flowers of vibrant colors like precious gems. After walking for what seemed like an hour, they stopped to take stock.

Rachel noticed that, although there was blue sky overhead, there seemed to be no horizon. Instead, the land disappeared into a dreamy, rose-tinged haze.

"Yes, I noticed too," said Trevor, as though reading her mind. "And what's more, the sun is still in the same spot in the sky—directly overhead."

Rachel shielded her eyes and looked up at the red sun. "How can that be?"

He shook his head. "Maybe this isn't our sun."

"But…but what else could it be?" asked Ka-Wing.

"Well, I know this sounds fantastic, but I think we may be in the center of Earth. This sun is too small and also seems to be much closer; probably less than three thousand kilometers away and…"

"So Charlie was right!" said Grace, clapping her hands together.

At the very moment she mentioned her husband's name, a being appeared out of the rosy mist. Behind the being was a second figure, his outline blurred by the mist.

"It's Ome!" cried Rachel.

Ome looked radiant, so different than he had at Shackleton Station.

He moved to one side and motioned to the figure behind him. The figure stepped forward into the sunlight.

Grace gasped. "Charlie!" she cried, running toward him.

Charlie laughed in joy and started down the path to

meet her. He swept her up into his arms and they embraced. He looked like he had hardly aged at all in the more than thirty years that had passed since he had fallen into the crevasse. His thick flame-red hair was still untouched by gray and his lean, handsome face smooth except for the smile wrinkles at the corners of his blue eyes; yet at the same time he looked years wiser than a young man. Even Grace looked years younger.

Rachel smiled and put her arm through Trevor's. The flowers, the meadow seemed even lovelier, if that was possible, than when they had started out from the river.

"Welcome," said Ome, spreading out his arms and greeting them in a soothing, singsong voice. "I am here to take you to the City of the Wise Ones."

A flying disc, similar to or perhaps the same one they had seen at the meteorology station, materialized out of the haze. Six beams of white light emerged from beneath it, reaching out to them, drawing them upward.

Chapter 37

It was the strangest sensation, like being suspended inside a giant soap bubble floating high above the landscape. The disc was transparent, at least looking from the inside out. What's more, no one seemed to be in charge of navigating it.

What is the City of the Wise Ones and where exactly is it? Rachel wondered.

Ome smiled. "It is the home of the noble and true Aryan beings accessible only to those we choose to reveal it to."

Accessible only to those chosen? What did that mean? Rachel had so many questions. Was that why the bioterrorists at the old underground Nazi base had been unable to find the home of the Aryans? She was about to ask when she realized Ome had not spoken at all; instead, he was communicating telepathically. She glanced around. Trevor, Grace, Charlie, and Ka-Wing were gazing out through the transparent walls of the disc, transfixed by the beauty of the landscape below.

"Tell me more about your people and the Wise Ones. Are you the ancestors of the ancient Aryans of India?" Rachel asked Ome, without using words.

Ome replied, "As we grow older—centuries in your terms—we become Wise Ones. Our bodies become lighter until we are truly one with the light. However, in reaching toward eternal life we have lost the power to procreate. We are slowly dying out, although we may long outlive the surface people if they continue on their current path of self-destruction. Our ancestors came here from the stars many millennia ago to bring new life to the human race. We tried genetically engineering children to carry on our legacy of peace. Your people—the surface people—are the offspring of these children, the true Aryans. But the surface people soon grew apart and forgot their roots."

Are we an experiment gone wrong? Rachel thought about the bioterrorists and their project to alter the human genome through a viral infection. Maybe it is wrong for humans to play God or mess with nature, she mused. She instinctively placed her hands on her belly as though to quiet some unknown force growing deep inside of her.

"There are no mistakes, only love," said Ome, reading her thoughts. "We learned long ago to live in the present, in love, and not to dwell in the past."

"What about my father? Hilde Braun told me I have Aryan DNA from one of your scouts."

"The DNA from your father is the *bija-bhaga* DNA all Aryans share in common. We are all your father. The ring you are wearing is a gift from us so you will never be alone or far from us."

She glanced at the small ring on her baby finger, then up at the sky filled with the earth's inner sun.

She was about to ask what he meant by "they came from the stars" when he said, "You are also more than us. We are no longer able to tolerate conditions on the surface—your sun, your air—can be toxic to us without our special protective robes or traveling in dark matter. Unfortunately, dark matter becomes fluid and unstable the closer we get to the surface because of the radiation from your sun. However, we no longer have sickness and suffering as long as we stay here."

"But not having children around. That's so sad," thought Rachel.

Ome smiled. "All will be well," he replied. "What is, is."

"How can everything be well if your people are dying out and there's so much treachery in our world," protested Rachel.

Sadness flashed across Ome's face. "Good will triumph in the end. Both the Nazis and bioterrorists started out with good intentions—to achieve purity and goodness. However, they became corrupted with power. A peaceful world cannot be achieved through destruction and domination."

Rachel gazed out at the mountains in the distance. She thought about the infants back in the nursery. All they had to look forward to was a life of misery and exploitation. If only they had been able to rescue some of the children and bring them here.

Ome smiled and nodded at her, as though reading her thoughts.

She glanced over at Trevor and felt filled with sweet longing. She reached out and took his hand. He smiled and squeezed her hand. Maybe someday they would have children of their own.

As the disc ascended higher, an inland sea bathed in a translucent light came into view. Music, faint at first, filled the air, drawing them toward it like a magnetic beacon.

They flew onward until they came to a great island suspended in the air above the sea as effortlessly as an albatross riding the thermals. Plasma streamers of rainbow colors billowed over the city. As they drew closer, Rachel could see pyramids gleaming golden in the sun. It reminded her of the description in Admiral Byrd's journal of the great city he stumbled upon when flying across Antarctica.

The disc descended and set down at the edge of a wide boulevard paved with gold and jewels and lined with rows of trees bearing golden fruit and beautiful flowers. The disc opened, and Ome escorted them outside.

The buildings along the boulevard were made of a crystal-type material that pulsated with the muted colors of the rainbow. Soothing music and rose-colored light emanated from the walls of the buildings. Light beings, similar to Ome, drifted by. Others swam effortlessly through azure blue canals that encircled the city in concentric rings.

Trevor took out his magnetometer. "This is incredible," he said. "An island city suspended between two intersecting magnetic fields acting as superconductors." He looked around. "My guess is the pyramids are situated between the centers of the fields and use crystals, like the ones we found in the grotto, to collect and direct the energy."

He checked another instrument and punched in some figures. "You're not going to believe this," he said, staring at his notes.

"Believe what?" asked Rachel, smiling at his enthusiasm.

He looked up at her and then over at his Aunt Grace. "I think we're directly under Lake Vostok, near the geographic South Pole. That would explain the extraordinary magnetic energy there."

"Just as you had suspected," said Grace to Charlie, with an air of self-satisfaction.

Charlie smiled. "That's right. Without the life-giving magnetic field radiating from here through the two poles, we'd become a dead planet like Mars." He took Grace's hand. "Come," he said. "There are other just as amazing things about this place we want to show you."

Ome motioned for them to follow him.

They moved effortlessly, almost floating, along the boulevard toward a magnificent temple where they were met by gossamer beings, some even brighter and lovelier than Ome. One of the beings led them into a courtyard where they were given warm drinks—elixirs—which tasted delicious like nothing Rachel had never had before.

After resting a while, they were taken to a great hall. The golden doors slid open noiselessly and the gossamer being beckoned for them to enter. Like Ome, the being spoke to them through thoughts. Only this time it was not just Rachel who was able to hear.

"Have no fear," the being said. "You are about to have an audience with a Wise One."

At the far end of the great hall Rachel could make out a form—a golden aura. A light being, too beautiful and wondrous to describe, approached them. Colors, like tiny crystals glittered in the air, moving to music so sublime that no earthly composer could ever put it down on paper.

The light being was ancient, yet ageless, with delicate, youthful features and years of wisdom engraved on his or her face. Rachel was overcome with awe as the being's mind penetrated the innermost depths of her heart.

The being said, "We have let you enter here because you are all of noble character."

Rachel recognized the words as the very same ones Admiral Byrd had used in his diary.

"There is much darkness on the surface world that has been brought on by human ignorance and greed," the being continued. "The answers are not in science or war. Unless humans change their ways, darkness and chaos will come and cover the earth."

The being gazed at each of them in turn with eyes full of love and compassion. "It is in your hands now to remember who you really are, to use your power and knowledge wisely. You have a choice: to stay here or to return to the surface world with this message of hope and peace." Then the light being fell silent.

Rachel was torn. Life here, it seemed, would be so much easier, yet… She glanced over at Trevor.

"What is your decision?" asked the light being.

Ka-Wing was the first to speak. "I want to return," he said, "and finish medical school so I can help people."

Grace looked questioningly at Charlie.

"I can't go back," he said, taking her hands in his and kissing them. "You don't know how much I've wanted to return, to be with you again. But if I go back, I'll die within minutes. My spine was severed at the neck by a bullet. Here injury and pain don't exist. But on the surface…"

"Then I will stay here with you," said Grace resolutely.

Rachel was touched by their love and commitment

to each other. She turned to Trevor. "And what do you want to do?" she asked him, already knowing.

He looked at her tenderly. "I can't stay. My family lives on the surface, and I have work to do there." He paused and took Rachel's hand. "And our own life together, until death do us part, for better or worse," he added, getting down on one knee. "That is, if you'll have me."

Rachel smiled. She placed her other hand on his.

But, of course, he already knew the answer.

They kissed, a kiss that gently sealed promises yet unspoken.

Grace laughed softly and gave them each a hug. "Oh, my dear children, I am so happy for you."

"Do you wish to return to the surface now?" the light being asked, looking first at Trevor, then at Rachel.

Trevor's face grew solemn. He stood again. "No, not just yet. First we have work to do just below the surface."

"The bioterrorists," said Ka-Wing, clenching his fists by his side.

The light being smiled and began to fade into the background. "Remember, compassion is your greatest weapon in the fight against darkness."

In an instant, they were alone again in the great hall. Ome bowed slightly and escorted them outside to a garden beside the temple. The air smelled sweet with the fragrance of flowers. Iridescent hummingbirds fluttered from flower to flower, gathering the nectar.

Rachel sat down beside Trevor on one of the marble benches and thought about the children in the nursery. Then she remembered what the gray had "said" to her about saving the children as it had passed her in the lab. Looking up at Charlie, she asked, "You know how you said you can survive down here, but not up on the surface because of your injury?"

Charlie nodded. "That's right."

"What about the children in the underground nursery—especially the ones who're malformed? What if we can find a way to bring them down here where they can be whole and healthy? They need a home and there're no children here now."

Grace seized upon the idea. "There's lots of love to go around here. And we've always wanted a family of our own."

Charlie smiled at her.

"But how can we get the children down here?" asked Ka-Wing.

"I haven't figured that part out yet," replied Rachel. She gazed at the ring on her baby finger. "But I just know there has to be a way."

Trevor rubbed his chin thoughtfully. "Maybe through the same wall that brought us into the grotto?"

"We can help you from this side of the grotto," said Grace.

"What about the bioterrorists?" asked Ka-Wing. "Won't they just keep making more deadly viruses?"

Trevor put his hand in his pocket and pulled out the plastic bag with the crystals from the grotto. "Not necessarily," he said. "I think I can shut down their power grid if I can find the power plant for the underground complex. I have an idea where it might be from a diagram I found next to the electrical box in the biohazard lab."

"How will you shut off their power?" asked

Rachel.

"When I was a child," he replied, "the whole Northeast power grid, including Ontario, went out because of magnetic activity associated with the aurora. Then the grid went down again in 2003 for a couple of days because of a power overload. I did a research paper in graduate school on the factors leading up to the two outages. I think I can reproduce the outage on a smaller scale in the underground power plant, using these magnetic crystals—and make the outage permanent this time."

Trevor looked at Ome. "Can you get us back?" he asked.

"I can," replied Ome. "We have infiltrators inside the complex with whom we are in communication. They can help you in accomplishing your mission."

"You mean the grays?" asked Rachel.

"Yes, the grays," replied Ome. "When the bioterrorists created them, little did they realize that the pacifism they programmed into the grays is genetically linked to telepathy and the ability to move between dark and regular matter. If it had not been for them helping you and your mother escape and quietly sabotaging the genetic experiments, there would have been a lot more children born with experimental deformities in their attempt to achieve an 'improved' Aryan race."

Ome stretched out his hands toward Rachel. "We must part ways once again, my daughter. Time on the other side is running out—the portal is beginning to shift. You must go now."

Chapter 38

Mist curled around Rachel's feet. The unpleasant odor of antiseptic and urine, and the harsh fluorescent lighting contrasted sharply with the ethereal beauty of the City of the Wise Ones. Trevor and Ka-Wing stood next to her. From down the corridor a gray motioned to them from the nursery door. The nurse in charge was asleep at her station as was the nurse's aide, drugged, Rachel suspected, by the gray.

Another gray approached and motioned for Trevor to follow.

"Don't worry," Rachel reassured him. "The gray will take you where you need to go." She pulled the ring off her pinkie and, kissing Trevor lightly on the lips, slipped the ring into his hand. "It's for good luck. And so you'll remember, no matter what happens, that I love you."

Trevor took her in his arms. "I love you too," he whispered.

A final kiss, and then he was gone. Once he was out of sight, Rachel entered the nursery, which was lined with four rows of white plastic bassinettes. Going to the bassinette farthest from the door, she looked down and saw a baby with a malformed head and webbing between his tiny fingers.

She hesitated. From deep inside she felt a stirring—like a nascent life. She put her hand on her stomach. Could it possibly be—? But it had only been a few days since she and Trevor had made love under the lights of the aurora.

The baby gazed up at her and cooed.

She gently lifted the baby from the bassinette and stroked his soft cheek. Cradling him in one arm, she proceeded to the next bassinette for a second baby. Ka-Wing followed her lead.

With the all-clear signal from the gray at the door, Rachel and Ka-Wing moved quickly down the hall with a baby in each arm. Another gray was stationed at the wall near Room 10. Rachel handed one of the babies to the gray and, pressing the pendant against the wall, pushed the other baby through. One by one, the infants disappeared into the shimmering wall.

Far away, deep in the Earth in the crystal grotto, Grace and Charlie, with the assistance of Ome and other ethereal beings, received each baby, placing each precious bundle on a cushion of warm, healing air.

****

Trevor hurried through the winding tunnels, following the gray. The gray came to a stop at the back entrance to the central power plant. Trevor opened the door a crack and peered inside. Three generators stood in the center of a large, dimly lit cavern. An armed guard was talking to a maintenance worker near the main entrance on the far side.

Trevor stepped inside and edged along the wall until he could hear them. “Possible intruders,” he overhead the guard saying. “Keep a lookout for anything suspicious and notify us immediately.”

The worker nodded and glanced nervously in Trevor’s direction.

Trevor quickly stepped back into a dark recess in the stone wall.

****

Back in the nursery, the gray raised its hand in a warning gesture. Rachel set down the baby she was holding and signaled Ka-Wing to do the same. Only four babies left. They ducked down and held their breath as a thickly-muscled, skinhead guard walked by and looked through the hall window. He scowled at the sight of the nurse sound asleep, but seeing the gray there watching over the children, he continued on his way.

After removing the rest of the babies, the gray then led Rachel and Ka-Wing to another nursery housing older infants and toddlers. Rachel stopped short and sucked in a deep breath as memories of her three years spend in this nursery resurfaced. Looking around, she noticed the absence of mothers there; she wondered where they were. Her mother had been allowed a one-hour visit each day. She shuddered as she recalled the mechanical surrogate mothers in the laboratory.

The nurse and the two teachers in charge were out cold. The toddlers were remarkably docile, probably lightly drugged by the grays. Unlike the children in the first nursery, these children seemed to be in exceptionally good health. Several of them were identical, and all of them beautiful, blue-eyed, and blond.

"What should we do?" whispered Ka-Wing. "What if some of them are clones of Hitler?"

Rachel hesitated.

The gray picked up one of the drowsy-eyed toddlers and held her out to Rachel.

Rachel took the child. “We should try to save them all,” she said resolutely. “They’re innocent victims too.”

****

Trevor waited until the guard and another worker returning with a tray of tea and pastries distracted the maintenance worker. Then Trevor quickly crossed the cavern to the row of generators. Two smaller, newer generators flanked the center generator, which was about three meters tall. Not a good sign, he thought; they’re probably in the process of expanding the facility. Looking around, he noticed, to his relief, that the air-regeneration system and pumps were connected to a separate backup system, a safety precaution, no doubt. Moving back to the center generator, he shined his penlight into one of the cooling vents in the outer casing of the generator. Fortunately, it was a standard design for an electromagnetic generator with a rotor coil wound around a central shaft.

The guard jerked to attention. He must have spotted the light from Trevor’s penlight out of the corner of his eye.

Trevor snapped off his light and stepped behind the generator.

The guard stared nervously at the spot where the light had been, a piece of Black Forest cake in one hand and his weapon raised in the other. After a few moments, seeing nothing else, he went back to his tea break and conversation.

Keeping the generator between him and the guard, Trevor considered his options. If he could somehow disrupt the rotor coil, it would disable the main generator, which would transfer the load to the remaining two generators. That, in turn, would overload them and they would shut down, causing a blackout. But how was he to accomplish that?

****

Once all the children were safely on the other side of the wall, the gray led Rachel and Ka-Wing to the genetic engineering laboratory. Rachel checked her watch. There was no way they could destroy the lab in the few minutes they had left before the dark matter and portal shifted again and became inaccessible to them.

Then Ka-Wing noticed a laser gun lying on one of the counters near the door. He reached for the gun.

"No," said Rachel, putting out her arm to stop him. "They don't deserve to die. There has to be another way."

"But there's no time," protested Ka-Wing. "We have to…"

"The walls of Jericho?" said Rachel, reading the gray's mind.

"The walls of what?"

"Music. It knocked down the walls of Jericho—and music was the key to the portal to the underworld where the Aryans live. I just need to…" She looked down at her hand. Her heart sank. The ring was not there; she had given it to Trevor.

****

Trevor reached into his pocket and selected the smallest of the crystals he had found in the grotto. He set it in his hand next to the small ring. If he just shoved the crystal through the vent hole, it would not have enough momentum to reach the rotor coil in the center. He would have to throw the crystal. He closed his hand around the crystal and began calculating in his head how far back he would have to be in order for the crystal to have enough momentum to reach the coil. As the crystal made contact with the ring, it began to glow. Trevor opened his hand and stared at the crystal.

This time the light was so bright the guard knew it was not his imagination. The worker with him stared incredulously at the shimmering rays of light coming from behind the main generator. Shouting something into his walkie-talkie, the guard took off in Trevor's direction.

Trevor quickly slipped the ring into his pocket. But even with the ring removed, the crystal kept glowing brighter and brighter. He gulped. The guard had reached the generator and was coming straight at him. There was no time for calculations or practice shots. He had only one chance, just like the time when, as a boy, he had won that stone skipping contest at Camp Algonquin.

His heart racing, Trevor stepped back and positioned the glowing crystal in his hand as though he was about to skip a rock. Taking a deep breath, he threw it at the vent.

The guard gaped in surprise as the glowing crystal flew past him, barely missing the barrel of his gun. The crystal disappeared into the generator's vent opening and the lights in the power plant flickered briefly, then came back on.

Stumbling backward, Trevor broke into a run toward the door.

The guard raised his weapon and aimed at the figure zigzagging across the cavern. He fired just as the lights flicked off and on again. The bullet whizzed by, grazing Trevor's arm. The guard took aim again.

****

Rachel was about to give up hope when one of the grays began singing a sweet, haunting melody. The scientists and technicians stopped their work and stared in astonishment. The grays were bred to be mute.

Rachel placed her hand on the pendant, which hung around her neck, and began softly singing along. She could feel the pressure rising, until her eardrums felt like they might burst. But still she kept on singing.

Chaos broke out in the lab as glass shattered and metal crumbled. The mechanical surrogate mothers collapsed inward with steely groans.

Suddenly the lights flickered out. A thick, eerie stillness settled over the lab. Then, a thunk and hiss, and the air pumps started up again. The emergency lighting flashed on, casting a reddish pall over the lab. The scientists and technicians stared in shock at the ruins of their life's work.

As the emergency lights came on, Rachel noticed the grays were no longer in sight. The portal! She grabbed Ka-Wing by the arm and raced toward the portal near the nursery.

When they arrived, the grays were already crowded together beside the wall. One of them placed a hand on the wall and motioned toward Rachel's pendant. In the distance, she heard muffled shouting and what sounded like gunfire. Removing the pendant from her neck, she pressed it against the wall.

"Come on," cried Ka-Wing, as the last of the grays disappeared through the shimmering wall. "We have to get out of here before the portal closes."

Rachel looked over her shoulder in the direction of the gunshots, the same direction where she had last seen

Trevor. “No,” she said, “we have to wait for Trev…” She broke off and stared at the wall. The shimmering had given way to a more sinister look, like a thick primordial slime struggling to give birth to some primitive life form. A damp chill was beginning to creep through the air. Fascination turned to horror as a hand—a mangled hand—then an arm, materialized from the wall.

“What the…” said Ka-Wing.

Rachel gasped and jumped back as Hilde suddenly emerged from the wall.

Hilde’s face contorted as she wrenched the rest of her body from the viscous wall. She struggled to get her bearings. Spotting Ka Wing, she seized him around the neck with the lightning speed of a cobra. Then she noticed Rachel. “You,” she shrieked as she yanked Ka-Wing toward her, tightening her grip on him.

Rachel froze, clutching the pendant to her chest.

“I want that pendant, freak,” she said through clenched teeth.

Rachel did not move.

Hilde’s eyes narrowed. “Give me the fucking pendant, or I’ll snap this little geek’s neck,” she hissed, thrusting out her gloved hand while still keeping her grip on Ka-Wing. Her other hand, which had been so brutally mangled by the powerful jaws of the leopard seal in the basin, hung limply by her side.

Fighting the choking fear rising up inside of her, Rachel frantically tried to collect her thoughts. From behind, she could hear the sound of footsteps getting closer.

“Please don’t let her kill me,” Ka-Wing wheezed.

Trembling, Rachel opened her hand and looked at

the pendant. After a moment's hesitation, her shoulders drooped and she extended her hand. "Here," she said in a subdued voice. "You win."

Hilde let out a triumphant laugh. "Toss it there—in front of me."

Rachel stretched out her hand but then hesitated. "How do I know you won't kill Ka-Wing even if I do give you the pendant?"

Hilde scowled and loosened her grip slightly on Ka-Wing as though in a good will gesture.

Seizing the opportunity, Rachel lunged forward, throwing Hilde off balance.

Ka-Wing broke free.

Stumbling to her knees, Hilde reached out and snatched Rachel's ankle. As she did, Rachel brought the heel of her free boot down on Hilde's injured hand. Hilde bellowed in pain and let go—but only for a split second.

Recovering her wits, Hilde reached inside her pocket with her good hand, fumbling for the gun. It was not there. Rachel came down hard on Hilde's shoulder with her knee, forcing her to the ground. Reaching over Hilde's flailing arm, she pushed the pendant into the wall. The pendant disappeared.

"You idiot," Hilde shrieked. Staggering to a crouching position, she threw herself against the wall just as the portal closed.

Just then, Trevor appeared breathless from around the corner. He gaped at the scene before him. Hilde was screeching in rage and clawing at the rock wall, her bloodied fingers leaving ragged red streaks on the stone.

Rachel rushed over and hugged Trevor. "Are you

okay?" he asked, stroking her hair. Not far behind, Rachel could hear the sharp rapping of boots against the hard floor, like automatic gunfire.

Trevor stepped back, looking for an escape route. Swinging around, Hilde glared at the three of them, her eyes wild with almost unbearable pain and hatred.

"We have to get out of here," Ka Wing pleaded.

"You're bleeding," Rachel said, noticing Trevor's shoulder.

Before Trevor could reply, armed guards appeared from around the corner.

"Grab them, you imbeciles," Hilde screamed.

The guards stopped in their tracks, too surprised to react. "M-Majorgeneral Braun?" one of them stammered.

Trevor pulled Rachel closer to him. There was nowhere to run, no escape route. They were trapped. "The ring," he said, thrusting it into her hand.

Ka-Wing gripped Rachel's arm, his eyes wide with fear. "How're we going to get out of here now without the pendant?"

"This time you're not going to get away," Hilde snarled as she lunged toward Rachel.

Rachel clutched her ring and closed her eyes. "Ome," she whispered. "Help us."

She could feel Ome's presence, but even more, her own power surging through her like a white light, embracing Trevor and Ka-Wing in its protective aura. As it did, she sensed the dissolution of all her tissues. Her arms, her fingers, became translucent, wavering in the dim, murky light of the underground complex. Then, the three of them vanished altogether.

Chapter 39

Rachel blinked. The bright light stung her eyes. Snow, sparkling in the morning sun, stretched in all directions. Behind her was the meteorology station. Trevor and Ka-Wing stood next to her, looking as bewildered as she. They were all wearing their parkas and boots. The rest of their gear was stacked in a neat pile beside them.

From above came the purr of an airplane. Rachel shielded her eyes with her hand and gazed up at the National Science Foundation Twin Otter ski plane. For a second it seemed to hang motionless in the sky. Then it slowly descended for a landing, its propellers stirring up the snowfield into a whirl of glistening crystals.

The door of the plane opened, and Caitlyn waved.

Once the propellers had spun to a stop, Caitlyn and Byrdie hopped out of the plane.

"Hey, guys," called Byrdie. "Glad to see you all made it to the meteorology station safely."

"You came back!" cried Ka-Wing. He grabbed his backpack and ran to the plane. Placing a foot on one of the plane's landing skis, he hoisted himself up into the small passenger cabin.

Byrdie took Ka-Wing's pack and tossed it into the back stowage area of the plane, then turned to Trevor and Rachel. "What did he mean by 'came back'?" Byrdie asked with a puzzled expression.

Rachel hesitated, not sure how to explain what they had just been through without sounding like they had gone off the deep end. Then again, maybe that was what happened.

"Well, whatever he meant," said Caitlyn cheerfully as she gave each of them a hug, "it's good to see you all safe."

Trevor reached into his pocket and pulled out the plastic bag holding the remaining crystals from the grotto.

"What's that?" asked Caitlyn.

He started to say something but instead closed his hand around the bag and slipped it back into his pocket. "What's the date and time?" he asked.

Caitlyn checked her watch. "March 3rd, 9:48 in the morning. Why?"

"But how can that be?" asked Rachel. Falling into the crevasse, the underground lab, the City of the Wise Ones, what Trevor had said about wanting to spend their life together—had it all been a dream? She glanced up at the sky—was it possible? But then she dismissed the thought. She rubbed the back of her neck and glanced over at Trevor.

"We must have gone through some kind of time warp," he said. "Remember how I told you time appears to be unstable in dark matter?"

"Dark matter? A time warp?" asked Byrdie. "What in the world are you guys talking about?" He gave Trevor a playful nudge in the ribs. "Hey, have you two been into that secret cache of weed up at the meteorology hut?"

Trevor laughed and shook his head. "Hardly," he said. Then he grew somber. "Can we use the radio in the plane?"

"Sure. But, why?" asked Byrdie.

"I have to contact the World Health Organization about a virus."

"Why, is someone sick?" asked Caitlyn.

"Hopefully not yet," replied Trevor.

Byrdie looked puzzled. "What's happening?"

"I won't know for sure until we find out more."

"Does this have something to do with why Dr. McAllister came down here?"

Rachel drew a deep breath and glanced over at Trevor.

"She's not coming with us," Trevor said after a moment's hesitation.

"Oh, why not?" Byrdie squinted up toward the meteorology station. "Where's she now? Is she still up at the hut?"

"She's okay. She decided to go on ahead." Trevor shouldered his backpack and turned to Rachel. "Are you ready to go?" he asked taking her arm.

But Rachel was staring up at the station. A flicker of movement in one of the windows caught her attention.

Was that a face in the window? A cold dread coursed through her.

"What is it?" Trevor asked, following her gaze.

"I…I…thought I saw a face—like Hilde's—in the window."

Trevor dropped the backpack, pulled out his binoculars and scanned the windows. "There's no one there that I can see," he finally said, picking up his gear.

"Come on guys," Byrdie called out. "Let's get moving." He glanced up at the hut one last time.

“There’s something about this place that gives me the willies.”

Trevor gave Rachel’s arm a gentle squeeze. “Hey, it’s okay. Everything’s going to be okay.”

Rachel smiled weakly but said nothing.

As the plane lifted off, she stared out the window at the hut until it was swallowed up by the great white expanse as though it had never existed.

A word about the author…

Judith Boss is the author of several short stories as well as five college textbooks, two of which are among the top sellers in their fields.

Prior to pursuing a career in academia, Boss worked as a writer/researcher for the Nova Scotia Museum. During her spare time she volunteers with the US Fish and Wildlife Services.

An avid traveler, she has traveled with students from Brown University Medical School to work with underserved indigenous people in Mexico and Guatemala. Her favorite travel destination, however, is Antarctica.

Boss lives in rural Rhode Island with her daughter, son-in-law, twin granddaughters, and corgi.

For more information go to:

www.judyboss.com

Thank you for purchasing
this publication of The Wild Rose Press, Inc.

If you enjoyed the story, we would appreciate your letting others know by leaving a review.

For other wonderful stories,
please visit our on-line bookstore at
www.thewildrosepress.com.

For questions or more information
contact us at
info@thewildrosepress.com.

The Wild Rose Press, Inc.
www.thewildrosepress.com

Stay current with The Wild Rose Press, Inc.

Like us on Facebook

https://www.facebook.com/TheWildRosePress

And Follow us on Twitter
https://twitter.com/WildRosePress

Printed in the USA
CPSIA information can be obtained
at www.ICGtesting.com
CBHW071114150324
5427CB00046B/815